PRAISE FOR

THE ART OF CRASH LANDING

"I fell in love with Mattie, the hero of *The Art of Crash Landing*, with all her sass, her snark, her badass ways. The best compliment I can give this talented new author? I wish I had written this novel. You nailed it, Melissa DeCarlo. And you deserve legions of very happy readers."

—Ellen Sussman, author of *A Wedding in Provence* and *French Lessons*

"Mattie describes herself as a natural disaster, and she may on to something. Accidentally pregnant and unemployed (too old and too smart for either), she's on the run from a past she doesn't really understand. In a few short months, she will figure out the riddle of her mother's death, learn that even the most powerful love doesn't always look pretty, and that sometimes there are very good reasons for very big secrets. Melissa DeCarlo's storytelling is strong and sure, genuinely moving, and genuinely funny. Like her unlikely heroine, she's a force to be reckoned with."

—Jacquelyn Mitchard, author of *The Deep End of the Ocean*

"*The Art of Crash Landing* is full of heart and sass. It's about forgiveness, self-understanding, and the complicated love between mothers and daughters. Readers will root for DeCarlo's goofy, sharp-tongued heroine. . . . This is a sparkling, funny, and moving debut."

—Edan Lepucki, author of *California*

"Behind the smart-ass mouth of Mattie Wallace, our troubled protagonist, is a whole lot of heart, soul, and humor. Mattie's only assets are a stolen guitar strap, a nearly dead 1978 Chevy Malibu, and her wickedly acute observations, which keep the reader completely and totally hooked. You won't stop reading *The Art of Crash Landing* until all the great mysteries of Mattie's messed-up life have been unraveled by the ever-wise Mattie herself."

—Jessica Anya Blau, author of *The Wonder Bread Summer*

"A dazzling debut that truly soars, about figuring out the tug of the past, about family mysteries and the marvels of forgiveness, and all of it features a spunky heroine readers won't be able to stop falling in love with."

—Caroline Leavitt, *New York Times* bestselling author of *Is This Tomorrow* and *Pictures of You*

THE ART
OF
CRASH LANDING

THE ART OF CRASH LANDING

A Novel

Melissa DeCarlo

HARPER

NEW YORK • LONDON • TORONTO • SYDNEY

HARPER

P.S.™ is a trademark of HarperCollins Publishers.

HarperCollins books may be purchased for educational, business,
or sales promotional use. For information please e-mail the Special
Markets Department at SPsales@harpercollins.com.

FIRST EDITION

Designed by Jamie Lynn Kerner

Library of Congress Cataloging-in-Publication Data

DeCarlo, Melissa.
The art of crash landing : a novel / Melissa DeCarlo.
   pages cm
   ISBN 978-0-06-239054-7 (paperback) — ISBN 978-0-06-239055-4
(ebook) — ISBN 978-0-06-241685-8 (large print) 1. Mothers and
daughters—Fiction. 2. Family secrets—Fiction. 3. Oklahoma—
Fiction. 4. Domestic fiction. I. Title.
   PS3604.E2372A37 2015
   813'.6—dc23
                                        2015010374

15 16 17 18 19   OV/RRD   10 9 8 7 6 5 4 3

*To my parents, Barbara and Don Freeman, who encouraged
my love of books, and to Leonard, Mike, Katherine,
and Stephen, who encouraged me to write one.*

THE ART
OF
CRASH LANDING

SATURDAY

A bad beginning makes a bad ending

CHAPTER 1

Twenty-seven minutes is, if anyone ever asks, exactly how long it takes to cram everything I own into six giant trash bags. Add that to the twenty minutes I'd already spent picking and losing a fight with Nick the Asshole, plus five additional minutes to stuff all the bags into my car, and then maybe a minute to eat the stale half a Slim Jim I found on the floor of the backseat, and you're still only up to fifty-three minutes. Most people would probably have a hard time totally fucking up their life in under an hour. But then again, I'm not most people. I'm amazing. I'm like some kind of fuckup savant.

I fire up the Malibu, put in a Black Keys CD, and light a cigarette with shaking hands. Three drags later I remember why I quit smoking. Slamming on the brakes, I open the car door and lean out to retch, depositing my half a Slim Jim and an earlier glass of orange juice in the middle of an oily puddle.

I am lying about the fifty-three minutes.

It's actually taken years to get things this bad. Even the current screwup started three months ago when I was late getting a prescription refilled. Or to be more specific, it began the moment I decided that missing six out of twenty-one pills was no big deal.

I drive around the block three times trying to think of somewhere I can go that isn't Queeg's trailer. Around and around I go, running through names in my head, trying like hell not to be what I am—a thirty-year-old woman with no friends. Sure, I have people I party with, but they're not my friends. If they're anybody's friends they're Nick's, and none of them would take me in. I used to have my own friends, of course I did, but it's like the dentist told me when I was a kid—ignore them and they'll go away. He was talking about teeth, not friends, but it's the same theory, and I can tell you it works. The friends part, anyway; I still have my teeth.

If there's an upside to not having friends it's that nobody depends on me for anything at all, which is exactly how I like it. For instance, I never have to help anybody move, and if you think that's not a big deal then you've never loaded furniture into a pickup on a Florida August afternoon. The downside? Well, that's pretty drive-around-the-block-three-times obvious.

When I merge onto the highway heading east, I turn up the music and try to ignore the familiar ache in my chest, a hollow sort of ache that's all sharp edges and empty air where something used to be. Dan Auerbach is singing *It doesn't mean a thing to me*, and I sing along. I know the words to this one.

I think about how I ought to call Queeg and let him know that I'm on the way, but I won't. Odds are, he'd tell me to come on over, but it's not a sure bet. Lately, I get the feeling that my stepfather is a little tired of dealing with me. God knows I am.

CHAPTER 2

When I reach the entrance to Two Pines the gate is closed, so I pull over and park on the far shoulder. Although it does have a few RV hookups, this is mainly a mobile home park, and a weedy one at that. I note the clotheslines sagging under bright beach towels, piles of shoes in front of every door, potted plants struggling to survive in the hot, salty air. I've been coming here since I was a little girl, and I would swear that the only things that change are the ever-expanding rust stains along the trailer seams.

My mother and I first met Queeg here at Two Pines, seventeen years ago. She and I were staying on the far side of the park, in the section filled with extra-shabby trailers owned by the management and billed as vacation rentals. Queeg had wandered back into that area one afternoon while my mother was sunbathing topless, and the rest is history. He hadn't lived at Two Pines long enough to know that the rental people were trouble.

I climb out of the car and stretch. The sun is low enough to be behind the treetops, and the storm has left a steady breeze, making the evening pleasant in that soft, faintly fishy way you can only find within a mile or two of an ocean. There's nobody in the courtyard, but Queeg's car is parked next to his trailer, so I know he's home.

His name is actually Herman Isaacs, and I remember laughing at that the first time I met him. I was thirteen years old, and the only Herman I'd ever heard of was a Munster. Luckily for this Herman, *The Caine Mutiny* by Herman Wouk was assigned reading for eighth-grade English at Booker T. Washington Middle School. By the time this dumpy, middle-aged Herman married my mother, I'd started calling him Captain Queeg, something for which he should be grateful since I wasn't all that thrilled with the idea of a stepfather, and Lily Munster's nickname for her Herman, Pussy Cat, was awfully tempting.

After the wedding Queeg sold his trailer and moved us all into a little house just a couple miles from here. But after their divorce he bought himself another double-wide and parked it right back here at Two Pines. I sometimes wonder if he still walks through the rental section to meet the people staying there. Probably not. He knows better now.

I eye the familiar fence and then take off jogging across the road, timing my approach to take one, two big steps and then with a hand atop the fence, I side-hop the four-foot chain link, landing on the other side with a crunch-skid on the oyster-shell gravel. *I've still got it.* I raise both arms and do a small Rocky Balboa prance for my audience, which numbers exactly zero. If you do something cool and no one is around to see you do it, are you still cool?

I walk past the dinner-mint-colored metal table and chairs that sit, exactly as they always have, on the empty slab behind the office trailer. Other than being perhaps a little paler pastel, they're frozen in time, still with a loose chain circling through the chair legs. No ordinary thief specializing in ugly metal patio furniture will be able to nab one of these chairs. No sir. Only one wily and strong enough to drag away the whole set will score these beauties.

Queeg's door squeaks open. My heart sinks a little at how carefully he descends the three cement steps.

"Mattie . . ." He starts toward me, slowly. "What a surprise."

I notice the absence of the word *pleasant*. "You know me, Captain. I thrive on doing the unexpected."

We give each other an awkward one-armed hug.

"Saw your little gymnastic maneuver there at the fence," he tells me.

Excellent! I had an audience. I am cool. "I've still got it," I say.

"Is it catching?"

"Not by you," I reply and it's the truth. Queeg is to cool what black is to white, what antimatter is to matter. When he walks into a room, he actually creates a coolness vacuum that sucks all the cool from everyone around him. He is a coolness black hole.

We look at each other and grin.

"You know," Queeg tells me, "that gate isn't locked. You could have opened the latch and walked in."

See? The Uncool Force is strong in him. "Where's the fun in that?"

"Not breaking a hip is fun."

"Okay, now you're talking like an old man."

He doesn't reply but I can tell we're both thinking the same thing. He is an old man.

I ask him if I can stay for a while, and although he tells me it's fine, there's a pause between my request and his answer—a long enough pause that, once I pull my car through the gate and around behind his trailer, I don't unpack. I can't always take a hint but I'm going to take this one. I promise him that it's only for tonight. I'll figure something else out tomorrow.

We cook together in his tiny kitchen and then sit knee-to-knee at his table. Over dinner we talk about safe subjects: his bowling league, my job. Freelance photography doesn't provide me with much of an income, but it keeps me stocked up on funny stories. So I launch into one about a recent photo shoot where the bride's dress wouldn't zip, an angry grandma threw her rosary beads at the groom, and the reception was held in the church gym where we had to take off our shoes before stepping onto the polished court.

It's good to laugh with Queeg again. He is the yin to my yang. We're complete opposites in every way and yet manage to hang together somehow. And I don't know whether yin or yang is the white tadpole but Queeg would definitely be that one, and I'd be the black one, because from the moment we met Queeg, life started to get brighter for my mother and me, and, I suspect, darker for him. Or maybe now that I think about it, the yin-yang thing isn't right at all. It doesn't leave any space for my mother. Maybe Queeg and I are bookends, each propping up a different side of the same terrible story.

The sky is a purple glow once we've finished cleaning up and stepped back outside. We walk over to the metal table and chairs behind the office. The chairs grind on the cement as we pull them out. Touching the chalky powder coating gives me goose bumps.

Queeg sets his beer on the table, and I set down my glass of ice water. I can see the question in his eyes—he's been nagging me about my drinking for years, and I'm sure he's never seen me turn down a beer before—but a question unasked is easy enough to leave unanswered.

"So . . . are you going to tell me what happened?"

I sigh. A question asked is harder to dodge. "Nick is an asshole."

"Isn't this the idiot I met last summer?"

I smile and shake my head. Last summer's idiot was named Chris, and Queeg got a chance to meet him when I talked Chris into a beach vacation. Rather than getting us a room at a hotel, I booked a trailer here. Even as I was on the phone, I knew making a reservation at Two Pines was a mistake, but I did it anyway. It was kind of like buying a Ding Dong at the 7-Eleven. You know they're gross, with waxy chocolate and that peculiar white goo in the middle, but you remember loving them as a child, so you buy one anyway. It was like that. Only I made Chris eat the Ding Dong, too.

And then it rained all week and there we were, screaming at each other in the cramped kitchen. The funny thing was, they'd put us in the same trailer my mother and I had usually rented when I was a kid. After I'd finally managed to make Chris hit me, I remember lying there facedown on the floor and taking a deep breath to see if I could find the smell of my mother's boozy vomit in the orange shag.

"No," I tell Queeg. "This one has a college degree."

"In what?"

"English."

"So what does he do?"

"He's in a band."

"Of course he is." Queeg knows and disapproves of my propensity to date musicians.

"But mostly he's an assistant manager at Pizza Hut."

"Another idiot."

Queeg has a simple classification system when it comes to the men I date. They're all idiots. I like to think it has something to do with them not being good enough for me, but I suspect it has more to do with them being stupid enough to date me.

"We had a fight," I say. I don't mention the start of the fight, which was me not having my share of the rent. Instead I start near the end of the argument. "He told me I was a slob."

Queeg doesn't comment on this. He knows me.

"And he said that I use too many *aphorisms*."

"Well . . ." Queeg pauses to take a sip of his beer. "If the shoe fits . . ."

"Shit!" I laugh. "I had to look the word up."

He laughs, too, but his turns into a cough. When he finally catches his breath he's still grinning, but his eyes are watering from the struggle. "You'd know lots of big words if you'd gone to college."

"Oh, come on. I know plenty of big words, just not that one."

"If you say so."

Queeg knows I'm right; I'm no dummy. But that doesn't stop him from giving me his raised-brow you're-not-living-up-to-your-potential look. I get it a lot from him. No matter how badly I screw things up I can always count on him to make me feel worse about it—not by being critical, but by being so certain that I could do better. He was only officially my parent for four years, but believing in me is a habit he can't seem to break.

"You're partly to blame, you know," I tell him.

"How do you figure that?"

"You were the one who taught me all those stupid sayings."

"You're the one who dates assholes."

He's got me there.

"Anyway," I say, "the fight got really big and I threw him out."

"I thought it was his apartment."

"Yeah." I lift my glass. Its moisture has made a perfect deep yellow circle on the faded tabletop. "I'd kind of forgotten about that."

He shakes his head, "Oh, Matt . . ."

"I know, I know . . ." And I *do* know. I'm in a serious jam, but I still start to laugh. "I should look before I leap."

"Out of the frying pan . . ." he says, but his smile is forced. He mostly just seems tired and worried, the way he always looks when we're talking about me.

"I haven't seen Minnie," I say, changing the subject. I'm referring to Min He, the old Asian woman who is both the park manager and Queeg's on-again, off-again lady friend. Their relationship is a long, complicated story that I try not to think about because it brings with it mental images of saggy, naked old people.

"She's at her daughter's. I'm picking her up tomorrow."

"I'll leave early." Min He hates me, and with good reason. Another story, but one that isn't particularly long or complicated.

I take a sip of my water and close my eyes, soaking in the moist Florida evening, the tree frogs and the crickets singing, the palms rustling in a breeze so soft I can't even feel it.

When I open them, I see Queeg watching me.

"What?" I ask.

He shakes his head and smiles. "Sometimes you look just like your mother."

"I don't look anything like her," I say, and we both know it's true. She was petite and soft. I'm tall and knobby. She had bright copper curls and green eyes that changed color with her moods. I have blond frizzy hair and blue-gray eyes that are a little larger than they need to be. My mother was striking, maybe beautiful. I, on the other hand, am nothing special.

"Mattie?"

"Yeah."

"What's really going on?" he asks.

I can't say I don't consider it, laying all my problems—broke, homeless, pregnant—at his Hush Puppy–wearing feet. Ten years ago that's what I would have done. Hell, an hour ago that's what I planned to do. But looking at him tonight I see a deep weariness I've never noticed before. It scares me.

"Nothing," I say. "Just my usual shit."

He smiles and gets a familiar look on his face. I know what's coming next.

"Well, sweetheart, when life gives you lemons . . ."

"Zip it, old man."

I can see from his grin that he's tempted to keep pulling my chain, but in the end he zips it, thank God.

For as long as I've known him, every single time I've had a problem, Queeg trots out Lemons to Lemonade. And every single time he does that, it annoys the shit out of me, which in turn amuses the hell out of him. We may not technically be a family anymore, but considering how much fun we have irritating each other, you'd never know it.

I've tried explaining to him why that particular aphorism is so annoying, but he can't let it go. Deep down, he is still of the opinion that all I need is a better attitude. My opinion of that opinion is *fuck that shit*. As far as I'm concerned, there are two types of people in this world: people like Queeg who, when life gives them lemons make lemonade, and everybody else. And although those smug, cheerful lemonade-makers think the rest of us just sit around all day bitching about not getting oranges, they're wrong. It's all about volume. When you're ass-deep in lemons, you start looking for a shovel, not a pitcher and a cup of sugar.

Queeg clears his throat and leans back in his chair, lifting one leg up and crossing it over the other. He still wears sock garters.

"So," he says. "Is your phone working?"

As usual, this afternoon I ignored a call from him, and, as usual, I feel bad about it. "As far as I know."

"Somebody's been trying to get in touch with you."

"Area code 918?"

He nods.

A 918 number has shown up on my phone a dozen times the past three weeks, but I've never answered it. If I've learned anything in my thirty years, it's that the surprises in my life aren't birthday parties and engagement rings. My surprises are visits to emergency rooms, flashing lights in my rearview, or more recently, a stupid blue line on a white plastic stick.

"I've seen that one come up a couple times," I tell him.

Queeg sits up a little straighter and frowns. "And you never answered?"

I shrug. "I don't usually answer when I don't know who's calling." This is the truth, but not the whole truth. There's more coming.

"You don't usually answer my calls either."

And there it is.

Bracing his hands on the table he pushes himself up. I grab the other side to hold it steady. At the edge of the concrete slab he upends his beer, pouring the last half into the weeds.

"You should at least set up your voice mail."

But then I'd have to listen to messages is what I think, but I don't say it. Instead I say, "You're right."

"The lawyer wouldn't tell me much, Mattie, but he did tell me that your grandmother is dead."

A quiet space opens between us. He's watching my face for the reaction I'm struggling not to show.

"Your mother's mother," he adds.

I don't know what he wants me to say, so I just nod. For years Queeg has been after me to contact my maternal grandmother, and for years I've been putting him off. *Ignorance is bliss*, I'd remind him. *Sometimes it's just ignorance*, he'd reply. I guess now it's too late to find out which one of us was right.

He tosses the bottle at an oil-drum trash can, and it goes in even though the can must be thirty feet away. "With your mom gone, it leaves you as the closest relation, so I think you've inherited something. Maybe you should give them a call." He steps down off the slab and starts toward his trailer. "I'm going to bed. The spare linens are in the cabinet under the TV. Don't forget to lock up when you come in."

The light is fading but there's enough reflecting off the clouds to make out some seagulls in the distance. They're so far away that they look like little checkmarks, the way I used to draw them when I was a child.

"Hey, Cap . . ."

He stops and turns back. "What?"

"What was her name?"

"Tilda Thayer. Her name was Matilda, too."

I feel a prickle as the hairs on my arms stir, and I shiver, just a little. I'm wondering if this is the first time he's told me her name, or if it's just the first time I've listened.

"Where is area code 918?" I ask.

"Gandy, Oklahoma. Where your mom grew up."

"Seriously? Who grows up in Oklahoma?"

He tilts his head to one side, and even though it's too dark to really see his face, I can imagine the look of exasperation that's surely there.

"Everybody grows up somewhere, Mattie."

I can't resist the setup. "Growing old may be mandatory, but growing up is optional," I say, even though Queeg and I both know that's not completely true. Not everybody gets a chance to grow old.

He nods, a little sadly it seems to me, then climbs into his trailer and he's gone.

CHAPTER 3

Two years ago, I came and stayed with Queeg for a couple of days over Christmas. At the time, I was living in a crappy duplex with two almost-strangers who rented me their couch for a-hundred-fifty a month. One of my roommates had finally gotten visitation rights, and her two kids were coming to spend a few days, so she needed the couch. She offered to pay me ten bucks for the two nights, but I told her not to worry about it. But later, when I noticed that I was out of cigarettes, I rounded up and slipped a couple packs of her Camels in my suitcase. I figured that was the best of both worlds—she felt like I was being generous, but I knew I wasn't, so there was no resentment on my part. Win, win.

It was the first time since I was seventeen, when Queeg left my mom, that my stepfather and I had spent more than a couple of hours together, and at first it was awkward, the two of us breathing the same air. Then we both got drunk and opened presents. We laughed about the crazy shit my mother used to pull. His only Christmas music was a Lawrence Welk album, and I wasn't about to let that happen, so he put on an old Gordon Lightfoot cassette tape and we sang "The Wreck of the Edmond Fitzgerald." Looking back at that Christmas Eve, it may be one of my favorites ever.

The next morning, my head still thumping, we drove down to Fort Pickens and parked at the last public beach lot. He pulled a big plastic tablecloth and a couple of old blankets from his trunk, and I followed him with the thermos of coffee down onto the sand. He'd slipped his loafers off in the car and was wearing socks, but I'd left on my sandals and wished I hadn't. Three steps, and the cool sand had worked its way between my skin and the leather. By the time we'd spread out the plastic and sat down, my feet had an angry pink outline of every strap.

I'd always loved an empty winter beach, and it was nice sitting there, wrapped up in a blanket, listening to the waves, my face to the wind. The seagulls swung overhead, their paths tracing lazy ellipses. As I watched they tightened their circles until we were the center. We had nothing for them, but they didn't know that.

After a few minutes Queeg broke the silence. "Penny for your thoughts."

Since my thoughts at that moment were of the kids sleeping on my couch and how much I hoped they weren't bed wetters, I felt confident replying, "You wouldn't get your money's worth."

"I was thinking about your mom," he said.

Of course he was. This was her favorite spot on the beach, the one she always used to pick if we got here early enough: just far enough over that the noise from the parking lot wasn't obvious, but not too far for a woman and a little kid to drag a cooler and an umbrella. Later, when Queeg was with us and he carried the umbrella, we could easily have gone further, where the sand was cleaner and the crowds thinner, but my mother still stopped here. She'd turn her back to the ocean and lift her towel, letting the wind straighten the stripes, before lowering it onto the sand.

"I always felt a little funny about how few people came to her memorial service," he said.

"I know." It hadn't surprised me it was just the two of us, her doctors, and the staff of the funeral home. But it had surprised my stepfather.

"I don't know that she would have wanted me to," Queeg said. "But I called and told her family."

I looked over at him, confused. *Her family*, I remember thinking, *is sitting right here*.

"I talked to her mother," he added. "But she said she couldn't come to the service. She didn't tell me why."

I turned my attention back to the sea, hoping he hadn't noticed my surprise. Whenever I'd asked my mother about her parents, she'd said they were gone. It was clear that my asking about them made my mother unhappy, so at some point I stopped asking. Eventually I stopped caring. Or at least that's what I told myself.

I didn't turn to look at him when I said, "She told me her parents were dead."

He paused so long before replying that I thought the wind had taken my words before they reached him, but finally he said, "She was wrong."

I remember thinking that was an interesting way to say *she was lying*.

He put his arm around me. "That August, it was so hot and so crowded . . ."

I smiled. I knew what afternoon he was talking about—*the* afternoon, the last time we would ever come to the beach together. Mom and me and Queeg—we'd finally finished fixing up the old Malibu, and we came out to celebrate. The day had been perfect. We'd filled the cooler with cans of Orange Crush and brought the old umbrella even though it had gotten too rusty to lock open.

We propped it up, leaning on the sand, to provide a tiny puddle of shade where we could crouch, drinking from the icy cans.

But Queeg was still talking. "I had to wait until dark."

And that's when I realized we were remembering two different August afternoons. Mine was the last truly happy memory I have with my mother. His was a last memory, too.

"It was windy so I couldn't really scatter her or she'd have ended up in the dunes. I had to carry the bag into the ocean and open it underwater."

Watching the waves rolling on the sand, I imagined the scene, Queeg easing out into the water, plastic bag clutched to his bare chest. I closed my eyes, but the imagined memory was still there. "She died in December, Queeg," I said.

"I kept thinking you'd come down so we could do it together."

My heart broke a little when he said that, and I whispered, "Sorry."

It was partially true. Although I wasn't sorry I'd missed dissolving my mother in the salty waves, I really was sorry that he'd waited for me, that he had depended on my help. He should've known better.

We were quiet for a minute, but Queeg was watching me, at least I think he was. I made sure my eyes stayed focused on the horizon, where I watched . . . something, bobbing in the waves. Was it a boat or a buoy? It's hard sometimes to tell the difference. I knew Queeg was waiting for me to say something, for me to explain why I wouldn't drive three hours to watch my own mother laid to rest.

A gull landed near the water's edge and picked its way up the sand to only a couple feet from where we sat.

"Shoo," Queeg said, waving his hand at the bird. "Get out of here." It hopped back a few feet, but continued to watch us with one flat eye, unblinking and as gray as the water.

"Flying rats," Queeg mumbled. I still wasn't looking at him, but I heard him sigh.

The bird heard it, too, cocking its head to one side and taking a hopeful hop closer.

"If only your mom were here," Queeg added. At the time I thought he was talking about how my mom always brought food for the gulls, but now I'm not sure. He might have been talking about everything else.

I nodded, not trusting my voice.

"Are you okay, sweetheart?"

Again, I nodded, keeping my face turned toward the sea. I didn't want him to see how the wind was making my eyes water.

SUNDAY

*A journey of a thousand
miles begins with a single step.*

CHAPTER 4

I'm awake by six fifteen. The light coming in from the edge of the curtains hits me right in the face, and the Herculon upholstery on Queeg's couch is itchy right through the sheet. There's no point in trying to fall back asleep. When I step outside, I see a few other residents up and about, but Queeg's car is gone—either he's already left to pick up Minnie, or he's gone to get doughnuts. I hope it's doughnuts.

I drag the lawn chair that's next to his trailer out into the sun and sit down. Then I turn on my phone to see how many missed calls came in last night from Nick.

There are many.

I call him, smiling as I listen to his phone ring and ring and ring. I'm waking him up. He hates that.

He answers with a groan.

"Good morning!" I use my most annoyingly cheerful voice.

I hear another groan and the rustle of bedsheets. I can imagine him sitting on the edge of the bed, sheet puddled in his lap, the morning light shining on his freshly waxed chest.

"Where is it?" he asks.

"Where is what?" I already know but don't want him to know that I know.

"The guitar strap."

"Which guitar strap?" I know this answer, too. Nick owns two guitar straps, but only one of them would make him call me fourteen times in one night. I'm asking because I want to make him say it.

Nick makes a soft angry-animal sound and then says, "My collector's-item-near-mint-condition-brown-leather-guitar-strap-signed-by-Jimmy-Page-and-Jeff-Beck." As always, he blends the description into one long word.

He's extremely annoyed. Excellent.

"Oh, *that* strap. I haven't seen it in a while." This is true-ish. I haven't seen it since I tossed it in my car yesterday afternoon.

"Bullshit. I know you have it, and I want it back."

"Why would I take that sweaty old thing?"

"Because it's worth a bundle."

"Really?" I took the strap to mess with him, but now I'm wondering how much, exactly, is a bundle?

"I'm gonna call the cops."

I laugh. "You'd better hide your bongs and air out that apartment before you let a cop inside."

There's a short pause during which I picture Nick taking an experimental sniff, and then he says, "You're at your stepfather's, aren't you?"

"Nope." Even as I say this, I see Queeg's white Toyota approaching slowly from the north. He's not alone in the car.

"I know you are. I'm getting in my car right now."

"Don't bother," I tell him. "I'll be long gone." It's three hours from his bed in Tallahassee to this folding chair in Pensacola.

He switches tactics. "Don't be that way, baby. You know you belong here with me. Come home."

My throat tightens. There's comfort to be found in the familiar, even when the familiar isn't all that great. But the thing is, once you've lived with someone, you learn their little tricks. Nick can do a pretty good *nice*, but it's not the real deal. His is a thin, watery nice, a niceness-au-jus drizzled over a great big asshole sandwich.

"I don't think so," I say.

He starts some name-calling, but by now Queeg has parked his car, so I end the call before Nick has a chance to get warmed up. I stuff the phone back in my pocket, and my loneliness back wherever it came from.

Min He is in the car with Queeg. This is going to get interesting.

Min He and Queeg were an item before he met my mother, so when he broke it off with Min He to date and then marry my mom, Min He, rightly I suppose, thought of my mother as a man-thief. And since I borrowed two hundred dollars from her three years ago and never paid her back, she thinks of me, rightly again, as a regular thief. Queeg has tried, on several occasions, to pay her back on my behalf, but she won't hear of it. I haven't given her the money either, partly because two hundred bucks is a lot of money, and partly because it's kind of fun having this miniature Asian lady so angry with me. Her skin is wrinkled and dark like an apple that's been left out in the sun, and she must wear dentures, because when she frowns—and around me that's all the time—her face folds up like a little brown fist.

As she climbs out of Queeg's car, she looks everywhere except at me. She's holding a box of doughnuts and when Queeg walks around the car to take them from her, she resists him for a second before letting go. He must have told her they're for me. He's carrying one of those little cardboard caddies for drinks in which there are three large Styrofoam cups. He holds it up and Min He pulls one out, then he walks to me holding the doughnut box in one hand and the drinks in the other.

"Good morning, Minnie," I say. She hates it when I pronounce her name like Mickey's gal.

"I am not as the mouse. My name is Min He, stupid girl."

I grin. There's something about this woman that always cheers me up. "And my name is Mattie, not *stupid girl*."

She narrows her eyes. "You are both."

Well, she's got me there.

Queeg lifts the drink caddy toward me. "There's a coffee and an orange juice."

My mouth starts to water; the pregnancy queasiness is starting up again. I take the juice and snag a chocolate frosted out of the box.

"Did you know that orange juice and Slim Jims mixed together tastes just like Thai food?"

He looks at me for a second and then asks, "Do I want to know how you discovered that?"

"Nope." I shove about a third of the doughnut into my mouth and manage to chew most of it and swallow before asking, "Do you have a computer and a printer?"

He shakes his head but glances at Min He. She knows what's coming and starts shaking her head *no* before I even ask.

"Oh come on, Minnie," I plead. "I only need it for five minutes."

"No way. You will find some way to steal—"

"I will not. Tell her, Queeg. Tell her that I've changed my ways."

"Her lips," Min He says, mysteriously, and then gestures with her hand holding the coffee, sloshing some onto her knuckles. "Ouch!" she adds. "This coffee is really hot."

"What about my lips?"

Queeg removes the lid from his cup and takes a cautious sip. "These Styrofoam cups work well."

I try again. "What about my lips?" I turn to Queeg. "Did she say, *lips*?"

"They're better than the ones at Starbucks," Queeg says.

"There are lips at Starbucks?"

He laughs. "The cups at Starbucks aren't as good. The coffee isn't as good either."

"Burnt," Min He says.

"Is somebody going to tell me what's—"

"She was trying to say that your lips were moving, Matt."

Now I understand. For years Queeg has said that he knows when I'm lying because it's when my lips are moving. I guess he shared that running gag with his girlfriend.

"Et tu, Minnie?" I ask.

Queeg laughs, but Min He frowns, pointing at the doughnut box. "I only ate one, stupid girl."

I wolf down another doughnut while Queeg negotiates with Min He. I am finally allowed to go into the office trailer, supervised by Queeg, to use the computer. It's not until I explain that I want it to print off driving directions that she relents.

I fire up the computer and then call back that 918 number and listen to their answering machine. *Barber, Smith and Franklin, Attorneys at Law.* I plug Pensacola in one slot and their address in Gandy, Oklahoma, in the other and print out the directions. Queeg stands over me as I do this, watching but not saying a word. I'm sorely tempted to download some porn just to annoy Minnie. That's probably why he's standing there.

He waits until I've grabbed the paper from the printer, and we've gone back outside before he asks. "You're going to Gandy?"

"Yup."

"Now?"

Min He is standing a little distance away to make it seem as if she's giving us privacy, but I see her interest pick up when she hears us talking about me leaving.

"Why not?" I reply.

"You're crazy."

He's right, of course. I am crazy, but I need to take my crazy somewhere else. Camping out on Queeg's sofa is going to make all of us crazy.

"Nah," I reply. "Just irresponsible. Undependable. Erratic, even."

Min He snorts at this, and I'm pretty sure she mutters, "And stupid."

"First you won't answer their calls, and now you're driving a thousand miles without knowing what they want?"

"Eight hundred," I tell him.

He points to my car. "You're driving eight hundred miles in that?" Now he's getting mean.

"It's an adventure."

He raises an eyebrow. "You complain about going to the grocery store."

"I complain about the shopping part, not the driving part." I am lying. I complain about both parts.

"But it's Sunday."

"I'll crash at a cheap motel there tonight. That way I can be at the lawyer's office first thing tomorrow to pick up my check."

"That's not how it works," he says. "There's going to be paperwork."

I wave away his concerns with my hand. I've stopped listening.

I understand that driving to Gandy today is a dumb idea, but Nick might well be on his way over here, and that's a confrontation I'd like to avoid. Besides, it's a cool, breezy morning, I'm riding a glazed-doughnut sugar rush, and I'm feeling a little loose and what-the-fuckish. Getting out of here sounds so good I can't stop myself.

"I'll be fine."

"What about your job?" Queeg is saying. "Don't you have anything booked next week?"

I think about my almost empty calendar and how easy it's been to watch my dead mother's business die. I didn't kill it, or at least it wasn't premeditated. One day I just didn't bother to return a call about a booking, and when I realized how much I enjoyed not having to take those pictures, I ignored the next call, too. My phone doesn't ring all that often anymore.

"Nope."

He frowns. "Your mother stayed busy when she ran the studio."

"I'm not my mother." This is my stock answer for any comparison to her. Unfortunately, it's not ringing as true as it once did.

Queeg sighs and then fumbles in his pocket, pulling out his wallet. I can see that there aren't many bills inside.

"Stop. I've got money." I don't mention that it isn't much and I'll need to put it all in my gas tank.

He pulls out the bills and glances at them. "Fifty-eight. Here."

He's holding the cash out toward me, and I'm shaking my head. "You should go shopping with that money," I say. "You need a new cardigan. You're starting to look like some down-and-out Mr. Rogers." I stick my finger through the largest of the holes in his threadbare sweater. "And stop smoking before you set yourself on fire."

"Don't lecture me," he says. "Either take this or I'm going to throw it away." He points to the trash barrel and Min He frowns. She's not going to let that money stay in the trash can.

I take the cash. "Fine. Thank you. I'll pay you back." At this I see Min He warming up on a speech regarding my promises to pay back loans, but before she can get started I turn and walk to Queeg's trailer. He follows me inside.

"Is there any way I can stop you from doing this?"

"Nope." I get my toothbrush from the bathroom and pick up yesterday's underwear off the floor.

He shakes his head and sighs. "You're a force of nature, Matt."

"What? Like gravity?"

"More like an earthquake."

I brush past Queeg, walk back out of the trailer and down the steps, heading toward my car.

My stepfather is right behind me. "A hurricane."

"Oh, come on—"

"Tornado, tsunami—"

"Okay, okay. I'm a disaster. I get the picture." I toss my stuff in the car and then walk back to Queeg. He's standing there with his arms crossed over his chest. He's acting like he's angry, but I recognize it for what it is. He's worried.

"I'm going, and that's that," I tell him. "I know exactly what I'm doing." That's a lie, and he knows it, but I can see in his face that I've won. Even Captain Queeg can't stop a hurricane.

Instead, he gives me a wry half-smile and says, "Your lips are moving."

And then there's one of those uncomfortable silences where we both realize that a Hallmark-card moment is just around the corner unless somebody acts fast.

"I'd better get going," I say. "And if Nick comes by looking for me, don't tell him where I've gone, okay?"

Queeg sighs again and shuffles his white old-man sneakers in the gravel. "I have a bad feeling about this, Matt."

When he looks up and his gaze meets mine, I take a moment to study my stepfather, the slight sheen of sweat on his skin even though the morning is cool, the way his cheeks have gone from lean to sunken, his wracking cough that rattled through the trailer all night. Maybe he should save one of his bad feelings for himself.

"Never put off until tomorrow what you can do today. It's one of your favorites, Queeg."

He's shaking his head.

"I'll be fine," I tell him. "I'll be back in a couple days."

He opens his arms, and I step inside. His familiar smell—wool and menthol cigarettes and Old Spice aftershave—makes my throat ache. "I'll call you tomorrow morning," I promise.

He doesn't reply so I pull back and look up at his face. He's not looking at me; he's looking at Min He. "Make it tomorrow afternoon," he says.

"What's going on tomorrow morning?"

"Just another damn doctor's appointment."

I'm not worried until I glance over at Min He. For once I see an expression on her face that's something other than rage. It's fear.

I take a step back. "*Another* appointment?"

"It's nothing."

"Define *nothing*."

"Everything is fine," he says, draping an arm around my shoulders. "Would I lie to you?"

If he thought the truth would hurt me, the answer to that is *yes*.

I glance over again at Min He. She's staring at me, expectantly. This is when a good daughter says she's not leaving, that she'll stay in town and drive him to his appointment tomorrow, she'll sit in the waiting room, later she'll go with him to talk to the doctor, to get the results. To hear the bad news.

We exchange glances, Min He, Queeg, and I. All of us know the truth of the situation. For all his bluster, Queeg wants me to stay. Maybe he needs me to stay. I feel a thick panic rising in my chest.

I open my car door and climb inside. "So, I'll call tomorrow afternoon." I pitch my voice to sound breezy, hoping Queeg will play along.

He does. "It's a plan," he says with a smile. He's always been good at hiding disappointment.

I shut the door and roll down the window. Queeg comes up beside the car and leans over. "Are you going to stop by the beach before you go?"

It's the closest thing to visiting my mother's grave, and he can't help but remind me about that once in a while. Now and then when we're winding up a telephone conversation he'll ask if I've been lately, and I always tell him *yes*, which is never really true. When I go to the beach, I avoid Fort Pickens, instead choosing Casino Beach or Opal Beach. I tell myself it doesn't really matter. It's all the same water.

"Not today," I tell him. "It's in the wrong direction."

He nods. For all that he's still sentimental about a woman he divorced years before her death, Queeg is a practical man. He understands an urge to go in the right direction.

"Drive safe, sweetheart," he says.

I turn the key and after an initial roar the engine settles down to a gentle rumble with only a faint rattling sound. Nothing I'll be able to hear over the radio.

Queeg steps away and Min He comes forward and leans in close to deliver her parting words.

"You are a bad one," she says in a voice pitched just loud

enough for me to hear over the engine. "You will get what you deserve. Someday . . ." here she pauses, frowning as she struggles with the words. "Someday, your roast chicken will come home."

When I laugh at her mangling of one of Queeg's favorites, she scowls and straightens up, crossing her arms over her ample chest. The engine noise drowns out her voice, but her lips move in one last "Stupid girl."

Queeg is grinning. That one, he heard.

I back the car up, turn it around, and am almost to the gate when I look over my shoulder at Queeg standing there, looking frail, his gray sweater blending into the backdrop of the cheerless, sagging trailers. He has an arm around Min He's waist, and I'm glad that he has her, even if it seems to me like she has a pretty wide mean streak.

I tap the horn and stick my arm out the window for one last wave.

"Hurry home," he calls out.

I accelerate, but slowly, checking my rearview mirror every few seconds. With each glance, Queeg grows smaller, the grip of his love for me less and less painful, until finally I can breathe again. One last glance in the mirror and he is just a speck on the horizon, his hand still raised in a farewell. Or a benediction. I'm not sure which.

CHAPTER 5

Anything that can go wrong, will go wrong Queeg likes to say, and
he's not even the one trying to drive eight hundred miles in a piece-
of-shit 1978 Chevy Malibu. It's around Hammond, Louisiana, that
I first notice something is wrong. A faint shudder when I accelerate, a minor lurch, then another. Forty-five minutes later I'm near-
ing Baton Rouge and the lurching has amplified and my progress
down the road is involving a bit more hopping than I would prefer.
It's only happening when I speed up or slow down, but that's not
helpful in the long run. It's not like I can drive another six hundred
miles without stopping even if I could forgo eating and drinking. I
don't have a bottomless gas tank or an astronaut diaper.

I pull off the interstate in Merrydale, a suburb of Baton Rouge,
which, for the record, seems far too dreary and flat to have inspired
its name. My lunch is unexceptional, but eating it averts my stupid
empty-stomach nausea. Things are looking up, in fact, until I put
the car in drive and find that I've lost my high gear completely.

My new maximum speed without redlining the rpm is thirty
miles per hour. The car moves smoothly, if loudly, in this gear, so

I decide to keep driving—not that there are many other choices on a Sunday afternoon with no money in the middle of a state where I don't know a soul. So, emergency flashers blinking away, I crawl along Interstate 10, mile after mile, just me and my piece of shit Malibu with the vinyl trim peeling in so many places that it looks like fur, rust on two fenders, backseat stuffed full of all my worldly possessions. Cars slow as they drive past, the driver and passengers ogling my little redneck melodrama. I give them each the finger—a little cherry to sit atop my white-trash sundae.

I stop a few times for soft drinks, gum, a bathroom. It's an interesting population at small town all-night convenience stores. Lots of tattoos and unwashed hair. Nobody in these sad places gives my car a second glance. These are my people, my mother's people. Not a single one of them looks interested in making lemonade.

As the night grinds on, I come to understand that twenty hours alone in a car gives a person a lot of time to think. I turn the radio off when the static starts and back on when I see a town coming up. I sing along when I know the song, I hum when I don't, and I sigh when every once in a while a song finds a crack and wriggles inside, causing memories to shift and slide. In a rare moment of clarity I see this loss of my high gear for what it is: a pretty damn good metaphor for my life.

When we are young we are limitless. I remember leaning into the wind and feeling as if I could run until the sand turned to water, swim past the horizon, and fly until the blue sky around me filled with stars. There was a time when I believed my whole life stretched before me, rich with promise.

Now?

Not so much.

CHAPTER 6

The summer I turned five years old, my mother and I moved into an apartment complex with few children, and I was lonely. Things weren't all that great for my mother either; they'd cut her hours at the Photo Gem and she'd had to take a second job at Woolworth's. During the summer, while she was at work, Mom left me with our downstairs neighbor, Mrs. Klapper. The old woman was nice enough, but deaf as a post and addicted to game shows, so all day long her television played at ear-splitting levels. Mercifully, she took a long nap after lunch, which gave me a chance to watch a few cartoons with the volume down.

Mrs. Klapper had a key to our apartment in case she needed something from up there for me, and I think I wasn't supposed to know that she kept it in a little silver bowl on the mantel. But, like most five-year-olds, I knew a lot of things I wasn't supposed to know.

That summer *Peter Pan*, the Disney version, was rereleased in theaters. We didn't have a lot of extra money, but my mother must have understood how long the days were for me, because the weekend it opened she called in sick and took me to the Saturday matinee.

I'm not sure if that was the first movie I saw on the big screen, but it's the first one I remember. The sticky floor, the salty popcorn, having to sit on my knees to see over the head in front of me—I remember it all. But mostly I remember wanting to fly.

It felt so obvious to me. With enough fairy dust and lovely thoughts anyone could fly. Lovely thoughts aren't hard to come by when you're five, and in our apartment dust wasn't in short supply. Unfortunately, even after several weeks of lovely thoughts and trying everything from flour to the dust from the windowsill, my feet had never lifted from the olive green carpet.

I started kindergarten that fall and underwent the usual strain of adjusting to school and trying to make friends, but I never gave up on my dream of flying. It wasn't long before Halloween appeared on the horizon, and I had an epiphany. I wasn't Wendy; I was Tinker Bell. What I needed were wings.

Convincing my mother that last year's costume, black leotard and tail with cat ears on a headband, would not work again this year, took all the whining I could muster, which, in all honesty, was a fair amount. I wasn't an easy child. But when you're five and you want to fly, the ends justify the means.

The day before Halloween, my mother brought it home. She pulled the folded package out of her purse, and carefully worked the costume out of the wrapper. Rather than cutting off the tags, she pinned them up inside.

Despite my best efforts to channel only lovely, flight-worthy thoughts, watching my mother's care with the costume brought an unhappy thought to mind. "Did you steal that?" I asked.

"No," she said. "I borrowed it."

"From who?"

"Whom. Come try it on."

I stepped into the shiny blue tunic, avoiding the pins. Tinker Bell's dress was green, but I didn't mention that to my mother.

I tried again. "Borrowed from whom?"

"It's a little big," she said. "But it will have to do."

"The pins are sticking me."

She shifted the pinned-up tags until they were less annoying and then slipped the wings on and adjusted their straps.

"There," she said. "You look like an angel."

"I'm a fairy," I said, although in truth the wings were shaped more like an angel's wings than Tinker Bell's.

"Take it off until tomorrow night." My mother eased me out of the wings and then the dress.

"Can I take it to school tomorrow?"

She shook her head.

"Just the wings?"

"You'll get them dirty," she said. "It's borrowed, remember? I have to take it back to the store Saturday."

I think I knew my mother was misusing the word *borrowed*. I was pretty sure that none of the other kids at school were wearing costumes their mothers had borrowed from a store without asking. But I didn't mention it again. I just hugged her tight and promised that I would be extra careful with the costume. And I meant it. Really.

The following afternoon, when the school bus dropped me off I went to Mrs. Klapper's as usual. I let myself in; she always left her door unlocked in the afternoons so that my arrival wouldn't interrupt her nap. That day, however, instead of going to the kitchen to eat the sandwich she had left for me, I reached up and plucked the key to my apartment from the silver bowl, then went back out, quietly shutting the door behind me.

The costume was right where my mother had hung it. Carefully . . . oh so carefully, I put it on. The wings were more difficult to get into by myself, but not impossible. I was cautious with the fairy dust, talcum powder this time, lightly dusting just a tiny amount on my arms and legs. I put just a little bit in my hair. More would have been better. In the movie, Tinker Bell had sprinkled it liberally over Wendy, John, and Michael, but my costume was borrowed. This would have to do.

The wind was gusty that afternoon, and as I walked out on our balcony, I remember hearing the whisper of dry leaves scraping along the sidewalk below. I swung my legs over the top of the wooden railing and sat cautiously, careful not to get a splinter. I looked at the browning weeds and grass directly beneath me, and then raised my chin to look at the green grass of the gated playground at the nicer apartment complex across the street. A breeze plucked at my wings, and I smiled. And I thought lovely thoughts. And I believed. And I jumped.

It was only a broken arm. It could have been much worse, but my mother had no lovely thoughts that Halloween. She was furious. Furious with Mrs. Klapper, with me, and with Walt Disney as I recall. I missed three days of kindergarten and the teacher had all the kids in my class donate some of their Halloween candy for me. Of course, they just gave up their reject candy, Bit-O-Honey, Sweet Tarts, Almond Joys. But I didn't mind. I would have done the same thing.

When my mother asked me why I had jumped, I told her about the wind and the fairy dust and how green the grass was in the playground across the street. It worked, I told her, for a few seconds I'd been flying. It wasn't until I took my eyes off the distant green grass and looked down at the weeds below me that I started to fall. I still remember how she frowned and shook her head as I talked. After a while, I stopped trying to explain. If she couldn't understand wanting to fly, then I couldn't teach it to her.

There was no more Mrs. Klapper. From then on I stayed

with Mrs. Roberts, and she never took naps and her apartment always smelled like broccoli. The costume was also gone, filthy from the fall and split along one side where the hospital had cut it off. My mother told me not to worry about it, but I did. As far as I know, she never got in trouble for taking the costume, but I understood that it was because of me that her borrowing had turned into stealing. When she told me that she couldn't return the costume, I asked her if we could just wash it and keep it—at least the wings—but she said no and threw it all in the trash.

And when she turned back around and leaned down to speak to me, I can still remember exactly what she said. "There's no such thing as magic," she told me. "You can *believe* all you want, but it's never going to do you any good. Nobody flies. We only fall."

It's after four a.m. by the time my whining Malibu and I finally reach the Gandy City Limits sign. There's a sad-looking motel with a red "vacancy" light on, but even if I had the money, I wouldn't rent a room to sleep for less than four hours, so I continue following the directions. A few houses start to appear as the state highway gradually turns into a city street. With every block the houses get older and smaller and closer together until eventually they're supplanted by businesses, one of which, thank God, has a sign out front that reads "Barber, Smith & Franklin PLLC."

I pull in, turn off the car, and get out to stretch. The silence is glorious. The only sound is a faint rustle of wind in the trees, the only light a hazy glow from a moon mostly hidden by fast-moving clouds. I need to sleep, but first I need to pee.

Once my eyes adjust to the darkness I walk along the edge of the parking lot. At the back, next to the rear of the building, there's a break in the pavement, a weedy patch between the parking lot and a privacy fence. I pick my way through some taller brushy plants and find a reasonably flat spot. I'm not one who normally answers the call of nature in such close proximity to actual nature, but some things simply can't be helped. After another glance up and down the street I drop my pants and squat, only to discover that I've chewed so much gum to stay awake that somehow even my urine smells minty fresh.

Back in the car, I roll the windows wide open and recline my seat as far as it will go. The cool darkness presses on my skin like water, and when I think of Queeg's *bad feeling,* a heaviness that is more than mere exhaustion settles on my chest. Is it the weight of not knowing anything about my mother's past, or the weight of knowing everything about my own? They say you can't take it with you when you go, but we all know that's not entirely true. You can carry your secrets to the grave.

I take a measured breath in and out, and try to relax. Phantom white lane-marker lines flicker behind my eyelids, and I feel a disorienting sense of motion, as if I'm still trying to get someplace, but I can't see where I'm going.

It feels a little like falling.

MONDAY

If it's too good to be true, it probably is.

CHAPTER 7

I wake, sweating, the sun shining straight on my face. I check the time; it's almost eight. Grabbing the pillowcase that holds my toiletries, I climb out of the car and look around. I'm on what seems to be the outer edge of one of those quaint, redbrick downtowns. The kind where it looks like you're in a *Leave It to Beaver* episode until you notice that all the shop windows are covered in paper, and the only thriving businesses are attorneys, bail bondsmen, pawnshops, and payday loans places.

Other than my Malibu, this parking lot is empty, as are all the other lots adjoining the similar office buildings nearby. But across the street there's a church with a car parked outside. I walk over.

The main door of the sanctuary is open and I step inside. It's cool and dark and has the familiar blend of candle musk and lemon wood polish I've come to associate with some of the longest Sunday mornings of my life.

A man is standing near the altar, his back toward me, but at the sound of my footsteps he turns and heads in my direction. As he gets closer I notice both that he is wearing a white-tab in his collar and that he is movie-star handsome.

"I'm Father Barnes," he says, holding out his hand.

The priest's voice is deep and his hand warm as it envelops mine. He's even better looking up close. Remembering that it's been twenty-four hours since I've last brushed my teeth, I try to angle my dragon breath away from his lovely face. "Mattie Wallace. I'm sorry to bother you, but no place else seems to be open this early. May I use your restroom?"

"Certainly, right this way,"

He leads me through a small door at the front of the chapel, down a narrow hall to the restroom. When I emerge a few minutes later, I walk back down the hall and find the Father in his office a couple doors down.

I poke my head in and say, "Thanks. I appreciate it."

"No problem." He glances up from his computer. "Anything else I can help you with?" Again with the sexy little half smile. His thick dark hair and long eyelashes are killing me. He doesn't look much like Richard Chamberlain, but I still find myself getting all *Thorn Birds* about the man. What is it about forbidden fruit that makes it so very, very tasty?

"Do you have any idea when the law office across the street opens?"

"Any time now. But I'm pretty sure Charlie Franklin is out of town."

"Maybe I can see Smith or Barber?"

"Smith moved to Florida six months ago."

"And Barber?"

"Went to be with the Lord a few years back."

"Really? Wasn't he a lawyer?"

The priest's lips curl into a smile. He's heard the joke before, but he's going to humor me anyway. "I've only been here for a few months, but from what I've heard, Randall Barber was a good man. Honest, kind. Not your typical . . ." He pauses here, seeming to search for a word.

I'm waiting for *lawyer*, but instead he says, "Presbyterian."

I laugh a little harder than politeness requires. This man is beautiful and clever. He's the perfect blend of completely out of my league combined with entirely unavailable, that in my experience guarantees a broken heart. In other words: exactly my type.

My stomach is empty, and I can feel the queasiness revving up, my mouth starting to water. At this point my only two options are getting something into my stomach immediately, or running back to the bathroom. Luckily, there's a candy bowl on the corner of the priest's desk, and luckily again, Father Barnes takes note of my rabid interest in said bowl.

"Help yourself," he says.

I take one of the tiny obviously Halloween-themed candy bars, only fleetingly concerned about how many months there are between October and June. I rip open the package, stuff the candy in my mouth, and then reach back in and take as many more as I can hold with one hand.

Father Barnes gives me a worried look as I power-load another candy bar into my mouth, and then he reaches into a desk drawer and pulls out a business card.

"I hope we see each other again," he says.

I want to answer "me too," but my mouth is so full that I opt for nodding enthusiastically. He's probably just being polite, but if Adonis really wants to hang out with me, I'm all about making sure that happens.

"And if I can help you with anything else, please let me know," he adds.

Never make an offer you don't want accepted. I swallow the wad of candy in my mouth. "You know," I say, "there is one thing . . ."

With a belly full of chocolate, I can now appreciate the fact that it's a beautiful morning—warm but not hot, enough wind blowing to fluff my sleep-flattened hair but not so much that I'd be afraid to wear a dress. You know, if I had a dress. I left Father Barnes my keys, and he's probably on the phone right now calling a garage with a tow truck. I should feel bad about dumping the car problem on him, but he's a priest; helping people with unwashed hair and no money is practically written in his job description. Maybe when I get my inheritance I'll surprise him with some new churchy doodad—an altar cloth maybe, or a fancy brass candlesnuffer.

There are now two cars parked next to mine in the parking lot of Barber, Smith, and Franklin PLLC, so I hustle across the street, toss my toiletries back in my car, and then push through the office's ornate wooden door. Once inside, I have to slow down and give my eyes a moment to adjust; everything about this office is the exact opposite of a sunny June morning. The room is paneled in dark wood, burgundy velvet drapes frame the windows, and the carpet is a vivid emerald and deep like quicksand. The whole place feels like a cross between a bordello and a putting green.

Cutting across the room at improbable angles are strips of hard clear plastic, forming walkways, I suppose. I slog over, step up onto one, and follow the path—with the green carpet it's impossible not to think of it as a cart path—to the reception desk near the center of the room.

Seated at the desk is an impossibly perky woman, her face lit in happy anticipation of our upcoming conversation. As I approach she pecks a few last letters into her keyboard with her sculpted fingernails and then twists her chair to face me head-on. Her white teeth gleam in the dimly lit room.

"Good morning!" she says—exclamation point hers, not mine. "How may I help you?"

I have no good excuse for what I do next, except for the fact that I am highly allergic to perk. "I'm here to see my dear Uncle Barber. We haven't spoken in years, but he's been like a father to me."

And just like that, her sparkle is replaced with a stricken expression that almost makes me regret just asking to see a dead guy. Almost.

"Oooooh." The furrows between her brows deepen. "Oh my God!" Even in suffering she manages to sound excited. "Hang on a second!" She jumps to her feet and scurries, high heels tappity tapping on the plastic runner to a door in the back wall. She doesn't knock before entering.

I follow her, not really so much to overhear the conversation—I can only imagine how many exclamation points are flying around in there—but because such bright sunlight streams from the open door that I'm drawn, like a lost soul, or maybe a doomed moth, toward the light.

As I peek around the doorjamb, two heads turn to face me. Perky, standing next to a desk wringing her hands and, seated at the desk, a man with red hair cut short and freckles covering his face. The man isn't in *Mad Magazine*'s Alfred E. Neuman territory, but he's definitely one of those extremely gingery gingers. Not that there's anything wrong with that.

This office has wood floors and pale blue walls and sleek blinds rather than drapes, a balm to the senses after Mata Hari's golf course out there. The man behind the desk waves me inside and without standing, gestures to the wingback chair in front of his desk. "I'm Luke Lambert," he says. "Please have a seat. Can I have Patty get you some coffee?"

"No, thanks, I—"

"Iced tea?"

"No, I don't—"

"It's pomegranate!" This is from Patty, practically on her toes in eagerness.

"Well, sure," I say, sitting down in the proffered chair, "if it's *pomegranate . . .*"

Patty nods, aiming a grateful smile at me and at Mr. Lambert before hurrying out the door.

"I hate to be the bearer of bad news, Ms. . . ."

"Wallace. Mattie Wallace."

"But Randall Barber passed some time ago."

"I know. I'm sorry. I was just having a little fun with your secretary."

"Assistant."

"Right. Anyway, I talked to Father Barnes, and he already informed me that Mr. Barber *went to be with the Lord.*"

Luke Lambert raises a brow and cocks his head to one side, saying, "Well, that's certainly the best of the options available."

Another clever man. Excellent. "While we're on the subject of Father Barnes," I say. "Are Episcopal priests all into the celibacy stuff like regular priests?"

He frowns and studies me for a second before asking, "*Were* we on the subject of Father Barnes?"

"Well . . . we could be."

Mr. Lambert leans forward, resting his forearms on his desk. He's wearing a shirt and tie, but something about the way that shirt stretches across his shoulders hints at a very muscular build. His eyes are a dappled green and the few lines around them look like smile lines. I consider having a little flirt, but at the moment he seems annoyed with me.

"If I'm not mistaken," he says. "Episcopal priests are allowed to marry."

"Oh. Okay." I'm a little bummed. A human wife or girlfriend isn't nearly as interesting an adversary as Jesus.

Mr. Lambert is still talking and still looking annoyed. "But since you're not here to see Mr. Barber, and I'm not here to discuss Father Barnes, perhaps you could tell me what we *are* here to discuss?"

"I guess I need to see Mr. Franklin."

"Well, he's out of town, I'm afraid. But I'm his paralegal, and it's likely that I can help you if you'll tell me what this is regarding."

"My grandmother died and you guys have been trying to get in touch with me. About an inheritance, I assume."

His frown clears and he smiles, revealing nice, even teeth, a small dimple in one freckled cheek, and just a bit of a resemblance to Howdy Doody.

"You must be Tilda Thayer's granddaughter. Charlie has been trying to reach you for weeks. We must have had a wrong number."

"No, it was the right one."

He gives me a puzzled look. "Well, anyway, it's a pleasure to meet you, Ms. Wallace."

"Call me Mattie."

He nods. "Then call me Luke."

Patty steps back in the door and sets one tall glass down on the table next to my chair and the other on Luke's desk. He thanks her, and she flashes her Crest Strips smile and tap taps back out of the office. Luke lifts his glass and takes a sip of his tea. I lift my glass to follow suit, but stop when I notice several green leaves floating on the top.

Luke sees me studying the flora in my beverage and says, "It's fresh mint. Patty picks it every morning for the tea. We have some in our little garden out back."

"You're not talking about that weedy patch at the back of the parking lot, by the fence?"

He nods. "It doesn't look like much yet, but this spring we planted some mint, a couple pepper plants, and we hope to have some tomatoes later this summer." He takes another sip and smiles. "Try it. The mint adds a really interesting taste."

I set my tea down carefully. I'm pretty sure I know what it's going to taste like this morning. "I think I'll save it for later."

Howdy pulls out a file and spreads the contents on his desk. "Here's a copy of your grandmother's will." He holds a stack of papers out toward me.

I stand and step closer to take them from him and immediately see why the man didn't get up and shake my hand when I entered and why he's not standing now. Even the cart paths in the outer office are making sense. Luke Lambert is in a wheelchair.

"Thanks." I take my papers and sit back down, determined to try really hard to be nice. I'm uncomfortable around people with physical disabilities. Now, with emotional cripples, it's a different story. It's only around them that I truly feel at home.

"Let's see . . ." He glances at the papers and then back at me. "The good news is, now that we've located you," he pauses, correcting himself, "or, more accurately, now that you've located us, we can get things rolling."

I chuckle a little before I can stop myself. Now I'm left hoping that he thinks I'm extremely happy that we're going to get things rolling, and not that I cracked up because a man in a wheelchair said *get things rolling*, which you have to admit is a little bit funny. Or maybe I'm just punchy from lack of sleep. Or maybe I'm a jerk.

He continues without missing a beat. "Your grandmother's estate isn't overly large, which will speed things up."

I look at the clock on his wall, and say, "Great!"

He must have noticed me check the time, because he shakes his head and looks apologetic when he tells me, "Three months."

I smile at his little joke. It takes me longer than it should to understand he's not joking.

"Sorry," he adds.

Three months? I examine his words from several different angles but still come up with the number *three* followed by the word *months*. As in ninety days.

I breathe in and out a few times, considering my situation: I'm knocked up, flat broke, and I've killed my car. I'm stranded in a town where I don't know anybody and with no prospect of cash for three months.

I wait for the feelings of disappointment, frustration, regret—the trifecta of side effects that I have come to associate with most of my leaping-without-looking escapades. I inhale, exhale. And again. The trees outside the window wave, and above them there are birds circling, waiting perhaps for the wind to ease and the branches to settle to make for an easier landing. The air conditioner in the room cuts on with a hum, Luke Lambert shifts his papers an inch to the left, an inch to the right and yet . . . I feel . . . Nothing. I feel nothing; I'm completely numb. Surely it's the exhaustion. It's hard to believe that at thirty years old I'm already permanently out of give-a-shit.

It dawns on me that it's my turn to speak. "So, is that the bad news, Mr. Lambert?"

"Luke," he corrects me. "And no, three months is good actually. Probate often takes over six months."

I nod and he nods and we both smile. I think his is a polite smile, but I'm not sure what mine is. I mean, my teeth are showing, but it doesn't feel like a smile.

"So, what is it?" I ask.

"What is what?"

Wheelchair or no wheelchair, this man is making me cranky. "Well, usually, when someone says, *the good news is* . . . it means that means there's also bad news."

"Oh . . ." He busies himself with the papers on his desk, lifting them and tapping the ends to straighten the stack. "Well, I wouldn't exactly say *bad* news . . ."

"Spill it, Howdy."

He looks up at me, surprised. "Did you just call me *Howdy*?"

"Sorry," I say, but I'm not sorry, and I think he can tell.

He shuffles through his papers until he finds the one he's looking for. He studies it for a second and then looks back up at me. "There are several claims against the estate, and more creditors will probably surface after we publish the combined notice."

"So that means what, exactly?"

"Your grandmother has outstanding bills that have to be paid out of the proceeds of the estate liquidation."

"And I'll get what's left."

"That is correct." He clears his throat and picks up his papers, repeating the tap-and-straighten process. There's more, I can tell, and I'm pretty sure I'm not going to like whatever it is.

"Is there going to be anything left?" I ask.

He frowns and looks back down at the paper. It looks to be a list—a long list. "There are quite a few creditors who have filed a claim, but I think there'll be something remaining," he says. "She did leave a house."

"She left me her house?"

"Technically she left it to your mother. But as the surviving heir it goes to you."

"A house."

"Yes. Her house and the Winstons."

"Cigarettes?"

"Dogs."

I pause, certain that I have lost the thread of this conversation somewhere. Luke is watching me with a strained expression on his face. Perhaps *this* is the bad news. "Did you say, *dogs*?"

"Yes."

"Let me get this straight . . . she left me more than one dog and a house?"

"Two," he replies. "Dogs, I mean. Just one house."

"A nice house?"

"I don't know. But I've met the dogs. They're nice enough."

I pause to let this sink in. Luke seems perfectly happy to sit quietly and let me think.

"So, we sell the house . . ."

"Yes. After the court hearing you'll be named the executor, and you'll liquidate the assets and clear the liens against the estate."

"And keep whatever is left."

"Correct."

"And there will be something left," I add.

He pauses, doing a little maybe-maybe-not thing with his head and then says, "Probably."

"And the dogs?"

He shrugs. "They'll be yours."

"Probably?"

"No. I'm certain you'll get to keep them."

Luke is still smiling, and I'm grinning right back at him, with a real smile this time. I can't help it. Sure my life is in the crapper, and this turn of events feels a lot like somebody pressing the flush handle, but at the same time this seems like the funniest joke ever. How can I not appreciate its flawless execution?

I flip through the stack of papers in my lap; the will is dated seven years ago, two years before my mom died. I wonder if my grandmother considered redoing it when Queeg called and told her about her daughter's death. Surely he told Tilda about me. Maybe she left it as it was, knowing that it didn't matter, that they'd find me, and I'd be sitting in this chair. Or maybe she was like me, and she waited and waited until one day it was too late to change anything.

"The dogs are both named Winston?" I ask.

He nods. "To the best of my knowledge."

"Why do you suppose she did that?"

"Well, the simplest explanation would be that your grandmother really liked the name Winston."

"But do you think that's why?"

He takes a moment to slide his papers back into their file. When he looks up at me his expression is serious. "It's been my experience, Ms. Wallace, that when it comes to human behavior, the simplest explanation is rarely the correct one."

I notice that the branches on the trees outside are still shifting to and fro, but the birds are gone, having either landed or given up. My throat aches, and the hollow feeling in my chest is back, so I pick up my iced-tea glass and take a big gulp. Not bad. Not bad at all.

CHAPTER 8

The memories of all my childhood beach vacations have, for the most part, melted into a slurry of heat and grit and the smell of Coppertone suntan lotion. We always stayed at Two Pines, we always went to the same beach, shopped at the same store, crabbed off the same pier. Always too much sun for me, too much gin for my mom. Every year we'd come back to Tallahassee dehydrated and cranky.

Of course a few events stand out. When I was thirteen and we met Queeg, for instance. Or when I was eleven, and my mother talked me into letting her use the clothes iron to straighten my hair but then accidentally left the steam on, raising painful blisters on my neck. Or when I was seven years old and I almost drowned.

The trip that summer—the summer of the near drowning—started out like the rest. On our first day at the beach my mom met a man; that year it was a tall, skinny guy named Curtis, and for the rest of the week he nipped at her heels. Every day he'd come to the trailer park and drive us to the shore in his Firebird. I'd play in the water, and they'd lie under the umbrella and flirt.

At night he'd come by the trailer to watch TV, or sometimes my mom would turn up the radio and they'd go outside and dance. To this day, anytime I hear Rick Astley promise me all the things he's never going to do, it puts me right back outside that trailer at Two Pines, watching my mother and Curtis dance. I joined in as best I could, doing the kind of silly skipping and hopping that seven-year-olds call dancing. I can still remember the feel of the gravel rolling around under my thin rubber flip-flops.

Curtis wasn't a bad guy, and it was obvious that my mother enjoyed his attention. But even if he hadn't just been visiting Florida for the week, he and my mother would have never lasted long. He was goofy-looking and nice, and she was still in the market for handsome and cruel.

The memory of my near drowning is clear but fragmented. Unsettling. The rule was simple: I was not to go past the first sandbar unless my mother was with me. I obeyed the rule. Mostly. But it was Friday, our last day at the beach, and I remember standing there on the first sandbar, the water calm and only up to my waist. I looked at my mother in her pink bikini, lying on her towel next to Curtis. I could hear them laughing. I turned to look out at the second sandbar where everyone else was swimming. There were lots of kids out there playing with their parents.

I started out toward the next sandbar, but that's the last memory with any clear connection to the rest. After that they're jumbled up, overlapping, out of sequence. Me on my tiptoes with the water at my neck. A wave knocking me over. Losing my footing. Finding my footing. Losing it again. Then the water was colder, deeper. Going under and back up. Again. And again. I remember scanning the beach for my mother, but I couldn't see her anymore. I wasn't far from the families playing on the sandbar, but I could spare no arm to wave for help, no breath to cry out. Wave after wave, under and up and under and up. I looked for my mother. I coughed and gagged, the salty burn in my throat, the water always trying to fill my gasping mouth.

And then I'm sitting in the sand drinking an orange soda. The towel wrapped around my shoulders is wet, and I'm shivering even though the sun is warm. My mother kneels next to me, frowning, one hand holding back her hair, the other helping me hold the icy can. Curtis isn't there. I think he was getting the car.

On the way back to the trailer we drove with the windows down, and the air blowing in was so strong I could hardly keep my eyes open. The radio was tuned to a country station, and I remember my mother kept trying to light a cigarette in the windswept car. Nobody even yelled at me when I vomited orange soda all over the backseat.

The next day, when we went home to our Tallahassee apartment, my mother told me she had something to show me, that she'd been waiting until I was old enough, but now it was time. I remember understanding that this had something to do with what had happened the day before, but at the same time not knowing what, exactly.

I followed her into her bedroom and watched while she opened her closet and reached up onto the top shelf, pushing aside a couple of shoe boxes. She turned around holding a snow globe. Inside it sat a lighthouse on a rocky island surrounded by a painted blue sea. But instead of snow, it was filled with white birds that, with just the right twisting shake, would spin around and around the plastic lighthouse. First high and fast and then slower, lower, until finally gently settling back on the painted rocks and ocean below.

She explained to me that it was her most prized possession. A gift from her father. She told me to sit on the carpeted floor, and then she sat next to me and put the snow globe carefully in my hands.

"Five times," my mother said and then she watched as I set the birds in motion. After the birds settled the fifth time, she took the globe from my hands and told me to go get ready for bed. The next day when she was in the shower, I slipped into her room and opened the closet door. The top shelf was empty. I understood that whatever window my near drowning had opened, was now closed. She'd hidden the snow globe from me again.

As an adult, my *The Day I Almost Drowned Because My Mother Was Busy Flirting* story has been in regular rotation with several others, like *Shoplifting Was How I Got New Clothes* and *The Time I Had to Hitchhike to School Because I Missed the Bus and My Mother Was Already Too Drunk to Drive Me*. The stories aren't exactly tragic, but they do illustrate the climate of exhausted, boozy ne-glect that characterized my childhood. Quite a few people have easily trumped my little anecdotes with some seriously fucked-up horror stories about their parents, which, I must confess, always made me feel better. Other people would just shake their heads in wonder and then buy the next round of drinks. That worked, too.

Once in a while, though, when I'm lying awake at night I think back on that afternoon in the water—my throat burning, my eyes frantically searching for a mother who wasn't there—and I wish I knew what happened to the largest of the missing pieces of that story. Maybe I've put it away until I need it. Or maybe I'll never know how I got back to shore.

And then, if I'm still awake—and I always am—I think about that snow globe.

It surfaced now and then during the frequent moves of my

childhood. Eventually it came out of hiding; for years it sat on my mother's dresser between a cigar box filled with tangled necklaces and the disembodied porcelain hand that held her rings. Once we moved into Queeg's Pensacola house, it ended up in the living room on a shelf next to his bowling trophies.

The thing is, there was no need for her to have kept it hidden. I never once asked to play with the snow globe again. I suppose it's possible that I'd come to associate it with the near drowning and because of that it made me uncomfortable, or maybe once it wasn't forbidden anymore it lost its appeal. Of course, the simplest explanation for my loss of interest is that once you've shaken them a couple of times, snow globes really aren't all that much fun.

And yet, as Luke Lambert, paralegal extraordinaire, so wisely said: when it comes to human behavior, the simplest explanation is rarely the correct one. Because when I'm lying there in the darkness thinking about that damn snow globe, I feel an itch in my chest, an emptiness, as if no matter how deeply I breathe there will always be a place that cannot get enough air.

And then I'm seven years old again, feeling the carpet scratch my sunburned legs, feeling the heat from my mother's body as she sits next to me. And I can smell her perfume and her gin, and I can see the look on her face, and not once does she glance at me as I cradle the glass orb in my little hands. Her interest lies only in the snow globe and in the birds. Those trapped, circling birds.

CHAPTER 9

The wind has picked up. On the way to the parking lot, a gust lifts my hair off my shoulders and swirls it into my eyes. I've got a key to my grandmother's house in my hand; amazingly I managed to talk Luke into letting me stay there until my car is fixed. Obviously nobody around here has run a background check on me.

A man crouches at the front of my car, attaching a winch to the frame. The other end of the cable stretches over to a tow truck so dented and rusty that it makes my Malibu look good. The words *JJ's Auto Works* are painted in a faded looping script on the door, and the flat twang of country music is pouring from the truck's open windows.

I walk up behind the man and say, "Thanks for coming out. I'm Mattie Wallace. You must be JJ."

He straightens and turns toward me. He's tall, thin, and middle-aged, I think, but it looks like years of hard living have done a number on his face. His nose is crooked from a poorly set break and deep wrinkles run from eye to chin and across his forehead. He reminds me of someone—Clint Eastwood? Bruce Willis? I'm not sure which action hero he resembles, but as he stares at my outstretched arm without lifting his own, I am pretty sure we're not going to shake hands.

"What's your problem?" he says, in a surprisingly soft voice.

"No problem. That's my car and I thought I ought to introduce myself. I'm Mattie."

"With the car. What's the problem with the car?"

"Oh." I lower my unshaken hand. "The transmission, I think."

He nods then climbs in his truck and starts up the winch motor. We both watch as my car assumes the position.

"Nice restoration job," he says.

"Thanks."

"You do the upholstery?" He's talking to me, but he's looking at the car.

"My mom did it."

"Not bad. But the paint looks like shit." He double-checks the connection and then, wiping his hands on his coveralls, he turns to me and says, "Am I giving you a ride to the garage?"

"Yes, thanks." I hurry to the far side of the truck and clamber in. A banjo has taken over the melody of whatever song is playing on the radio. I can practically hear gap-toothed hillbillies seducing their nieces. And nephews. Hey, I've seen *Deliverance*.

"Yee haw," I mutter, not quite under my breath.

He gives me a hard look and then turns off the radio.

"Sorry. Turn it back on. I was just kidding around. I like music."

He responds with only a grunt and then we pull out of the parking lot. The music stays off. He looks straight ahead, the truck picking up speed even as we approach the stop sign at the bottom of the hill.

"Stop sign! Stop Sign! Stop Sign!" I press my foot to the floor-boards and frantically glance both ways while we blast through the stop. "Holy Shit! Didn't you see that?"

"I saw it."

"Are you trying to kill somebody?" *Like me,* I think but don't say. "Aren't you even worried about getting a ticket?"

He reaches over with an arm covered in gnarly gray hair and switches the radio back on. "I work on the sheriff's car for free."

I notice but don't comment on his lack of response to my other concern—the sudden, tragic, gone-before-her-time concern. Faster and faster we go, engine roaring through a yellow light and three more stop signs. We hit a dip and I catch a few inches of air before slamming back down on the seat. Just as I snap the seat-belt buckle, we take a tire-squealing left turn at what must be thirty miles an hour. Glancing back I see my car whipping out behind us like a water-skier hotdogging for an audience.

Before long, we reach a part of town where the buildings have boards over the windows, and the railroad overpass has inventively obscene graffiti. As we pass a house with appliances in the yard and a sofa on the sagging front porch, I notice that there are ac-tually a few chickens strutting around the scraggly grass and into the street. JJ leans on the horn and the birds flap and scatter back up into the yard. One, the rooster, I suppose, stays on the curb and crows an admonition.

When we pass a vacant weedy lot, JJ slows the wrecker and pulls into a dodgy-looking gas station. He drives past the building, stops, slams the gearshift into reverse, and then, with a deft spin of his steering wheel, backs the car into the open bay. When he switches off the ignition and turns to face me, it's the first time I see him smile, and I'm pretty sure it's at the sight of my clammy, pale face. For a second I search for the snappy response his per-formance deserves, but in the end, I respond in the only manner I am able—I put my head between my legs and vomit on the floorboard.

I apologize with a promise to clean it up and then hurry inside where, in the most vile service station bathroom I have ever seen, the Father's chocolates and Luke Lambert's iced tea finish disembarking.

Prepregnancy, I had long stretches, years-long stretches, between vomiting episodes, including some pretty impressive hangovers. I am extremely disappointed in this new sickly me. Shaking and disgusted, I trudge back out to the tow truck, slowly of course, in the hopes that JJ will have already cleaned up the mess by the time I arrive. No such luck.

Thank God for removable rubber floor mats.

I coil the hose back alongside the building and go check on my car. JJ has the hood up and already seems to have some parts taken out and lying on the cement floor.

"Well?" I ask.

"Looks like you need a new transmission."

"Seriously? Shit."

He rocks back on his heels and tucks his hands up under his arms. "So what I'm thinking is . . ." He pauses and chews awhile on his lower lip. I get the impression that thinking is a struggle for the man, so I don't interrupt. Of course it's possible that I'm being too judgmental. I'm sure lots of really, really smart people listen to banjo music.

"What I'm thinking is you should give me some money."

Without being obvious, I look up and down the street. Seeing as how this neighborhood is one big cry for help I'm not sure who I think would respond to mine, but I still start measuring the distance to the closest house.

"So . . . is this, like, a robbery?"

He scowls. "Hell, no. It just looks to me like you don't have a pot to piss in, and I'm sure as hell not putting seven or eight hundred dollars of parts in a car if I'm not getting paid."

"That's ridiculous. Of course I can pay." I pull out my Master-Card and wave it in front of his face.

"Great. Come on in the office and we'll run it through."

"You expect me to prepay?"

"Just the parts."

I'm pretty sure that he and I both know things are about to get ugly, but I can't stop myself from trying again. "Don't be silly. It would be easier to pay one time. Once the work's done we'll settle up."

"You pay for parts now, and labor later."

"No . . . I don't think so."

He narrows his eyes, engaged apparently, in that difficult thinking stuff again. He picks up a Styrofoam cup and spits a glob of brown goo inside. "You don't have the money, do you?"

It seems Albert Einstein here has a firm grasp of the obvious.

"I have money. Or I will have soon. I just inherited my grand-mother's house." I don't mention the creditors and I don't mention the three months.

"Miss Thayer's house, right?"

I nod.

"How old are you?" he asks.

"Thirty. Why?"

He shakes his head. "No reason."

"How old are you?" I'm just being obnoxious; I don't give a shit how old this asshole is.

He looks annoyed. "Fifty-four."

For all his weathered looks, he's a year younger than my

mother would be if she were still alive. "Maybe you knew my mother . . ."

JJ studies me for a second before answering, "I knew her."

Wiping his hands again on the rag, he walks out of the garage bay and into the office. Through the window I can see him sorting through some papers scattered on the counter.

The door beeps when I push it open. "So are you going to fix my car?"

He shakes his head. "You bring me the money, we'll talk."

"Oh come on, what am I supposed to do? I don't have the cash, but I'm good for it."

"It's company policy."

"What is?"

"We don't work on vagrants' cars without some money up front."

"Vagrant!"

"Homeless. Broke. Destitute."

I sigh. "I know what *vagrant* means, and I'm not one."

"You've got a lot of crap in that car."

"What's that supposed to mean?"

"Looks to me like you're living out of it."

"I'm in the process of moving."

"Where to?"

"I'm not sure."

"I rest my case."

"Come on, what am I supposed to do without a car?"

"I need money up front to buy the parts. Company policy."

"Show me where that's written down. I don't see that posted anywhere."

He uses his spit cup again. "I didn't write it down," he says, wiping his chin, "because I couldn't decide whether to put a hyphen between *dead* and *beat*."

"Nice. Very nice."

I'm wondering if the man is just an evil fucker or if he's smarter than he looks. I glance around the waiting area. The whole room smells like burned rubber. There are two orange chairs and between them a table piled with tired-looking newspapers. Above one chair is a framed print of John Wayne, above the other a framed print of Ronald Reagan. Perfect.

"So tow me to another shop."

"Fifty bucks will cover the tow. Pay me that and I'll do it."

I pull out my wallet and count bills. I count change. I dump my purse and count that change: $23.74. I look up in time to catch a smile on JJ's face. He's shaking his head.

"You could sell it to me."

"What?"

"The car. I'll take it off your hands."

I feel clammy, nauseated, sitting in one of the orange chairs, staring at the meager wad of cash in my hands.

Sell the Malibu?

I take my time shoving everything back into my purse, hoping the asshole can't see that I'm furiously blinking back tears. I wasn't always certain what my mother thought about me, but there was never a question about how much she loved that car. She would hate for her car to belong to an asshole. Well . . . an asshole who wasn't related to her, I should say. We're all assholes sometimes.

"I can't sell it," I tell him, and it's the truth. My hands are shaking as I zip up my purse.

"I'll make you a fair offer."

"Sorry."

"Can you afford to keep it? It's going to be a couple thousand to fix this, then it's only a matter of time before the next thing goes out."

"I know." I lift my gaze to his and add, "But it was my mother's."

I'm not sure what he sees in my eyes, but whatever it is, something hardens in his.

"Suit yourself." He turns back to the paperwork lying on the counter.

"What am I supposed to do?" I ask. "I don't see a bus stop around here."

"Not many buses in Gandy. You could rent a car." He doesn't look up when he says this, but there's a little smirk at the corner of his mouth.

"Tell me, is there a hyphen between *douche* and *bag*?" That gets rid of the smirk, but doesn't get me out of this smelly office.

"Well, then I guess I'll just hang out here with you." I lean back in my seat beneath Ronald Reagan and cross my legs. "What's your sign? I'm a Gemini. I bet you're an Aries, right? All the real jerks I've known have been Aries. Or Capricorns . . ."

After less than five minutes of my sparkling conversation, he gestures for me to follow him. We walk around to the gravel lot behind the building. He opens the passenger-side door of a white Taurus.

"Where are we going?" I'm thinking that it might just be to a shallow grave in the woods.

"Back to where I found you."

"What about all my stuff?"

He shrugs. "Not my problem."

"Hold on a minute." I run to my car and grab my toiletries pillowcase and shove in some clean underwear, my phone charger, Nick's guitar strap. I also grab my mom's camera bag.

I hurry back to the Taurus before the asshole changes his mind. "I'm staying at my grandmother's house." I dig in my pocket for the slip of paper with her address. "I've got the address—"

"I know where it is. Get in."

"Maybe I should drive."

"Maybe you should get in the damn car."

I climb in, fastening the seat belt before I shut the door.

"Thanks for the ride—"

"You can thank me by not spewing in this car."

"Why are you so mean?" I ask, sounding a little whiny even to my own ears. "I thought you said you knew my mother."

"I never said I liked her."

He pulls out of the lot and heads back the way we came. The chickens are back out in the street and JJ honks at them again. As the car passes the flock, the rooster and I lock eyes. I have a funny feeling that Minnie might just be right this time. Maybe my chicken finally has come home to roast.

CHAPTER 10

JJ slows the car and turns onto a neighborhood street. The homes are older and small, but look well taken care of, their neatly manicured lawns lining up one after the other. A sidewalk runs along each side, clean and straight except for a few buckled spots where tree roots have fought for space and won. We pull into the driveway of a tidy two-story tan-brick house. JJ turns off the car and opens his door the same time I open mine.

"Thanks for the ride. I've got it from here," I tell him.

"Got what?"

I gather up all my crap and climb out of the car. "I can take it from here."

"Take what?"

Refusing to try again, I walk toward the house. I don't notice until I am on the front porch that the numbers hanging next to the door don't match the house numbers on my little scrap of paper. I turn around to tell JJ that we're at the wrong house, only to find him standing directly behind me.

"This isn't it."

He steps around me, swings open the storm door and puts a key in the doorknob, giving it a twist. From inside there's the sound of dogs barking that grows louder as he pushes the door open and starts edging in.

"This is your house?"

"Yup," he replies.

"But I thought you were taking me to my grandmother's—"

"Right there." JJ points at the house next door.

"That's her house?"

"Yup."

"You live next door?"

He nods. "You'd better do something about your lawn, by the way. Your dandelions are going to seed."

"My lawn? My dandelions?"

"And now that you're here, I'm sure the dogs would like to go back home."

"Wait a minute, nobody said anything about taking care—"

JJ shuts the door. I hear the lock turn.

"Shit!" I pound on the door, but the only thing that gets me is a chorus of barks from within. Wonderful. I stomp off the porch and walk next door.

My grandmother's house is similar in size to JJ's except that it's redbrick rather than tan, and the porch steps and trim could use a coat of paint. And of course the yard needs to be mowed by someone who isn't me. But there's a wide, welcoming porch, windows with shutters, and a big maple tree in the front. It looks like what a kindergartener would draw if handed a box of crayons and instructed to draw a house. All that's missing is scribbled smoke rising from the chimney.

The lock opens easily, and with a nervous flutter in my belly, I step inside. I find myself trying to be quiet; this feels like breaking and entering, not coming home.

I flip the switch near the door and am relieved to find the electricity still on. I open the drapes and a window to let in some light and fresh air. There's a small blue sofa, a wingback chair upholstered in a floral brocade, and next to that an old sewing machine. A grand piano takes up the rest of the small living room. Everything looks mostly clean, but there's a faint odor of moth-balls and something sweet, Fig Newtons maybe? Whatever it is, it smells like old people.

I dump my stuff on the coffee table and make the down-stairs circle—living room to dining room to kitchen. Through the window over the kitchen sink, I notice a detached garage, and let out a little "Whoop!" Everyone knows what belongs in a garage, right? I hurry outside and after several minutes at the fence, strug-gling with an extremely uncooperative gate, I open the garage door.

Shit. No car. Half of the garage is filled with lawn and garden supplies, the other half—the one that, judging from the oil stain, did at some point house a car—now holds only a bike, pink with a banana seat and a white basket on its wide handlebars. Un-fucking-believable. Standing here in this dimly lit garage, it takes very little imagination to hear Queeg's voice whispering, *Now you're up a creek without a paddle.* His voice in my head is laughing as he says this, by the way.

When I step back outside, I'm unpleasantly surprised to see JJ in his backyard, standing next to the chain-link fence that sepa-rates the properties.

"Did you find the lawnmower?" he asks.

I fight my way through the weeds to him, saying, "I think the yard looks fine. If you don't like it, feel free to mow it." In truth, the yard is a mess—weeds, old piles of dog crap, cigarette butts. I'd never admit that to him of course. When I finally get to the fence, I point at the two squatty animals standing at JJ's feet. "What exactly are those supposed to be?"

"Dogs."

"They're pretty ugly."

"The smallest one farts a lot."

"Great."

"Are you ready for me to bring them over? I'll just grab their food—"

"No no, not now. I have some things to do."

"Things? What sort of things?"

"Errands."

He gives me an unpleasant smile. "How're you going to manage that?"

"Fuck you. I'm very resourceful."

Cue dramatic exit. I spin on my heel and take a few quick steps toward the house, only to discover that my feet have somehow become tragically tangled in an evil spiky vine that winds through the tall grass. I lift up a knee, and the barbs embedded in my jeans pull a whole wad of greenery along with me. Next step, the same.

I look back at the neighbor-from-hell. He's grinning like an idiot.

"You were right," he says. "Your yard looks great."

I resume my graceless march, responding only with a single-finger salute over my shoulder.

He laughs. "I'm headed back to work," he calls out. "I'll bring the Winstons over when I get home."

As much as I hate repeating myself, I flip him off again, only to hear more laughter followed by the sound of a door closing. Step by slow step I struggle across the lawn, cursing, trying to rip the green creeping bastard off my legs without making too many holes in my hands or my jeans. Once I manage to reach the patio and fight my way free of the last few grasping tendrils, I glance over at JJ's house. I see a curtain move. What a douche.

Back in the kitchen, I take a few deep breaths and decide to reconnoiter. The very first thing I notice is the little opening in the base of the door I just used. It's a small dog door, maybe a foot and a half tall, its plastic flap grubby from use. Hopefully this means that if I really do end up with those ridiculous dogs for a couple days, the only bowel and bladder issues I need to worry about are my own, which is, in my opinion, exactly how it should be.

The refrigerator is empty and the freezer contains only ice trays and a few frost-coated TV dinners. There's a small pantry with a collection of dusty soup cans and half-empty cracker and cereal boxes. Sigh. I'm relieved that nobody cleaned out the kitchen; obviously, I'm not going to starve to death. But mealtimes are going to be pretty grim unless I can scare up some pity-food.

I dig in my pocket for the card given to me by Father Barnes and punch in the numbers.

His phone rings, once, twice. The plastic flap of the dog door clicks open then shut with each gust of the wind. Ring, click, ring, click . . . three rings . . . four . . . five. The sun cuts a bright rectangle across the blue Formica countertop and as I stand here with the phone pressed to my ear, everything takes on a slow, dreamlike quality. On the wall just inside the pantry door I see a series of pencil marks, horizontal lines with initials and dates. Two sets, I think, one more faded than the other, suggesting that two generations grew up right here, in this house. The flap on the dog door clicks again, the Father's phone rings again, and I'm having a hard time looking away from those penciled-in lines. Until I was fourteen years old, I'd never lived anyplace longer than six months.

An answering machine finally picks up, and although I've already mentally rehearsed a humorously pathetic plea for a dinner date, when I open my mouth to speak, it's all I can do to squeeze my name past an unexpected lump in my throat. I end the call, deeply embarrassed to have left a message so authentically pathetic.

After a handful of stale crackers, I get up the nerve to go upstairs. Each step creaks softly as I ascend. To the left is a bedroom that, judging from the fussy chenille bedspread and an abundance of potpourri in little bowls, must have been my grandmother's. On the dresser is a jewelry box that looks both full of shiny objects and small enough to fit in the bike basket. I pull the pillowcase off my grandmother's pillow and drop the box inside.

In addition to the bathroom there are two other rooms upstairs, their doors closed. I open the first door. It's a bedroom, surely my mother's room. I stare in amazement at the dozens of black-and-white photographs pinned to the walls. Not once had my mother ever mentioned taking pictures as a hobby. She made it clear to me that photography was her job, not something she enjoyed. I never saw her take a picture she wasn't getting paid for. Not even of me.

There are tie-dyed drapes at the window, a denim bedspread, a Pink Floyd poster on the closet door, and a healthy-looking spider plant hanging from a macramé plant holder in front of the window. A pair of brown sandals is on the floor next to the bed, and I walk over and pick one up—size seven, my mother's size. I drop the shoe and back out of the room, my heart pounding. This is a museum—a fucking time capsule. The edges of the photos on the walls are curled, and the curtains and the side of the bedspread closest to the window are faded, but otherwise I have a feeling that the room looks as if my mother had just stepped out for a minute. Thirty-five years ago.

Back out in the hall, I look at the final door. I'm reminded of dreams I've had—surely everyone has had them—where I'm walking down a familiar corridor and suddenly see a door I've never noticed before. That instant of wonder mixed equal parts with fear—there's been an echo of that feeling with every step I've taken through this house. But now, my hand turning this last doorknob, the feeling is strong enough to take my breath away. Even though I already know what I'm going to find.

CHAPTER 11

The summer I turned eight years old, my mother worked as an assistant at a photography studio. More often than not she brought me with her to work, since her boss didn't mind and the only other option would have been to pay a babysitter. Mr. Nester, her boss, had Brylcreemed black hair and oversize dentures that gave him a Jerry Lewis smile. He had a dozen telephones in his office, and he was always talking in code when he was on one. Looking back, I now understand that he was a bookie and the shoddy photography studio was just a cover, but back then I found him mysterious and oddly compelling. He was loud and always laughing, friendly on the outside, but dark on the inside.

Mr. Nester was one of those people who dislike children but pretend otherwise when in the presence of other adults. He would be all "Hello, sweetheart" when I walked in the door, but on the occasions he and I were alone together, he delighted in terrifying me. No sexual stuff—thank God—yet there was something wrong with Mr. Nester. He prided himself on being a practical joker and thought an eight-year-old was an appropriate target. The pack of gum that snapped shut on my finger, the shock pen, the fake blood, the rubber foot he left sticking out from under his desk . . . And when I invariably screamed and cried, Mr. Nester would laugh, his yellowed Chiclet teeth glowing in the dim light. He'd say I had no sense of humor, then a phone would ring and he'd disappear back into his office.

He liked to say "If I were a bettin' man" before most of his declarations. It was years before I could tie that joke in with the bank of phones. At the time I thought he was saying "If I were a *bitten* man." I couldn't imagine who would possibly be brave enough to bite somebody who was so mean and had such massive teeth.

It was fun watching my mother take photographs, but when it was time for her to develop them, I was faced with the choice of staying with Mr. Nester or following her into the darkroom. I chose the darkroom, but I'd hesitate long enough at the threshold that my mother would grab my arm and pull me inside so she could close the door. When it was time for total darkness, she'd sit me in a chair and put something in my hands, a pen, her keys, a Coke can, whatever was nearby. "Hold on to this for me," she'd say. "Don't drop it." Then she'd turn off the lights.

When the safelight could stay on it wasn't so bad. The amber light made it hard to sit and play quietly; it was too dark to look at picture books, but the muted light made the darkroom almost cozy. My mother was right there, and I could watch her moving back and forth purposefully. But there were times, of course, when there could be no light at all in the darkroom, and in those minutes that felt like hours, I sat cocooned in an airless black so complete that it was hard to tell if my eyes were open or closed.

In that thick darkness I held tight to whatever talisman my mother had handed me. Sometimes through the thin walls I could hear Mr. Nester shouting into his phones, and over that I could hear my mother's voice, singing gently, reminding me that she was there, promising me that everything was going to be okay.

If anything, it's a little too warm in my grandmother's house, but I have goose bumps, standing here in the hallway, looking into this room, its contents only vaguely revealed under the safelight's glow. I stick my arm further inside the doorway and find the switch that turns on the overhead light. I can now see that the darkroom equipment is cobbled together with thrift store finds: a washstand, a long desk lined with trays, brown glass jugs setting underneath, plywood nailed over the window, the Velcro strip across the wall above the door that once held the heavy black fabric now folded on the floor. There's a wire hung diagonally across the room, and a light box on a card table set up in the far corner. I walk over and pick up the jug of stop bath, cracking the lid for only a second. The vinegar odor that escapes—so sharp I can taste it—burns my nose and makes my knees go wobbly. For a second I'm back there in the dark, waiting to see my mother again.

The pillowcase containing Nick's strap and the jewelry box fits snugly in the bike basket, but I still take off my belt and fasten it around the whole thing to avoid spillage during the inevitable falls. My bike riding skills are rusty and rudimentary to say the least. I walk the bike down the driveway and onto the street, put my feet on the pedals, ride a few wobbly yards and then put my feet back on the ground, considering the downhill slope before me and the stupid thing I'm about to do. The shitty thing. I know that it's not okay to sell stuff that doesn't belong to me. It's not that I'm lacking a moral compass, it's that I've found life to be easier when

I leave it in my pocket. It's no mystery who taught me that lesson. Even Mr. Nester knew.

"If I were a bettin' man . . ." he used to tell me, showing me his yellow teeth in what I'm sure he thought was a smile. "I'd say the odds are you're gonna grow up to be just like your momma."

CHAPTER 12

The good news is the pawnbroker didn't call the cops. The bad news comes in two installments. First, I still have no idea whether or not Nick's guitar strap is actually worth a *bundle,* because I made the dumb mistake of nodding when asked if the strap belonged to me. It took the broker about two seconds to figure out that I don't know jack about guitars, which made me having the strap seem more than a little suspicious. The second piece of bad news is that my grandmother's jewelry is all *total crap*—his words not mine. The pawnbroker went on to explain—quite emphatically—that he didn't buy stolen goods or total crap. I quickly refuted the latter, pointing out that he does, in fact, sell total crap because not only was there an Incredible Hulk cookie jar displayed in the window, but on a nearby table I noticed a boxed set of Lawrence Welk DVDs. Sadly, the broker didn't think that was nearly as funny as I did.

So here I am back out on the street, still in possession of my grandmother's total crap jewelry and a collector's-item-near-mint-condition-brown-leather-guitar-strap-signed-by-Jimmy-Page-and-

Jeff-Beck. It's not easy coming to grips with the fact that I've just been thrown out of someplace called Ye Olde Pawn Shoppe. I swear, if this shit were happening to anybody else I would be totally laughing my ass off.

I take a couple of deep breaths, shake off this most recent humiliation and come up with an alternate plan. As Queeg likes to say, there's more than one way to skin a cat. I rode right past a bank on my way to the pawnshop. As a matter of fact, I fell and deposited a bit of elbow skin on a curb near there. Unfortunately, the bank is near the crest of an impressive hill and there's no way I'm going to get up there on a bike. So I pull the bike close to the building, behind a sagging baby swing, and then pop my head inside the pawnshop and tell the broker I'm leaving it parked outside for a few minutes. Before he can open his mouth to argue, I sling the pillowcase-bundle over my shoulder and hurry away.

Even though the day isn't overly warm, I'm sweating by the time I reach my destination. When I open the door of the First National Bank of Greater Gandy—the name of which can't help but make me imagine, with a shudder, the existence of a Lesser Gandy—the air-conditioned air feels like heaven. I tell the woman at the main desk why I'm here, then I grab a cherry Tootsie Pop from the big bowl on the side table and settle down on the sofa to wait. Mere seconds after I put the candy in my mouth, a woman comes over to get me, so I rewrap my pop and slide it into my pocket as I follow her to a glass-walled office.

A man stands when I enter, smoothing down his tie over his shirtfront. The sign on his desk says, *Gordon Penny*, a perfect name for the man. Penny because he's a banker, of course, and Gordon because he looks like the name Gordon sounds, no sharp angles, just soft doughy curves arcing one into the other.

He looks me up and down, his gaze registering my damp shirt and the pink pillowcase in my hand. When he takes my hand in a limp, moist grip, he twists his wrist to where his hand is underneath and mine on top. For a crazy second I think he's going to kiss my hand, but instead he just pumps it up and down. Mr. Penny must think he's being gentlemanly, but it feels more like he thinks I'm a dog.

We sit facing each other across his desk. Mr. Penny's shirtsleeves are rolled up to the elbows, the folded cuffs cutting deeply into his forearm flesh. His tie is loosened, top shirt button mercifully open, but the buttons around his middle are working overtime.

It's only three o'clock, but it's already been a long day, so I get straight to the point. "I've inherited some property in Gandy, but my car has broken down and I'm a little short on cash. I'm here to see about getting a loan."

"Using the property as collateral?"

"Exactly. Can that be arranged?"

"You betcha. We just need the paperwork from the probate hearing."

"That could be a problem."

"There'll be a copy on file at the courthouse."

I explain my situation, playing down the three-month wait, and of course not mentioning any claims pending against the estate. Mr. Penny asks who's handling the probate, and I tell him.

He leans back, his chair groaning in protest. "Well, I need to have me a chat with old Charlie first. But he's off on a fishing trip as I recall."

I nod.

He chuckles. "That man doesn't fish to live, he lives to fish."

"Is that right?"

"You betcha. I bought him a T-shirt for Christmas last year that says *Women love me. Fish fear me.*" Mr. Penny is smiling, but his narrowed eyes belie his friendliness. "This wouldn't happen to be Matilda Thayer's place we're talking about?"

"It is," I say.

"That's a mighty nice little house." Still leaning back, Mr. Penny laces his hands behind his head, props a foot up on an open drawer and begins to rock back and forth. As he continues to talk, the screams of metal fatigue grow stronger. "I took piano lessons from Miss Thayer."

I nod along, still waiting for him to get to a point of some kind.

"Can't say as I ever had a knack for it. It was mostly so I'd have a chance to see Genie once in a while."

"My mother."

"You betcha."

He studies me, chewing on his lip, continuing to rock his chair. Squeak, squawk, squeak, squawk. The credenza behind his chair looks solid and just far enough away to cause a head injury the day that chair gives way. Instead of buying T-shirts for his friends, Mr. Penny would be wise to invest in a helmet.

"You don't really favor your momma," he tells me. "Maybe a little around the edges."

Ugh. I don't know where my edges are exactly, but I do know that I don't want this man looking at any part of my body.

"Genie was a looker, all right. That blond hair, those big green eyes . . ." He sighs and licks his lips with his thick tongue. "She had a spark, like she was special. Know what I mean?"

He pauses, brows raised. He's looking for an answer to that question, but he's out of luck. I'm still back at *blond*. My mother was a redhead.

"Running around with that camera," he continues. "Acting like she was the next . . . I dunno. Who's a famous lady photographer?"

It takes me a minute to realize that he's waiting for an answer to this one, too.

"Diane Arbus?" I say. "Annie Leibovitz?"

"Never heard of 'em." He frowns as if this were my fault. "And there was her music, of course."

"Music?" I wonder if he's about to ask me to name some famous musicians. In fact, I'm so busy compiling a mental list of musicians that a man like Gordon Penny would recognize, that I almost miss what he says next.

"Hell, you've heard her play the piano."

I work at keeping my face neutral. I never saw my mother so much as touch a piano.

"She was such a big deal with her music scholarship to some-wheres back east." He pauses to heave a deep sigh, pink flesh winking from between the straining buttons on his shirt. "I'm sure you know the whole story . . ."

"Sure." I shrug, struggling to seem casual. "But I'm interested in your opinion."

My mother never went to college. Or so she claimed.

"My opinion . . ." He smiles again, his eyes narrowing un-pleasantly. "Is that your mother was too big for her britches. She paraded around this town, carrying on, laughing . . ." He shakes his head as if laughing were a bad thing. "And then bang. One day she was gone."

I wait, hoping he'll say more. There are all sorts of ways to be *gone.*

"When she first left, everybody thought she'd just gone on back up to school. But then she stayed away that Christmas and again that next summer . . ."

He pauses here, and I watch him watching me. I'm trying to hide my confusion, but I can't imagine that I'm successful. I knew my mother's point-blank refusal to discuss her past was strange, but I'd always chalked it up to a garden-variety unhappy childhood. It had never occurred to me that there was anything actually mysterious about her silence.

"Eventually people started asking questions, but her momma wasn't talking, and nobody else had a clue. That last summer Genie had been all hot and heavy with Trip, but even he claimed ignorance. No surprise there." He lifts a lip in a little sneer at the word *Trip*, so I suspect that it's a nickname for some good-looking boy. I furthermore suspect that good-looking is something Gordon Penny was not.

"This is a small town, Miss Wallace, a hard place to keep a secret. I nosed around about your momma, believe you me." He leans forward and looks me straight in the eyes for perhaps the first time. "But I never sniffed a whiff of whatever happened."

I feel a chill at the cruel pleasure I see in Gordon Penny's eyes.

"A few years back I heard that Genie passed. I am deeply sorry for your loss." He doesn't look sorry.

I clear my throat and manage an uncomfortable, "Thank you."

"Ms. Wallace, may I ask you a personal question?"

I hesitate before nodding. I can't imagine wanting to tell this man anything personal.

"How old are you?"

What is it with these people and my age? "Thirty."

"Any older brothers or sisters?"

I shake my head.

"Well, I'll be. I guess I was wrong. All this time I thought she'd gone and got herself in trouble." He curls his thick fingers in air quotes around *in trouble*.

The age question is making sense now, but unfortunately I have to disappoint all the fine citizens of Gandy who want me to be the solution to the mystery of my mother's disappearance.

My mother was twenty-five when I arrived, a product of one of her many doomed, short-term relationships. And though I never really knew him, the identity of my father is well established. He was, depending on how much my mother was drinking when asked, either a *bartender with a sensitive soul*, a *redneck asshole who took advantage*, or my personal favorite, *M. Y. O. Fuckin' B. Now bring me my cigarettes.*

Mr. Penny is still looking at me expectantly, waiting for me to give him some clue as to why she left. I compare the girl he described with the woman I grew up with, and I feel a prickle of anxiety. She wasn't pregnant with me, but that doesn't mean she wasn't in trouble. There's more than one kind of *trouble*.

I clear my throat and say, "About that loan . . ."

He shakes his head. "You don't legally own that property."

"But—"

"We might could arrange a signature loan, depending on your credit rating of course." He can't resist a quick glance at the pillow-case under my chair.

I don't have to reply; he knows checking my credit rating isn't going to improve this situation.

"Have you got anything else to use for collateral?" he asks.

"My car, maybe."

"Some payroll-loan places offer auto title loans. You give them the title, they loan you some money. Of course, the amount depends on what your car is worth."

My car title is in a file cabinet in Queeg's trailer with all my other too-important-to-be-accidentally-thrown-away paperwork.

"How about a guitar strap?"

"Excuse me?"

I dig in the pillowcase at my feet, pull out Nick's strap and then set it on Mr. Penny's desk.

"It's a collector's-item-near-mint-condition-brown-leather-guitar-strap-signed-by-Jimmy-Page-and-Jeff-Beck."

Under the fluorescent lights the sweat-stains on the leather look especially grim, each amoeba-shaped spot outlined in a darker brown. The ink of the signatures looks purple and cheap. Gordon Penny leans forward to look at the strap lying across his desk, but he's careful not to touch it. After a few seconds he looks back up at me with a question in his eyes. I'm not sure what the question is, so I start answering all the ones I can think of.

"Jimmy Page was the guitarist for Led Zeppelin. Jeff Beck was . . . is . . . well, he's a famous musician, too. It's near mint condition . . ." I'm watching the banker's eyes to see if anything I'm saying is having an effect, but so far it doesn't seem like it is.

"How much is this worth?" he asks.

"A bundle," I reply.

"Maybe you should try a pawn shop."

Well, shit. I sigh and then put on my most winsome smile. "Couldn't you bend the rules for the daughter of an old friend?"

He shakes his head. "I'm sorry, Ms. Wallace."

Apparently, the smile works better with clean hair.

He stands, and so I stand and shake his extended hand, again the good dog. Woof.

As I'm stuffing the strap back in my bag, he says, "Once you get that paperwork on the house, you come on back here, all right?"

"You betcha," I reply.

He fishes a business card out of a little brass tray on his desk, and then makes a show of writing a phone number on the back. "I'm truly sorry about the loan, but I might be interested in buying your grandmother's house once it's on the market. If you'd like to get in touch, here's my personal number . . ."

I can't say for sure that he's hitting on me, maybe he really just wants to buy a house, but I find myself fighting to keep revulsion off of my face as I lift the card from his fingers and tuck it in my pocket. I turn to leave, but before I can make my escape Gordon Penny clears his throat, saying, "And, Ms. Wallace, just so you'll know . . ."

I look back. "Yes?"

"Your mother and I were never friends."

CHAPTER 13

There's a nice shady spot on the sidewalk outside the bank. When I sit on the curb, the Tootsie Pop stick gives me a little jab in the ribs. I pull it out of my pocket, but it seems I didn't wrap it thoroughly enough; it sticks to the inside of my jean's pocket, pulling it out as well. I pick off the worst of the lint and then, because I'm starting to feel sick again, I put the still-fuzzy sucker in my mouth. Speaking of suck, man oh man, this day sucks. I mean, things usually suck, but today takes the suck-cake. It wins a gold medal at the Suck Olympics.

I pull out my phone to check the time; Queeg will be home from his doctor's appointment, finished with lunch, and probably watching a game show, or rereading one of his Louis L'Amour books. I don't want to call, but it's time.

Queeg got on the subject of quantum mechanics once, and told me about Schrödinger—the guy who said that if you poisoned a cat while it was in a box, the cat wasn't alive or dead until you opened the box and looked inside. At the time, I thought that was funny as hell. I mean, even if the cat was very quiet—which it wouldn't be, by the way—within a couple days you'd know for sure if it were dead, especially if the box was outside and it was summer. Queeg tried to explain that Schrödinger's whole point was to prove that some other dude's theory was flawed, but I was laughing too hard to listen.

But, the thing is, I get it now. While I hold my undialed phone in my hand, Queeg is still just fine. But once I call him, he's going to tell me what the doctor said, or more likely he'll lie to me about what the doctor said and that's going to be even worse.

I dial his number. When he picks up, his voice sounds hoarse, as if he's been asleep.

"Were you taking a nap?" I ask. Queeg never naps.

He coughs. "Of course not." I think he's lying and that scares me.

"What did the doctor say?"

"Nothing interesting."

"I don't care if it's interesting. I want to hear it anyway."

He sighs. "They scheduled a biopsy."

"Another one? When is it?" Last year Queeg had a prostate biopsy, and I thought I'd never hear the end of it.

"Thursday. And it's a different body part, thank God."

"Which part?" I ask.

"Mattie, it's no big deal."

He's not exactly lying, but he's getting close. "It's your lungs, right? You're getting a lung biopsy."

He sighs a nonanswer that is answer enough.

"Oh, Queeg . . ." I lean forward and rest my head on my knees. Just saying the words *lung biopsy* made me feel sick.

"I'm fine. Don't worry about me."

As if.

"Getting old stinks," he tells me. "But I guess it's better than the alternative."

"You guess?" The thought of Queeg with a needle in his lung is terrible. The thought of him dying is unbearable.

Queeg is quiet for a second, and I think I hear a metal *chink*. Like the sound of a cigarette lighter.

I swipe at a tear that's poised on my lashes. "You're not *smoking*, are you?"

"Nope," he says, pausing long enough that I'm certain he's taking a drag. "So, how are things going out there?"

And here it is. The empty slot in this scene just big enough for me to tuck in all my problems, and then ask him to send me some money.

"I met a Lawrence Welk fan," I say.

"I like Lawrence Welk."

"Don't remind me."

I hear him chuckle, and that makes me smile.

"And I've been talking with some people about Mom," I tell him.

"Really?" He sounds surprised and pleased. He always wants to talk about my mother. I always refuse.

"Not on purpose."

"Ah . . ."

"She was different when she was younger."

"Sure she was. People change."

"No, this seems like more than that."

"In what way?"

"Nothing. Never mind," I say, adding, "We'll talk about her later," which isn't true and we both know it. I understand that my mother is always there, her heart beating beneath all of our conversations. But understanding something isn't the same thing as accepting it.

"And when will *later* be?" Queeg has long since caught on to this dodge.

"I don't know," I reply. "But don't hold your breath."

There's an awkward pause. I'm wishing I hadn't told a man who might have lung cancer, *don't hold your breath*, and I think Queeg is wondering if he needs to remind me that *later* will someday be too late. As usual, neither one of us says what we're thinking. Instead Queeg asks me how the visit with Tilda's attorney went.

I gloss over everything, telling him that I signed papers and should know more in a few days. I don't mention the list of creditors waiting for the first bite, and I don't mention the dogs, and I don't mention the three months. Instead, I tell him that it's so nice here that I'm going to hang around a few days and that everything is just great. As I'm concocting this fairy tale, I can picture him exactly. He's sitting on the edge of his sofa, his hair standing up in tufts, his shirt twisted from his nap, probably a goddamn cigarette between his fingers. *Happily ever after* is what he needs to hear.

Queeg laughs softly, pleased by the story. "Now I'll be the one hitting you up for money," he says. "I have a feeling my visit today cost a pretty penny, and they haven't even punched a hole in me yet."

He's playing this off as a joke, but it's not. And he's not really talking about money. Unlike me, he's got health insurance. No, Queeg is giving me a heads-up, reminding me that the time is coming when we'll switch places, he and I. He'll be the one calling me, depending on me for help. Sadly, he's spinning a yarn equally as far-fetched as the one I just told him. I'm pretty sure we both know that he's never going to be able to depend on me.

"We'll jump off that bridge when we come to it," I say. I keep it light, where it needs to stay.

He shifts the conversation to Min He's hemorrhoids, and I'm grateful for the subject change even if disgusted by the topic. When my phone beeps a call waiting, I don't even look to see who it is. I just tell Queeg I have another call and to put out his damn cigarette, and then I click over to the other call before he has time to argue or say good-bye.

It's Father Barnes on the phone, and I immediately launch into an exhaustive recounting of my troubles, sparing no painful details except the part about me being pregnant, and the part about me trying to sell things that don't belong to me. I don't even know what I'm hoping to accomplish. Am I looking for a date, or just trying to shake him down for some cash? At this point, it just seems like I should be able to get something from somebody even if it's only sympathy.

Father Barnes "Hmmm"s and "Oh, dear"s at the appropriate moments, and I'm sure I'm golden right up until he ends the call with, "Well, Mattie, the good news is the Lord must have something very special planned for you, or he wouldn't have given you all these difficulties." Then he invites me to lunch tomorrow, see you at the church at noon, take care, etc., etc. . . . click. Terrific. I guess I got my date, but it doesn't save me from tonight's meal out of my grandmother's pantry.

I shift around and lean back against a parking meter. The sidewalk is warm beneath me; the wind is shuffling the leaves in the trees. I close my eyes and turn my face to the sun. Maybe Father Barnes is on to something. If there really is a God, he does indeed seem to have something special planned for me, and so far it's an extended ass-kicking. For some people God may be a shepherd leadething them beside still waters, but lately he seems a lot more like Mr. Nester, tauntething me with a mound of fake doggy-doo.

At the sound of a car slowing to a stop next to where I'm sitting, I open my eyes and turn my head to see who has come to gawk at my misfortune. It's Luke, the paraplegic paralegal behind the wheel of a silver Accord. I wave, half hoping that he'll drive on so I can get back to my comfortable pity wallow. Yet the other half—the one that includes my tired legs—hopes that he'll offer me a ride.

Luke lowers his window, and I stand and walk over.

"What's that?" He's looking at the pillowcase in my hand.

"Worthless crap," I reply.

From his puzzled yet worried expression, I can tell that he's curious as to why I would be carrying around a pink pillowcase full of worthless crap, but can't quite decide if asking would be rude.

I decide to help us both out by changing the subject.

"How did you do that?" I point at what must be Luke's wheelchair, but is now a pile of aluminum rods and wheels in the backseat.

"Years of practice. Need a lift?"

His tie is off and his shirtsleeves are rolled up on his forearms, showing some of the muscles I thought were hiding under his clothes. I smile. I am a sucker for the white-collar type even if I only seem to date the asshole-musician type.

"Got room somewhere for a bike?"

He nods. "The trunk. There's a bungee for the lid."

"Perfect. Hey, can you open it and let me toss this inside, too?"

He pops the trunk, but not before glancing again at the bulging pillowcase in my hand. But he doesn't ask so I don't have to lie. Excellent.

When we pull up outside the pawnshop, I see an ample, middle-aged woman in regrettably snug spandex shorts closely inspecting my bike, as in searching-for-a-price-tag inspecting. In retrospect, I shouldn't have left the crappy bike parked in the middle of all the pawnshop's crappy sale items.

I walk over to the woman. "Excuse me," I say, taking the bike by the handlebars.

"Hey!" She straightens up and puts her hands on her generous hips. "What do you think you're doing?"

"I'm taking this home," I tell her.

"I saw it first!" She follows me, shouting "Stop!" as I wheel the bike to the back of Luke's car. She's taking little tiny steps, each one causing her spandex-covered thighs to make a *zip zip zip* sound. I'm glad the car is close by; I'm a little afraid she's about to start a fire.

"It's not for sale," I tell her.

"What does that mean?"

"Is English not your native language?"

Luke has popped the trunk and is watching this little brouhaha with an enormous grin on his face. How lucky for him that I am around to provide him with quality entertainment.

"You can't take that without paying for it."

"Back off, lady," I say.

The woman grabs the handlebars, forcing me to pry it from her grasp in order to lift the rear wheel and angle the bike into the trunk. The woman is ineffectively pushing at me while I'm struggling to slide the rubber tire over the trunk carpet. Either the drive here, or the ongoing tussle over the bike has caused the jewelry box to slide partially out of its pillowcase. The woman notices this and reaches in to push the pillowcase away from the initialed lid.

"Hey . . ." the woman says, reaching for the box. "This isn't yours . . ."

"The hell it isn't." I bump her aside, give the bike a final shove, and strap on the bungee cord. "All this shit is mine."

"Bullhonky," she says. This woman must be the type of person who, no matter how angry, is not willing to use profanity.

"Fuck off, pork chop," I reply. I am not that type of person.

I hop in the car, and Luke pulls away. When I look back, she's still standing in the street, shaking her fist in the air and shouting, "Thief!"

When we're a block away he turns to me, laughing. "What was that all about?"

"I left that bike parked there less than an hour ago. I don't know what in the hell was wrong with that lady."

"Pork chop?" He's laughing again. "Oh my God."

"What?"

Instead of answering he shakes his head, still grinning. "So what'd you find out about your car?" he asks me.

"It's the transmission."

"Ouch."

"Yup." I slump down in the seat and prop my feet on the dash. "Unless you'd like to loan me a couple grand, it looks like I'll be here awhile, Howdy."

It's not that I actually expect him to give me any money, but I figure I'd be a fool not to drop the hint. I wait for him to refuse or laugh it off or tell me to get my feet off his dashboard, but he does none of those things.

He just frowns and says, "What's with calling me *Howdy*?"

"Howdy Doody . . . you know . . . red hair . . . freckles . . . cute smile . . ."

"I guess it's better than calling me a random cut of meat," he says. "But calling me by my actual name would be even better."

The smart thing to do here is to apologize and then shut my damn mouth. But when do I ever do the smart thing?

"That's true. You have a good name," I say. "*Luke Lambert* is an awesome name, in fact."

He gives me a quick look and then asks, cautiously, "*Awesome* because . . ."

"It sounds like a Superman villain."

He laughs. "Good Lord. What is *wrong* with you?"

I laugh, too, mostly because I'm relieved that he's laughing. "It's a long list. Right now, I think it's low blood sugar. I'm so hungry . . ."

He offers to feed me, of course. When we get to the order-window of the fast-food deli, Luke looks a little disconcerted when I ask for a foot-long meatball sub, but he repeats my request into the speaker-station without comment. And when we drive up to the next window, he pulls out his wallet and pays the total, and I don't argue. Tacky? Absolutely. But standard operating procedure for someone with a wallet as thin as mine.

I notice a "help wanted" sign, and so on a whim I lean past Luke to ask the teenager at the window for an application.

The girl hands it to Luke who passes it to me along with the enormous sack holding my sandwich. "I think I can find you a job you'd like better than this one."

"Really?"

"Sure." He doesn't look at me; he busies himself putting his Coke in the cup holder, pressing on the plastic lid to make sure it's snapped into place.

"Why would you do that for me?"

Still concentrating on his hands, he unwraps a straw and pops it through the lid. "It's not a problem." I see his ears growing a little pink. "Really," he adds, still not looking at me. "I like helping out."

"It's your daily good turn. What a nice Boy Scout." I reach over to ruffle his hair.

He ducks away from my hand, grinning, his face now such a remarkable shade of raspberry, that I can't help but laugh again.

"What's so funny?" he says.

"It's nothing. Just . . . thank you. Really." I sit back in my seat and smile. God, there's nothing like embarrassing a ginger to improve my mood.

Luke pulls back onto the street, using the hand controls as effortlessly as I do the pedals of my car. I'm curious about how long he's been in a wheelchair and why, but I don't ask. A little teasing is one thing, but digging into someone's past is different. In my experience, the past is rarely as harmless, or as far away, as we'd like it to be.

CHAPTER 14

Like most kids, I wanted a pet. At first this longing was vague, species-wise. Dogs, big ones at least, frightened me with their red toothy mouths and sharp eyes. Cats seemed calm enough, but I had a tendency to get itchy if I spent too long petting one. Fish . . . boring. Snakes . . . ick. But I knew that out there somewhere was the pet for me. It wasn't until my stint in Mrs. Baxter's fourth-grade class that my ambiguous pet-ownership urge found its focus—on a fat ginger and white guinea pig named Buttercup.

Buttercup had the dubious, possibly hazardous, honor of being Mrs. Baxter's classroom pet. Daily, she suffered pokes and prods by dozens of tiny fingers pushed between the metal bars of her cage. She made the best of the situation, nibbling on her pellets and greens, shuffling around in slow circles, and—most telling of her innate intelligence—spending much of her time watching us from the far corner of her cage, tucked inside the empty twenty-two-ounce can that had once held crushed tomatoes and now served as her refuge. Buttercup made lovely little chortles and *ooooweek* sounds throughout the day. The whole room smelled faintly of cedar shavings.

Buttercup was to Mrs. Baxter's class the proverbial carrot to a donkey. Unlike the girls in Mrs. Wilson's class, the girls in our class did not spend their time during math lessons writing notes and drawing pictures of Strawberry Shortcake on our notebooks. No, the girls in Mrs. Baxter's class worked every bit as hard in arithmetic as the boys, because whoever made the highest grade on the Friday math quiz got to feed Buttercup the following week.

When Christmas approached, Mrs. Baxter began discussing a class "Maptastic Geography Bee." To make the contest even more exciting, the winner would be allowed to take Buttercup home to care for over the Christmas break.

Oh how I studied state capitals, rivers, mountains, estuaries. I was determined to win. I was certain that if my mother had the chance to get to know the sweet little guinea pig and see how responsible I could be, she would allow me to have a Buttercup of my very own.

The Bee was scheduled for Wednesday morning. That afternoon the winner would take home a permission slip outlining the responsibilities of caring for Buttercup, to be brought back to Mrs. Baxter on Thursday. On some level I must have known that, no matter how many geographic facts I managed to stuff into my frizzy-haired head, the real hurdle would be Wednesday night, not Wednesday morning. But I was nine years old and not yet ready to give up on miracles. If I won the Geography Bee my mother would have to let me bring Buttercup home.

Wednesday finally came, and just over an hour into the contest only two of us were still standing—me and Ronnie Richter. Ronny was smart and cocky, and he was also the tallest boy in class. Some of the girls thought Ronnie was cute, but one afternoon during reading time, I noticed that he had visible earwax, so I was immune to his charms. Even then I had standards.

Anyway, thanks to a last-minute brushing up on my deserts, I knew, and Ronnie did not, that Death Valley was in California not Nevada. Everybody cheered my win, even the girls who I thought liked Ronnie, which made me wonder if they'd noticed his dirty ears, too. Mrs. Baxter gave me a hug, a one-hundred-piece puzzle of the United States, and the permission slip. On the way back to my seat I glanced at Buttercup. At that very moment she stepped out from inside her tomato can and looked straight into my eyes, letting out a little squeak. Even Buttercup was glad I'd won.

It wasn't until I was walking home from the bus stop that I started to consider the outcome of handing the permission slip to my mother. She knew about the Bee, of course, since I had to give her a reason for my sudden enthusiasm for schoolwork. But I hadn't mentioned the prize.

The next morning, eyes swollen from crying, I handed Mrs. Baxter the unsigned permission slip. After a quick squeeze of my shoulders and a whispered, "I'm sorry," Mrs. Baxter sent Ronnie Richter to the office to call his mother and see if Buttercup could spend the holidays at their house. Naturally, his mother said yes.

As it turned out, it was a difficult holiday. The day before Christmas, my mother and I came home from the grocery store to a dark, cold apartment with a yellow eviction notice taped on the front door. We spent Christmas day and the day after shuttling our belongings from that apartment to another one across town. New school, new teacher, this one with no class pet. My mother was right after all; it would have been a mistake to trust us with the beloved guinea pig.

But when I think back on that autumn and Mrs. Baxter, the Geography Bee and that sweet, fat little guinea pig, what I remember most clearly is the pained look on my mother's face when I gave her the permission slip. She'd glanced at it, and then handed the unsigned paper back to me, saying only, "We're not Buttercup people."

Waiting on my grandmother's porch is a surly mechanic, two squatty dogs, and a black plastic bag. JJ starts in with detailed dog-care instructions, and I try to pay attention, but all I can think about is how I wish my mother could see me now. If we weren't Buttercup people, I can promise you we would never be Winston people.

Finally JJ shuts up and hands me the leashes. I drag the trash bag, the dogs, and the sack of their food into the house. Looking in the trash bag, I'm pleased to see that it's one of the six that were stuffed in the backseat of my car. I guess I have to admit it was decent of JJ to bring me some clothes, but unfortunately it's the bag that was on top, in other words the last bag I packed, filled with things I almost didn't bother to bring—old or uncomfortable shoes, stuff that's too small, sweaters with snags.

I turn to the dogs, pat their wide little heads and unhook the leashes. It's time to make friends. I go into the kitchen, cut off a section of my sandwich and feed each grinning monster a piece. Once they happily wolf down their snack and then lick that part of the floor clean, they fix their beady brown eyes on mine and wag their stumpy tails in what I'm sure passes for charming when you're a freaky-looking dog. I eat the rest of the sandwich quickly, furtively, feeling their stare with every bite.

One is a little larger than the other, but overall the Winstons look alike—tan fur, short legs, stubby bodies, batlike ears. They snort and trot around like little pigs, and already there has been significant fartage. I'm hoping it's the sandwich and not the natural

THE ART OF CRASH LANDING   105

state of affairs, although it would explain the bowls of potpourri everywhere. JJ informed me, when he dropped them off, that they are French bulldogs, which has led me to reassess my opinion of the French. They may know a lot about making wine and fries, but they don't know jacques-merde about making dogs.

Nick the Impregnator calls twice, but I don't answer. I can't avoid him forever, but I can avoid him tonight. By nine o'clock, the dogs have gone in and out of their doggy door a couple times, and since the cable is still on, the dogs and I have passed the evening watching several hours of crappy television. The three of us are settled on the sofa, the dogs, one on each side of me, are snoring and twitching happily, but I'm feeling restless.

I wander upstairs to my mother's old room. On the wall next to the closet are the types of photos you'll see in any photographer's collection of favorite shots—flowers, landscapes, shadows cast by buildings. But I'm interested in the pictures thumbtacked over her bed. There are groups of smiling teenagers, and in a few of these I'm relieved to recognize my mother. There was a moment back at the bank, when Gordon Penny talked about my mother's blond hair, that I worried this would all turn into some Movie-of-the-Week drama about mistaken identity.

I pull one group-shot off the wall. The girls in the photo look happy—my mother looks happy—a sense of mischief, a lightness in her expression that I don't remember ever seeing. And her hair really was blond. Even from the earliest snapshots of her on this wall, her hair is a cap of blond curls rather than the red hair I remember so well.

She'd always been so proud of her hair, agonizing over the first few gray strands, yet refusing to cover them up with dye for fear it would change the color of the rest. And when she lost it all, clump after clump in the shower and on her pillow, she mourned her hair harder, I swear, than she seemed to mourn the future she might not have.

There are pictures of other people, too, an elderly couple, standing in front of this house, or one that looks just like it. There's a square photo with the ripple-cut edges you find on pictures from the 1950s. It's faded, but it's easy to make out a young man, a teen-ager maybe, wearing a suit that looks a little too big. He's standing by a car with the oversize tailfins of that era, and he has one hand raised to shade his eyes. He's smiling, looking slightly away from the camera.

I take a step back and look again at the wall, at the photos of all these people, and I realize what's been bothering me. It's not what I see, but rather what I don't see.

I gather up the pictures of the young man by the car, my mom posing with her friends, the elderly couple, and carry them to the desk. Before setting them down, I run my hand over the dark wood. There is dust, but just the lightest coating. My grandmother Tilda cleaned in here, watered the plant hanging in the window, left her daughter's shoes sitting next to the bed. How must she have felt to be the caretaker of this room, its walls filled with photos of everyone, it seems, except her.

Relationships are complicated, none more than that of a mother and her daughter. I, of all people, know this to be true. But still, the absence of that photo weighs heavily on me.

I check the closet and the dresser—both completely full of clothes. There's a suitcase in the corner of the closet. I pull it out and unzip and inside there's another and then another—a whole set of nested suitcases. They look practically new. There's a small bookshelf with the usual paperbacks, but also a stack of what look like college textbooks—a history book, a psychology book, two on music theory. In the desk, some spirals filled with my mother's handwriting. I skim through them but they're class notes, nothing personal. There's a notebook of sheet music paper, half of it filled in with penciled dots and scribbled annotations. In other drawers there are tons of photo negatives, some loose, some in manila envelopes. In the bottom drawer there is only a shoe box.

The rubber band securing the lid crumbles in my hand. I open the box, peer inside, and then let out the breath I hadn't noticed I was holding. It's just a conch shell. I set it on the bedside table and close the drawer. There are no answers in this room. Only questions.

Back downstairs, I lock doors, turn off lights. When I get to the living room, I pull out the piano bench and sit for a minute, looking out the window. A streetlight shines through the maple out front, casting a shadow shaped a little like an upturned fist. I shiver in the darkness even though the room is not cold. On the piano there's a collection of silver-framed photos, most of them black-and-whites of a boy and then that boy as a young man, the same guy, I think, who was posing by a car in that old photo upstairs. There are a handful of framed pictures of my mother as well. In one she's seated at this very piano.

I lift the piano fall and gently press a few keys. Then I take out my phone and call Queeg.

He answers on the third ring.

"I have a question," I say.

I hear a shuffling sound and a cough, and I wonder if I have woken him up. "What?" he finally replies.

"This is going to sound strange but . . . did you know that Mom could play the piano?"

There's a pause before he answers. "Yes."

"Why didn't I know?"

"I only found out by accident," he says.

"Tell me."

"We were shopping at an outlet mall. I was trying on trousers, and your mother was restless, bored. I told her to go on to another store and I'd catch up with her. She told me to wait there and she'd be right back." He pauses and coughs again. "Sorry. Where was I?"

"She told you to wait . . ."

"Right, but I didn't wait. When I got finished, I went looking for her. A few doors down there was a music store and as I walked past it, I glanced in the window and there she was, playing a piano. She had her back to me but it was her. And she was terrific, Matt. I mean, she wasn't just fooling around. Everybody in that store had stopped what they were doing to listen. I'm not sure I'd have been more surprised to see her sprout wings and fly away."

"So what happened?"

"I don't know if she felt the air move when I opened the door, or she just felt me looking at her, but as soon as she noticed me, she jumped up and came outside."

"Didn't you ask—"

"Of course I did," Queeg says. "I asked her why she'd never told me she could play like that. I wanted to go right back in there and buy her one of those keyboards for the house. But she wouldn't hear of it. The more I talked the angrier she got."

"So . . ."

"So I dropped it."

As I watch, the wind is moving through the maple, flexing the shadow fist.

"I don't know why I never told you about that," he says.

"It's okay," I tell him. "I'm sitting on a piano bench, in the house she grew up in."

"That's good."

"It's a nice house, Queeg. Really nice. In a nice neighborhood with big trees and sidewalks. Mom went to college for a year. She had a music scholarship."

"I never knew that," he says.

"She was going to be somebody."

"She was somebody, Matt."

"Not what she could have been."

"How can you know that?"

I stand and walk to the window. The temperature has fallen since the sun went down; the glass feels cool against my palm. "Because the people who lived here were Buttercup people."

Queeg is quiet, and then I hear a rumbling sound and I know he's holding the phone against his chest while he coughs. When he speaks again he's a little out of breath.

"I don't know what that means, Matt, but I do know that your mother did her best."

I consider that for a few seconds. "No. She left her best here," I say. "We just got what was left."

He sighs, and then he says, "It was enough."

"No it wasn't."

There's another painful silence, and I picture him sitting on the edge of his bed, trying to think of something to say that will make me feel better. Or make him feel better.

"Queeg?"

"Hmmm?"

"I'm gonna let you down. You know that, don't you? Just like she did."

"I haven't given up on you yet, kiddo."

There's such tenderness in his voice that I can't bring myself to say what needs to be said: that he's making a mistake; that he should have given up on me a long time ago. I did.

The silence sits there between us for too long. Finally he says,

"I don't know what's going on with you, sweetheart, but it scares me."

It scares me, too, but that's not what he needs to hear. So I tell him not to worry, that I'm just tired. When we say our good-byes, he tells me that everything is going to be all right. He's wrong, but I don't argue.

I walk through the dark, quiet house, looking for the dogs. I find them asleep on the floor in my grandmother's room. On the dresser there's a ratty gray quilt that looks like something that's been used by dogs, so I fold it into a rectangle and lay it on the floor near where they're resting. Immediately they stand and move to the blanket, circle a few times, then snuggle together on the quilt. The dogs have the right idea. I look at my grandmother's bed, but it looks uninviting, hastily made up; besides, I'm too spooked by the idea that she might have died in it to sleep here. I consider the couch downstairs, but then remind myself that I'm a grown woman and I'm being ridiculous. There's another perfectly good bed in this house.

It's a clear night, and there's plenty of moonlight so I leave the lights off while I exchange my clothes for an old tank top. I reach to pull the thin curtain closed. I pause. There was something, for just a second in the darkness outside. I see it again: a flash of red and then it's gone. I stand motionless, my heart speeding up, and watch the same spot. There, again, a brief red glow. Someone is outside smoking a cigarette. JJ, it has to be, standing in his yard, smoking, facing this house. Somehow I know he's looking up at this window, and I can't help but wonder if he knows that I'm looking down at him.

The sheets on my mother's bed smell stale, but I'm too tired to look for a fresh set. Instead, I lie on top of the bedding and wrap the comforter around me, the back of my head resting on my dead mother's pillow. This is hard. Nights are always hard, but tonight is harder than most. There's not enough light for me to see the details of the photos tacked to the wall above my head, but I can feel them there, the pictures of my mother. In them she's laughing, happy. Whole.

I take that girl in the pictures, the same one Gordon Penny at the bank knew, and hold her up against the brittle, damaged woman I remember, and my heart breaks. Because something happened to change that girl into the woman she became. And the terrible truth is that the one thing I *know* happened to her was me—her unplanned-for, unwanted, child. For five long years I've struggled to stay afloat under the weight of my mother's death, and now I wonder if the blame for her unhappy life rests with me as well. It's possible. It's unbearable.

And yet . . .

Mr. Penny's account of how abruptly and completely my mother severed all ties to her past gives me hope. If she really abandoned her life in this town five years before my birth, maybe I didn't start my mother's downward spiral. Maybe I was just along for the ride.

Queeg has warned me more than once, that those who do not learn from history are doomed to repeat it, and here I am lying in my mother's bed, my head resting on her pillow. I am pregnant with an unwanted child just as she once was with me. Like her, I am bitter, lonely, broke. Broken? Perhaps.

I reach over to the nightstand and lift the conch shell, holding it to my ear, knowing as I do that my mother once cupped it just so. After all, she's the one who taught me to listen for the ocean's secrets. I don't believe in ghosts, but I want to. I want to hear my mother's voice whispering to me, telling me what happened to her and why and when. I want to know. I think I need to know.

Either the shell is warming or my skin is cooling, because I can no longer feel its chill on my cheek. I'm still listening but the shell holds no comfort for me. There are no answers here, only echoes of my own childhood—the sigh of the surf, the wind stirring the sea grass on the dunes, and the gulls. They're always there, of course.

TUESDAY

A half-truth is a whole lie.

CHAPTER 15

A thin curtain over an east-facing window pretty well guarantees some early-to-rise crap happening. I'm awake at six thirty, by seven I've fed the dogs their kibble, scrounged in the pantry, and am sitting at the table feeling sad and lonely. Sad, because dry, stale Cheerios and a glass of tap water are a decidedly noncheery breakfast. Stupid Cheerios. Stupid water. Lonely because my usual breakfast companions, coffee and cigarettes, are no longer my friends. I thought about trying some coffee this morning—there's a coffeemaker and some Folgers—but just smelling the can almost made me puke. Stupid coffee. Stupid pregnancy.

I hear excited yaps from the backyard and look out the window to see Tweedle Dumb and Tweedle Dumber race across the yard. JJ is squatting on his side of the fence, one hand reaching fingers through the chain links to pet the dogs, the other holding a fucking cup of coffee and a cigarette. Stupid dogs. Stupid JJ.

I open the door and step outside. "Good morning," I call out to him. "Can I ask you a question?"

He stands and takes a sip out of his mug, watching as I approach the fence. This time I carefully avoid the viney weeds.

"There are some plants inside the house."

"That's not a question," he replies.

I ignore him and continue. "The soil is a little damp."

"Okay."

"My grandmother died a month ago."

"Is there a question coming?"

God, this man is a dick. "Do you have a key? Have you been watering the plants?"

He looks away and takes a drag from his cigarette, letting the smoke drift out of his nose. He holds the cigarette between his thumb and first finger, cupped in his hand like a tough guy in the movies.

"Nope," he finally replies.

"No you don't have a key, or no you didn't water the plants?"

"Yes."

"Yes? So does that mean you did or—"

"So then, *no*. Whatever. I don't have a key and I didn't do jack."

I'd feel better if he'd look at me; it's hard to read a lie in profile. "Okay," I tell him. "Well . . . thanks."

"Anytime." And with that he walks away. At the door, he glances back at me and then his gaze moves upward and for an instant he focuses on something above my head. When he disappears inside, I turn to see what he was looking at. It's the window of the room I slept in last night.

My grandmother's bathroom is clean but cramped, the showerhead over the tub so low I have to crouch to get my head wet. There's a bottle of shampoo and a bottle of conditioner, both formulated for thinning gray hair. Great.

I'm sitting on my mother's bed, toweling dry my presumably thicker and less gray hair when my phone rings. It's not a number I recognize, but I like to think that I've learned something about the foolishness of ignoring calls, so I pick it up and say, "Hello?"

"Good morning." It's Luke; I recognize the voice. "It's Luke," he adds unnecessarily.

"Howdy," I reply.

There's a pause during which I think he's trying to decide if I'm giving him a cowboy-flavored hello, or if I'm back to the name-calling. In the end he lets it slide.

"I've got good news," he tells me, pausing for effect.

And just like that, I realize I have no idea what *good news* means to me now. Sitting in Luke's office yesterday morning, good news would have meant a big fat check, but that's not true anymore. I feel an echo of last night's longing, and I look over at the photos pinned on the wall, all those smiling faces, every single one a stranger. Even my mother. I can't leave yet.

"I've found you a job," Luke tells me.

I take a deep breath. I still don't completely understand my feeling of relief, but it's genuine.

"It's at the library." He's pleased with himself; I can hear the smile in his voice.

"Uh . . ." is all I say. I'm trying to picture me working in a library.

"I hope that's okay," he adds.

"I don't have much experience with libraries." This is an understatement.

"You can read, can't you?"

"Of course I can read. I can also drive a car, but that doesn't mean that I should work in a garage."

"You'll do fine," he announces. "You start this morning. Need a ride?"

The answer to that is *yes*, but what I actually say is "Gosh, I hate to cause you more trouble . . ." I am so coy.

"The library is just a couple blocks from my office. No big deal."

Excellent. I'll be within walking distance of my lunch date with Father Barnes. I thank Luke profusely and take him up on his offer for a ride.

I slap on a little makeup and finish scrunching my wild mop of hair into the closest thing to a hairstyle I can achieve without hair gel or a blow dryer, neither of which I have. The fact is, getting ready by eight forty-five sounded like plenty of time until I remembered that I only have one sixth of my belongings with me, and that small fraction is still wadded up in a trash bag.

Last night I hauled the bag upstairs and shoved it in a corner of my grandmother's room. Unfortunately, even as I stand here surveying the lump of black plastic, I know that I could dig through it all day and still not find anything remotely librariany. Even the bags still in my car don't have what I need. I'm a low-rent photographer, for Christ's sake, I don't own anything except old jeans, tight black pants, funky T-shirts, skimpy club-wear, and one tatty old skirt for situations that absolutely require one. Nary a tweed to be found.

In my grandmother's closet, however, I find an ocean of wooly tweed. Perfect. The trousers won't work, they're way too short, but the skirts fit pretty well, although I suspect a fair amount shorter and tighter than Granny wore them. And a white blouse, the too-short sleeves rolled up, looks fine. It pulls a little across the chest, but I'm not in skank territory.

Her shoes are too small, so I tear through the bag of my stuff until I find a pair of pumps. In the full-length mirror, I analyze the finished product. Kicking aside the pile of clothing and plastic with my four-inch black patent stilettos, I cock a hip, and open another button on the blouse. Not bad. I've managed to achieve a reasonably arresting librarian-on-the-skids look.

Just as I step outside and lock the door, Luke pulls up. He grins appreciatively when I sashay down the walk, but is too much of a gentleman to stare as I climb into the car, struggling to keep my too-tight, too-short skirt from showing him the goodies.

Once I get settled and belted he turns to me and says, "You look nice."

"Thank you."

"Your hair looks good. What did you do to it?"

"I washed it," I say.

"Ah . . ." He frowns and chews his lower lip, his face turning an impressive shade of pink. I turn away to hide my smile.

When we get to the T-intersection at the base of the hill, I say, "Help me get my bearings." I point to the direction I took yesterday to get to the pawnshop. "To the right is toward downtown?"

"Correct."

"And to the left?"

"To a four-lane loop that goes around this side of Gandy. It's usually faster than driving through town, but it's all strip malls and car dealerships. I like to drive through town where you can see stuff."

"What kind of stuff?"

"Normal stuff."

At the intersection stop sign Luke comes to a complete stop and then looks both ways. Unexceptional behavior, I know, but after the ride with JJ yesterday, I vow to never take it for granted again.

I point at the copse of trees straight ahead where I think I can see part of a paved trail. "And that?"

"The park."

We turn right, toward downtown. He continues, "It's wooded on this end, but further along it opens up. There are trails that go under a couple of streets. The whole thing winds along the creek almost all the way downtown."

"I bet it's a great place to walk."

"You're probably right," he replies, accelerating with his hand control.

Shit. Now it's my turn to blush.

"So . . ." I change the subject. "How did you manage to get me a job?"

"The head librarian is sort of my aunt."

"Sort of?"

"Well, I call her Aunt Fritter, but she's not my aunt. She and my mom have the same great-great-great-grandparents. What would that make her?"

"I have no idea."

He slows and waits for a man walking his dog to cross the street. "Anyway, she was a friend of your grandmother's, so I called and explained your situation. She was . . . um . . . happy to help."

I take note of the pause in the middle of that last sentence, but I don't ask for any details. I'll meet Aunt Fritter soon enough.

We ride in silence for a while, and I notice that Luke is right, coming this way I do see *stuff*. A lady in a jogging suit pushes a stroller, an elderly man leans over to pick up his newspaper, a rope swing hangs from the limb of a huge tree. It's all nice stuff, but it's not *normal* stuff. I don't see any cars on blocks, or old ladies walking to the store, dragging a saggy-diapered grandchild behind them. There are no tough kids in hoodies, hands deep in their pockets, eyes narrowed, watching for someone's carelessness to exploit.

"Hey, I was wondering . . . who has keys to my grandmother's house?"

He frowns and shakes his head. "I'm not sure. Is everything okay?"

"Everything is fine," I reply. "There are a couple plants inside that look pretty healthy. Somebody has been watering them."

"I'll ask when I get to the office."

"Thanks."

I don't much like the idea of keys floating around, but I'm careful to keep my tone casual. I'm probably not the only person who's noticed that most overly suspicious people are themselves untrustworthy, and I don't want Luke reconsidering his decision to let me stay at the house.

Eventually the residential area gives way to businesses, and as we approach a stately redbrick building with the words *Public Library* engraved in a pseudo-Latin script above the door, Luke slows the car. We're here.

"Before you go in . . ." He puts the car in park and turns to face me. "Fritter is pretty scrappy, but she's getting old. She overestimates her stamina."

I'm not sure where he's going with this. I hadn't planned to challenge the woman to a foot race.

"She's got a niece staying with her, or actually I think probably a great-niece. Anyway a niece—"

"Sort of."

He grins. "Exactly. Anyway, every summer Fritter tries to rehabilitate one of the family's teenagers. Her *summer project*, we all call it. I don't know if she watched *Boy's Town* one too many times or what, but she seems to think she can cure what ails today's youth."

"Tall order."

"You have no idea," he says, but he's wrong. Queeg tried the same thing with me—still trying, come to think of it.

"Anyway," Luke continues, "from the looks of this year's project, I'm afraid she may be more than Fritter can handle. I was hoping you could maybe help her out with that."

"You don't think the niece will be more than I can handle?"

He laughs softly. "I get the feeling that you can handle just about anything."

Hmmm. While I appreciate his vote of confidence, nothing could be further from the truth. I look up at the white columns and take a deep breath. I'm actually feeling pretty nervous about this gig.

"Well . . ." He sneaks a glance at his watch.

I take the hint and climb out of the car only slightly more gracefully than I got in. "Thanks again," I say.

He must sense my worry, because when I reach in to get my purse, he grabs my hand and says. "Mattie, everything's going to be okay."

"Dewey Decimal isn't going to know what hit him," I reply.

He laughs. "That's my girl."

I shut the car door and walk up the wide, shallow steps. Before I open the door I glance back and lift a hand to wave, but Luke is already gone. Oh well. I'm sure Howdy is a nice enough guy, but he doesn't know a thing about me. I'm nobody's girl. And it's much too late for everything to be okay.

CHAPTER 16

I'd always assumed that a job in a library would, if nothing else, at least smell better than a job at a fast-food restaurant, but it seems I was mistaken. Inside I find the expected odor of musty books, but beneath that there is a faint, disconcertingly fecal odor.

There's a little girl slouched at a desk straight ahead, and five dumpy middle-aged men—the Gandy intelligentsia, I'm sure—sitting at a bank of computers on my right. When the heavy door thumps closed behind me, the computer users lift their gazes, momentarily disregarding whatever research they had just been engaged in—googling the success rate of penile-enlargement surgery, watching YouTube videos of women crushing beer cans with their breasts, hunting for an extra-large camo thong for the little woman's birthday.

As my high heels clackity-clack on the marble floor, the girl behind the desk straightens, watching me approach. At first glance, with her close-cropped black hair, pale freckled face, and tiny birdlike frame, she'd looked to be about ten years old, but when I get to the desk I reassess my estimate. The surly expres-

sion, black lipstick, and the metal rings and studs protruding from
her lips, nose, and eyebrow surely puts her age closer to sixteen or
seventeen. She's got one hand flat on the desk in front of her, palm
facing up. In the other she's holding a red Sharpie. This explains
the *how* of the red pentagram on the girl's palm, but not the *why*.

"Hello," I say, and we both flinch at the echo my greeting sets
up in the high-ceilinged room. I drop my voice to a whisper. "I'm
here to see . . ." At this point I realize that Luke didn't tell me Aunt
Fritter's last name, and for all I know *Fritter* could be just an affec-
tionate food nickname given to her by her family, like Pumpkin
or Dumplin'.

Satan's pixie is giving me a doubtful look by the time I finally
ask for, "The person in charge."

"No soliciting," she says.

"I'm not selling anything. I'm here about a job."

"We're not hiring." She turns and walks to a stack of books on
the cabinet behind her.

"Excuse me," I say in a stage whisper. There is no response
from Goth-girl, so I increase my volume just a teensy bit for the
next one. "Excuse me . . ."

At this, she spins around with a "Shhh!" that's much louder
than my voice had been, then turns back to her stack of books.

I've had enough. "Listen, Morticia, your aunt Fritter is expecting me."

She lets out an enormous sigh and turns back around. "*Great-
great*-aunt," she tells me.

"I'm sure she's spectacular."

"No, I mean that she's not really my regular aunt, she's—"

"I know what you meant. Can I please talk to her?"

"Whatever." She steps out from behind the desk and shuffles
to a flight of stairs.

I follow her up the steps, amazed that her tiny hips can support the baggy black jeans that hang from them and drag the ground, puddling over her flip-flops. As if to make up for the largeness of the pants her black T-shirt looks several sizes too small. I would suspect that it was a child's size except I've never seen anything in the children's department stenciled with a bloody skull complete with maggots in the eye sockets. If this is the employee dress code I am way, way overdressed.

We stop in front of a door; the girl raps her knuckles three times, pushes the door open, then without a word shuffles back to the stairs.

I was expecting an office, but instead it's a room with book-shelves along two walls and a table in the center. A small, plump, gray-haired woman bends over the table holding a partially decon-structed book.

She looks up as I enter and lifts a gloved hand to push away the strands of hair that have escaped her bun. For a few seconds she stares at me, seeming to take my measure, and then she nods. "I'm fixing a spine. Come make yourself useful."

Under her instructions I hold the cover up as she paints glue on two tabs sticking out of a white strip of some kind of cloth tape. She uses a ruler to press everything together, slides waxed paper on either side of the glued area and then wraps a couple of rubber bands around the book and we're done.

"Thank you for that," the woman says. "I'm Fritter Jackson. And you are . . ."

"Mattie Wallace." I hold out my hand. "Your nephew told me—"

"You're Genie's girl," she replies, stripping off her gloves and shaking my outstretched hand. "Luke and I discussed you, but he didn't tell me your name was Matilda."

"Probably because I don't go by—"

"Luke is not my nephew, by the way. Most people would hardly consider us related. He's my fourth cousin twice removed."

"Okay," I say. She's looking at me like she expects a more elaborate reply, so I add, "I've never understood all the numbered cousins and the *removed* stuff."

"I'm sorry to hear that. It's not very difficult."

Yikes.

The old woman opens a filing cabinet, pulls out a sheet of paper, marks on it, and then hands it to me with a pen. It's a standard employment application, but she has put an X next to the questions she wants me to answer which are: my name, my social security number, and my birthdate.

"I'll be paying you off the books. The social is just for me to keep in case there's any criminal activity. I already know your local address," she says. "And I suspect that your qualifications are none."

It's pretty obvious that she's feeling a little employer's remorse. "Listen, don't feel like you have to hire me—"

"Fill in these blanks and sign it, please."

I finish with the form and hand it over. She glances at it and then quickly looks back up at me. I get the feeling it was my birth date she was most interested in seeing. I'm starting to wonder if I need to wear a sign that says *No, I am not the reason my mother left town.*

Fritter spends a few minutes explaining my duties, which seem to be limited to reshelving books and light cleaning. I ask about the hourly pay and she quotes a discouragingly low number, and then she explains my schedule: nine to five with thirty minutes for lunch. When I mention my lunch date today with Father Barnes, she frowns.

"While I do appreciate the impulse to seek out a church home . . ."

I'm pretty sure that's not what I have in mind, but I nod anyway. Seeking out a *church home* sounds more respectable than seeking out *sexy man-flesh*.

"You must take your duties at the library seriously," she continues. "I'm hiring you as a favor for someone important to me."

"My grandmother, right?"

Fritter doesn't reply to that. Instead she studies me for a few seconds and then says, "You favor your grandmother. She never looked much like a *Matilda* and neither do you."

I don't know what she thinks a Matilda looks like, but I've always thought that I look a little like Gene Wilder, except with longer hair and a vagina.

Suddenly, I'm worried that this old lady is waiting for me to reciprocate and tell her she doesn't look like a *Fritter*. The only problem is, with her rounded, compact build and tanned, wrinkled flesh she actually does look a little bit like a fritter. Or a tater tot.

"I go by Mattie," I say.

"Well, you don't really resemble your mother," Fritter tells me.

"Just around the edges."

"What is that supposed to mean?"

"You'd have to ask Mr. Penny at the bank. That's what he told me."

Fritter shakes her head. "Gordon Penny was a little shit as a child, and he grew up into a big one."

I nod, but Fritter seems to be waiting for me to say something more. If this is a job interview it's the strangest one I've ever had.

"While we're on the subject," I say, for lack of a better idea. "Do you guys have a plumbing problem or something? Because it smells pretty bad downstairs . . ."

"Oh, not again! Come with me."

I follow her out of the workroom and we start down the stairs. She is surprisingly nimble for an elderly fritter-shaped person.

"This is the fourth time, damn it."

"Fourth time for what? Wait . . ." I'm struggling not to fall with these stupid high heels on the slick steps.

At the foot of the stairs she stops and waits for me to catch up. "That a visitor has done this."

"Done what?"

"Believe it or not, they aren't unheard of in the world of public libraries," she tells me. "One librarian's blog refers to them as *rogue turds*."

"Librarians blog?"

"Shhh," she replies.

I follow Fritter as she walks toward the spooky girl at the desk.

"I, however," she whispers over her shoulder, "have been referring to them as UFOs."

"Unidentified . . . ?"

"Fecal Objects," she explains. "Seems classier than turds."

I can't argue with that. Just about everything is classier than turds.

"The last one was in the Reference section. On a shelf next to the OED."

"On a shelf?"

At this point we've reached the counter and Fritter raises a finger at me just like my first-grade teacher used to, and it still works. I play the quiet game. Fritter walks up to the desk; it's almost chest high to the squat woman. She gestures to the teen, who leans forward to hear. "Tawny, can't you smell that?"

The girl's name is Tawny? Oh, my. If there was ever a word less descriptive of the vampirically pale teen at the desk, I can't think of it.

"Smell what?" the girl replies.

"Sweet Jesus on a Triscuit," Fritter says, walking through the little swinging half-door at the side of the desk. "You need to stop smoking." The woman puts her hands on Tawny's shoulders and pushes her out from behind the checkout area. "Go on. You know the drill . . . bag, gloves, cleaner, and paper towels. Chop chop."

Fritter and I watch as Tawny slouches her way past some bookshelves and around a corner.

"Now," Fritter turns to me. "What was your question?"

"How could someone take a . . . leave a *fecal object* on a shelf."

She shakes her head. "Good question. Of course it was on one of the lower shelves."

When Tawny reappears with the cleaning products, Fritter announces, "Follow your nose."

With the old woman leading the way we begin to weave through the library.

"Should we split up?" I say.

"Excellent idea," Fritter replies. "I'll take Reference and Audio. Tawny, you and Mattie take Fiction and make a quick run through Periodicals."

Tawny and I dawdle a bit in our search efforts; the speed of the hunt does depend on whether or not you want to find what you're hunting. Unsurprisingly Fritter locates the prize.

We hear a quiet "Ah ha!" from a few aisles over and head in that direction with the cleaning supplies.

"It's not very large," Fritter says, frowning. Indeed it is an unexceptional poo, on the floor immediately in front of a large window looking out into a coffee shop parking lot.

"The culprit is not modest," I say.

"Perhaps one of you could speak to the people at that shop and see if anyone saw anything unusual."

Tawny and I look at each other and in that instant we find a tiny patch of common ground. She may have a bad attitude and five or six more holes in her face than I do, but on one thing we agree—neither one of us is going to go into a coffee shop to ask if anyone happened to look this direction and see a naked ass.

"We'll take care of it," I say.

"The last one was quite a bit larger." Fritter dons the gloves and places the turd in the bag, then sprays the floor liberally with cleaner. "Perhaps we have more than one miscreant."

"Really? You actually think there is more than one person in this town who would take a crap on the floor of a library?"

Fritter shrugs. "Lots of people urinate outdoors."

She's hitting a little close to home now. "Only when a bathroom isn't available. You do have a bathroom here, don't you?"

"Of course."

"Then this is not an act of necessity," I say.

"You're right," Fritter tells me, her blue eyes now twinkling with either anger or amusement. Or both. "This is an act of war."

"Cool," Tawny says. It's the first time I see her smile.

CHAPTER 17

At eleven forty I make my escape from the library's fluorescent gloom. Even in my too-high heels, the sunshine puts a spring in my step. It is a beautiful day here in the armpit of America. I turn left at the corner and head downhill toward the Episcopal church. There's a crowd gathered in the church parking lot for some reason, and I have to weave my way through it, garnering a couple of wolf-whistles from the motley crew.

I push open the main door and slip inside the cool, dark sanctuary. It's empty, but I hear voices drifting up from somewhere, so I retrace yesterday's steps through the small side door. Since Father Barnes's office is empty, I continue to follow the noise until I reach its source: a large kitchen.

My empty stomach rumbles as I survey the scene: steaming pots on an industrial range, stainless-steel counters with tray after tray of rolls, paper cups and plates stacked along one side, and, in the far corner, Father Barnes, holding court with a group of hairnet-wearing women.

One sturdy middle-aged woman working at the stove looks in my direction. Even through the steam on her glasses, she sees me standing at the door. "Sorry, hon. Fifteen more minutes. You'll have to go on back outside."

"No, I'm here to—"

"Hon, we can't have folks in the kitchen."

The woman looks a little familiar. I take a step closer saying, "But I was invited to—"

She pulls off her fogged-up glasses, saying, "Health regulations, h . . ." and then her voice dies out and she stops smiling. I think she might have been going to add another "hon" but at that moment we recognize each other. It's the woman who wrestled with me over the bike yesterday. The one I called Pork Chop.

"Listen, I'm sorry," I say, "but Father Barnes—"

"Is busy at the moment."

"But—"

"And he'll remain busy until after we finish serving today's hunger outreach lunch."

I'm not liking the direction this is heading. "Wait a minute, I'm not some homeless person."

"Not all the people we serve are homeless. They're just down on their luck, perhaps unemployed, and every Tuesday and Thursday—"

"I'm not some unemployed deadbeat." I don't add *anymore*. "Father Barnes invited me to lunch."

"And lunch you shall have. But you need to go back outside and—"

"Ladies?" Father Barnes has come up behind us. He is beaming. "I see you two are getting acquainted. You remember Tilda Thayer?" He's asking Pork Chop this. She nods.

"She was one of our favorite congregants," he says to me with a wink. Then he turns back to the other woman. "This is her granddaughter, Mattie Wallace. Mattie, this is Karleen Meeker, one of our tireless custodial engineers."

Karleen stares at me for a second, then turns to Father Barnes with a fawning smile. "I was just explaining that we're not serving yet."

"And I was just explaining," I say, "that I don't need to wait outside, because you and I are having lunch together."

Father Barnes puts his hand on my shoulder. "When you called yesterday, Mattie, you sounded like you needed a little fellowship and perhaps a hearty meal. We're providing both here today for a group of folks just like you."

Learning humility is never fun, and for the last couple days the lessons have been coming hot and heavy. There's only one way to handle his embarrassingly correct assessment of my situation. I start lying.

"I'm so sorry we had a misunderstanding," I say with a smile that certainly outsparkles Pork Chop's. "But I'm doing great. I'm working at the library, and I'm staying at my grandmother's house. Everything is fine. I was just a little upset yesterday."

"Oh, well I'm glad to hear that."

"I just thought it was important for me to find a local *church home*," I say, grateful to Fritter for providing the lingo.

"Wonderful!" he says. "This is one of our most active ministries. Volunteering here you'll meet some of the outstanding women at this church."

And that's how I go from an intimate lunch with a dishy man to dishing out lunch to strangers.

I'm stationed next to Pork Chop and, frankly, am surprised at how nice she is to all these people in stained T-shirts and dirty work boots. She exchanges a few friendly words with each, calling a few "hon," but obviously remembering most of their names. There's Frankie with a porn-star mustache, and Juanita missing a lens in her glasses and a couple of teeth. There's even an Elvis, a feral-looking older man with twigs and leaves twisted into his matted hair. He leans in and asks quietly if he can have a little extra for Colonel Parker. I laugh, but Karleen just gives him a wink and serves up another small chunk of meat loaf.

Over and over again, I drop a blob of mashed potatoes on the paper plates passed to me and do my best to smile even though the body odors mixed with food odors turn my stomach.

By twelve forty the crowd has passed through the line. Karleen puts a hand on my arm and says, "Why don't you make yourself a plate and sit down. I'll finish up here."

"I'm fine."

"You're looking a little peaked. You need to eat something."

I would argue, but she's right. She hands me a plate with a slab of meat loaf and I serve myself some potatoes and green beans. There are empty tables, but I need to get away from the oppressive food smell, so I take my plate outside. There's a picnic table by the door, but it's occupied by a group of men having a quiet conversation in what sounds like Spanish. So I walk past them out to the parking lot and perch carefully on one of the air-conditioner units.

The meat loaf is as bad as it looks, and the instant potatoes are like rubber, but after a few bites my nausea recedes. The sun feels good on my back and shoulders. The metal is warm under my legs. A hearty weed that has forced its way through a crack in the cement tickles my left calf with each breeze.

I've eaten what I can—about half of what was on my plate— when I see Karleen coming around the building toward me. She's carrying a glass of milk.

"You didn't bring out a drink," she says.

I'm not a big milk drinker but I nod my thanks and take it from her. She's not wearing her plastic gloves anymore, and I notice an angry, red circular mark on the back of her hand.

I look up at her, surprised. I've seen that sort of mark before. "Cigarette?"

She pulls a pack from her apron pocket, taps one out, and then holds the pack out for me. I shake my head and look pointedly at the wound on her hand. "No, that burn."

"It's nothing," she says, angling herself away from the wind to light her cigarette.

"I bet it hurts."

She shrugs and sucks in a lungful of smoke. "God," she says, exhaling. "I hate how much I love to smoke."

"I know what you mean."

"Sure you don't want one?"

I shake my head.

"So, you quit?"

"I guess," I reply.

"How?"

"Just lost a taste for it."

"Lucky . . ." she says taking another long drag, "Even when I was pregnant I loved smoking."

"Who said anything about me being pregnant?"

"Not me," she says, looking at me with a smile. "Are you?"

I hold out my hand for her cigarette, and she passes it over. I take an experimental puff and hand it back. Fuck. It's awful.

"I'm sorry about that whole thing with the bike yesterday," I say. "I was rude."

"Me too. I don't know what I was thinking. My granddaughter won't be old enough to need a bike that size for years."

"I shouldn't have left it parked in the middle of all that shit for sale. And the jewelry box was my grandmother's. I should have just explained. I apologize for the whole situation."

"Me too."

The air conditioner cuts on and we both startle. I hop off the unit, and we step away from the blast of warm air. Karleen leans over and puts her cigarette out on the ground and then slips the butt into her apron pocket. "You were good help today," she says, pitching her voice loud enough to be heard above the noise. "I'm glad you came."

"Well, it was nice to discover where Elvis has been hiding all these years."

She laughs. "You know, he told me once that his name really is Elvis, but I don't know that I believe him."

"And Colonel Parker?" I'm remembering the extra serving of meat loaf.

"Well, if your name is Elvis, what else are you going to call your cat?"

We look at each other, grinning. I don't know what she's thinking, but I'm thinking about how fluid the border is between *crazy* and *interesting*, and how hard it is to decide who belongs where. Hell, most of the time I can't answer that question about myself.

"You coming to help again Thursday?" she asks.

I'm not sure why, but I say, "Okay."

She takes the plate, plastic ware, and cup from my hand and smiles. "Have a nice afternoon."

"Thanks." I turn and take a few steps and glance back. She's still standing in the same spot, looking at me.

"I knew your mother," Karleen says.

"Me too," I reply, wishing it were true.

CHAPTER 18

When I was eleven years old, my mother dated Dewayne, a baseball cap–wearing NASCAR fan who was a welder and a deacon at a small Pentecostal church that met in a rundown strip mall. The name of the church was the Holy Jesus Apostolic Tabernacle of the Solid Rock of Ages, or something like that, and it was no ordinary listen-to-organ-music-and-pray-it's-over-soon church. No, this was an old-school, out-of-tune-piano-with-the-minister-playing-a-tambourine, "Amen!"-shouting, tongues-speaking church. The only thing missing was snake handling and there was talk of starting that up.

Every Sunday that spring and early summer, we sat in the third pew from the front, Dewayne next to the aisle, and then my mother next to him and then me stuck next to an overweight man who wore the same dark gray three-piece suit every week. Sure, there was a lot going on, with old Mrs. Bettencourt's speaking in tongues, the preacher's fist-pounding sermons, and the bad music. But two hours is a long time to sit in a church with inadequate air-conditioning, and mostly I remember sitting there, dazed, focused on counting the number of sweat droplets that beaded, trembled, and then fell off the nose of the fat man next to me.

Although my mother had a long track record as a serial dater-of-losers, I really think she tried to avoid the dangerous ones. She wasn't always successful. She shielded me from as much of the actual violence as she could, but it was harder to hide the results. *You win some, you lose some*, she'd say as she iced a twisted wrist or blotted blood from a split lip. Love was a game for my mother. Sometimes it was a contact sport.

As June slid into July, things started to get ugly between my mother and Dewayne. Then there was an incident one Saturday night—I never found out exactly what happened—but it marked the end of their relationship. She came home earlier than usual from her night-shift waitressing job, shaken and angry. I remember that she threw her purse on the couch and went straight to the refrigerator for a beer. When I asked her what happened, she told me she'd lost her job and it was Dewayne's fault. She refused to elaborate but I saw something that looked like a cigarette burn on her forearm. When she noticed me looking at it, she crossed her arms and told me to go to bed.

We never went back to the Jesus Apostolic Holy Solid Tabernacle of the Rock of Ages, or whatever. No more tambourines or sweaty Mrs. Bettencourt's *hubbadahubbada*. Our Sunday mornings were rededicated to the ancient, yet satisfying rituals of the eating of pancakes and the doing of laundry, just like they'd been before.

My mother stopped answering the phone. But Dewayne didn't stop calling.

We were packing our bags for our annual trip to the beach, half watching a *Gunsmoke* rerun, when there was a loud banging on the front door. It was Dewayne.

He shouted about *punishing whores* and their *bastard children*, his voice echoing in the concrete breezeway. We waited a little while, hoping he'd give up and go away, but his voice and the pounding grew in strength. He started using his foot on the door; the latch shook. It was only a matter of time before he either broke it open, or thought of trying the window. My mother made a decision.

She pulled out the baseball bat she kept under the sofa, then turned to me and said, "Go to your room."

I shook my head. The only thing more frightening than what was about to happen would be listening to it happen from another room.

She must have understood that, because she nodded and said, "Just stay back."

Luckily for both of us, Dewayne must have finished off his nightly pint of Jim Beam before coming over, because when my mother whipped open the door, he stumbled in, badly off balance.

I'm sure it all happened quickly, but when I think back on the moment, my memory is in slow motion. My mother brought the bat past her right shoulder and then, with a wide smile on her face, she swung a clean arc, catching Dewayne's elbow with a resounding crack.

He cried out, falling to his knees, his left arm hanging limp. Eyes wild and watering he shouted my mother's name and came to his feet, taking a lurching step toward where we stood. For a second I thought he would keep coming for us, but after that one step he seemed to finally focus on the situation. He froze, staring at my mother. She stood in the center of the room in a loose batter's stance, the bat raised and ready.

"One more step and it'll be your head," she told him.

Without a word he turned and left.

My mother shut and locked the front door then turned around, laughing. "All-Star Softball team, 1977."

"You could have killed him," I said.

She nodded. "If I'd wanted to." And with that she tucked the bat back under the couch and said, "Now stop crying and get ready for bed."

Until she said that I hadn't even noticed I was crying. I wiped at my damp cheeks.

"I didn't even know you played softball."

"There's a lot you don't know about me," she said.

CHAPTER 19

Back at the library, Tawny is sitting at the circulation desk, her head resting on her arms. As good as a nap sounds, it's probably a bad idea for me seeing as how it's my first day on the job. So since I'm not sure what my duties are for this afternoon, I look around for Fritter. I find her in Reference. She's scanning the shelves, shaking her head.

"What's wrong?" I ask.

She points up at a gap in the Book of Knowledge series. "K through L is still missing."

"Maybe somebody checked them out."

"It. One volume, two letters."

"Maybe somebody checked *it* out."

"It's reference, it doesn't leave."

"Well, it has to be around here somewhere."

"Then where is it?" She stares at me as if she expects me to pull the missing book out of my ass.

"I don't know, but who would steal it? Nobody reads encyclopedias."

"They most certainly do."

"Name one person you've seen using these in the past year."

She frowns, but doesn't answer.

"And why K through L?" I ask. "They're boring letters."

"Boring?"

"Come on, they got both letters into one book, right? Name something interesting that starts with a K or an L."

She frowns a little harder.

"See?" I ask.

Fritter takes a deep breath, shakes her head and smiles, yielding, obviously, to my superior line of reasoning.

"How was your lunch *date*?" she says.

I hesitate before answering. From the emphasis she just put on the word *date*, I'm pretty sure that when I talked to her about lunch at the church this morning, she knew exactly what it really was.

"Fine," I reply, hoping she'll get the hint and drop the subject.

There's a *gotcha* twinkle in her eyes, but she plays along. "Now that you've returned, I'd like you to clean all the tables, restock the pencils and papers, and place any unshelved books on the cart next to the circulation desk. And while you're at it, please be on the lookout for poor K through L, even though it does cover an *exceedingly* dull portion of the alphabet." She pauses to gesture overdramatically at the two-inch break in the row of books. "Its absence leaves such an *unsightly* gap in these *useless* resources . . ."

Sarcasm is not as attractive in the elderly as it is in someone, say, my age, but rather than point that out, I promise to search for the missing book.

She turns away but I stop her before she walks off. "Can I ask you something?"

"I'm certain that you can," she replies. "Are you asking if you *may*?"

Wow, this woman is tiresome. "*May* I ask you something?"

She nods.

"You knew my mother, right?"

"It's a small town," she tells me, as if I hadn't noticed.

"I'm staying at my grandmother's house, and my mother's room is totally full of her stuff. Her drawers and closet are full of clothes, her suitcases are still here, her bookshelf is full of books—"

"If you'd like to donate the books to the library we would be happy to oblige. The hardbacks, anyway. We have to be selective with paperbacks—"

"No. I mean, okay. But what I'm asking is—don't you think it's weird that my mom left everything here?"

"Well, she went back to college—"

"Without any of her clothes? Her luggage?"

Fritter blinks a few times and then smiles. "Hmmm. There might have been some nice young man back east."

"But still, surely she'd pack up—"

"People do impulsive things. I suspect you have some experience with that."

From her intonation and the look on her face, she's trying to bait me for some reason, but I'm not taking it. "But my mom had a scholarship. It's strange for her to just give that up, right?"

"She must have had a good reason," Fritter says, taking my hand in a dry bony grasp. "But I have absolutely no idea what it was." Her voice is breathless, hurried. "Now if you'll excuse me . . ." She gives my hand a squeeze, just hard enough to hurt a little, and then she hurries away.

As I stand here, watching the old woman's retreating back, I realize that I can think of one interesting word that starts with the letter "L." Liar.

I don't like being lied to—who does? Yet at the same time, a tiny voice deep in my secret heart has started to sing. I think some-thing *did* happen to my mother when she lived here—something bad. And I think Fritter knows what it was. Beneath every lie, a buried truth is hidden. It's time to start digging.

I make a show of obedience; I wipe down a few tables and make a perfunctory pass through the main room, collecting loose books and putting them on the cart. I even help an elderly man wearing green Sansabelt pants print out his receipt for the two cases of fiber-bars he'd just purchased online. I'm a disgruntled employee, not a total jerk.

A few minutes before five, I wander back to the Reference section. I like the blocks of uniform colors and shapes, the size of the books, the way that when I'm back here, nobody can tell that I've taken off my shoes because my feet are killing me. On the bottom row, I notice a sequence of yearbooks. I pull out the Gandy High School 1977–78 volume.

At a table I sit down and flip through the book. I find my mother in the senior section, near the end of three pages of young men and women with collars peeking out of identical black robes. Although the photo is black-and-white, I fill in the colors. The upper edge of the collar sticking out of my mom's gown doesn't look white, I'm betting it's blue, her favorite color. She's blond in the picture, of course, and has done her best to tame her wild hair; it's center-parted and hanging in two wavy sections on either side of her face, but you can tell that it's fighting her efforts. I would bet that within an hour after that photo was taken, her hair had lifted and re-formed into a bramble of curls. She's looking at the camera, at me, with an openmouthed smile on her face, as if she'd just been laughing. As if we had just been laughing together.

I find the athletics section and there's the softball team with my mother in the front row. She's got her arm thrown over the shoulder of the dark-haired girl standing beside her. I check the names under the photo. Karleen Harden is the girl's name.

I turn back to the portraits and find Karleen. She's pretty, with a Mona Lisa smile and a sparkle of mischief in her eyes. I can tell from the upturned nose and the arched brows that this girl is the woman I watched serve meat loaf today. But I can't imagine this girl calling anyone "hon."

Gordon Penny is in the book, too, with the sophomores. His rounded features are unchanged. I go through the book looking at everybody whose name starts with a J, but there is no one who resembles my surly neighbor, JJ. Of course it's been over thirty years, and I'm not sure I'd recognize him if I saw him. I grab the 1976–77 book and flip through it as well.

The library closes in just a few minutes, so I take the yearbooks up front and give them to Tawny.

"Do I need to fill something out to get a library card?"

Tawny passes back the books shaking her head. "These are reference."

"Shit. Do you suppose if I ask Fritter she'll—"

"No exceptions."

I sigh. I don't even know why I wanted to take them home to look at them. It's just . . .

"For God's sake," Tawny interrupts my reverie, taking the yearbooks from my hands. She rubs them across a metal plate on the desk and then opens the backpack at her feet and slips them in.

"I don't think you should—"

"I didn't have you pegged as a Goody Two-Shoes," she says.

"That's good, because I'm not."

"Getting your panties in a wad about lifting some lame books nobody has looked at in a hundred years?"

"My panties are not—"

"Spending your lunch hour, feeding the homeless . . ."

"Hey, I had an ulterior motive for that."

"Whatever."

"Have you *seen* Father Barnes?"

She rolls her eyes. "Get your stuff, we need to go."

"We?"

"Apparently, I'm now your chauffeur."

"You don't have to—"

"Yes I do. Fritter told me to do it, so I'm doing it. You want a ride or not?"

"Okay, hang on." I hurry to the back room and get my purse. When I call Luke to tell him I don't need a ride home, he sounds a little disappointed, but that's okay. He doesn't know it yet, but he's better off not having to deal with me.

Tawny and I walk out the back door to the parking lot, but there's no sign that Fritter is leaving. I ask Tawny and she tells me that Fritter often stays late.

"In the summer anyway," she adds. "Probably not in the winter. She won't drive in the dark."

"People get that way as they get older," I say.

Tawny raises an eyebrow, looking at me.

"I'm not there yet," I tell her.

"Whatever. Anyway, she gets home in time for supper. Except for Wednesdays and Fridays when she goes to see her brother in the nursing home. She stays and eats with him, so those days I don't have to make her dinner."

"You cook?"

Tawny explains the conditions of her summer employment. She gets a steady job, free room and board, but she has to cook dinner five nights a week and clean the bathrooms.

"Not bad," I tell her.

She shrugs. "Could be better."

I follow her out to a mostly primer-colored truck that I think was green in a previous life, except maybe the hood, which might have been black. It's a piece of shit on the inside, too, trash on the floor, upholstery shredded. There are keys dangling from the ignition and a large book on the driver's-side seat. Before Tawny settles her ass on the book, I'm pretty sure I see *K–L* printed on its spine.

The truck's transmission is a three on the tree, and the girl struggles to keep a foot on the clutch as she muscles the gearshift into reverse. Even perched on the book she's almost too short to see over the steering wheel.

"Are you okay driving this?"

She slams it into gear and gives me a look I recognize. It's a you're-not-worth-the-trouble-it-would-take-to-say-fuck-off look. I think we're bonding.

"Never mind," I say, trying to settle in. I have to shuffle my feet to find a spot for them in the pile of trash on the floor, and the bench seat is pulled so far forward that my knees bump the glove box. I fish around for a few minutes looking for a seat belt, before I realize there isn't one.

Tawny shifts the truck into first and we lurch over the curb and into the street. My knees ram into the glove box, and I take a moment to give Tawny some constructive criticism of her driving skills. When I'm finished she takes the opportunity to share her opinion of my critique. It's surprising, really, how many four-letter words we know between the two of us.

"Don't get your panties in a wad," she adds. "I'm an excellent driver."

"Have you considered . . ." I put one hand on the dash and one on the door, bracing myself as we approach a pothole. "That I might not be wearing any panties?"

She shoots me a dark look. "Gross."

CHAPTER 20

When Tawny and I pull up outside the house, I'm pleased to note the absence of JJ's truck next door. Maybe he's out harassing someone else. Maybe he's in his shop fixing my car for free. Maybe he's finally run one stop sign too many and is in the hospital in traction. Hey, a girl can dream.

"You got those funny dogs inside?" Tawny says.

Surprised, I look over at her, but she doesn't meet my eyes.

"Yeah. Want to come in and play with them?"

Still looking away, she shrugs, saying, "Whatever." She hesitates, probably weighing the ramifications of letting me see her be friendly, and then finally she turns off the truck, grabs her backpack, and hops out.

"The keys . . ." I say.

"Who'd steal it?"

The dogs are thrilled to see her, ecstatic. Thing One hops up and puts his front paws on Tawny's knees as she leans down to ruffle his ears. Thing Two spins in circles stopping every third turn to nudge the girl's hands. They like me okay, but they love her. Of course they also love to lick their asses, so I'm not sure how much to read into this display of affection.

"They love me," she says.

I reply, "Whatever."

I excuse myself and go upstairs to change out of my librarian costume. Barefoot, in a T-shirt and jeans, I return to the living room dressed as myself. Tawny is sprawled on the sofa with both dogs in her lap. She is holding a beer.

"Where did you get that?"

"In the fridge," she tells me.

I don't remember seeing beer in the refrigerator, but I didn't exactly look for it. I'm trying to visualize my grandmother—her closet filled with tweed—tossing back a longneck.

I sit in the chair next to the sofa. "How old are you?"

"Old enough," she says, effectively telling me that she is not of legal drinking age. I decide not to respond—I'd like to keep the conversation away from the wadded or unwadded state of my underpants.

The girl reaches in her bag, brings out the yearbooks and sets them on the coffee table. Then she pulls out a pack of Marlboros. "Mind if I smoke?"

"Yes."

With some eye rolling she returns the cigarettes to her backpack. It's almost physically painful to watch her heavy-handed efforts to be cool.

"So you've been here before."

"Why would you say that?" She's petting a dog with each hand.

"You knew the dogs—"

"I knew *of* the dogs."

"You knew how to get to the house without any directions, you knew there was beer in the refrigerator . . ."

We stare at each other for several seconds. I win.

"I came once with Fritter when your grandmother was sick."

This brings up a question I've been wanting to ask someone. "I was wondering . . ." I try to keep my voice casual. "Did my grandmother die here? In this house?"

Tawny grins. "Scared of ghosts?"

"Just curious."

I lean over and pick up her beer. It's cold all right, and it looks untouched. I wonder if Tawny only opened it to bolster the I-belong-in-juvie image she's going for. I take a tentative sip. Fuck. It's awful. I scoot a coaster over and set the sweating bottle on the cork.

Tawny puts her feet up on the coffee table. The smaller, stinkier dog takes the cue and walks out onto her legs and lies down, facing the table.

"You've got the wrong end of that dog pointed at you," I tell her.

She reaches out to scratch him just above the tail. He squirms with delight and stretches his back legs further out.

"About that room upstairs with the orange light . . ." Tawny says.

"The darkroom."

"It's for making pictures, right?"

I nod. "My mom must have set it up when she lived here. She was a photographer."

Tawny gives the dog's rump another scratch. "What does she do now?"

"Nothing. She's dead."

Tawny picks up the beer. I watch her face as she tips it back and takes a swallow. She grimaces.

"So we have something in common," the girl says, setting the beer on the wood, not on the coaster. Her look dares me to move it back to the coaster, but I just smile and lean back in my chair. What the hell do I care?

"Your mom died, too?" I ask.

"No. But she does nothing. I wish she was dead."

A small space opens up in the conversation. Tawny pets the dogs, the beer sweats on the table, and I think about how much I loved my mother and how much I hated her. How much I wish I could go back and do things differently. I could try to explain it to Tawny, tell her how it feels from this side, but I won't. People like Tawny and me never understand anything until it's too late.

"The photography thing is cool," Tawny says. "In the old movies where they swish the paper in the water and pictures magically appear."

"There's no such thing as magic," I tell her, and it's the truth.

She keeps a casual tone in her voice, but it's obviously forced. "Do you know how to do it?"

"Yes."

"Can you teach me?"

I can think of nothing I would rather not do. "First you have to take pictures with a regular camera that uses film, not a digital one."

"Do you have a regular camera?"

Upstairs, in the corner of my mother's room, sits the camera bag I brought with me. One of the things inside that bag is my mother's old 35mm Nikon.

"No," I say.

"Bummer." Tawny sighs and takes another shot at becoming a beer drinker. This attempt looks no more successful than the last.

The fat Winston noses the girl's arm until she sets down the bottle and turns her attention back to him, scratching him under his chin and behind his ears. The little dog grunts with pleasure.

Tawny smiles. "I had a dog," she says.

"What kind?" I'm not particularly interested, but it's something to say.

"Just a mutt."

I ask the next appropriate question. "What happened to it?"

She shrugs. "My mother's new husband isn't a dog person. They told me my dog ran away, but I'm not stupid."

"Oh man . . . I'm sorry."

"Yeah, well fuck 'em." She gives each dog a pat on the rump and then sets them carefully on the floor. "I'd better get going."

I don't want to do it, but the thing about her dog got me feeling sorry for the girl. "Look, there are a bunch of old negatives upstairs," I tell her. "I could show you how to make a print from one of those. That's what you're thinking of. When you put the paper in developer, and the picture appears."

Her face lights up, and for a second she almost looks like the kid she is. "Cool!"

"We need paper and chemicals. Is there a photography store in town?"

"There are still lots of bottles up there."

I pause, surprised that she looked around the darkroom long enough to have noticed the containers stored under the desk. "Fresh would be better."

"I'll buy some. I've got money."

She stands, so I stand. I'm already regretting my offer to print the negatives, but when she promises to pick me up for work in the morning, I can see that it's in my best interest to not piss off this teenager.

"She didn't, you know," Tawny tells me.

"Who didn't what?

"The old lady didn't die here. She went to the hospital and died there."

"Good," I say. "Thanks."

Tawny smiles. "No ghosts."

I look around at the room, at the yearbooks, the sewing machine, the piano. "I don't know about that," I reply.

CHAPTER 21

Sometimes it's not possible to tease out the beginning of the end, to find the origin of a break, to know whose finger knocked over the very first domino.

But sometimes it is.

The summer I turned seventeen three things happened, and they happened in this order: my mother came home from a ninety-day stay in rehab, Queeg bought her a 1978 Chevy Malibu, and I broke her heart.

Her stay in an inpatient facility had been at Queeg's insistence, but I think it was a relief for us all, even my mother. For the first year of their marriage, she'd managed to hide the extent of her drinking problem, but eventually Queeg couldn't help but notice how quickly the booze disappeared and how often my mother was either enraged or incapacitated. Finally, Queeg threatened to leave if she didn't quit drinking, so she packed her bags, he took out a loan, and they found a place called Meadowbrook with an open bed.

After all that drama, it stands to reason that their third wedding anniversary, falling as it did only a week after my mother's release from rehab, would have a giddy over-the-top quality for all of us, especially Queeg. He woke us up early that June morning, urging us to come outside. There in the driveway sat the Malibu with its flaking blue paint and patches of rust. Queeg had stuck a silver bow on the middle of the hood. When I pulled it off, it brought a chunk of paint with it.

I remember being surprised by how much my mother loved both the car itself and the fixer-upper aspect of it. Newly sober, she had too much time on her hands and she seemed thrilled at the prospect of a project. We were quickly assigned roles—Queeg was in charge of getting the engine running, and my mother would remake the shabby upholstery. Me? I ended up in charge of everything else. Laundry, cooking, cleaning—it all fell on my resentful seventeen-year-old shoulders.

While my mother was at Meadowbrook, Queeg had purged the house of alcohol, searching for and finding all of her stashes, except one. He never checked behind the dryer, and I never pointed out the unopened bottle of gin tucked in that dusty corner. Was it because I planned to swipe the booze someday to take to a party, or was I leaving it there to test my mother? At the time I told myself it was the former, but in retrospect I think it was the latter. All summer I checked on that bottle at least once a week. The lint surrounding it disappeared, making it clear that my mother knew it was there, however the seal remained unbroken. Perhaps she left it there as a test as well. Or an insurance policy.

For the most part, my memories of those two months are happy ones of a peaceful but messy home—the mess a result of my negligence and of my mother's insistence on making tuck-and-roll upholstery for the car. Scraps of leatherette littered every surface, and the ancient heavy-duty sewing machine she bought for the job took up the entire coffee table. Only someone who wanted a piece of sewing-machine needle in her foot went barefoot in the house that summer.

Toward the middle of August, the Malibu was looking good. Thanks to a $99 check to Earl Scheib, the car was candy-apple red, and thanks to my mother and Queeg, the black tuck-and-roll upholstery was installed and the engine rumbled in an even pitch. I can still smell the fresh rubber of the seats, the lemony shampooed carpet. And the day it was finally finished, even though it was much too hot to be outside, we headed for the beach.

When I think about that afternoon—and I do think about it—I always slow the memory down at the same spot, a moment polished smooth from years of fond handling. The three of us unpacking the car and then shuffling through the sand. I can still feel the tingle of the impossibly hot sun on my skin, still smell the soft, salty air. I looked over at my mother walking next to me, holding the other handle of the red cooler we carried between us. Her eyes met mine and she smiled. She was squinting in the sunlight, her face full of happiness.

But tides rise and fall, and one domino tips into the next and again, and again: click, click, click . . .

There's no stopping time, not even when it's in the past. Even that afternoon at the beach, my favorite memory, has no choice but to tip over into all that came next.

CHAPTER 22

I follow Tawny to the foyer and hold on to the Winstons' collars as she opens the door and steps out. Blocking the dogs' exit with a foot, I squeeze out behind her.

JJ is in the front yard, looking inside the cab of the old truck. Tawny walks toward him and I follow.

He looks up as we approach. "You ever clean this out?"

"Screw you," the girl replies.

"Don't you know there's a city ordinance prohibiting public eyesores?"

"Then you'd better get inside your house before someone sees your ugly face."

They both laugh.

"I take it you've already been introduced," I say.

They turn and look at me as if they just noticed my presence. JJ's smile disappears.

Tawny nods, still grinning, and says, "Unfortunately." She climbs up into the truck. "So long, fartknocker," she says, presumably to JJ who is, surely, a fartknocker, whatever that is.

"Later, runt," he replies.

She cranks the truck, leaning a little hard on the starter, making both JJ and me flinch at the squeal. The truck trundles down the street, shuddering a little as she shifts into second, and then she turns left at the corner and is gone.

Suddenly it's weird to be standing here in the yard with JJ. I try for friendly. "So, how do you two know each other?"

Friendly doesn't work.

"You come up with any money?"

"Not yet."

"The parts will be in by this afternoon. I'll have the car ready tomorrow."

"You went ahead and ordered them? I thought I had to pay first."

He laughs. "I figure it'll be my car before long, anyway."

"Why would you say that?"

"There's an abandoned vehicle ordinance . . ."

"You wouldn't dare."

"Thirty days, lady."

"Come on . . ."

"My offer to buy it still stands. Of course, it's getting lower every day."

"I already told you that the car was my mom's," I say.

"And I still don't give a shit." JJ turns and walks away.

"Why do you have to be such a jerk?" I ask his retreating back. He doesn't answer. "And stop throwing your cigarette butts in my yard," I add.

JJ stops on his porch and looks back at me. I'm waiting for his response, which will be, I presume, either a gesture of the one-finger variety or a few words of the four-letter variety, but instead he just smiles and walks into his house. An entirely unsatisfying reply.

Back inside, I dump some kibble in the dog bowls, and then get on my phone to find a local photography store. With a quick call, I establish that they sell what we'll need, so I write down the address for Gandy Graphix, and then get back on my phone for another quick search. It has occurred to me that although my car can sit at JJ's for twenty-eight more days doing nothing more tragic than gathering additional rust and a slightly funkier smell inside, my other issue is more pressing. I may be too stupid to avoid getting knocked up, but I'm not stupid enough to wait until it's too late to do anything about it.

I find a local women's clinic and make the call, hoping that someone is still answering phones at five twenty-five. Although the receptionist, in her aggressively ivy-league accent, offers me an appointment in two weeks, I start making up dire symptoms until I manage to get an appointment tomorrow afternoon. I scribble down the address and ask for directions.

"Will you be arriving via public transportation? I can give you directions from the bus stop," she says.

I consider my options and then smile, remembering Tawny's truck with its ugly paint and its beautiful keys left dangling from the ignition.

"No thanks," I reply. "I'll be arriving via public eyesore."

I rummage through the dusty, stale contents of the pantry and then look in the freezer: Five Cheese Cannelloni, Four Cheese Rigatoni, Three Cheese Chicken, Double Cheese Enchiladas. The options don't excite me, but they do explain the jumbo jar of Metamucil by the sink. Sigh.

After spending a few minutes microwaving and then choking down some freezer-burned cannelloni, it occurs to me that I have another long evening ahead with only basic cable and two squatty dogs for entertainment. I walk to the front window and look outside. A faint haze of cloud cover edges everything toward sepia and softens the lengthening shadows. There's plenty of light to go for a walk.

The instant I pick up their leashes, Fred and Ginger begin a crazed scrambling dance at my feet and by the time I manage to grab each squirming dog and clip leash to collar, I'm sweating and cursing. Outside, they immediately begin to pull me, sled-dog style, down the hill toward the park, which is fine with me because that's where I'm going anyway. They're gasping, strangling themselves as they strain against their collars. For dumpy little freaks they've got some spunk.

Somebody is grilling, and the smell of meaty smoke makes my mouth water and fills me with envy. There's a sprinkler in the yard across the street, tick, tick, ticking its way in a lazy arc. JJ's truck is in his driveway but he's nowhere in sight. Thank God. He's got his windows open and his stereo playing classical piano music. Hmmm. The banjo suited him better.

At the bottom of the hill, where we cross the street to get to the park, the dogs notice a lump in the center of the road, and they drag me closer to investigate. It's a turtle, head and legs drawn in at our approach. There's a car coming, so I pick the turtle up, careful to grab him well away from his head. Once we're all under the trees I set him down in a grassy spot that looks appealing, at least what I think a turtle might find appealing.

He pushes his leathery head and legs out of his shell, then looks up, opens his mouth and hisses a warning. His pursed beaky little face and bad attitude remind me of my tenth-grade history teacher, Mr. Newcomb. He was a cranky old man who'd lost whatever love he once had for teaching. Day after day he endured our inattention, our halfhearted efforts, our murmured laughter when he turned to write on the board. If you'd asked me about him back then I would have told you how much I disliked the man, but now all I feel is pity. He was miserable in his job, probably miserable with his whole damn life. The dogs tug at their leashes, trying to approach the turtle, but I pull them away from him and back to the asphalt path. Poor old Mr. Newcomb has had enough.

There's an interesting cross-section of humanity on the trail. Joggers with their short-shorts and earbuds, other dogs dragging their owners, families on bikes, elderly people, androgynous in primary-colored windbreakers that whisper with each swing of their arms.

The Winstons and I weave and dodge along, making good time, and before long the trail dips down to follow a creek. The brush is thick along the bank, and in it I hear the crickets start their evening song. Up ahead is a playground with tall metal swings and a wooden climbing fort with gravel beneath. Just past the playground the path splits. One half goes up a steep hill to a bridge next to the main road; the other half continues to follow the creek under the bridge. There are no kids in the playground, but there is a balding man sitting alone on a bench, reading a newspaper.

I give the creeper a wide berth and lead my pigs up the path to the street level to look around and get my bearings. The hill is steeper than it first appeared and I'm panting along with the dogs by the time we reach the street. I stop and take a few deep breaths.

I'm happy to see that I know where I am; the distinctive spire of Father Barnes's church looks to be not more than three or four blocks away. I'm less happy to see a small child sitting on the bridge railing on the far side of the road. Of course, the good news is that this probably means the bald guy at the playground is her father and not some random child molester, but the bad news is that this little kid is going to kill herself if she's not careful.

I drag the Winstons across the street. She hears us coming and twists her body to watch our approach.

"You'd better get down," I say.

The girl is stocky and wearing jean shorts and a red shirt with a picture of some cartoon character I don't recognize. Judging by the brown smudges covering her cheeks, chin, and the front of her shirt, she has had a recent close encounter with something chocolate.

"Or what?" she replies.

"You might fall."

"So what? It wouldn't hurt."

I look over the railing, down at the rocky slope on one side of the shallow creek and the sidewalk on the other. The ground is much farther away than I expected. I've heard it said that there are two types of falls: the ones that solve all your problems, and the ones that cause you more. I suspect the distance to the culvert below is right at the sweet spot. It could go either way.

"You're wrong," I tell her. "It would hurt a lot."

She swings one leg back on this side of the railing. "What are their names?" She's looking at the dogs who are wriggling from head to toe in happiness at the sight of her. Obviously they have a higher opinion of small bratty children than I do.

"Ben and Jerry. Want to pet them?"

She clambers down from her perch to kneel on the sidewalk next to them. "Their names are like the ice cream," she tells me. "I like chocolate ice cream."

"So I see."

"My name is Shandy, like the drink, or that's what my dad says, but my mom says it's short for Shannon but when you say it it's not any shorter so I don't know why, but my dad likes to call me Shandy anyway." She stops and takes a breath, finally.

"Is that your dad down there at the playground?"

"Yeah, we had to come here because when he got home my mom told him that she needed a break and so he should bring me here and play with me, which is good because the park is nice but mostly when we're here he just reads."

"I can see that." The dogs have finished cleaning the girl's face and have started in on her shirtfront. "Well, Shandy," I say, "it's been nice to meet you, but—"

"Are you married?"

"No."

"Are you a mom?"

I now see why this girl's mother needed a break. I'm tired of her, and we've been talking for less than a minute. "No."

"You know what? You don't have to be married to have a baby. How it works is that the man has a banana, and milk comes out of it and gets all over a lady's eggs and inside her stomach the eggs turn into a bun in the oven except that it gets way bigger more like a watermelon."

Wow. I'm not sure what to say at this point, so I ask the obvious question, "Is your dad a grocer?"

"No, he's a funeral director which means that he takes care of dead people, but he says that he likes the job because it's quiet which makes sense because he's always telling me and my mom that he needs some peace and quiet in the house. Have you ever seen a dead person?"

"No," I tell her and it's true, though I wish it weren't. What we don't see with our eyes, we see in our minds. I know my mother looks worse in my imagination than she really did on that steel table, but knowing something isn't the same thing as believing it.

"My dad lets me come to work with him sometimes," the girl is saying, "and you know what?"

I don't bother to respond. She's going to tell me anyway.

"Dead people are colder than you think and they're hard, which means that people are more like bread than fruit because old bread gets hard but old fruit gets soft."

We're on the food again. Maybe she's hungry. "So your dad lets you touch dead people?"

"He tells me not to but it's no big deal because it's not like they care and mostly I just sit in his office and play on the computer but once I got to see him put clothes on a dead person and do you know what? They cut the back open and just put it on and don't close the back so the dead person is really naked on the bottom."

I'm all for Take Your Daughter to Work Day, but this kid can't be older than seven and she knows more about corpses than I do. "How old are you?" I ask.

"Old enough," she replies.

"I've heard that once today already."

She is hugging the dogs against her as they slobber on her shirt. "So why are your dogs so ugly?"

"Nobody knows," I tell her.

"So if they're ugly why do you have them?"

"I don't know that either."

She looks up at me and cocks her head to one side. "You know what? My dad says that people and their dogs look alike which means that you're ugly, too."

Okay, I've had about enough of this. "Yeah, well, your dad named you after a really terrible drink, so what does he know?"

"He knows everything, dumbass." She pushes the dogs aside and stands. "And you know what? He's way better than your dad."

Well, if she's talking about my biological father, she's got me there. "You shouldn't call people dumbass," I say. "It's not nice."

"I don't give a shit," she says, skipping across the street to the sloped path that leads down to the playground.

"You know what?" I shout after her. "I've already heard that today, too." She turns back and flips me the bird before disappearing down the slope.

I cross the street to watch from the bridge as she runs past her father and climbs on a swing. She pumps her legs hard, back and forth, sending the swing higher and higher. She calls out to her father, "Look at me!" He never looks up from his paper. I wonder if he isn't listening, or if he isn't interested. I wonder if there's any difference.

CHAPTER 23

My mom, Queeg, and I got home from the beach that August afternoon tired and sunburned, and before we'd even washed the sand off of our feet, my mother and I were in an argument. It was one of many that summer, the by-product of a newly sober mom trying to make up for lost time. Seventeen years of disinterest, and suddenly my mother was ready to *parent*. Is it any wonder I balked? Sadly, the fight wasn't even about anything all that special: there was a party, I wanted to go, my mother said no. Embarrassingly predictable, really. Thinking back, sometimes I wonder if I would feel any better about what happened next if the argument had been over something more important. Probably not.

Queeg was working the graveyard shift, so my mother and I were alone in the house that evening. She spent the hours watching a *Baywatch* marathon on TV. I spent them sulking in my room.

Here's the evening I wish I remembered: me pouting in my room until I fell asleep. Or better yet, me apologizing to my mother and then sitting next to her on the couch. Maybe I'd eat some caramel corn. Maybe I would have laid my head on her lap so she could play with my hair. That would have been nice.

Instead, I waited until my mother was in her bed asleep, then I came out of my room and tiptoed down the dark hallway. I'd like to think I was going to the kitchen for a snack. Maybe I didn't really intend to go to the bookshelf in the living room; I was just walking past it and some reflected light from the snow globe's glass surface caught my eye. Maybe what happened next was an impulsive act, an unpremeditated spasm of cruelty. That's what I wish I could believe. But the truth is, I left my room and walked straight through the darkness to the bookshelf where the snow globe sat. I remember noticing the shelf was dusty. I remember that when I lifted the snow globe the tiny white birds inside flew erratically, frantically.

I carried it to the kitchen and turned on the small light above the sink. After a swirl or two to get the plastic birds circling in unison, I lowered it and tapped the glass on the countertop. Nothing happened. And again, harder. Still nothing. The Formica was too forgiving. I can still remember looking over at the red cooler next to the back door, and feeling my anger almost soften into something else. And then I turned back to the sink and tapped the globe once more, this time on the metal faucet.

With a barely audible pop the snow globe exploded, the water and birds escaping down the drain. I stood there, holding the base with its jagged glass walls, and I reached in to touch the little lighthouse. It was plastic, of course.

I was careless when I scooped the mess out of the sink into the trash can, the fragments of clear glass becoming harder and harder to see as my eyes filled with tears. When I'd cleaned out the sink, I turned my attention to my hands. My blood mixed with the water as I washed out my cuts, rubbing hard with the soap, waiting to rinse until I could stand the stinging no longer.

The next morning I woke to the sound of shouting and followed the noise to the kitchen. My mother was yelling at Queeg, accusing him of carelessness. It went on and on, her lurching, drunken dumping of blame, and I remember standing out of her line of sight, looking in through the kitchen doorway, watching her back as she screamed and flailed her arms. She must have dug the snow globe pieces out of the trash because fragments of glass were scattered on the table. On the counter sat that bottle of gin, opened and half empty.

Queeg looked past my mother, at me, standing in the doorway, and for several long seconds our eyes met. I was the first to look away. I don't know what he saw on my face. Gloating? Dismay? I was feeling both. The expression on his face was despair.

I went back to my room and waited until I heard Queeg leave the house, and then I waited awhile longer until I was fairly certain that my mother had either gone back to bed or passed out on the couch. But when I returned to the kitchen, there she was, seated at the table, smoking a cigarette, drinking a mug of something I knew wasn't coffee. She was sifting through the ruins of the snow globe, pushing the shards of glass this way and that. Each piece made a soft scraping sound on the tabletop. Sensing my presence at the door, she glanced up, and then she held out her hand, palm open.

She took a long drag from her cigarette and then exhaled, looking at me through the smoke. In her outstretched hand were two white slivers of plastic. "They remind me of our summers at the beach," my mother said, reaching out a finger to touch one bird and then the other. "There's only two left. One for you, and one for me."

She looked at me, her eyes red from crying. I looked away. Seconds passed with soft clicks from the kitchen clock. A water drop trembled, shining on the sink faucet. She waited, needed me to tell her everything could still be okay. She needed to believe that she and I were bound by a knot too strong for the gin in her coffee cup to unravel. She needed me to take one of those damn birds.

The moment balanced there, her hand outstretched, my hands behind my back, fingers clenching and unclenching, the Band-Aids whispering against each other. My next move would shift the balance. I could walk across the room and pour the rest of the bottle down the drain and apologize for breaking the snow globe. I could lift one tiny bird from her hand and hold it in my own. I could tell her that I loved her, that everything was going to be okay. I knew that if I did that, our unsteady little family might still turn out okay. After all, we'd had a good summer, and she could climb back on the wagon if we helped her. Queeg would forgive her, and she would forgive me.

But God help me, I was seventeen years old and so filled with shame that all I wanted to do was hurt somebody.

And I chose her.

Pulling my mouth into a cruel parody of a smile, I said, "No thanks. You can keep them."

She flinched, though she tried to hide it. I watched her face for the rage I knew would come, but instead I saw only a deep sadness so terrible that to this day the memory of it is physically painful. Standing there in that kitchen, it was all I could do to keep the tight smirk on my face until I turned away. As I left the room, I saw her take a long drink from the coffee cup filled with gin. I wasn't smiling anymore.

CHAPTER 24

The dogs and I continue along street level awhile, walking the length of the overpass and then two or three blocks up the street until we reach the turn I would take to go to the library. Although I hope I won't have to use my newfound knowledge of Gandy geography, it's nice to know that if push comes to shove I could walk or ride the bike through the park to get to work.

By the time we turn around to head back, the light is fading and the wind has picked up. At the bridge over the park I glance down, looking for Shandy and her father, but they're gone. From here I can see that the playground is deserted; the swings hang empty, swaying slightly. I watch a jogger bounce past and a couple walking steadily, their feet striking the pavement in such confident unison that I imagine they've been together for years.

In the distance I hear a child shriek and laugh. I'd like to think it's Shandy. Maybe her father has tickled her ribs or picked her up and swung her around. They're on their way to their car, to their home, to where a mother who needed a break will be waiting, happy to see them. It's not a scene from my past, so there's no excuse for the sinking pressure of homesickness in my chest. But knowing that doesn't keep me from feeling it.

The dogs are urging me toward the path down to the park, but I pull them back over to the other side of the street where Shandy had been sitting. Stepping up until my thighs touch the railing, I lean over the edge, angling out as far as I dare. In the gathering shadows, the creek is a dark smear, the clumps of scrubby brush alive in the wind. I close my eyes and let the breeze tug at my hair. The leaves and the water whisper to me, and I shiver, thinking of how easy it would have been for that little girl to slip off her perch, how easy it would be right now for me to loosen my grip on the railing.

I may not know much about the beginning of my mother's life, but God help me, I know how it ended. I haven't forgotten anything. I remember how to fall.

WEDNESDAY

A drowning man will clutch at a straw.

CHAPTER 25

Up and at 'em this humpday and once again I am feeling like shit. I feed the dogs and then scrounge in the pantry for a sad little match girl breakfast of my own. God, I am pitiful.

When they finish eating, the dogs trundle outside, and after a few minutes leaving deposits I fear I must at some point clean up, they come charging back in through their flap. Cheech has something in his mouth and Chong follows him close behind. I take up the rear of the rollicking cha-cha line. Thanks to my longer legs, I quickly catch up to Cheech. Thanks to my opposable thumbs, I am able to pry open his mouth and extricate whatever delicacy resides within.

It's a cigarette butt. Charming.

"Like you don't snort and wheeze enough already? You've got to give them up, buddy. They'll kill you."

Both dogs smile up at me, wagging their tail stumps in agreement, so I declare the intervention a success. After disposing of the slobbery butt, I wash my hands. I look through the kitchen window but see no sign of JJ, the littering peeper. The day is looking up already.

Deciding that I don't need to dress up as much as I did yesterday, I put on my moderately grimy jeans, and then dig through my trash bag of clothing to find my brown lace-up boots, which are ugly but mercifully low-heeled. Back in my mother's room I look in her closet for a clean shirt. The garish polyester within is so out it's in again, or at least that's what I tell myself as I slip on the peasant blouse printed with a pink and olive geometric pattern. I tuck my jeans in my boots, and the shirt in the jeans, and then check the result. Perfect. Little House on the Kick-Ass Prairie. On LSD.

I grab the photos I took down from the wall Monday night—my mother with friends, the elderly couple, the guy with the old car—and stow them in my purse. Then I smooth out the bedspread and push my crap into the corner, so I can at least walk through the room without tripping. The plant hanging in the window looks pretty droopy—it needs water—but the sound of a horn blasting outside tells me the plant will just have to tough it out a bit longer.

Tawny is very prompt for a disaffected teenager; perhaps I shouldn't have been so quick to judge. Just because she has a face full of metal, and holes in her ears I could stick a finger through doesn't necessarily mean she's irresponsible with anything other than a piercing gun.

As soon as I settle myself in and swing the truck door shut, she turns to me and says, "What the hell is that?"

She's pointing at my shirt, laughing. This from a girl who's wearing another black mini-tee, this one with the words *Good-bye Kitty* under a graphic of Hello Kitty hanging from a noose, and either the same or an identical pair of giant black cargo pants. I am still overdressed.

She starts down the hill, and I brace myself, keeping one hand on the dash and one on the door, watching for potholes. I'm not the only one who should be worried about getting jostled; a cigarette dangles from her lip, a good half-inch of ash trembling on the end.

"Are those pants fire retardant?" I ask.

She glares, but takes the hint and taps the ash into a Red-Bull can in the cup holder.

"You do know that smoking is bad for you, right?"

Tawny gives me a derisive snort. "Live fast, die young, leave a good-looking corpse."

With a lurch we turn left, toward the loop. I am unsurprised that Tawny takes the shorter, less scenic way. She doesn't strike me as someone who'd want to cruise through suburban neighbor-hoods unless it were to case them for later criminal activity. When we pass the trailhead where I crossed last night getting to and from the park, I see a small dark lump in the middle of the road.

"Wait, slow down," I say. "Stop."

She slows marginally.

"Stop!" I say. "It's Mr. Newcomb."

She pulls over, looking at me like I'm crazy. The truck is still rolling when I hop out, check both ways and trot out to the turtle, only to discover that meaty flesh bulges from a crack running through his shell. Ants swarm everywhere. I leave the turtle where he is and hurry back to the truck.

"Too late," I say, climbing back in. My voice sounds a little thin and high.

Tawny glances over at me, puzzled. I clear my throat as if that had been the problem, and return her stare, trying really hard not to look like the sort of crazy loser who'd cry about a turtle.

Tawny shakes her head and tosses her half-smoked cigarette out the window. "That was a snapper," she says.

"I know."

"Mr. Newcomb?"

"Long story," I tell her.

She wrestles the gearshift into first. "I would never help a snapper," she says. "They're mean."

Twisting in her seat to watch for a break in the traffic, she grips the wheel with both hands, rising partially off her encyclopedia booster seat. It's easy to imagine her without the piercings, her hair its natural color—which I'm guessing is strawberry blond—in a Hello Kitty shirt that doesn't feature a noose. All her studied fierceness seems so carefully constructed that I'd be willing to bet she practices it in the mirror. Tawny is still a girl, an innocent. She isn't yet a disappointment to herself. She hasn't spent years sleeping with forgettable men, waking up every morning in a cold sweat, head and heart pounding, mouth dry from the booze or the drugs. She hasn't lived long enough to understand the downhill tumble of a disturbed stone, how each mistake leads inexorably to the next. She still thinks the choices she makes are her own.

"It's their nature," I say. "They can't change what they are."

She glances over at me, and from the look in her eyes I think she understands I'm not really talking about turtles.

"Fuck 'em," she replies.

When Tawny and I arrive at the library, Fritter gathers us into a huddle for a quick rundown of the things to get done this morning. Number one on the list is to find volume *K–L*.

Before she continues to the next item I say, "Tawny and I were just discussing that book."

Fritter looks at me, surprised. Tawny scowls.

"She thinks it could be misshelved over in the Children's section," I say. "And she was hoping you'd let her reorganize that area today . . . you know, take everything off the shelves, clean up the books a little . . ."

"That's a terrific idea," Fritter says, beaming at Tawny.

"And I can check Periodicals," I offer. This not only allows me to dawdle out of sight and read magazines, it's close to the bank of computers and their clueless users. Yesterday, I heard one man ask another if the past tense of *tweet* was *twat*.

Tawny is pissed, but doesn't dare argue. Once Fritter is out of earshot, the girl whispers, "I can't believe you did that."

I shrug. "It's my nature."

"God, you're such a dickbag."

I laugh and watch her sulk her way toward the sticky mess that is the Children's section. First *fartknocker* and now *dickbag*. Working in a library is certainly enriching my vocabulary.

After spending an hour catching up on my magazine reading, I decide it's as good a time as any to start poking around the edges of Fritter's knowledge of my family. If I can figure out what she's willing to talk about and what she isn't, it might help me decide what to do next. I get the photos from my purse and take them to the circulation desk behind which Fritter sits, assessing some damp, slightly rippled books.

"I didn't find K through L in Periodicals, sorry," I tell her. "But can I ask you something?"

She pauses her tut-tutting over the book in her hand. "I don't know. *Can* you?"

Here we go again. "*May* I?"

She nods.

"Who are these people?" I hold out the photo of the elderly couple.

"Burneel and Carter Wallace," she tells me. "Eugene's parents."

"My great-grandparents." I look to her for confirmation, but she's returned her attention to the book in her hands.

"It looks like the picture was taken in front of the house I'm staying in."

"That's because it was their home. When Tilda turned up pregnant, her parents disowned her. Burneel and Carter took her in."

This is an unexpected development. "My grandparents weren't married?"

She raises one eyebrow. "Your mother never told you that she was born out of wedlock?"

"My mother never discussed her past."

Fritter pauses, seeming to consider the implications of that statement. "Interesting."

"Is it?" I ask.

She clears her throat, but doesn't reply. She's looking at my hand, at the next picture, the one with the young man standing by a car.

"Is this my grandfather?"

I pass the photo to her and she sets it in her lap. Her mouth curves up a bit at the edges, a small smile.

She nods. "Wasn't Eugene handsome? All of us had our caps set for him." She's quiet for a few seconds, still looking at the photo. I bite my lip to stay silent, hoping she'll say more, and finally she does.

"It drove a wedge between us, you know, Tilda and me. It's not easy for friends to share a crush."

"So what happened?"

"He chose Tilda, of course." The old woman shrugs her rounded shoulders. "She was beautiful—blond curls, big blue eyes. She sang like an angel and played the piano like it was on fire." She hands the photo back to me and picks up a book, fanning through it as if searching for her next words. "I grew up next door to Gene; he and my older brother Jonah were friends. I spent my childhood tagging along behind the boys, but summers of playing hide-and-seek don't count when everyone starts falling in love. I had no claim on Eugene at all. None of us did."

Fritter slams shut the book in her hands, and I jump at the sound. Lifting it up to inspect the spine, she says, "I guess I was the lucky one. Being an unwed mother in 1959 was no fun."

"So Eugene just knocked up my grandmother and left town?"

"No." She sets the book down and picks up the next. "He died."

I watch as her age-speckled hands move around and around on the book, and I take a minute to consider what she's just told me. My mother never met her father; he died before she was born.

Fritter seems not to notice my surprise, or perhaps she's giving me a moment to recover, because she pointedly keeps her attention focused on the book in her hands. She must find some moisture in it as well, because she puts it with the other damaged ones. When she shakes her head and says, "A terrible tragedy," I'm not sure if she's talking about the book, or my grandfather's death.

"So what happened?" I finally ask.

"Your grandmother did the best she could in the circum-stances. She moved in with Gene's parents and raised your mother in their home."

"And named her Genie."

Tilda nods. "That was a kindness. Burneel and Carter had lost their only child. I think your mother growing up in that house helped to mend their broken hearts."

"So what happened to them?"

"What happens to everybody. They got old and died."

I think of Eugene, who must have died in his twenties, and of my mother, who died at fifty. Not everyone gets old.

Fritter holds her hand out for the last photo, the group shot of my mother with friends. She touches one face with a bony finger. "That's your mother."

I nod. "Her hair looks blond."

"Your mother was a blonde."

"She bleached it though, right?"

The old woman shrugs. "It's certainly possible. She dyed my dog."

"Excuse me?"

"I once made the mistake of asking your mother to watch Frida, my miniature apricot poodle, while I was away for a weekend."

The scowl on Fritter's face is the only thing keeping me from laughing at this point.

She continues, "I came home to an animal with irritated skin and sickly yellow fur."

I swear I don't laugh or even smile, but something in my eyes must reveal my struggle to keep a straight face.

"It's not funny, young lady," Fritter says to me. "She was so ashamed . . ."

"My mother?"

"Frida."

At this I do smile. To my relief, Fritter smiles a little, too.

"Oh, I was so angry. I don't know what possessed your mother to do such a thing, but I do know that Harden girl was also in on it." Fritter taps the photo again, this time pointing to the girl standing next to my mother. "That young lady was trouble on a stick."

"She's Karleen Meeker now," I say. "I met her at the church yesterday."

When I tell Fritter this, she glances up at me. She looks alarmed, but trying to hide it. "I should have known she would frequent a soup kitchen."

"No, no," I'm quick to explain. "She works at the church."

"Regardless of employment, trash is trash."

"She seems nice enough—"

"Stay away from that woman," Fritter says, perhaps a bit too forcefully. She must sense that she's gone too far, because her tone is now one of feigned nonchalance. "I don't know if you planned to go back to that soup kitchen, but I think it's best if you don't. You ought to associate with persons of a higher class. Besides, you can't take such long lunch breaks. If you're short on food, I'll have Tawny pack you a lunch tomorrow."

I have a feeling I'd end up with a lugie sandwich so I refuse the offer, but I do agree to stay away from the church. It's a promise I'm reluctant to make, not so much because I enjoy dishing up slop, but because Fritter's weird insistence that I stay away from Karleen makes seeing her again irresistible.

Apparently satisfied with my sincere-sounding assurances, Fritter lowers herself off the high stool, and then gathers up the stack of damaged books.

Before she leaves, I say, "Was it an accident?"

"I don't think so." She frowns at the damp books in her arms. "I think those hoodlums discard their soft drinks in the night depository on purpose." Her voice is shaking with emotion—this from a woman who takes rogue library turds in stride.

"I meant my grandfather," I say. "Did he die in an accident?"

Fritter pauses, then replies, "I wouldn't say that."

"Well, what *would* you say?"

"I would say, if you're finished in Periodicals, can you please go help Tawny in Children's?"

"There's no doubt that I *can*," I reply. "Are you asking me if I *will*?"

Her mouth curls into a thin smile. "Actually, I'm not asking at all."

CHAPTER 26

My mother wasn't going to tell me. I don't remember how I learned that she was sick and bleeding, or of her doctor's appointment. It could have been from Queeg, but they'd been divorced for years, and he was no longer a reliable source of information about my mother. Or I could have noticed something at the studio. I was working there at the time; a life dedicated to the pursuit of happiness—and by happiness I mean kick-ass parties and badass boyfriends—makes it hard to maintain steady employment, which is how I ended up working for my mother. Of course, by working for her I don't mean to imply that we saw much of each other. She just took more jobs and farmed out some of the easier ones to me, so we tended to go our separate ways.

Actually, now that I think about it, I'm pretty sure I found out because of the Malibu. The car had suffered yet another nervous breakdown, and at the last minute my mother needed a ride to her appointment.

The doctor's office was on the seventh floor of a tall, mirrored building near the hospital. I followed my mother to the receptionist's window, then to a set of empty chairs. Sun streamed in through the wall of windows, potted plants glowed with green health, and the chairs were filled with women whose bellies swelled with promise.

I looked at my mother as she sat filling out forms and noticed for the first time that her belly, too, was swollen. Not the soft pooch of a *menopot*, as my mother called the potbellies of middle-aged women, nor was it the thickened middle I had come to associate with her alcoholism. And certainly it was not the happy roundness of the mothers-to-be around us. No, my mother's bulge looked low and firm and, judging from the way she shifted the clipboard as she tried to write, uncomfortable. How long had she had this? Nobody had said the word *cancer* yet, at least not to me, but still I felt a knot of fear in my own flat stomach.

I didn't say anything, but my mother must have sensed my worry. She leaned over toward me and whispered. "It's just a D and C. They're no big deal."

I could smell the booze on her breath.

"You've had one before?"

"I never said that." She turned her attention back to the forms in her lap.

I remember wondering if she'd had an abortion at some point in her life, and if so, if it had been before or after she had me. And I wondered if she wished she'd had one instead of having me. I didn't say any of that to her.

When a nurse came out and called her name, my mother stood and then I stood. She looked at the nurse and then at me.

"Are you crying?" she asked.

I shook my head. "It's just too bright in here."

She reached in her purse and pulled out her ridiculously large Jackie O sunglasses and handed them to me, watching expectantly until I slipped them over my eyes.

"I'll be right back," she said and then followed the nurse through the door.

The only reading material available was parenting and pregnancy magazines and, surprisingly enough, a few bridal magazines. I picked up one and was thumbing through the photos of frothy gowns, when a strange squeaking and clanking noise made me look up. From the left side of the room a roped platform appeared outside the floor-to-ceiling windows. Inch by inch it lurched farther and farther along the wall until finally the man standing on the platform became visible. He wore heavy coveralls and a thick harness around his waist from which a rope extended to a clasp on the platform railing.

Squeegee in one hand, sponge in the other, bucket at his feet, he smeared fluid in sweeping arcs, then pulled it off with the rubber blade. Back and forth, up and down, then a pause and the platform eased over a few feet, stopped, and he repeated his motions. The man wore wraparound mirrored sunglasses that in turn reflected the mirrored windows, which gave his face the illusion of being two sections of flesh divided by a strip of sky. I pulled the painter's name from a distant memory—Magritte. I could still remember the breathless feeling in art class when our teacher showed slides of his work. Painting after painting of people who were not quite whole, their missing pieces filled with blue and clouds.

I stood and walked to the window, stopping when the man and I were less than three feet apart. Wet and wipe, across and down, he never paused, never acknowledged me standing there.

"It's mirrored," a woman behind me said. "He has no idea what's going on in here."

"Lucky him," I replied.

CHAPTER 27

This afternoon I am operating under a theory I deduced at an early age: it is easier to ask for forgiveness than permission. Once Fritter leaves to spend the afternoon with her brother at the nursing home, I encourage Tawny to take the first lunch break. When she returns, I tell her I'm going to walk to the diner for lunch, then I snag someone's apple from the fridge and go out to Tawny's truck. Just as I expect, the keys are in the ignition. Unfortunately, the seat is still jammed all the way forward and the adjustment lever seems to be rusted in place, which leaves me driving hunched over with my legs spread and the steering wheel practically touching my ribs. Ah well, needs must when the devil drives.

I approach the small gray brick building with apprehension, and when I step through the clinic door, the medical disinfectant smell within weakens my knees. Nothing good has ever happened in a place that smells like this. I actually consider leaving, but the receptionist notices me standing frozen at the door, and gestures me in.

"Sign in." She pushes over a piece of paper and a pen with a plastic flower taped to the end. Her nasal voice sounds familiar;

she must be the same woman I spoke to when I made the appointment yesterday. She asks if I have insurance, and I tell her no. With a Tawny-worthy eye roll, she pushes herself up out of her chair and crosses to a filing cabinet against the far wall. I notice that though her legs and arms are thin, her middle is round and tightly packed. I smile, finding comfort in the knowledge that this rude woman will someday be one of those unfortunate old ladies shaped like a tick.

I fill out the required forms, and before long I am escorted to an exam room. A few minutes later, sporting the paper vest and drape de rigueur, I am flipping through an illustrated pamphlet on the latest and greatest STDs when the door opens. A woman of average height, in her mid-forties, I'm guessing, with short salt-and-pepper hair and a white coat, enters.

"Ms. Wallace? I'm Dr. McDonald."

When we shake hands my paper garments rustle.

"So what seems to be the problem?" She looks down at the pamphlet in my hand.

"Not an STD," I reply without thinking it through. In all honesty, I have contracted the ultimate sexually transmitted disease.

"I'm pretty sure I'm pregnant."

"Have you seen a doctor?"

I shake my head. "Pee test."

We go through the expected questions regarding my last period, then she has me lie down on the paper-covered table, place my feet in stirrups, and scoot, scoot, scoot to the edge.

The fluorescent light overhead hums and has a flicker that I sense more than see. There's a constellation of dead bugs in the fixture's plastic covering. The Bug Dipper. I squint my eyes and try to decide which one is the North Moth, the moth by which I could find my way home.

After a few minutes of intimate poking and prodding, the

doctor tells me to sit up, scoot back onto the table, and lie back down. She lowers the paper blanket covering my middle and squirts some slime onto my lower abdomen. It's cold and I startle a little as it hits my skin.

"Sorry," she says, not sounding terribly sorry, and then she reaches into a drawer and pulls out a plastic gadget with what looks like a thick pen attached by a twisty cord to a walky-talky base. She puts the walky-talky speaker to her ear and the flat end of the pen into the goo on my belly and starts moving it around. A few seconds later she pulls the speaker away from her ear and turns up the volume dial with her thumb.

There's a roaring static noise, but underneath that a fast, rhythmic whooshing. The doctor's eyes meet mine. "There's the heartbeat," she says.

I look away.

After turning off the machine, the doctor wipes my belly with a Kleenex and tells me to sit up. She looks at my paperwork, then pulls a small cardboard wheel from the pocket in her white coat and fiddles with it for a few seconds. "I put your due date in mid-December."

It's either my sigh, or the look on my face, that prompts her to put a hand on my arm and say, "Why don't you get dressed and come visit with me in my office," rather than "Congratulations."

A woman in scrubs leads me to Dr. McDonald's office. The room is small but cheerful, with white walls and a narrow clerestory window behind her desk. A bookshelf holds comfortingly large medical volumes on the lower shelves with a top shelf filled with photos of young children displayed in matching silver frames.

The doctor smiles at me. When I sit down, she pushes the box of Kleenex on her desk closer to me.

"I'm not going to need that," I tell her.

"Okay," she replies, but she leaves the box where it is.

"You don't happen to have a farm do you?"

She shakes her head. "About this pregnancy. I get the impression that it wasn't anticipated."

"Correct," I say.

"Would you like to spend a few moments discussing your options?"

"I give birth or I get an abortion. Doesn't that about cover it?"

"Well . . ." She picks up a pen lying on her desk and clicks the button a few times before answering. "I would have added adoption in there."

"That would certainly be a part of the give birth process. For me anyway."

She clicks her pen a few more times. "If you do decide that an abortion is the right decision for you, I'm afraid that it will have to be surgical."

"Surgical?"

"Before eight weeks it's possible to do what's called a medical abortion. Oral medication is used to induce a miscarriage. I think you're around ten weeks, possibly eleven."

"So the surgical one is what, like a D and C?"

"Exactly. It's very safe."

"You think so?"

"You don't? Have you had one?"

My mother was the one lying on the paper-covered table while I sat in a waiting room hiding my eyes. Of course getting a cancer diagnosis wasn't what killed her; hell, it wasn't even cancer that killed her. But that doesn't stop my heart from skipping a beat as we discuss the procedure.

"No" is all I tell the doctor.

"Don't worry." She sets down her pen. "It's a simple procedure performed at a clinic under light sedation. The decision you need to make shouldn't be focused on the procedure itself. A surgical

abortion is ten times safer than childbirth; I can show you studies to that effect. But terminating a pregnancy brings with it certain ethical implications and a number of emotional issues. That's
where your focus needs to be."

"I shouldn't be anybody's mother," I tell her.

She nods. "I understand how you feel."

I glance up at the photos on the shelf and then back at her.

She answers my unasked question. "I have children. But I still
worry about being a good mother."

I'm not sure how to respond to that, so I don't. She's not too
far from the age my mother was when she died. I wonder if
this woman waited until her late thirties to start a family; that
wouldn't surprise me. Or perhaps she just prefers to display photos
of her kids as young children, before they began to disappoint.
That wouldn't surprise me either.

"Adoption is a valid option," she is saying. "There are lots of
couples who are unable to conceive, but desperately want to be parents."

"How much does it cost?" I ask

"Well, if you go with an open adoption, the adoptive parents
generally assume the financial burden—"

"No, I mean an abortion. How much do you charge?"

I watch her face for a flicker of disappointment, but see none.
She is good. "We don't do them here, but I can refer you to a clinic
in Tulsa. Once there, state law now requires the clinic to provide
you with a state-directed counseling session followed by a twenty-
four-hour waiting period prior to the procedure."

"But how much will it cost?"

"Hard to say exactly. It's an hour drive to the clinic, so there
would be transportation expenses there and back each day. All
that aside, however, the cost of the procedure would be approxi-
mately $600 to $700 right now."

"Right now?"

"In another two weeks you'll be in your second trimester. At that point, the procedure itself often takes two days—the first day a dilator is inserted, then the second day the curettage is performed. Still perfectly safe and reasonably painless, it's just somewhat more expensive."

"Somewhat?"

"It's around $1,500."

"That's more than somewhat."

She picks the pen back up, but thankfully does not begin to click. "Women often get help with the cost from the father of the child."

I run a trial conversation with Nick through my mind. Although I'm pretty sure he'd be in favor of an abortion, he is unpredictable at best, cruel at worst.

"How long do I have?" I say.

"Legally? Eight more weeks, maybe nine. It's legal until the fetus is twenty weeks, but I would strongly recommend sooner rather than later. It gets more difficult the further along you are. Physically and emotionally."

The window behind her desk stretches the length of the wall, up close to the ceiling. From where I'm sitting all I can see is blue sky and a steady procession of clouds blowing past from right to left, misshapen cotton balls on a conveyor belt. I look again at the doctor. She looks at me. She's leaning forward, her arms resting on the desk, her fingers knitted. She's waiting for me to say something, to make some sort of a decision.

"Any more questions?" she says. Her tone is friendly, but at the same time it's clear that she doesn't have all day.

The thing is, even though I can't imagine staying pregnant for seven more months, I can't seem to focus on taking any action to become unpregnant. The harder I try to think about it, the faster the idea slips out from under my attention. It's like trying to eat a peanut with a fork.

"Do you guys use window-washers?" I ask.

"Excuse me?"

"You know, the guys that stand on the platform that hangs from the roof and they use that squeegee on the glass . . ."

She studies me with a worried look on her face before saying, "This building only has one floor."

"Right," I say, feeling my face flush. "I don't know what I was thinking."

She seems to realize that she's not getting a decision from me today, because she just nods and stands, so I stand, and then we observe each other across her cluttered desk. I glance again at the photos on her bookshelf. In one, Dr. McDonald and a tall man are wearing Santa hats. Seated between them, on a fence rail, are three dark-haired children. A horse stands on the other side of the fence, its liquid eyes looking at the camera from between the middle-size and smallest child.

"Nice hats," I say.

"We took it for a Christmas card."

"Taken at your place?"

"We have a few acres. It's not really a farm."

"And a horse?"

"Two," she replies.

I smile. "E-I-E-I-O." Reaching down, I push the Kleenex box back to the center of the desk. "Told you I wouldn't need those."

"You were right," she says. She echoes my smile, but hers looks a little sad. I have a feeling mine does, too.

CHAPTER 28

I pull into the back lot of the library and find Tawny slouched against the brick wall, waiting for me with a cigarette between her lips and fury in her eyes.

"You're lucky I didn't call the cops," she tells me, which is exactly the cue I've been waiting for.

I brush past her, saying, "Don't get your panties in a wad."

For the rest of the afternoon Tawny sulks behind the circulation desk, and I read some magazines and take a nap. Things are certainly more relaxed with Fritter gone. About four o'clock a group of teenagers show up and settle in behind the computers. The arrival of the after-school crowd seems to be the lifeguard's whistle signaling the end of adult swim; a line quickly forms in front of the circulation desk. Tawny gets busy checking out books while I reshelve the ones lying on the tables. I make a quick pass through the aisles reminding anyone still browsing of the time, and before long it's five o'clock. Once we manage to run off the last of the teenagers, we lock the doors and leave.

Tawny doesn't mention my truck borrowing again, but she does insist on today being the day we pick up the chemicals and go back to my grandmother's house and print photos. Since I suspect the only way I'll ever get her off my ass about it is to go ahead and do it, I reluctantly agree.

The idea of facing another dinner out of Tilda's freezer makes my already queasy stomach churn, so I insist on a stop by a grocery store before we go to the photography supply store. While the truck jerks along, hitting every pothole, it seems, I turn on my phone and check my messages. I'm unsurprised to see several missed calls and a dozen new text messages, all from Nick. He's given up on threats; these text messages are along the lines of *please come back home*. Anybody who didn't know better would think I was crazy to leave a guy who wanted me so badly.

My sigh must be louder than I intended, because Tawny glances at me, curious.

"Problems with the ex," I tell her.

She nods with a world-weariness that would work better on someone who looked older than twelve.

"What kind of problems?"

"He says he wants me back."

"And that's bad?"

I nod.

"Is he dangerous? Are you scared of him?" Tawny seems to be enjoying this.

I think of Nick and his friends in their skinny jeans and hand-rolled cigarettes and soulless irony. The answer to that question depends on your definition of *danger*. He wouldn't hurt me physically, not much anyway. The danger to me, I think, lies in how easy it would be to do what he's asking, to be the rat jumping back on that sinking ship.

"Yeah," I reply. "I am a little scared."

Ten knee-bruising minutes later, we pull into the parking lot of Chandler's Food Mart. This store has seen better days; weeds sprout through cracks in the pavement and the parking lot is so littered with carts that Tawny has to work to find an empty space.

I watch a tall, nicely built man in a navy sport coat climb out of a dark sedan and walk toward the store. When he passes the truck I see that it's Father Barnes. I think about how strange Fritter is acting about my grandfather's death, and I remember the priest had claimed that my grandmother was one of his *favorite congregants*. And I notice how nicely he fills out his trousers.

"You know what?" I say. "I don't know what time Gandy Graphix closes." I dig a scrap of paper out of my purse and start writing. "Just give this to someone who works there."

"But—"

"Here. You go buy everything on this list, and I'll run in here and grab some food. Then you can swing back by and pick me up when you're finished."

She looks at me, her eyes narrowed. My sudden change in plans has aroused her suspicion, but unable to find a flaw in my logic, she agrees. Almost before I can slam the door shut, she's pulling away in a cloud of blue smoke.

I hurry into the store, grab a cart, and push it past the row of tired cashiers. They have the look of prisoners of war with their thousand-mile stares and slumped shoulders. As I walk by, one after another looks past me and chirps an overly energetic greeting, yet the instant the "Good evening!" passes their lips, their faces fall back into slack misery. By the fifth mechanical greeting I'm starting to feel vaguely homicidal.

I go up and down the aisles, grabbing a few easy-to-prepare

non-cheese-based food items. And some oranges and apples to avoid rickets or scurvy or whatever you get from eating only TV dinners.

It is a delicious coincidence that I find Father Barnes in the meat section.

"That looks good," I say.

He jumps and almost drops the t-bone back into the display case. "Mattie! Nice to see you." He looks down at the package in his hand. "I was thinking of making a nice steak . . ."

"For your wife?"

"No. I'm not married." He puts the t-bone into his cart, and then glances at my lonely girl load of Coco Puffs, bread, lunch-meat, and fruit. "What are your dinner plans?" he asks.

"You're looking at 'em," I reply, gesturing toward my pitifully bare cart. "I haven't gotten my first paycheck yet." Which is true, but it's also true that my selections were chosen with an eye for pathos.

"Why don't you let me cook you dinner," he says, right on cue. "You look like you could use some meat."

Could I ever! is what I think. "If you're sure it wouldn't be too much trouble . . ." is what I say.

"Put your groceries in." He adds another steak to his cart and shifts all his items to one side. "You can stash them in my fridge until you go home."

We wander companionably through the store finding items on a list he untucks and retucks into his divinely snug back pocket. His items are all grown-up boring things like laundry detergent and cornflakes—no Hostess Cupcakes or bologna or aerosol whipped cream. Pity.

When we get to the checkout, I hope he'll offer to pay for my groceries, but no such luck. He unloads his onto the belt, then places the little wooden divider stick down and unloads mine on the other side. After he pays for his, he puts the bags into the cart and turns to wait for me.

"Go on out and get started loading," I say. "I'll be right there."

I watch until he's out of earshot, then I ask the cashier, "Are you going to be here awhile?"

She sighs and nods, letting her rhythmic gum smacking take the place of an actual reply.

"In a few minutes, an angry-looking teenager dressed like an extra in a vampire movie is going to come in here looking for me."

"That will be $14.78," she says.

I hand her a twenty. "So would you please tell her that something came up and I'll see her in the morning."

She puts the receipt and change into my open palm. "Thank you for shopping at Chandler's. Come back soon," she says, mechanically, before turning her attention to the next customer in line.

"So will you tell her?"

She seems surprised to see me still standing here. "Tell who?" she asks.

"The teenager."

"The vampire?"

"Right. Tell her I need a rain check. Tell her Mattie will see her tomorrow."

"Is it raining?"

"No. Rain check means that I need to do it later."

"Do what later?"

"It doesn't matter. Just tell her what I said."

"Who's Mattie?"

"Good God." I dig in my purse and pull out a pen. On the back of my grocery receipt I scribble the message, fold it up, and hand it to the cashier.

"That's your receipt," she says.

I scan the immediate area for a more competent-looking employee. No such luck. "Listen, just give this to her."

"To who?" she says.

The man behind me is starting to get impatient. He nudges me gently with his shopping cart and clears his throat. Turning to the cashier he says, "To *whom*."

Giving up, I grab my bags and leave. I can't decide if I'm relieved or sorry when I see Tawny's truck idling just outside the door.

When she sees me coming, Tawny rolls down her window. "I got everything, and by the way, the store didn't close until eight."

"Oh, okay . . . well . . ." I see Father Barnes pushing his empty cart back in this direction. "I'm going to need a rain check," I say.

She leans forward and looks up at the sky, then back at me. What is it with these people?

"I know it's not raining. That's not what—"

"I know what a rain check means. I just think it's a dick move to bail on me—"

"Listen, I ran into someone in the store and he invited me over to his place for dinner. So we'll need to work on those photos tomorrow night. Okay?" I pause. I'm not actually waiting for her permission, but I am trying to not come off as a total douche here. If anyone will understand this situation, a teenage girl will.

"You picked up some random dude in the grocery store? What a slutbucket."

It seems she understands a little too well. "He's not exactly random," I point out. She's correct about the picking up part and the dude part, but surely a man of the cloth doesn't fall into the category of *random*.

Before I can explain further, the dude in question has come over to see who I'm talking to.

"I don't believe we've met," he says to Tawny. "I'm Father Barnes."

"I know who you are," she replies.

"And you're Fritter's niece, right?"

Tawny corrects him. "Great-great-niece."

"She's not that great," I mutter.

"I invited Mattie over for dinner. Would you like to join us?"

I can see the smile forming in Tawny's eyes. Oh how she would like to fuck with me here. Thankfully, either her grudging respect for the girl-code of not horning in on dates, or her reluctance to spend the evening with a slutbucket and her random dude kicks in. She shakes her head, and charmingly replies, "I'd rather vomit blood."

Father Barnes tells Tawny it was a pleasure to meet her, which I find impossible to believe, and then takes the bags from my arms and starts walking out to his car.

I lean toward the truck and say, "Thanks. So, are you picking me up in the morning?"

She laughs and shakes her head. "No, I think I'm going to need a rain check."

With that, she puts the truck in gear, pulling away with a squeal. I watch with grudging admiration as she manages to hit no fewer than seven carts on her way to the exit.

Father Barnes has the groceries stowed in the trunk by the time I get to his car.

I climb in and shut the door. "Sorry about that."

"She's a nice kid."

I look at him, expecting to see some trace of sarcasm, but there is none.

Once he pulls out of the parking lot and into traffic—hitting exactly zero shopping carts, I might add—I say, "Well, thank you for this, I'm looking forward to a home-cooked meal."

"I'm looking forward to the company."

On the car stereo Tammy Wynette exhorts me to *stand by my man*, which, as much as I am enjoying sitting by this one, is decidedly not in line with my taste in music.

"Can I change the channel?" I ask.

"It's a CD." He reaches past me and opens the glove box. "Pick out another one."

I pull out a zippered CD case, but unfortunately, it's slim pickens inside, and I say this not only because the choices are bad, which they are, but because there actually *is* a Slim Pickens CD inside. There's also Merle Haggard, Hank Williams, Patsy Cline, and John Denver.

"Did you buy this car used?" Surely there's an old lady in Arkansas who's missing her CD collection.

"No. Why do you ask?"

I sigh. "No reason." I exchange Tammy for Patsy and turn the volume down.

After a couple of turns I realize we're driving almost exactly the same route Tawny and I just took from the library to the grocery store.

"So you live downtown?"

He nods. "Just a couple blocks from the church."

Father Barnes goes on to explain that the church owns not just the parsonage, but several other houses in the neighborhood, which it rents to low-income families and church employees. And then he continues to discuss church real-estate holdings in more detail than I would have believed possible. Patsy Cline is singing about how crazy she is, and I can empathize. Father Barnes is still talking. And talking. He mentions that Karleen Meeker and her husband live across the street from the parsonage, and that's mildly interesting, I suppose, since I've at least met the woman, but when he starts naming off everybody else who lives on his street, I reach over and turn up the volume on the stereo until he gets the hint. I know that Queeg's aphorisms, a source of pleasure to him, can be a source of irritation to me, but there are times when nothing else will do. *Don't judge a book by its cover* has never been more apt. Father Barnes looks like a romance novel, but I'm afraid he belongs in the Reference section.

Before we get downtown, he pulls into a crowded parking lot and turns off the car. "This will just take a minute. Want to come in?"

I look up at the sign for Bill's Bottle Shop and tell him I'd rather wait in the car. He leaves the keys in the ignition so I can listen to the music, but I turn it off as soon as he shuts his door.

Father Barnes disappears into the store right as another man exits. I watch as people go in with empty arms, come out cradling brown paper bags. *Expectation is the root of all heartache,* Queeg has told me time and time again, and I know he's right. But I keep forgetting.

When I was a kid I spent a fair amount of time sitting in liquor store parking lots, and now here I am again. What do I expect to happen tonight? Do I actually believe Father Barnes knows something important about my grandmother? Of course not. This has nothing to do with that, and everything do with the melancholy emptiness I start to feel whenever things get too quiet. Or maybe I'm getting hungry. I reach over and turn on the music.

Patsy falls to pieces while we're waiting, but I just sit quietly.

CHAPTER 29

The aggressively landscaped flowerbeds outside West Florida Oncology did nothing to make the utilitarian building more welcoming. My mother seemed to like the flowers, but I hated them. They smacked of overcompensation. As far as I was concerned, all that show-offy beauty on the outside guaranteed a grim interior, just like how when you see a truck all jacked up with a lift kit and monster tires, you *know* the guy behind the wheel has a tiny dick.

And it *was* grim inside. Sure, they put a few plastic ferns in the corners, but what I remember are sterile, chemical-smelling rooms filled with beige vinyl recliners, the same sickly oatmeal color as my mother's skin. It was always the same nurses and often the same patients, but nobody made friends like you see in the movies. For the most part everyone just sat in their recliners reading or watching one of the two televisions hanging from the ceiling. The woman in the next recliner crocheted skein after skein of yarn, blue, then green, into strips of color that piled on the floor. I never did figure out what she was making.

Right next to the cancer center was a combination liquor store and cafe, Pop's Bottle Shop and Pizza. While my mother sat in that chair with a needle in her arm, I'd tell her I was hungry so she'd give me money to have lunch at the pizza place. I'd walk over there and buy myself a pack of cigarettes and a couple Jose Cuervo minis. I wasn't hungry. I was sad. I was thirsty. At first it felt funny being the one sneaking the booze, but I got used to it. What's good for the goose is good for the gosling.

The eight months my mother was in chemo she was sober, believe it or not. It was by far the longest stretch of sobriety that I can ever remember her having. The doctors had insisted that she quit drinking before she started chemotherapy, and so she did—just like that. No problem. Thinking about it still pisses me off, even if I have a hard time understanding why.

I smoked a lot of cigarettes standing in front of the cancer center, and yes, even at the time I saw the irony. I'd light up and lean against the wall, the bricks warm in August, cool in November when my mother had her final treatment. As I stood outside watching, workers in their pink scrubs would walk through glass doors coming out, going in. Patients and their families climbed out of cars and walked to the building with that heads-down stride you see in old videos of coal miners approaching the shaft.

Seven minutes—that's how long I learned to make a cigarette last. When I could put it off no longer, when my mouth was filled with the bitter taste of the filter, I'd grind the butt with my foot and kick it into the closest flowerbed. I still remember how the blue plumbago was planted so close to the marigolds that just looking at the contrast made my eyes water.

Just as I expected, Father Barnes knows nothing at all about my grandmother; *favorite congregant* is apparently his way of saying *quiet old lady who sat near the back*. Other topics he discusses include: that he's from Nebraska and is interested in the Cornhuskers, sudoku, gardening, Jesus, and global warming. Until recently he was engaged to his high school sweetheart, a schoolteacher in Lincoln who hadn't been able to relocate to Gandy until her contract was up. Then, just two weeks ago, she called to inform Father Barnes that she'd renewed her contract for another year—oh and by the way she was dating the basketball coach.

I make a salad while he puts potatoes in the oven, steaks on the grill. We talk, or I should say he talks, about his life, his interests, his recent heartbreak. And as we prepare and eat dinner, he works his way through one bottle of wine and then another with a speed and efficiency that makes my heart sink. Father Barnes is not only good-looking, smart, and lonely, he's a drunk, or at least a drunk-in-training. Perfecto.

Every relationship has a balance of power, and it's usually not hard to predict how things are going to work—who's the hammer and who's the nail. And sitting here with my glass of iced tea, stone-cold sober, I have no doubt that seducing this man is going to be a piece of cake. Shooting fish in a barrel. I don't know if they do the whole confession thing in the Episcopal Church, but if they do, by God, I'm going to give him something to talk about.

After dinner I help clear the table, and I offer to do the dishes, but Father Barnes won't hear of it. He clatters the plates into the sink, pours himself another drink, and sits down on the sofa, patting the seat beside him. I join him there and rest a hand on his knee. There's a vase with a couple of cut flowers sitting on the coffee table. They're slightly past their prime; a few white petals have fallen on the tabletop. When he sees me looking at them, he says, "Peonies."

I nod. "So how did you get interested in gardening?"

"All we've done tonight is talk about me," he says. "Let's talk about you."

"Let's not."

"Come on. Tell me about your family. Where'd you grow up? Any brothers or sisters? What's your favorite movie?"

He thinks he wants to get to know me better. He's wrong.

"*The Exorcist*," I say.

His eyes widen. "Really?"

I laugh and shake my head. God, this man is easy.

He smiles, taking my teasing in stride, and then he finishes his wine in one gulp and sets down the glass. He hesitates just long enough to betray his nervousness, and then he leans over to kiss me.

You reap what you sow, Queeg likes to say, and it's true. Not that I'm a strict believer in some cosmic bean counting tit-for-tat, but I'm smart enough to understand that what you put into life determines what you get in return. And yet, time after time I sow the seeds of shitty behavior, only to feign surprise when there's nothing to harvest but a bumper crop of poo.

And so it would be nice to attribute what happens next to a moment of clarity, or mercy, but it would be a mistake. I'm sure it's the overripe smell of the peonies, or maybe the taste of wine on his tongue that makes me pull away, swallowing hard against the gorge rising in my throat.

"I should go," I say.

For a second Father Barnes looks hurt, but then he just looks relieved. I watch him search for his keys, and once I'm sure he won't find them tonight, I tell him I've already arranged a ride home. He hesitates, and I can see that he's considering asking how that could be possible, but in the end he decides to pretend I'm telling the truth. When he excuses himself and staggers to the restroom, I open the front door and slip outside.

I lean against the house and wait for my eyes to adjust to the darkness. The night is cool, but the bricks still hold the afternoon's warmth. I could walk home if I had to; this house is less than a block from the church, and I could find my way to the park from there and take the trail back to my grandmother's house. But I don't relish the thought of walking that far alone in the dark, and besides, over at Karleen's house the lights are on. In fact I can see her from here, sitting alone at a table, smoking a cigarette. As I watch she turns her head and looks out her kitchen window, but it's dark. She's looking at a reflection of herself, not at me.

The katydids fill the trees with their longing, and the air is heavy with the scent of flowers it's too dark to see. When I finally step out from under the porch and into the night, I find a sky full of stars. I stop, lift my face and take a deep breath.

Star light, star bright . . .

I can't decide which is the first I see tonight, so I close my eyes and wish on them all.

CHAPTER 30

Wow!" I say when Karleen opens the door. Not the usual greeting, I realize, but her left eye is swollen almost shut with a reddish lump already darkening to purple. "You should put some ice on that."

"What do you think I was doing when you knocked?"

"Smoking."

"Well." She holds the door open. "That too. Come in."

I look around the corner of the doorjamb cautiously before I step inside.

"He's gone," she says, correctly interpreting my hesitancy. "Off licking his wounds."

"*His* wounds?"

"I got in a swing or two."

She leads me to the kitchen where there is, in fact, a bag of frozen peas on the kitchen table.

"I will say that your wound would be hard to lick," I tell her.

She grins. "His, too, now that I think about it."

From her satisfied smile I assume that she's the type to go for

THE ART OF CRASH LANDING

207

the 'nads. I have no problem with that, except that in my experience a broken nose gets a man's attention just as fast and has the
upside of making a mess of his face. But a girl's got to play to her
strengths.

Thinking of this, I tell Karleen about my mother's baseball
bat adventure with Dewayne the Pentecostal. She laughs at the
story, and I notice, on the side of her face not obscured by a bag of
vegetables, that her smile takes years off her face.

"Your mother always was a power hitter," she observes with a
sigh. "The ball would fly off her bat."

"She did a pretty good number on drunk assholes, too."

"I don't doubt it."

"How about you?"

"I know a little about batting," she replies. "And a lot about
drunk assholes." She sets down the frozen peas and knocks a cigarette from the pack. Her hands shake when she picks up the book
of matches. I pass her the bag of peas and take the matches from
her hand, strike one, and lift it to her cigarette.

"Thanks." Karleen takes a lungful of smoke, then asks, "So,
to what do I owe the honor?"

"I need a ride home," I tell her.

"How did that happen?"

"It's a long story."

"Well, it's a short drive, so you'll need to talk fast." She stands
and grabs her purse from the counter. "Let's go."

In the car I tell her about running into Father Barnes in the
store and his subsequent dinner invitation.

"And?" she inquires.

"We had dinner."

"Only dinner?"

"Yup."

"It's after nine."

"He's not a fast cook," I say and it's the truth. Efficiency is not enhanced when the chef is attempting to cook and consume two bottles of wine simultaneously.

"You know, his fiancée just dumped him."

"So he mentioned."

"He's pretty vulnerable."

"It was only dinner."

She frowns at me, probably trying to decide if I'm lying. "And why is *he* not driving you home?"

"He couldn't find his keys."

"That's strange."

"Sometimes it happens," I reply. This time it happened because I hid his keys in his coffee canister when he opened the second bottle of wine. Living with my mother taught me a trick or two.

Karleen and I are silent the rest of the way home, each lost in our own thoughts. I don't know what hers are, but mine are about my mother and how much I wish Karleen would talk about her, and yet how hesitant I am to ask. I watch Karleen's profile in the dark, her face softly lit and then shadowed, then lit, and then shadowed as we drive past the streetlights. She pulls out a cigarette and then pushes in the dashboard lighter. It's so quiet in the car that we both jump when it snaps out. She lights her cigarette and rolls her window down an inch.

We pass the park, a large swath of darkness to my right, and then turn up the street and into the driveway of my grandmother's house. There's a light on inside.

My heart picks up speed.

"I didn't leave any lights on," I say.

Karleen turns to me in the dark car. "Are you sure?"

"Pretty sure . . ."

We sit and stare at the house for a couple of seconds, and then she looks over at me with a grin on her face. "Let's go see who paid you a visit." She's got some fight left in her tonight.

My pulse roars in my ears. I stop at the door. Karleen is right behind me. I reach out and try the knob—it's locked. I dig in my purse for the key.

"Nice! A burglar who locks up after himself . . ."

"Shhhh . . ." I open the door and push it open. I step halfway into the foyer, and Karleen squeezes in behind me.

Now that I'm inside, I can tell that it's the kitchen light that's on, and I think back on the sun streaming in through those windows this morning. If the light had been on then I certainly wouldn't have noticed, but why would I have turned it on?

I take another step inside. There's something wrong, but I can't put my finger on it.

"Do you smell smoke?" I whisper.

Karleen snorts a quiet little laugh. When I turn to look at her she waves her lit cigarette at me.

We stand, listening. The house is silent, empty. I switch on a lamp and look around the living room. Nothing seems to be disturbed, and yet . . .

"Shit! The Winstons!"

I hurry through the kitchen to the back door, which I notice is also locked. I run out to the backyard where I whistle and call and make those kissy noises I hear other people make to dogs. I run over to check the gate; it's standing open.

Karleen is in the kitchen when I come back inside. "If you want a cigarette I have some," she is saying. "They're Camels, though."

I grab her arm and pull her to the front door. "Let's go."

"We just got here."

"We have to find the dogs."

"You have dogs?"

"I'll drive," I say, grabbing the leashes and opening the door.

She digs her keys out of her purse, but when I hold out my hand she hesitates.

"How many dogs are we talking about?"

"Two," I reply. "Very small." I don't mention their gastric issues.

We make a slow circle around one block and then the next. I shout "Winston!" out the window about every five seconds, but no luck. I pull over at the park trailhead and climb out of the car. The streetlight illuminates the first few feet of trail, but the rest of the park is a void. I walk a little ways into the trees, then whistle and shout, straining to hear a bark or a jingle of dog tags. There's nothing but a distant car alarm and the lonely sound of the wind in the leaves.

When I get back to the road, Karleen has her window rolled down. I can't see her face in the dark, but I can feel her watching me stumble back to the car. "What's the other one's name?" she asks as I climb in.

"They're both named Winston."

"Why?"

"Beats me." I immediately wish I'd used a different phrase. With the door open and the interior light on I get a good look at Karleen's eye. It looks worse than it did just a few minutes ago.

She leans her head back against the seat. She seems tired. "There used to be a music store in town named Winston's."

"It's as good a guess as any," I reply. "My grandmother played piano."

"Yes, she did."

I can think of no place else to search tonight, so we return to my grandmother's house. I turn off the car and glance over at

Karleen. Her eyes are closed, and for a second I think she's fallen asleep, but before I can reach over to wake her, she starts to speak.

"It's where I met Trip, you know."

I remember Gordon Penny mentioning a boy named Trip. I wait, hoping she'll keep talking, and she does.

"Your mother loved to play the grand piano at Winston's." Karleen's voice is so soft I have to lean closer to hear. "She said it was because it was a Steinway, but it was really because she loved an audience. When she left for college I was so lonely for her, I used to go to Winston's and just thumb through the sheet music. There's a particular smell in a music store, don't you think? Is it something they use to oil the instruments?"

"I don't know," I say, even though I don't think she expects an answer.

"It was a Saturday in March," Karleen continues. "I was back in my usual corner pretending to shop, when a boy came in and sat down at the Steinway. It had only been a couple of old ladies playing that piano since your mother left, nobody my age, not when I was there anyway, but there he was. Young, handsome, and he could play."

She looks at me with a wistful smile. "We left the store together that day, and for the next three months Trip and I were inseparable. He had some issues, I mean, he'd dropped out of high school and gotten in some trouble with the law, which was why he'd come to Gandy in the first place. But he was kind and smart and funny. I really thought that he was *the one*."

"So what happened?"

"Your mother came home for the summer." Karleen's voice is matter-of-fact, as if what happened next was inevitable. "In high school, Genie and I thought it was fun to steal other girls' boyfriends. It wasn't as much fun when she did it to me."

"I'm sorry."

She sighs. "Genie comes all the way home to break my heart, and then in August she runs off and breaks Trip's heart, too, not to mention her mother's . . . She ruined everything for everybody for no reason at all."

"I'm sorry," I say again. I can't seem to help myself; at this point I can't even tell if I'm apologizing or empathizing. "Why don't you come in and have a beer."

"Nah, it's late—"

"Come in for just a few minutes. Please?"

She frowns, or at least I think she's frowning; it's dark and I can't be sure. "Why?" she says.

"I have questions."

Karleen shakes her head and turns away, looking out her window. "You don't want my answers."

"Yes I do."

I wait for several heartbeats, but she doesn't look at me and she doesn't answer, so I tell her good night and climb out of the car. I'm on my grandmother's porch when I hear a car door slam, and then Karleen's footsteps behind me.

CHAPTER 31

I wrap ice cubes in a wet towel and hand it to Karleen where she sits at the kitchen table. Pressing the bundle gingerly to her swollen face, she asks, "Is beer the only option?"

"As far as I know." I open the fridge, hoping that Tawny didn't drink the only one. The bright emptiness reminds me that I left all my groceries over at Father Barnes's house.

"Crap," I say.

"Not even beer?"

"I don't know. Hang on." Although there's nothing in here that I want to be in here—like food—when I open the crisper drawer three bottles of Budweiser roll forward stopping at the front of the drawer with a clank. "Found it," I say.

I turn to hand the bottle to Karleen, but she's no longer at the table. "Never mind," she calls out from the other room. "I just remembered something."

I go in the living room and find her climbing the stairs. I follow her up. When we get to my mother's bedroom, she stops at the doorway. "Wow," she says. "The land that time forgot." She stands there, holding on to the doorjamb, staring at my mother's room, and then she crosses to the window and opens it a crack. Immediately a cool night breeze pushes into the room and dilutes the thick staleness.

Karleen pauses to look at the conch shell on the nightstand. She lifts it carefully and carries it to the dresser, and then scoots the nightstand away from the bed, grabs the corner of the mattress and starts tugging.

"Help me with this."

When we get the mattress pulled halfway off the bed, Karleen crawls up over it to the far corner and plunges her hand into a slit in the box springs. She pulls out a large Crown Royal bag. Turning around, she opens the drawstring and dumps the contents. A handful of photo negatives slide out followed by a baggie.

"Bingo," Karleen says, handing me the baggie. Inside is a handful of grayish-brown dust and some loose rolling papers.

Surprised, I laugh. "Are you kidding? I'm not smoking this moldy old shake."

She plucks it from my hands and leaves the room saying, "More for me."

I turn off the light, but before I go back downstairs, I pause and look around the bedroom. A cool breeze sucks the curtains against the screen and then pushes them back toward me. From somewhere in the distance I hear a few notes of music . . . I listen more closely—something classical, but I can't make out the melody. I shiver although the breeze isn't cold, and feel a faint prickle of . . . what? Apprehension, perhaps?

From somewhere downstairs, I hear Karleen call for me, so I shake off my strange mood and go down to find her. I'm imagining things. There's nothing wrong. I'm sure I just left the light on and didn't shut the gate firmly enough.

Karleen is seated at the kitchen table with the baggie open in front of her.

"This is harder than I remember," she says. She's struggling to roll a joint.

"That shit's gonna make you so sick."

She sniffs at it. "It smells pretty bad."

"Please just drink the beer."

She sighs. "God, it's been so long since I got high. I was really looking forward to this." She pushes the mess away from her and picks up the beer with a grimace.

"Wait . . ." I go in the pantry, grab a Kool-Aid packet and toss it on the table. "Pink Lemonade. Add it to your beer and you'll have a shandy."

Karleen laughs. "Shit, even I'm not that desperate. Who would even think of drinking a shandy?"

"Who would even think of smoking thirty-five-year-old weed?"

She laughs again and twists off the beer cap. "You're not having one?"

I shake my head.

"Then, make yourself some damn lemonade. If I wanted to drink alone I'd have gone back home."

I get a glass out of the cupboard, drop in some ice, and then fill it with water. "I don't drink lemonade."

"Who doesn't like lemonade?"

"I like it okay. It's just the principle of the thing."

"Lemonade has a principle?"

I could try to explain, but I don't. Instead, I sit down across from Karleen and lift the glass to my lips. The ice is stale and makes the water taste like cardboard.

"Last night I met a little girl named Shandy," I say. "That's what made me think of it."

Karleen digs in her purse and pulls out her cigarettes. "Who names a kid after a drink?"

"I went to a school with a girl named Mary. We all called her Bloody."

"Yeah, but nobody named her that."

"Tom Collins, Rob Roy, Margarita . . ." I'm on a roll now.

"Tequila Sunrise," Karleen adds. Noticing what must be a puzzled look on my face, she explains. "She's a dancer up at the Bare Trap. But she also bakes terrific cream pies. I can get you one if you're interested."

I run through about five obnoxious replies all involving the words *cream* and *stripper* before I settle on, "No, thanks."

"Your mother loved lemon meringue."

I nod. "I remember."

"She also liked lemonade."

"Not as much as she liked gin."

We sit in silence for a while. Karleen dabs at her face with the ice. The house is quiet except for the sound of the wind outside. The little magnets on the dog door flap make their little *click, click* sound with each gust.

"Can I ask you something?" I say.

She nods.

"Did you and my mom really dye Fritter's dog?"

Karleen throws her head back and laughs. Her laughter is throaty and contagious. By the time she quiets down I'm laughing, too.

"Oh my God, I'd forgotten all about that."

"Fritter hasn't."

"I bet." We're grinning at each other, but as I watch, Karleen's smile fades. "Can I ask *you* something?"

I say, "Okay," even though I'd rather she not.

She reaches back into her purse for her lighter, then she knocks a cigarette out of the pack and lights it. I can see her relax with the first inhale. "Why are you here?"

I get up and open a cabinet to grab a little china saucer for an ashtray and then sit back down, setting the dish in the middle of the table. "Tilda's lawyers called, so I came."

Karleen reaches out and pulls the saucer toward her. It's quiet enough that I notice the sound it makes on the tabletop. Karleen is staring at me with the eye that's not covered up by the ice pack, and it's pretty obvious that she's calling bullshit on my answer.

"You know the conch shell upstairs?" she asks.

I nod.

"Your mom and I found two of those at a garage sale, priced just a quarter," she tells me. "We each bought one and then gave it to the other—a symbol of our pact. We were going to California. Your mom was going to play music, and I was going to be an actress. We were going to sunbathe on the beach and meet men. Nice men." Leaning back in her chair, she takes a drag and exhales the smoke slowly, angling her lips and head away from me. "So she moves to Florida and I'm still here. Fifty-five years old and I've never even seen the fucking ocean."

I weigh the blue water in Karleen's imagination against the salty burn at the back of my throat, her version of my mother's life against the truth.

"Things aren't always what they seem," I tell her.

She lowers the ice pack and looks at me through both of her eyes. For a long second she watches me, taking my measure, and then she asks me what I knew was coming. "Why are you *really* here?"

Watching the cigarette in Karleen's fingers, I feel a desperate longing to have one in my own, to fill my lungs with burning smoke. To stall for time. I want to answer her question, but I can't. I thought coming here would change things for me, but

I'm starting to worry that I've done what I always do: mistake a distraction for a chance at redemption. How can I explain that to Karleen? Would someone who's never seen the ocean believe me if I were to tell her how easy it is to mistake a buoy for a ship?

"I don't know why I'm here" is what I tell her, and it's true enough.

She sets the ice pack on the table; the skin around her eye is bright red from the cold. "The thing about your mom and Trip . . . I mean, what they had together, it was . . . Hell, it's hard to explain."

She hesitates, but I just wait. It may be hard to explain, but she's going to.

"One time I saw them," she says, "in Winston's. I don't think they saw me. They both sat on the bench at the Steinway, shoulder to shoulder, each with one arm wrapped around the other's waist, and the other hand on the piano keys. I don't know the name of the song they were playing, but I do know it was complicated and fast, and they were flawless. Perfect. When I closed my eyes it was impossible to believe that it wasn't one person." Karleen lowers her cigarette to the table, tapping its ash into the saucer. "I don't go for all that soul-mate crap, but I'm telling you there was something there. You could see it. You could feel it. Even when Tilda found out about them and blew her top, forbidding Genie to see Trip, it didn't change a thing. If anything it added fuel to their fire."

"But I still don't understand—"

"I'm trying to tell you that I don't know. All summer long, Trip and your mother were Romeo and Juliet. Then one day she was gone."

"So nothing happened?"

She shrugs. "Every day something happens. Today you ate dinner with a priest, I got a black eye—shit happens. That's life. If you're asking me if I know why she left town, the answer is *no*."

"Gordon Penny thinks she was pregnant."

Karleen gives a little snort of disgust. "You shouldn't believe anything that man ever says about your mother."

"Why? What'd she do to him?"

Karleen waves the question away. "Genie wasn't pregnant."

"Are you sure?" The possibility of having a half brother or sister out there somewhere had never occurred to me before talking to people around here, but now that the idea has been suggested, I'm having a hard time letting it go.

She takes a drag from her cigarette and studies me. It feels like she's trying to decide whether or not to tell me something. I bite my lip to keep from begging.

She nods. "I'm sure. Now, tell me about your father."

I'm disappointed with the change in subject, but I do my best to hide it. "He was a bartender named Rocket."

She smiles. "Rocket?"

"He went by *Rock*."

"I would imagine so," she says, still smiling.

"He worked at a bar called Cock of the Walk."

"You're kidding me."

"Nope."

She's laughing a little now and shaking her head. "Well, what was he like?"

I was eight or nine when my mother took me to meet him. I remember that the bar was dark and almost empty and smelled like floor polish. She ordered me a Coke and told me to stay there, then she and the bartender walked to the far end of the room and talked. My barstool was wobbly, and every time I moved it made a dry little squeak. I'd only finished about half my soda when my mother came back and pulled me off the stool. She pointed at the man behind the bar and said, "Mattie, that cheap bastard is your father." I looked up at him, but he was rinsing my glass out and didn't look in my direction. He had pale hair and sad eyes. He needed a shave.

"I never really met him," I tell Karleen.

"You know, I can't picture someone like your mother looking twice at a man named Rocket."

"Someone like my mother? Oh, please." I've been trying hard to be extra agreeable to keep Karleen talking, but this is total crap. "As far as I could tell, my mother woke up every morning looking for a new way to fuck up her life. I realize that everyone in this town thinks that she was something special, but I've got a news flash for you. She was nobody, and she didn't do shit with her life."

Karleen nods. There's a faint hiss when she drops her cigarette butt into the beer bottle. "Well, I can see you're doing all sorts of terrific stuff with yours."

Ouch. "Touché," I reply.

She gives me a wry grin that lets me see she was talking as much about herself as she was about me. We're peas in a pod, Karleen, my mother, and I.

Karleen stands, stretches, and then picks up her bottle and carries it to the trash. It lands with a clink against Tawny's from yesterday.

"Don't go." I want to keep her talking, so I ask a question she might answer. "Tell me what happened with Gordon Penny. Why the grudge?"

"Oh, nothing really. He just can't take a joke."

She starts talking, using that voice we all use when we're making excuses for our bad behavior. The story gets convoluted and long, something about a costume party, and my mother tagging little Gordon with a nickname, and I have to admit my attention wanders. I'm tired and her complicated telling of the story reminds me of how often I've tried to soft-pedal my own bad behavior and casual cruelty. It's funny how when it's somebody else telling the story it's easy to see that *He can't take a joke* is just another way of saying *I'm a jackass.*

Eventually Karleen's story winds down with the usual, "We were just stupid kids." Lifting her purse from the back of the chair, she slings it over a stooped shoulder. "Thanks for the beer."

"Wait—"

"No, it's getting late."

"But—"

"Mattie, stop. I need to get to bed."

"I have more questions about my mom."

She smiles a little sadly. "I know. Will I see you tomorrow?"

She's reminding me that I agreed to help with the soup kitchen lunch again, and although Fritter has forbidden me to go, I tell Karleen that I'll be there. My mother isn't the only person who has an adverse reaction when people start forbidding things.

I start to stand, but Karleen gestures for me to stay. "I know my way out."

She's at the kitchen door when I stop her again, "Hey, about Romeo and Juliet . . ."

Again, she turns back. "Yeah?"

"Have you read it?"

"Your mother went to college, not me."

"It doesn't end well," I say.

"One of them dies, right?"

"They're both dead by the end."

She gives me a sad smile. "That sounds about right."

A few steps and she's out of my sight, a few more seconds and I hear the front door open and close. She's gone.

CHAPTER 32

I'm tired, but before I head upstairs to bed I go back outside and prop the gate open wide in case the dogs come back. Then I put fresh water and food in their bowls. I walk through the downstairs and double-check that the doors and windows are all locked and then go upstairs. It's only ten thirty, but it feels like the day has been going on forever.

My cell phone rings. It's Nick, so I ignore the call. Then I dial Queeg's number.

My stepfather answers with a cough.

"Are you asleep?" I ask.

"Not anymore."

"Sorry."

"It's okay," he says. It's what he always says. "So, how is everything?"

My throat squeezes tight. "I'm fucking everything up as usual."

"What happened, sweetheart?"

"I picked up some random dude at the grocery store, then he

gets too drunk to drive me home so a friend of Mom's does, but when we got here the dogs were gone, and we looked and looked but couldn't find them anywhere."

It's quiet on his end as he tries to select the best response. I was betting he'd hone in on the *random dude* part or at least ask me if I'd been drinking, too. Instead he chooses, "You have dogs?"

"Not anymore."

He doesn't reply, and I can picture him lying in bed, trying to figure out what I'm talking about. If I wait long enough he's going to ask me to explain, and right now I can't bear to talk about the Winstons.

"Do you remember that snow globe of Mom's?" I ask. "With the lighthouse and the birds?"

There's another pause while he follows the subject change. "Of course," he finally says.

"Did she ever tell you why she liked it so much?"

"Her father gave it to her."

"She told me that, too, but it's total bullshit." I go to the open window and lean down to put my face against the screen. The cool air smells wonderful. "Her father died before she was even born," I tell him. "She never met him at all. Plus, I found out that he and my grandmother were never married."

While I wait for Queeg's reply, I survey the jumbled mess that Karleen left of the bed. The musty-sheet smell is stronger now, so I decide to change the bedding.

"Are you still there?" I gather up the strips of negatives and put them back inside the Crown Royal bag on the dresser.

"I'm not going anywhere," he says. How I wish that were true. "Well then?"

"What do you want me to say?" he asks.

I pull one sheet and then the next off the bed. "She was a liar."

"I loved her," he says.

My mother's mattress pad is soft and stained with faded, nickel-size brown spots in the center. I can hear Queeg breathing. He's waiting for me to say that I loved her too. I ought to be able to give him that much.

"Mattie?" he finally says when he's waited long enough. "Next time you call, can you please call earlier?"

I gather the dirty sheets in my arms and carry them to the hamper in the hallway. I'm suddenly missing Queeg with a sharp pain in my chest. "I'm so sorry."

"It's not *that* big a deal, Matt. Call if you need to, but I'm usually in bed before ten—"

"No, for the snow globe. For breaking it."

"I know," he replies.

"And for everything that happened after."

I hear him sigh. "Oh, sweetheart, none of that was your fault. There's nothing you could have done to stop her."

He's wrong, but I don't tell him that. Instead, I just close my eyes and let his kindness break my fucking heart all over again.

My voice is only a whisper when I ask him, "What time is your biopsy tomorrow?"

"Nine. I should be home by late afternoon."

"I'll call."

"I know," he replies and then adds, "I love you." I start to repeat the words back to him, but I wait just a second too long. There's a click and he's gone.

It's not until I've put fresh linens on the bed, brushed my teeth, and have my hand on the light switch, that I realize what had been nagging me earlier about this room. My mother's camera bag is gone. And so is Nick's guitar strap.

I look around . . . I know they were setting in the corner by the bookshelf, but there's nothing there now. I lift the bedskirt and look under the bed, then in the closet, then under the desk . . . nothing. I walk through the rest of the house with a critical eye. Everything looks okay, the jewelry box is right where I'd put it, back on my grandmother's dresser, the television is in the living room, along with the DVD player.

My phone rings again, and again it's Nick. This time I answer. "Hi Nick."

At first he doesn't respond. Probably he's so surprised I actually took the call that he's momentarily forgotten what he wants to say.

"Mattie, it's me," he finally says.

"I know."

"I want my strap back."

I answer with complete honesty. "I don't have it, Nick. I swear to God I don't know where it is."

There's background noise on his side of the call, but over that I hear him sigh. "Fuckin' Rico. If it wasn't you, it has to be him."

Rico was Nick's roommate before I moved in. Last I heard he was in jail, but apparently that's old news. I shouldn't be surprised. Nick knows my opinion of Rico and rarely mentions him.

"Well, you can't trust a junkie," I say, which is true enough, even if not exactly applicable to this particular theft.

"Yeah, I know."

We listen to each other breathe for a few seconds, and I realize that I recognize the background noise I've been hearing. He's in a bar.

"You coming home soon?" he asks.

"Maybe," I say. "I was wondering . . ."

"What?"

"Do you ever want kids?"

He laughs. "Hell, no. And neither do you, remember?"

"I know," I reply.

The noise behind him swells; I'm guessing that some team scored a home run, or a bar favorite walked in the door. I can't really hear how Nick ends the call, but I think he says, "I miss you."

I could be wrong.

The breeze from the window billows the curtains and sways the hanging plant ever so slightly. In fact, the plant looks better than it did this morning. On a hunch I go stick my finger into its pot. The soil is wet, extremely wet. As in, just-watered wet.

I open my mother's closet, but nothing looks amiss, her dresser, the same . . . or do the contents look a little stirred up? I go through the rest of the dresser and then the desk, opening drawer after drawer. It takes me a minute to realize what's wrong—all the negatives are gone. The loose ones, the ones in envelopes—all missing. The only photo negatives left are the ones Karleen pulled out from the box springs an hour ago. Quickly, I slide the mattress off the box springs, tuck the Crown Royal bag full of remaining negatives back into its hiding place, and then push the mattress back onto the bed.

Who would steal a shabby camera bag, a guitar strap, and a bunch of thirty-five-year-old negatives, but leave everything else? Not to mention watering the plants and locking back up before leaving.

A gust of wind puffs the curtains and again brings with it the sound of faint music, a piano playing something slow and melancholy. I turn off the light and walk to the window, the moody soundtrack playing as I push aside the curtains and look out at the night. There are no cars on the street, no people, no dogs. I look over at JJ's backyard. Although I stand and watch for several minutes, I see no ember—only darkness. I'm on my own tonight.

CHAPTER 33

Everything is familiar, but at the same time slightly off, the way dreams often are. For instance I'm back at the Pig Pen wiping down a greasy table with an equally greasy rag, yet there's classical music coming from the jukebox, and I can promise you that never really happened.

Still, the dimly lit room glows red from the "Exit" light above the door, just like it used to. Robby has turned off the beer signs on either side of the door, but he's left on the big neon "Bass" sign over the bar. The "B" burned out a couple of weeks ago, and now it's just a big red triangle with "ass" written across it so he won't turn it off for anything. I watch him shake glasses dry, giving them a quick smear with a bar towel before stacking them on the shelves, and I wonder if he realizes that having the word *ass* floating directly over his head every night is, in fact, an excellent example of truth in advertising.

He has a beer waiting for me when I slip onto my usual stool. Slick is here, too; the three of us always used to close on Friday nights, and when we did, we usually stayed an extra hour to complain about our lives and lower the levels on the beer kegs a little. Slick is in the middle of some story about his ex-wife when I sense someone on the bar stool next to me. Surprised, because up until that moment Robbie, Slick, and I were alone, I turn and see my mother sitting there. It's not the woman my mother was when I was nineteen and working at the Pig Pen, it's my mother the way she was years later, during the worst of the chemo. She's bald and wearing a faded snap-front housedress, the kind she wore when her steroid-bloated belly could no longer fit into anything else. Her arms are too thin; drapes of extra skin weave their way from under her sleeve to her elbow that rests on the bar.

She turns to me and says, "A normal heart is the size of a fist." She holds up her hand, to demonstrate, I suppose, but her expression is angry, and I flinch as she waves her fist between us.

She drops her hand back to the bar. "I don't feel so good," she tells me. "Can you help me to the bathroom?"

I stand and put my arm around her waist and feel hers wrap around mine. A few shuffling steps and we're to the bathrooms, stopping in front of the door labeled "Sows." I push the door open, and my mother goes inside, but I don't follow her in. Instead I take a few more steps and open the door marked "Boars."

The bathroom smells of sour urinal cakes and shit. Nick stands just inside the door, smiling his crooked smile, running his fingers through his hair. Although in reality I didn't meet Nick until years after I quit my job at the Pig Pen, in the dream it makes sense, somehow, that he would be here. He grabs my wrist and pulls me to him, reaching around behind me to lock the door.

A few sweaty, gasping moments later I'm facing the mirror, my pants at my knees, Nick behind me. The whole time this is happening, part of me knows that I'm dreaming because although I see Nick in the mirror, standing behind me, thrusting, I'm not feeling anything except the cold of the porcelain sink I'm leaning on. There's a crumpled-up yellow receipt on the floor and a gray plastic film canister, and next to it a small white something . . . a rock? A shell?

The tile is grimy white and the grout cracked and gray, but as I watch, one fat, black fly and then another appears, crawling across the floor. A dark liquid begins to ooze from the wall and run along the grout line. It soaks into the yellow receipt, which I now know is from a bookstore, and if I were to pick it up it would say that *The Caine Mutiny* was purchased for $17.95. The dark puddle surrounds the film canister, pooling around the small white object that cannot be a rock or a shell, because it's a tooth. The fluid is black, but I know that it's blood.

I straighten and push Nick away. He shouts something, but there's such an echo I can't understand the words. All I know is that my mother is in the bathroom next door, and the blood is hers and it's all my fault for letting her go in there alone. I start to cry and tug my pants back up to my waist. I'm having trouble fastening the buttons, and as I'm fumbling, Nick turns me around and pulls me to him, pressing his lips against mine. I push against his chest and twist my head, my mouth filled with a metallic salty taste.

I get to the door and try to twist the knob but my hand slips on the metal and I realize that there's blood on the doorknob and on my hand. *It's my fault*, I keep thinking. I'm sobbing and my heart is pounding so hard that I almost don't hear Nick when he quietly calls my name. I turn to him to ask him for help. He's smiling. There's blood on his chin and between his teeth.

When I startle awake in bed, I'm still weeping. My heart gallops in my chest and the nauseating metallic taste remains in my mouth. Stumbling in the dark, I find my way to the bathroom and heave my stomach contents into the toilet.

After a few minutes resting my forehead on the side of the cool tub, my heart has slowed to an almost normal pace and I've stopped crying. When I stand and switch on the light, I'm relieved to have an explanation for why the taste of blood followed me out of my dream. In my reflection I see a red smear on my upper lip and a fresh rivulet starting down from my left nostril. It's just a nosebleed.

I go back to the bedroom, strip the bloody pillowcase and pull a clean one over the pillow and its fresh browning stain. Tucked back in bed with the pillow balled up under my neck, my head leaning back, I try to relax. Although there's only a faint light outside, morning noises are starting up, a few early birds, the occasional car somewhere in the distance. Someone's unhappy cat is crying. It sounds just like a baby.

I close my eyes and slow my breathing to try to catch another hour or two of sleep. But my mind won't leave me alone; it pokes and prods at the past like a tongue that has discovered a chipped tooth. All my mistakes—things done, things left undone—they're here with me tonight. The Winstons, the unwanted child in my belly, Queeg's biopsy, my mother. A parade of regrets marches past, and I am helpless to do anything other than relive them all as I lie here with my chin pointing at the ceiling, my nose stuffed with toilet paper, my ears filling slowly with tears.

THURSDAY

Time and tide wait for no man.

CHAPTER 34

I must have fallen back asleep after the dream, but when my alarm goes off, I'm still exhausted. The nosebleed has stopped, however, and once I've showered and eaten a couple handfuls of dry cereal, I still feel shitty, but that's as good as it gets these days. Sometimes my entire life has felt like one long exercise in lowering my expectations.

After checking that there's still water and food in the dog bowls in the kitchen, I go out and put some on the front porch as well, then go to the backyard and make sure the gate is still propped open.

Music is playing in JJ's backyard this morning—Frank Sinatra, in fact. However, once you get past his music selection, the scene gets a lot less classy. A card table is set up on his back patio and on it is an ancient boom box, its extension cord running into the house through a window. JJ stands next to the table with a paint roller in his hand and a cigarette dangling from his lips. He's wearing faded, sagging jeans and a white undershirt. Each lift of his arm reveals a thicket of pit hair and a deeply set yellow stain in the tank.

"What a douche," I whisper to nobody. I miss the dogs.

The grass is dewy and cool on my feet as I approach the fence, carefully avoiding the weeds and the dog turds. I'm walking quietly, with a smile on my face because it's obvious that my asshole neighbor hasn't noticed me yet. I wait until he has the paint roller fully loaded and is holding it directly overhead before I speak.

"Good morning!" I say much, much louder than necessary.

JJ startles vigorously enough for a large dollop of paint to drop on his head and, I'm especially gratified to see, on the toe of one of his newish-looking cowboy boots. But without so much as a glance at me, he sets his roller in the tray, wets a rag at the outside faucet and wipes the paint off his head and boot. Sadly, the leather seems to come completely clean.

He sets his cigarette down on the edge of the table and comes to the fence.

"Listen . . ." I hate to have to tell him, but I'm sure he's already noticed their absence. "The dogs got out last night."

He glances pointedly at the open gate.

"The latch is messed up," I say. He looks unconvinced. "But I don't know that it's my fault anyway, because someone was in the house last night."

"Other than you?"

"Yes. Someone who doesn't belong there."

"Like I said, *other than you?*"

God, this man is a jerk. "While I was out, somebody broke in and stole a camera bag and a guitar strap. I think whoever it was took the dogs, too."

"Guitar strap?"

"You know, so you can play a guitar standing up."

"You're a musician."

"No."

He says "Hmmm" in a neutral tone of voice but he looks surprised.

"What?"

"Your mother was."

"Not when I knew her."

He frowns for a second and then asks, "Is that it?"

"Is *what* it?"

His eyes narrow. "Is that all they took?"

"Well . . . and some old negatives. And there were two cameras in the bag."

He's giving me a you're-crazy look and I don't blame him. It sounds crazy to me, too.

"Listen," I say, "all I know is that the negatives, the strap, the camera bag, and the dogs are gone. The dogs could have run away on their own, but the other shit couldn't have."

I study him, looking for a sense of discomfort, some sign that he's hiding something. It's probably just because I don't like him, but if this were a TV crime show, JJ would be my prime suspect. He was her neighbor, he'd kept her dogs—it would make sense for him to have a key. Plus he's a jerk.

He glances at his half-painted wall and says, "I better get back to work," but he doesn't walk away. He just stands there like he's waiting for one of us to say something. So I do.

"Did you ever hear anybody talk about my grandfather? My mother's dad?"

"Just that he died."

I nod. "So weird."

"Not that weird. Everybody dies."

"But he died before my mom was even born, and she never told me that."

He's giving me another puzzled look, and I can see why. Even I'm not sure why it bothers me that she kept his death and the whole born-out-of-wedlock thing a secret, but it does. And of course the fact that Fritter is so tight-lipped about it all just makes me more curious.

I don't try to explain. I just shrug and say, "Never mind."

When I start to walk away JJ's voice stops me.

"Did your mother really give up her music?"

I turn back around. "She gave up everything."

He doesn't respond, but I can see the question on his face.

"She left it all here," I explain. "Her clothes, her books, her friends, her family, her music. And nobody will tell me why. Do you know why?"

He's shaking his head.

"Somebody knows," I say.

"Not me. I don't know and I don't care."

"That's not surprising," I say. "As far as I can tell, you're an asshole who only cares about himself and his yard."

"Speaking of yards, you ever going to mow yours?"

"Speaking of assholes, are you the one who broke into my house last night?"

He takes a step toward the fence, saying, "You listen to me." He's angry, and although I don't get the feeling that he's really threatening me, I still catch myself reflexively taking a step back.

"First of all," he says, "don't you ever call that *your* house. You don't deserve that house. You never once came to visit your grandmother when she was alive. Second of all, Miss Thayer had those dogs for seven or eight years, and they were fine, and I kept them for a month, and they were fine. Two days . . . you had them for two days and now they're gone."

"Fuck you!" I am embarrassingly close to tears. "I never asked for that responsibility. I was doing my best."

"And I've never broken into anybody's house, so *fuck you* right back."

We stare at each other across a barrier of chain link and a grudge I don't understand. He picks up the rag and wipes his hands. I know I should walk away before he says something else mean, but instead I just stand there watching him watch me for several uncomfortable seconds.

When JJ finally does speak, all he says is, "Your car is ready. The repairs came in just under eighteen hundred," he says. "I was fair. I kept the price down the best I could."

"Okay. Thanks."

JJ nods and then returns to his porch. Lifting the paint roller he holds it suspended above the tray as the paint drips slow to a stop.

"I'll keep an eye out for the dogs," he says without looking back at me.

I sigh, reminded anew of my latest failure. "Thank you."

"Save your thanks. I'm not doing it for you."

Sinatra sings the "In the Wee Small Hours of the Morning," and JJ runs the roller up and down the wall, and I stand here in knee-high grass, off balance and unsure of what to do about the dogs, of what the hell is going on with JJ. Unsure about everything. The sensation I had last night—that I'm missing something—is back again, but for the life of me I can't figure out what it is. I close my eyes and breathe in the smell of paint mixed with the sharp, green scent of the broken weeds beneath my feet. I wish I'd gotten more sleep last night, but sleep can be hard. Frank is right; it is in the wee small hours of the morning that I miss her most of all.

CHAPTER 35

There are nice things about riding a bike to work, like not having to bother to fix my hair. It's also fun to watch hapless pedestrians on the trail flee before me as I zip past, zing zinging the little thumb bell on my handlebars. Unfortunately there are also not-nice things about riding a bike to work, like sweating and the way that my newly swollen boobs—as tightly wedged as they are into my bra—jiggle painfully with every bump. Needless to say, by the time I arrive at the fount of all knowledge that is the Gandy Public Library, I am damp and cranky.

Tawny opens the door as I'm parking my bike at the back entrance.

"You're thirty minutes late," she says.

"My ride didn't show."

"Awww, that's a shame." She's all pleased with herself and smirky, probably mostly because she's the reason I'm late, but it's possible that some of the smirk is about my hair. It is pretty windy.

She glances at the bike. "Maybe I'll borrow that later without asking."

"Go right ahead," I say. "But the air whistling through all those holes in your face is going to make a damn racket."

She makes a noise like an old man, "harrumph," and then under her breath she calls me, and I couldn't make this up if I tried, a *twat waffle*. Truly, this girl's potty mouth is a work of art. *Twat waffle*. It's amazing. Better than *fartknocker* and way better than *dickbag*. I hurry inside to find a pencil and paper to write this one down. It's a keeper.

Fritter is nowhere in sight to witness my tardiness, so I act casual, grab the cart of books to be reshelved, and head out into the aisles as if I've been here all morning. Unfortunately, I haven't ventured far before I once more detect an odor of poo. Since I have no interest in volunteering for another turd hunt, I ignore the smell and get to work.

A woman about my age, attractive in a well-put-together way—a look that I have never managed to achieve and therefore find highly irritating—approaches me as I wheel the book cart into the Biography section.

"Excuse me," she whispers, "I don't want to be rude but . . ."

I stop and wait for her to finish. Whatever she says next will be rude, of course, because anytime someone begins a sentence with "I don't want to be rude but . . ." what comes next is invariably rude.

The woman knits her perfectly plucked brows and says, "Do you smell dookie?"

"No. Sorry," I reply in my best adenoidal voice. "Allergies."

My next stop is the Children's section. By this time I've habituated a bit to the smell, but obviously it hasn't gone anywhere. I see one young mother lift her squirming toddler's diapered fanny to nose height and take a sniff. I quickly shelve the two books in my hand and continue on my rounds before this woman doesn't want to be rude, but . . .

Once I finish with the books on the cart, I go to the Reference section; I want to take a look at some of the really old high school yearbooks. I have an idea. And of course, it is there, in the Reference section, that the dookie lurks. It's on the small side, like the last one, and this time it's balanced on a shelf rather than on the floor. In fact, this UFO isn't just on any shelf; it is placed neatly in the gap left by the yearbooks I swiped Tuesday. Someone isn't just shitting in the library, someone is messing with me.

To avoid alerting Fritter to the missing yearbooks, I grab some paper towels, disinfectant, gloves, and a plastic bag from the back room and clean it up myself. I notice as I'm picking up this firm, brown beauty that there is something embedded in the poo. Lifting it up as close to my face as I dare, I look closer. It's a cigarette butt. Very interesting.

I toss the UFO in the Dumpster in the parking lot, and then while I'm out there I make a stop at Tawny's truck, which is locked, of course. It's certainly possible that this is merely a reaction to my liberal borrowing policy, but it could also be because of the bundle lying on the passenger-side floorboard. It's well camouflaged by a mound of crumpled fast-food sacks; in fact, if I hadn't been in the truck yesterday, I probably wouldn't notice the mysterious addition. There's a filthy towel covering the lump that just happens to be the size of, say, my mother's camera bag and Nick's guitar strap nestled snugly together. I go around to the passenger's side and lean against the window, cupping my hands around my face to see inside. The towel is mostly tucked in on this side, too, but from here I can see the rounded tip of something brown leather outlined in stitching. It looks a little like the end of a belt, barely visible between a wadded-up Burger King sack and a Coke can. If I were a bettin' man like Mr. Nester, I'd bet that's the tail end of a collector's-item-near-mint-condition-brown-leather-guitar-strap-signed-by-Jimmy-Page-and-Jeff-Beck.

As tempted as I am to go grab one of the bricks lying by the Dumpster and smash the truck window to retrieve my possessions, I really want to know why Tawny took them in the first place—especially all those random photo negatives. She spent a long time riffling through my mother's desk drawers to collect all those. Why would she bother? Not that the camera bag, cameras, and the guitar strap are necessarily valuable, but she could have just swiped those to piss me off. But all those negatives? They're worthless. I think with a little finesse I can get my shit back and find out why she stole it all in the first place. In fact, a plan for dealing with this juvenile delinquent is starting to take shape, but it will have to wait. First I need to go back inside and look at those old yearbooks.

In the senior chapter of the 1958 book, I find my grandmother Matilda "Tilda" Thayer, *Most Talented Girl*. And there's Fritter Jackson. Under her name it says, *Our Little Firecracker*. I suppose I can see someone describing Fritter as a *firecracker* if by *firecracker* they meant enormous pain in the ass.

I look in the index to find more photos of Tilda and Fritter, and I come across a picture of the two of them posing with their dates—the girls in taffeta, the boys in suits. The caption underneath reads, *Tilda and Fritter bringing a couple of familiar faces to the prom. Welcome back, Gene and Dick!* The boy with his arm around my grandmother is clearly the guy that Fritter identified as Eugene. The other boy, the one next to Fritter, I don't recognize.

In the 1956 volume, I find Eugene Wallace in the senior section. *The Lone Ranger* it says beneath his name. It doesn't take long for me to find Fritter's date, Dick, in this book as well: Richard Hambly, also a senior. *Tonto* is written beneath his name.

Hmmmm . . . If *Little Firecracker* won't tell me what happened to *The Lone Ranger*, maybe *Tonto* will.

Just a couple shelves above the yearbooks are the Gandy phone books for the past several years. I find Richard Hambly's listing, and after looking around to make sure I'm unobserved, I rip out the page, stuff it in my pocket and then quickly replace the phone book and the yearbooks back on their shelves. Next, after making sure Fritter wasn't lurking anywhere nearby, I wander back to the far corner set apart from the rest of the room with its beige cabinets and little row of microfiche readers. Once I figure out how to use the filing system it doesn't take me long to find the correct microfilm reels and suss out how to run the projector.

I get lucky; news of Eugene Wallace's death appears about halfway through the second reel. I'd been checking the obituaries, so when that turned up, *beloved son, dear friend, leaving behind parents, Burneel and Carter Wallace, fiancée Tilda Thayer* etc. . . . I went backward looking for the report of the initial accident or whatever it was that caused his death.

And I find nothing. Not a mention of an accident, not a mention of an illness. Nothing. I zip forward and backward through the dates surrounding the obituary, but don't see the name Eugene Wallace anywhere.

I'm still sitting there in front of the monitor, defeated, when Tawny wanders over.

She grabs the chair next to me, turns it around backward and straddles it. "Whatcha looking at?"

"Old newspapers."

"Why?"

"I'm not sure," I reply, still turning the wheel, watching page after page sliding by. "Either I'm making a big deal out of nothing, or I'm trying to uncover a well-hidden secret."

"Cool."

"Cool?"

"Secrets are awesome."

I turn to look at Tawny. She's wearing a wide grin.

"*My* secrets aren't awesome," I tell her, and it's the truth.

"Not to you, because you already know them," she replies. "But they'd be awesome to me."

From the sparkle in her eyes, I can see that the girl believes what she's just said. She would love to have a secret of mine—my worst one, in fact. She wants to hold it in her hand and weigh my pain against her own. I wonder how long it's been since I was young enough to think that was a contest worth winning.

I shake my head. "Most people's secrets are just sad. Some are terrible."

"They're still irresistible," she insists, "like a scab you can't help but pick."

I turn back to the microfiche reader.

Tawny watches me read for a second or two and then says, "Somebody named Karleen called for you. She sounded pissed."

I pull out my phone and check the time: one thirty. Shit!

"Is she still on the phone?"

"Nah, it was like an hour ago. When I told her you'd gone to lunch, she just hung up."

"But I didn't go to lunch. I was here!"

"How was I supposed to know that?"

"You could have looked around for me."

"I could have, I guess," Tawny says, and then she shrugs. "Oh well."

I feel myself swell with rededication to my plan to mess with this most irritating teenager. Revenge may be a dish best served cold, but when you're really hungry, the temperature isn't all that important.

"I was actually just about to come talk to you," I say, wearing my most disappointed face. "I'm afraid that tonight isn't going to work well for developing pictures either."

"Is that right?" Tawny's smirk from earlier this morning is

back. She's waiting for me to talk about last night's break-in and how there aren't any negatives left to develop.

"Yeah, I've got another date. We'll need to put off the darkroom lesson until tomorrow. Okay?"

She's confused but trying not to show it. I imagine that she's thinking it's possible I haven't yet noticed the missing negatives, guitar strap, and camera bag, although she's got to be wondering how I could have missed the dogs' absence.

"So . . ." she draws out the word, buying herself a little time to decide how to play this scene. I don't interrupt her; I'm enjoying it too much. Finally she says, "So, everything else is okay? You just need another rain check?"

"Yup. Everything's great, thanks. And last night I found a bunch of hidden negatives. We'll print those tomorrow. No telling what's on them."

If I had even the slightest doubt that Tawny was the burglar, it is put to rest when I see her startled reaction and how quickly she tries to hide her surprise.

"So are we on for tomorrow night?" I say.

"No problem." She's careful to keep her face neutral, but her cheeks are flushed, and in her eyes is just the tiniest glint of mischief. She's not a terrible liar, but she's not as good as I am. She'll get better though, if she keeps working this hard at it.

"I really am sorry to cancel, but if we did it tonight I'm afraid we'd have to rush. I'll be at the house until eight o'clock, but then I'll be gone until midnight at least." I'm laying the time specifics on a little thick, but I don't feel like I have a choice. If things go my way, I'll be making a quick excursion this afternoon right after work, and I need the girl's upcoming criminal caper to happen when I'm back at home waiting.

Tawny stands up, stretching like a cat. Her T-shirt lifts enough to show a thick metal barbell through the skin above her navel. "So, are you going to take your lunch break now?" she asks.

"In a minute," I say, turning back to the microfiche reader. *Eugene Wallace, beloved son, dear friend, leaving behind parents, Burneel and Carter Wallace, fiancée Tilda Thayer . . .*

Tawny stands behind me, reading over my shoulder. I'm ready for her to leave, and I can tell she senses that, which is why she lingers.

She leans down and whispers, "Like I said, *irresistible*."

"I don't pick scabs," I reply.

Tawny laughs. "Don't be stupid. Of course you do."

I open my mouth to argue, but I'm too late. She's already walking away. Before I turn off the projector and put away the film, I read the obituary once more. In fact, I read it several more times. I'm glad Tawny isn't here to watch me do it.

CHAPTER 36

The sky is a mixed bag this afternoon, almost too blue to look at in spots, but there are also some scattered clouds, gray and swollen, chugging past. I step from sunlight to shade to sunlight again as I walk down the hill toward Luke's office. It's refreshing right now, but I imagine it's not much fun when a real storm hits here, adding heavy rain to this ceaseless wind.

Since I have only a half-hour lunch break, it's time to get started, so I set my phone to private caller and dial Richard Hambly's number. An old man answers, and once I verify that the voice is that of Mr. Hambly, I feed him a line of bullshit about me being from the gas company and that we need to work on his gas line. He's a good citizen so he agrees to be home this afternoon between five and seven, so I thank him and quickly hang up before he could start wondering why the gas company would have its phone set as a private caller. Now all I need is a ride.

Pushing open the door of Barber, Smith, and Franklin, I find myself momentarily disheartened. The gloom of the outer office, the sight of perky Patty sitting behind her desk exactly where she was the last time I came in—for a second it feels like I'm starting this craptastic adventure all over again.

I head straight to Luke's office, tossing a "He's expecting me" over my shoulder.

I stop at his door and tap my knuckles on his doorjamb.

He glances up from his computer and laughs. "Look at you!"

I make a quick clothing inspection, but nothing seems to be hanging out anywhere. "What?"

"Your hair . . . it's um . . ."

"Yeah, well, it's windy in case you haven't noticed."

"I like it."

"Really?" I put up a hand to pat at the fluffy mess that is, to be honest, a bit more out of control than I'd realized.

He grins. "I've always been a Bon Jovi fan."

I tell him to fuck off—in the nicest possible way, of course. He laughs, and I'm laughing, too, although I'm also trying to get my fingers through my hair to calm it down a little. I'm not overly vain, but . . . Jon Bon Jovi?

"I'm glad you stopped by," Luke says. "I asked Patty about the keys to your grandmother's house, and you don't have anything to worry about. We had the locks changed right after your grandmother passed, so there are no keys floating around. You have one, and we have the other."

"Uh . . . okay . . ." I'm momentarily dumbfounded. All the doors and windows were locked last night when I got home; unless perky Patty is Tawny's partner in crime—which seems highly unlikely—somehow Tawny does have a key.

"What wrong?" he asks.

I consider explaining to Luke how I know that he's wrong about the keys, but then he'd probably call Fritter and there would be a *thing* with Fritter and Tawny. And although I'd probably get all my stuff back, I might never find out what all the sneaking around was about. Plus, the alternate scenario, the one in which I catch Tawny in the act, wrestle her to the ground, and sit on her head until she talks, is simply too tempting to relinquish.

"Nothing," I reply.

"What is it?"

I laugh and shake my head. "Everything is fine. Trust me." This is always bad advice coming from me, but surprisingly enough, Luke seems to take it.

"All right, then. Oh, and Patty watered the plants last week, but it's probably time to water them again."

I nod. "It's already done."

"Thanks," he replies.

"It was no trouble," I say which is absolutely true since I wasn't the one who did it. "But I do have a favor to ask."

I pull the phone book page from my back pocket, and set it in front of Luke. He frowns at the crumpled paper on his desk and it occurs to me that tearing a page out of a phone book is probably not the sort of thing he would do. Furthermore, as he tentatively begins to unfold the page, I see that I have somehow also passed along another slip of paper that was certainly not meant for him. Now, not only does my casual phone book vandalism make me look like an asshole, I look like a crazy asshole.

"I should have written the address down instead of tearing the page out," I admit. "Sorry."

He nods, but his attention is on the other piece of paper. There's an awkward pause while both of us try to come up with what to say about a piece of paper upon which is written only the words *twat waffle*.

"I'm trying to decide on my rapper name," I tell him.

Luke grins up at me with an expression of bemused wonder, but he hands the slip of paper back to me without further comment.

"You mentioned needing a favor?" he says.

"I need to go someplace after work, but I still don't have a car . . ."

"Where?"

I flatten out the crumpled phone book page and point to Hambly's address. Luke deliberately picks up a pen and writes the address on a Post-it note.

"I'll pick you up at five," he tells me.

"I'll also need a ride home after."

"Naturally."

"Sorry."

"No trouble," he replies, but I don't think either of us believes that.

He passes back the phone book page and then watches without comment while I carefully fold it up and slide it back into my pocket. I'm not sure why I bother—it's not like I can *untear* it out of the book.

"When we're finished this afternoon," he says, "do you want to go get some dinner?"

The invitation catches me off guard. In every single interaction with this man I have come across as nothing but a big hot mess. What is he thinking?

"Sorry, I have plans for later tonight." This is true, assuming Tawny takes the bait I so elaborately dangled before her, but I worry that my reply sounds like a blow off, so I quickly counter with, "How about tomorrow?"

He agrees and then offers to cook me dinner, which I accept. We make a few minutes of general small talk—he asks how it's going at the library. I give him the highlights without mentioning any of the really important stuff, such as Fritter's stonewalling or Tawny's burgling.

I haven't eaten since breakfast and my stomach is dangerously empty, however I'm enjoying the banter, so I ignore my mounting queasiness and launch into the story of the Unidentified Fecal Objects. We're both laughing as I explain how, based on the size variation and the cigarette butt, I figured out that they're actually dog turds that Tawny is bringing in to torment Fritter. I don't mention the fact that I'm pretty sure the turd du jour was from my grandmother's backyard. If I did, Luke might ask why Tawny would be at the house, or ask how the Winstons were doing, and then I'd have to lie. Instead I just skim the surface of the mystery, keeping the dog shit generic and telling him that I'm going to put a stop to it, which is true enough.

When he asks if my job description includes "other related doodies," I laugh like I'm supposed to, but my heart's not in it. I'm feeling sick enough now that I've started to sweat.

"So, I was right about Tawny," he says.

"In what way?"

"She's too much for Fritter to handle."

"Nah. She's not that bad. Sometimes it's just easier to act like a badass than admit you're unhappy."

With a concerned expression, Luke reaches over to where I'm perched on the edge of his desk, and puts his hand on top of mine. He's acting as if I've said something overtly personal. Or maybe I look as terrible as I feel.

"Are you okay?" he asks gently.

"Where's your bathroom?" I reply.

By the time I leave Luke's office it's two thirty. The church parking lot across the street is empty, save a handful of cars and a couple of disheveled men crouched near the Dumpster. I walk across the street, keeping a careful eye on the Dumpster divers as I grow closer. I needn't have bothered. When they see me heading their way, they stand, pocketing handfuls of cigarette butts, and they walk away. Following a few steps behind them is a gray cat—Colonel Parker, I'm guessing, since I recognize one of the men as the feral-looking Elvis I met Tuesday. As he walks past, Colonel Parker studies me with one green eye, the other matted shut with pus.

I step up to the window by the door and peer through the cloudy glass. I can see Karleen cleaning out the food service area in the far end of the room. A teenager, probably some poor community service volunteer, listlessly smears a mop across the floor, and at a table in the corner sits Father Barnes staring into a coffee cup. He looks a little hungover. I'm not surprised.

The day is bright, so the glass presents me with two scenes superimposed one on the other—a double exposure: the people inside the dining room and a reflection of me standing outside in the parking lot. Everyone in there looks like a ghost. Or maybe I'm the ghost.

I could go inside. I could pick up a rag or a mop. I could apologize to my mother's friend for not showing up when I said I would. I could be a friend to Father Barnes, a man who has been nothing but kind to me. Or I could walk away.

At this very moment, as if my thoughts were words able to penetrate glass, the teenager mopping the floor looks up and sees me through the window. I step back, but not fast enough. When her eyes meet mine, she raises a hand.

Walking back to the library, I replay the girl's gesture and parse it for meaning—arm lifted, palm out. Was it a greeting? Had she been inviting me in? Probably not. I think she was just making sure I understood that I was much, much too late.

CHAPTER 37

Monday, December eleventh dawned cold—for Florida anyway—with a hint of rain to come. I had the whole day off and my mother's appointment with her oncologist wasn't until the afternoon, so I decided to do some Christmas shopping. I can remember as I hurried through my errands wondering when my mother would be able to drive herself again. I was ready, more than ready, to get my life back.

First, I made a quick stop at the liquor store to pick up a few bottles of Maker's Mark as gifts for my hardcore party friends. Then I swung by the mall, where I burrowed through the crowds and bought a few odds and ends for my mother, a video game for my then boyfriend, and some soap and lotion baskets for the coworkers who I feared would buy me something. I was especially proud of the cigars I scored from a dark, wiry man skulking around the parking lot behind Sears. He pulled the box out of his trunk, took my twenty-dollar bill, and promised me they were genuine Cubans. The man was Cuban, I could tell that the minute he opened his mouth. The cigars? Who knows? They might have

THE ART OF CRASH LANDING

been from Cuba. I hoped for my boss's sake that they weren't laced with anything too poisonous.

Then I went to the bookstore for the pricey, hardback edition of *The Caine Mutiny* I'd special ordered for Queeg. He'd recently admitted to me that although he'd seen the movie, he'd never actually read the novel. All those years he'd been answering to the name of a character from a book he'd never even read. The novel's Captain Queeg was even crazier than Humphrey Bogart's, and I could hardly wait to see how much reading this book would annoy my Queeg. I remember laughing as I ran out to my car, my arms clutching the book while trying to hold my jacket closed against the cold.

It was sprinkling by the time I reached my mother's house. When she got in the car, with only that fine halo of postchemo stubble on her head, I remember thinking that she needed the soft wool hat I had just bought her. But it was in the back of the jeep, jumbled up with all the other gifts; it would have been a hassle to get out and pop the hatch and dig around for it. Looking back, I wish I'd bothered. I wish I'd climbed out of the car to find that damn hat. She would have liked it; it was almost the same color green as her eyes.

At the clinic they took blood, did a couple scans, and then the doctor came in and poked around on her stomach a little. It would be a few days, he said, before all the results would be in and our next step—those were his words, *our next step*—could be discussed.

I remember thinking at the time that my mother didn't have many *next steps* left. Whatever the tests would reveal, it was pretty clear that she was finished with chemotherapy. The chemicals they'd pumped in to poison the tumor had poisoned everything else as well, giving her vicious sores in her mouth, weakening her kidneys, and even attacking her heart. Swelling it, the doctor told us, "from the size of a fist to the size of a softball."

When he said that to her, she asked, "Mush ball or fast pitch?"

The doctor frowned, scribbled on her chart for a few seconds, and then said "I'll see you next week" as he left the room.

I lifted her clothes off the hook behind the door. She sighed and slipped the hospital gown off of her shoulders as I handed over her bra.

"It was a valid question," she said to me. "A fast pitch ball is only eleven inches around. A mush ball is sixteen."

Once she fastened the hooks on her bra, I pulled her shirt over her head. The fuzz covering her scalp was velvety soft against my palm.

My mother was always cold, so I was hot and sweating in the car on the way home, wishing I'd taken my coat off. It felt like I'd spent all afternoon at the doctor's office, and next Monday we'd be back there to get her results, to find out if the chemo had worked. My mother clutched the appointment card in her hand and stared out the window. The cancer may or may not have receded, but either way she looked tired and pale. Her illness was all around us in that stuffy car.

So I was surprised when, as we pulled into her driveway, she turned to me and said, "I think I could drive if I had an automatic."

Sitting there in my jeep with its automatic transmission, we both looked at her Malibu parked right next to us in the driveway. I knew her next words before they came.

"We could trade cars," she offered. "Just until I feel better."

Her Malibu was certainly more fun to drive than my jeep, and from the tone of her voice I could tell she thought she was doing me a favor. But she was wrong. For me, her Malibu was a painful reminder of the happy family that Queeg, my mom, and I had once been, but were no longer. I took a second before I replied, to measure that pain against my desperate need to gain some distance from my mother.

Finally I said, "Okay."

She took her keys out of her purse, pried one off the ring, and handed it to me. "I still need your help at a shoot Friday morning."

"No problem."

The windshield wipers moved back and forth bringing her house into and out of focus. I remember wishing she would just hurry up. It felt like we'd spent a lifetime sitting in that hot stuffy car.

"It's a funeral."

I sighed, annoyed. It was just like her to not tell me that little detail until after I'd agreed to help. My mother had recently come up with some harebrained idea that funeral photography was some new unexploited market she could take advantage of. I laughed the first time she mentioned it, but amazingly a few people actually answered the advertisements she'd placed in the paper. So far I'd been lucky enough to avoid assisting her on those jobs, but now it seemed that my luck had run out.

She wrote down the address for the funeral home and handed it to me. "Don't be late," she said.

"You know me."

"Yes, I do." She frowned a warning. In the past year, since she'd stopped drinking, my mother had for the most part gotten her shit together. My shit, on the other hand, was still all over the place.

I asked if she needed anything out of the Malibu and she told me *no*, that her tripod and lights were in it, but since I would be meeting her at the funeral home anyway, that wouldn't be a problem.

She glanced back at all the packages piled in the back of the jeep. "You want some help moving all this stuff?" she asked.

The rain beat steadily on the roof. I took the Malibu's key from her and then turned off the jeep and laid its key in her open palm.

"I don't need any of it this week. Let's wait and swap everything out Friday after the funeral."

"You sure?"

"Sure I'm sure. Everything will be fine," I said.

CHAPTER 38

Richard Hambly's overdecorated, overheated home is filled with dusty antiques and uncomfortable-looking chairs. Mr. Hambly points me to a wingback chair, and I pick my way around the coffee table, step over a metal magazine rack overflowing with issues of *Arizona Highways*, and settle myself gingerly on the chair's faded, sagging seat.

"That upholstery is genuine horsehair," Mr. Hambly tells me.

"Super," I reply, grateful that I'm wearing jeans today; it's nice to have something between my legs and the itchy seat. I'm in no mood to ride bareback.

Luke sits on the perimeter of the furniture grouping, grinning at me from his clean, nonhairy wheelchair.

"Can I get you some tea? It will have to be instant iced, I'm afraid. There's a problem with my gas line." He frowns and adds, "I wonder if I should put out the pilot lights on my stove and hot water heater . . ."

"I'm sure everything's fine," I say. "You know how those people at the gas company are . . ."

Hambly frowns, wondering, I suppose, about my insider knowledge about gas company employees, but he doesn't ask me to explain further. He just excuses himself and goes into the kitchen.

Luke gives me a questioning look. He's smart enough to have picked up on both Mr. Hambly's surprise at our arrival and the strangeness of that last exchange about the gas company. I give Luke a wide-eyed *beats me* shrug, grab an issue of *Arizona Highways* and settle back in my prickly chair to thumb through the magazine's pages. Acting casual is the key to deception.

The dish-clattering noises from the kitchen stop, and the old man reappears carrying what looks to be a heavy tray. I hurry over and take the tray from him, against his protests, and then set it on the coffee table. Hambly crosses to a settee and leans hard on its carved wooden arms to lower himself into the seat. He waves his hand at the plate of cookies and three iced-tea glasses on the tray, so I hand Luke a glass and take one myself. My stomach is empty and I'm grateful for the Lorna Doones, no matter how stale they may be, which is very. The tea is sweet enough to remove the enamel from my teeth but I take a couple of polite sips anyway.

Mr. Hambly clears his throat. "Latter Day Saints? Jehovah's Witnesses?"

Luke and I both laugh. I think he's laughing out of surprise, but I'm laughing because Luke, in his white dress shirt and dark tie, really *does* look like a religious door-knocker, which is probably what gained us entrance into the Hambly home in the first place.

Luke introduces himself and me. As soon as he mentions that I work at the library, the old man scowls.

"Library?" he says, but in a tone that's suggestive of something more along the lines of an organized crime syndicate.

"What I'm here to discuss has nothing to do with the library." I try to move us back to more neutral territory. "I'm looking for some information."

His frown deepens. "Young lady, I'm getting so old and forgetful, I could probably hide my own Easter eggs. I can't imagine what sort of information you think I possess."

"About my grandparents."

"Your grandparents? Do I . . ." He stops, his eyes slowly widening in recognition. "You're related to Tilda Thayer."

I nod. "She's my grandmother. I'd like to know more about her and my grandfather."

"I wouldn't have much to say about that." He crosses his legs and looks around the room. He's giving me the impression of someone trying a little too hard to act casual. "Tilda looked like you, fair, curly hair. Your grandfather Eugene was the opposite. Dark, straight hair. Dark eyes. They were betrothed." He reaches over and fiddles with his tea glass, centering it on its little coaster. "I really don't know what sort of information you're looking for."

I decide to ask him straight out. "I want to know how my grandfather died."

He exhales as if he'd been holding his breath. "No." He shakes his head. "No, no . . . I'm sorry, but no."

"Please?"

"No."

"Pretty please?"

"That was a lifetime ago," he says.

"I want to know what happened."

He shakes his head. "Water under the bridge."

"What water? What bridge?" It comes out more irritated than I'd intended. I pause for a moment and then try again. "It's my family, but no one will tell me anything."

Instead of replying, the old man looks down at his lap and smooths the crease in his trousers with an unsteady hand.

I try a smile. "Pretty please with a cherry on top?"

He hesitates, seeming to consider something, which is a step up from *no*.

Finally, he says, "You work at the library?"

I nod.

"Then I have a proposition for you."

I have a feeling this ancient man's proposition isn't the type I'm used to getting. I say "Let's have it . . ." and then sit back, curious as to what he has in mind.

"There used to be a used bookstore not too far from here," he says.

"Okay."

"It closed last year."

"I'm sorry to hear that." I have no idea where this is going, but since Mr. Hambly seems to, I play along.

"So I'd like to start utilizing the public library."

"Good idea."

"There's only one problem," he says.

Here it comes.

"I don't have a library card." He's smiling when he says this, and I smile in return, relieved that his problem can be solved so easily.

"Well, just come in and fill out the form. All you'll need is—"

"No, no, no." He's shaking his head. "That will never work."

Hmm . . . I wonder if maybe it's not just his house that's dusty and jumbled, but also the space between Mr. Hambly's ears. I keep my tone gentle when I say, "It works for everyone else."

"That may well be," he says with a look on his face that tells me he noticed my patronizing tone. "But *everyone else* isn't banned from the library."

"Banned?"

He nods.

"You got *banned* from a library?"

"That is correct."

I search the old man's face to see if there's any indication that he's joking, but he seems sincere. I ask the obvious question, "How do you get banned from a library?" Oh, fingers crossed that this story is as funny as it promises to be. Surely poop won't be involved, right? I glance over at Luke and see him grinning at me. He's thinking the same thing.

"It's a long story from a long time ago," Hambly replies. "Which, interestingly enough, involves your grandfather."

"Come on, you have to tell me." I'm wheedling now.

He lifts his shoulders in a little noncommittal shrug. Suddenly, I understand what's going on.

"You want your library privileges back," I say.

Now there's a little twinkle in his eyes.

"Tell me what you know about my grandfather, and I promise I'll get you unbanned."

"Are you certain that you—"

"No problem at all," I assure him. I'm lying, of course, but it's for a good cause so I plunge ahead. "Trust me. A few minutes of your time now, and you'll be able to use the library whenever you want."

"Well . . ." He does that shrug thing again.

"And I'll increase your maximum checkout. You can have six books at a time instead of five."

"Ten."

"Seven."

"Eight."

"Deal!" Generosity is easy when you have no intention of ponying up.

Hambly grins, triumphant. I'm pretty sure he would have settled for seven. He takes a sip of his iced tea, and then settles further back into his chair.

"How should I start . . ." he says, pausing for effect. He's swinging his crossed leg, his fingers knitted and resting on his knee. Just as I'm starting to wonder if his fussy mannerisms and home-decor preferences hint at something more than old-man fastidiousness, he drops the bombshell.

"Your grandfather and I were lovers."

I'm pretty sure my eyebrows touch my hairline at this pronouncement, but at least I hadn't made Luke's mistake of taking a sip of tea at that very moment. Luke coughs and sputters loud and long enough that Hambly and I both stand to go to his aid. Luke manages to get a breath and croak "I'm fine" as he gestures for us both to sit back down.

Hambly waits until Luke's struggles fade into occasional throat-clearing noises, before he starts to talk of Gene, and how their boyhood friendship had blossomed into something more in high school.

"But this was the fifties," he says. "In a small town in the middle of the Bible Belt. All we knew of homosexuality was what we'd read in the Bible. So Gene dated your grandmother Tilda, and I dated her best friend, Fritter."

Luke makes a little half-cough at this one as well, but it didn't catch me completely off guard. I'd already seen the photo in the yearbook.

"Of course, dating the girls," Hambly explains, "was a total sham."

"A total sham?" I ask.

"A ruse."

"Mr. Hambly, I know what *sham* means. I was questioning how it could have been a *total* sham?"

"Well, obviously you're right. I suppose it wasn't a sham for Gene, because here you are—his progeny." He gestures at me with a magician's flourish. "But it was a sham for me."

Hambly stops and pulls a handkerchief out of his pocket.

Rather than use it, he sets it on his lap, folding and unfolding it three times before continuing.

"We had talked, you know, Gene and I, of moving away together. To the East Coast, or the West. Someplace large enough that we could live as a couple. I talked about it, anyway. Gene just listened. But I hoped that someday . . ." Hambly stops and looks down at his gnarled hands for a second. When he looks back up his eyes shine with unshed tears.

"Neither one of us went to college. After high school, Gene went to work for his dad—tractor supply. I got a job and a small apartment in Woodall."

When the elderly man pauses for a sip of his tea, Luke says for my benefit, "It's a town about thirty miles north of here."

Hambly nods and continues. "Anyway, having my own place made things easier, but still we were careful. Nobody knew me in Woodall, I could drop the girlfriend pretense, but Gene was still here, living in his parents' house . . . he just couldn't seem to find a way to break it off with Tilda." Hambly looks around and tries to smile. "Does anyone need more tea? How are we doing with cookies? I have some Oreos if you'd prefer."

Luke and I both shake our heads and reassure him that we're fine. After a few awkward seconds Hambly takes a deep breath and starts talking again.

"We managed to see each other some, but not as much as either one of us would have liked. Then there was his twenty-first birthday party and, well . . ." The old man smiles. "That took care of the Tilda issue. Or at least I thought it did."

"What happened at the party?" I ask.

Hambly shakes his head and chuckles. "Oh, I really shouldn't . . ." but luckily he does. He tells us of the birthday party for Eugene at his parents' house. There'd been a large crowd and a fair amount of drinking. "Gene's dad was mixing some powerful drinks in the kitchen. Gene rarely drank, but I'd talked him into a couple Gibsons, and he'd gotten pretty silly." Hambly smiled. "That night was the first time Gene told me he loved me."

Hambly fiddles with the hanky in his lap and then sighs and goes on with the story. "We went up to his room. We locked the bedroom door, but for some reason forgot the door to the jack and jill bath."

"Uh oh," I say.

He nods. "It was all so trite. Tilda walked in, there was a scene, as you can imagine, and she ran back out. By the time Gene and I got dressed and downstairs, Tilda was gone. Jonah drove her home."

"Jonah was . . ."

"Fritter's brother. So of course Fritter knew something was up. She cornered us, asking Gene what he'd done, that sort of thing. He stammered something or another but Fritter isn't stupid. One look at our red faces and she guessed what had happened."

"She was pissed, I bet."

"She was furious. She was livid. She was . . ." He shrugs and leans forward, lowering his voice. "She and I had dated, so I'm sure she found it degrading on that level. Plus, everyone knew she'd always had a thing for Gene. Her outrage was as much for her sake as for Tilda's."

"Did she tell anybody?"

"Oh no. There's no way she'd bring that humiliation on herself. Or on Tilda, I suppose. She never told a soul."

"So that's why Fritter banned you from the library," I say.

Hambly looks away and sighs. "No. I'm afraid there's quite a bit more to it than that."

I wait, hoping he'll continue when he's ready. He does.

"She banned me because I killed him," he says in a quiet voice. "I killed your grandfather."

CHAPTER 39

I glance at Luke and find him staring at me. He looks over his shoulder at the entry hall, and then back at me and the jumble of closely packed furniture between us. I'm pretty sure he's trying to calculate an escape route should our somewhat effete host become murderous.

"You killed him?" I say. "Like, with a gun or a knife—"

"Don't be stupid. I didn't *attack* Gene. I would never . . ." There's another shaky pause. "But his death was my fault. It was entirely my fault."

He makes a squeaking sound, abruptly stands and walks into the kitchen, leaving Luke and me to sit and listen to the old man's muffled sobs. It's obvious to me, and to Luke if I'm correctly interpreting the glower he's sending in my direction, that this is too much for Hambly. At this point a nice person would go apologize to the old man and then leave. Unfortunately for poor Mr. Hambly, Luke is marooned on his small island of clear space and can't make it to the kitchen. And I'm not all that nice.

Hambly comes back with a small plate of Oreos. "Found them!" he says, his voice cheerful, his eyes still wet.

I don't want an Oreo, but I take one, and when it turns out to be even staler than the Lorna Doones, I smile my approval and thank him anyway. I'm not nice enough to leave before my curiosity is assuaged, but I'm not a complete jerk.

Hambly sits back down and clears his throat. "It happened in Tulsa."

His voice steadies as he tells us that just a week after the fateful birthday party, Gene's father decided to let his son handle a sales call on one of their largest accounts. "Gene had just turned twenty-one, you see. His father wanted to increase his responsibilities."

When Gene told Hambly about the planned trip, Hambly talked his lover into letting him come along.

"We were careful, of course," the old man says. "At the hotel, Gene checked in alone. I didn't go up until later."

He goes on to tell us how Gene wanted to stay in for the evening, but Hambly insisted on going out. "The opera was in town and I really wanted to go, but Gene wouldn't hear of it. He was afraid one of his father's clients would see us there. But I pouted, and he let me talk him into going somewhere else." He takes a slow breath and exhales between pursed lips. "There was one bar in Tulsa that was rumored to be frequented by the homosexual crowd." The old man is shaking his head as he continues. "Gene was afraid to go. 'Let's just stay in,' he said when I suggested it. But I insisted, and he didn't want to disappoint me. You see, I thought it would be fun, it would give us a taste of what it might be like to live somewhere else, where there were other people like us."

The afternoon sun has slipped down far enough in the sky that the light from the window now catches the edge of the silver tray on the coffee table. An arc of reflected light illuminates Mr. Hambly's sagging throat. I see it move as the old man swallows, fighting tears.

"We got to the bar and it was exactly what I'd been hoping for.

We danced," he tells us. "I know it sounds stupid, but at the time it was a big deal, holding him in my arms, being out on the dance floor with other couples . . ." His eyes are closed and he's smiling and swaying ever so slightly. Then he sighs and opens his eyes.

"It got late and Gene had an early meeting the next morning, so we left. It was raining outside . . . not hard. Soft rain. It was March and neither one of us were wearing jackets. We started toward the car—it was parked just down the street—but when we came to a coffee shop with a cigarette machine, Gene ducked in to grab a pack. I waited under the awning. He didn't have change, I guess, because through the window I saw him go up to the man behind the counter and say something. The man shook his head. Then Gene turned to two men sitting on stools at the counter, but they just stared. They kept staring as Gene walked right past the cigarette machine and out the door. He said 'Let's go' and continued toward the car. I caught up and asked him what happened. He didn't answer me."

Mr. Hambly leans back a little and the reflected light moves to his face. It's not in his eyes, but he notices it anyway and turns his head to find the source. With exaggerated care, he scoots the tray to the far end of the coffee table to knock out the glare.

He settles back into his chair and continues in a soft voice. "We walked fast. We should have run. Two people stepped onto the sidewalk between us and the car. It only took me a second to realize they were the same men I'd seen through the diner window. They must have gone out a back door and run to get ahead of us. They were both just wearing trousers and white undershirts that were almost transparent from the rain. I remember . . ."

Hambly stops for a second, running one thumb across the other, pushing the loose skin to the knuckle and then back down. He looks up at me. "I remember thinking that they must be cold. I wasn't afraid yet—it hadn't occurred to me that they had stripped to keep from getting blood on their good shirts and jackets. I was shivering and wishing they'd get out of our way. I remember turning to Gene and asking him if he had a towel in his car. He didn't answer me, though. He kept his eyes on the men.

"I hadn't even noticed that the tall one was holding something until he moved his arm out from his side. The streetlight near us was burned out, but the light across the street was enough for me to see the pale wood of the baseball bat. That's when I remember getting scared. Looking at the wooden bat tapping the puddle at that man's feet.

"I thought it was a robbery," Hambly says. "I pulled out my wallet and tossed it to the shorter man. He grabbed it out of the air and laughed as he stuck it in his pocket. He looked at the one with the baseball bat and said, 'I wonder if faggot money spends as good as human money?' "

Hambly runs a shaking hand through his thin hair. "Before I could even take another breath, the short one grabbed me by the hair and threw me to the ground. I heard Gene shout 'Hey,' and then I heard a crack that sounded like a home run, and Gene fell to the ground next to me. I managed to get up and get a couple licks in, but it didn't take them long to get me back on the ground. They kicked and swung the bat, and at some point they must have hit my head, because that's the last I remember of that night, or any other day or night that week."

Hambly's voice is almost a whisper as he talks about going in and out of consciousness in the hospital. He tells us he remembered once asking about Gene, and a nurse replying, "Is that your wife? Should we call her?" At some point he was lucid enough to tell someone his name and his hometown, and the next day his mother appeared by his bed.

"By the time I found out about Gene, he'd been in the ground for two days," Hambly says. "I never even had a chance to say good-bye."

He goes on to talk about his injuries, the weeks spent in the hospital and his eventual return to Gandy to finish healing at his mother's house.

"Didn't the police investigate?" I ask.

Hambly gives a dismissive snort. "Right before I was discharged, a cop came and took a statement. He stood at the door, and didn't write anything down. From the look on his face I'm sure he thought Gene and I had gotten exactly what we deserved. The Tulsa newspaper never even mentioned anything about the attack. It was as if it had never happened."

According to Hambly, nobody in Gandy put two and two together—Eugene's death and, several weeks later, young Richard Hambly coming home with injuries.

"No one knew?"

"Well, my mother knew, but she wasn't talking. And of course I'm pretty sure Tilda figured it out. And Fritter."

He looks over at me with a tired smile. "The thing is . . . as broken as my heart was by Gene's death, I was comforted by the fact that he loved me, that even if he lived a lie with everyone else, he was honest with me." Hambly clears his throat. "And then Tilda Thayer gave birth to your mother. All along he'd wanted it both ways. Gene may have loved me, but he made love to her. He just couldn't resist the opportunity to live a normal life. Normal from the outside anyway."

He's not fighting the tears anymore. They roll down his withered cheeks. "He would have married her. He would have kept up the charade."

Dust motes drift through the shaft of sunlight cutting across the room. The three of us sit there, feeling the pause stretch thinner and thinner until it seems as if our breathing is too much.

"Why did you stay here?" I ask. "This can't be an easy place to live as a gay man."

"Around here homosexuals of my generation are referred to as *confirmed bachelors*." He smiles. "And no. It wasn't always easy, but it's better than it used to be. However, to answer your question, I'm not sure why I stayed. It was familiar, maybe that was it. Or it could be that I wanted to punish myself. Gene was gone; why should I deserve happiness?" He reaches down to straighten his trouser cuffs. "Eventually, of course, I let go of that kind of thinking."

I open my mouth but before I can say anything, Luke asks my question for me, "How?"

Hambly and I both turn to look at Luke, surprised at the note of urgency in his voice. His face flushes pink under our attention, but he goes ahead and finishes his question. "How did you do that? How did you forget?"

I consider Luke sitting there, and I wonder again what put him in that wheelchair. I feel a quick stab of guilt when I realize I'd given no thought at all as to how this little emotional hoedown might be affecting him.

Hambly shakes his head. "I never said anything about *forgetting*." And then he glances at his watch and stands. It's time to go.

He holds the front door open as Luke exits and I follow. I thank Hambly, and he nods politely. Luke continues wheeling his chair to the car, but I pause next to the old man and whisper, "By the way, there's nothing wrong with your gas line."

He gives me a knowing look and nods.

Luke and I are almost at the car when Mr. Hambly, still standing in the doorway, says, "Young man?"

It takes Luke a second to maneuver his chair around on the

narrow walkway, but Hambly waits until we're both facing him to continue.

"I never forgot Gene or what happened. But there came a day when I understood that he was gone, but I was still here with a whole lifetime ahead of me. And I knew that as much as I loved Gene, until I let go of him, I'd never be able to grab ahold of anything else." To illustrate his point, Mr. Hambly holds out a trembling, age-spotted hand, open, palm up.

The old man is talking to Luke, but I'd swear he's looking right at me.

CHAPTER 40

When my alarm went off that Friday morning—the morning I was to help my mother photograph the funeral service—I hit the snooze button and spent a few minutes listening to raindrops hit the window and wishing to God I'd had less to drink the night before. I weighed my options: going wet and hungover to help my mother, versus listening to her give me shit for-fucking-ever about blowing off the job. It was a close call, but keeping the peace with my mother won.

As I got dressed, I weighed my next two options: arriving without coffee but on time, versus arriving with coffee but having to listen to my mother give me shit for-fucking-ever about being a little late. Coffee won that round.

By the time I got in my car—or rather, my mother's car—it had almost stopped raining. I hit one green light and then another. When I pulled into Dunkin Donuts, there were only two people in front of me, and they both moved through quickly, which never happens when I'm in a hurry. It was as if the universe was conspiring to help me both be on time and get caffeinated. *Karma isn't always a bitch*, I remember thinking, right before I saw the blue flashing lights in my mirror. Apparently, even good karma can't make up for running a stop sign next to a doughnut shop.

I watched in the side mirror as the policeman levered himself up out of his cruiser and ambled toward me. When he leaned over and peered in my car, I could see the powdered sugar on the front of his uniform shirt. I could also see my face reflected in his mirrored sunglasses. I looked pissed.

"License and proof of insurance."

I popped the glove box, digging through all the crap my mother had stashed inside. It wasn't until I had her insurance verification card in my hand that I knew what I was about to do.

I handed him the paper, and then made a little show of digging around in my purse before I said, "Oh my gosh! I'm so sorry. I left my wallet in another purse. I can give you my driver's license number. And my social . . ."

"You shouldn't be driving without a license."

"I know. I'm soooo sorry. It's just that my mom's got cancer, and between taking care of her and working I've been so tired . . ." My hangover made it easy to act exhausted and ill.

He sighed and then turned and walked to his car, leaned in through the window and then came back carrying a pen and his clipboard-box. I gave him my mother's name, license number, and social security number without missing a beat. Helping her fill out all those insurance forms had some benefits.

It worked like a charm. The cop sat in his cruiser for a few minutes and then came back with a ticket, which I signed with my mother's name. He told me to drive safely, and I nodded and smiled, then stuffed the ticket into my mother's glove box. I'd get that paid before she found out about it, I decided. Surely I would. Probably.

I arrived at the funeral home half an hour after the service was scheduled to begin. My only parking options were either up at a covered entrance where I'd be blocking the hearse, or at the far end of the parking lot. Seeing as how I was late and had another trip to make with equipment, I parked in the covered drive, with a vague plan to move the car before the service ended.

Just inside the door was a sign with the names and locations of the funerals in progress. The McLeod funeral, which was the one I was looking for, was being held in the Serenity Suite. I remember thinking that was funny. The *Serenity Suite*? As opposed to what? The *Agitation Suite*? I hurried along the carpeted hallway and eased open the door labeled *Serenity* and stuck my head inside. A man who looked a little like Jeff Bridges, his hair slicked back in a ponytail was speaking from the podium; next to him was an open casket in which rested Mr. McLeod, I presumed. My mother was standing along the left side of the room, her camera poised. She saw me in the doorway and welcomed me with a frown. Several guests noticed her scowl and twisted in their seats to find its cause. Me.

I hurried out to the car and grabbed the rest of her gear. When it was all piled in the hall, I slipped back inside the room. My mother's camera bag was on a seat in the last row of folding chairs. I moved it under the chair and sat down.

I concentrated on being invisible. My mother moved around silently, first on one side and then the other taking photos of Mr. McLeod in his casket, and the minister—I'm assuming he was a minister, even if he did have a ponytail—at the podium. The family was up front, so I couldn't really get an idea of what they looked like, but glancing around the room I saw a lot of long stringy gray hair, and some tall eighties bangs. I counted three mullets. I remember thinking I had entered some tragic bad-hair time warp, but I also remember feeling relief. I looked like shit that morning, but I was dressed more appropriately than most of those people. My black slacks might be getting shiny in the seat, but they weren't skintight leather or acid-washed denim.

I sat quietly in hangover misery, sipping my coffee and counting the heartbeats thumping in my head, ignoring whatever The Dude of God was saying up front. I noticed that I needed to take my shoes to the shop and get new heels. I noticed that the woman sitting in front of me was wearing underwear a good three inches too tall for her low-rise jeans. I noticed that the arm of the man sitting next to me was covered in a thick pelt of wiry gray hair with a bald strip on his wrist where the stretch-band of his Timex sat. How many years had it taken for that watch to pull all that hair out, one strand at a time? I focused on the jump of the second hand of his watch. I noticed that my coffee was half gone, and I didn't feel even one bit better.

When the minister finished talking, he made a little motion, and a woman in the front came up to the podium. She was heavy-set, in her fifties, and had black hair with a few short spikes on top, the rest falling to her shoulders. She wore a red blazer that looked about twenty pounds too small, a tight miniskirt, and converse high-tops. There was a shuffling sound throughout the room. I wasn't the only one who sat up straighter as this super-size Joan Jett settled in behind the microphone.

She spoke in a pack-a-day growl introducing herself as Candy and then thanking us for coming to say good-bye to Bowser. I really think she said his name was *Bowser*. She started talking about meeting him at a Moody Blues concert and then drifted off into some riff about all the concerts they'd attended. As she droned on about show after show, I imagined that I could almost smell the marijuana—although it might have actually been coming from hairy-arms sitting next to me. Candy kept talking about this and that, Rolling Stones, Queen, Harley Davidsons, Jack Daniel's, lung cancer . . . blah blah blah.

Just when I thought I might have to go outside and have a cigarette—references to lung cancer always gave me the urge—the woman broke down in big showy sobs and left the podium. Some crackling from the speakers in the ceiling hinted that music would now begin. *Finally, the closing hymn,* I remember thinking. And I lifted my cup of coffee to my lips, just as the sound system played a distinctive guitar and drum riff.

The music was loud, but not loud enough to cover my bark of laughter. The man next to me shouted "Hey!" when I spewed coffee on his arm, and low-rise, sitting in front of me, jumped up when she felt moisture hit the exposed small of her back.

Still coughing and snorting, I hurried to the bathroom. I spent as long as I could blotting the coffee from my roommate's white button down, but eventually I emerged, finding the Serenity Suite doors open and Bowser's friends milling in the hallway. I weaved my way through them and back into the room to join my mother. She was taking photos of the family posed around the casket. I carried over the tripod and the lights, then followed her curt instructions as she took various groupings with and without the deceased guest of honor.

When things finally wound down, I waited quietly for my mother to finish packing up her camera, and then I picked up the tripod and lights and followed her. The lobby was tiled and had an aggressive fountain right in the center, so everyone had to raise their voices to be heard over the terrible acoustics. Everyone except my mother, that is, because she wasn't speaking to me.

"I'm sorry," I said.

She frowned, saying nothing.

"I'm sorry I was late."

More frowning.

"I'm sorry I coughed."

The frowning continued, but now with narrowed eyes.

"Okay, laughed," I admitted. "It was wrong, I know it was, and I'm really, *really* sorry."

Her expression eased a little, and I couldn't resist adding, "But, come on . . . who plays 'Another One Bites the Dust' at a funeral?"

She glared at me, but to this day I would swear that I saw just the slightest twitch at the corner of her mouth. When she finally spoke, however, all she said was, "Your shirt is ruined."

I shrugged. "It's not my shirt."

She gave me a look that told me I had once again confirmed her low expectations.

"The oncologist's office called," she said. "They have a cancellation this afternoon."

"I have to work tonight . . ."

"The appointment is at one thirty. Let's go get lunch and then go hear about my test results. We'll be finished in plenty of time for you to get to work."

I put on an apologetic expression. "I can't do it. There's a mandatory meeting at work this afternoon." I told her this because it sounded better than the truth, which was that I had a voluntary lunch date with Eddy the new bartender. The date was in his apartment, and I figured that if things went well, Eddy and I would probably both be late for work.

"But—"

"Just keep your appointment for Monday."

"I'd rather go today."

"I'm off work Monday. If you want me to go, it will need to be then."

While my mother and I were talking, I'd been watching a man in a gray suit and a name tag work his way methodically through the crowd, saying a few words and then moving on. I was pretty sure I knew who he was looking for.

"I already took the appointment for today," my mother said, "but I do want you there."

"Then I guess you'll have to untake it." I picked up the tripod and tucked it under one arm.

"But—"

She was interrupted by the gray-suited man who'd finally reached us. "Excuse me," he said.

I looked at his slick dark hair, tidy mustache, and pale skin and wondered if he'd resembled a member of the Addams family before he worked at a funeral home, or if the job had caused it somehow.

"Do either of you drive a red Malibu?"

My mother and I both said "yes," which seemed to confuse him, but only for a second. "You must move your car, immediately," he said.

My mother made one of those exasperated sounds that mothers do so well, and then said, "Where did you park?"

Before I could answer, the man said, "She parked in the porte cochere!" His horrified tone of voice making it sound as if I'd done a naked interpretive dance in his fancy French covered parking rather than just leaving a car sitting there.

"It was raining," I explained.

"You know," my mother said to me, "you still need to get all that crap out of the back of your jeep."

"Excuse me! You really *must* move your car right now."

My mother continued to talk to me, ignoring the man. "I'm parked on the north side of the building. Pull the Malibu around and we can swap out everything in the cars while we finish our conversation—"

"Ladies, *please!*" The man was bouncing on his tiptoes with impatience.

When I think back on that day, I can't help but dwell on how easy it would have been to just do what my mother asked. To drive the Malibu around to where she'd parked my jeep. We could have traded out all the crap in our cars. Given a few more minutes to work on me, she probably would have convinced me to postpone my date with Eddy, and that would have been just fine. A Saturday nooner is every bit as much fun as a Friday one. But I was tired and hungover and still cranky about the whole funeral-in-the-rain thing. I'd had enough of my mother for one day.

"I don't have time," I told her.

"I simply must insist!" the man shouted, his black mustache twitching.

"Settle down, Gomez," I said, then I turned to my mother. "I'll come over tomorrow. We'll clean out the cars then."

"But—"

The man grabbed my elbow and began tugging me in the direction of the door. I went along without a struggle since he was escorting me to my car, which was where I wanted to go anyway.

"I'll see you tomorrow," I called back to my mother.

I was at the door when I heard her say, "Mattie!"

I slowed and turned. "What?"

She said something in reply, but with the fountain noise and the hum of conversation I couldn't hear it.

"What?" I called back again. Gomez was still tugging and the crowd was pushing us farther apart. I had to struggle to keep my mother in sight.

"Be careful," she shouted. I heard "remember," and then something else I almost made out, but by that point I was out the door and could only hear bits and pieces of her parting words. The last word was "upholstery."

I looked down at the tripod in my arms and saw that it was missing the rubber tip on one leg. I was annoyed, of course I was. Her precious fucking Malibu with its stupid tuck-and-roll upholstery. I considered shouldering my way back in there to tell her she could just drive her own damn car if she loved it so much, but the crowd was thick and the hearse was now surrounded by several men in suits, all glaring at me. So instead I just yelled "Everything will be fine" in my mother's direction as I opened the car door and tossed in the tripod.

I never looked back to see if she heard me.

CHAPTER 41

Luke doesn't say much on the way home from Richard Hambly's except to ask if I'm hungry. We drive through a McDonald's, which wouldn't have been my first choice, but for once in my life, I keep my damn mouth shut. I'm not always good at picking up clues, but I can tell that Luke is annoyed, and I don't blame him. First he had to drive me to the middle of nowhere and then he had to watch me make an old man cry.

When we pull up in front of my grandmother's house, Luke turns to me and asks, "So, did you get what you wanted?"

I'm pretty sure he's not talking about the Quarter Pounder and large fries in the bag on my lap, but I'm not sure how to answer his question. Mr. Hambly's story didn't shed any light on what happened to my mother, but it did explain Fritter's refusal to discuss my grandfather's death. In the end, the visit with Hambly was a little like ordering a Happy Meal but ending up with a Big Mac Combo. I didn't get what I wanted, but I got more than I expected.

"I'm sorry I dragged you into this," I tell him. It's not answering his question, but it's what he wants to hear.

He tips his head in acknowledgment of my apology. "Is hanging out with you always this interesting?"

I grin. "I've been compared to a natural disaster."

"Which one?"

"All of them."

Luke snorts a little laugh. "I'll shore up the levies for tomorrow night." This is his way, I think, of making sure that our date for tomorrow is still on.

The evening sunlight illuminates the left side of his face, accentuating his cheekbone and chin, while casting a shadow across his full lips. He's turned toward me, one very muscular arm draped over the steering wheel. Good Lord. He's actually quite handsome. How could I not have noticed before?

"We may need extra sand," I reply, reaching over to ruffle his hair, just the way he hates it.

Once inside the house, I notice that my already filthy jeans now have a grease spot on one leg. I can put off doing laundry no longer. After eating, I go upstairs to try on some of my mother's old jeans, but they are way too small. The only pants that fit are a pair of groovy aqua velour sweatpants, so I put those on, gather up a load of clothes, and trudge out to the garage. The washer and dryer are circa *I Love Lucy*, but I persevere.

I call Queeg to check on him, but Min He answers his phone. She reports that his biopsy went well, but he's sleeping now. When I ask her to please let him know that I called, she asks why I didn't call earlier. If I had a good answer to that question, I'd give it to her, but since I don't I tell her that it's none of her damn business. She hangs up without saying good-bye.

It's time to start my stakeout, so I turn off all the lights and sit on the sofa to wait. Sigh. There's enough of an evening glow coming in through the windows that I can kind of read, so I pick up a magazine from the coffee table. I flip through the pages, mostly thinking about how quiet the house is without the dogs and how much stakeouts suck. But I also find myself wondering: is it marketing genius or some more subtle cosmic force that makes every elderly person on the planet subscribe to *Arizona Highways*?

It's full dark when a noise startles me awake. Once I remember where I am and why I'm asleep on the couch, I sit up and rub my face and listen for the sound that woke me. I hear it again; it's coming from the kitchen.

I pad to the kitchen doorway and peer around the corner. There's just enough ambient light for me to see what's making the noise. It's Tawny wedging herself through the little doggy door. I watch in wonder as she inches her way forward. It's exactly like childbirth, but only if babies emerged from the womb fully clothed and cursing under their breath. She has one shoulder through the door, and as I watch, she squirms until the other pops through. I wait until she's struggling to get her hips in without losing her pants, and then I turn on the light.

The look on her face is priceless, simply too good not to save. I pull out my phone.

"Smile!" I take the picture even though her expression could in no way be mistaken for a smile.

I grab her a beer and set it on the kitchen table, pull out two chairs and then sit in one and wait. Meanwhile, she's rocking back and forth, pausing to pull her pants up every so often until she finally gets the rest of her body on this side of the door. Standing, she brushes herself off and then comes over to sit at the table.

"You should join a circus," I say.

She twists the top off the Bud and gags down a swallow.

"How'd you figure it out?" She's trying to act cool, but I can tell she's secretly pleased that I've discovered how clever she is.

"You're not as smart as you think you are."

"Whatever."

"You were careless. Leaving my stuff in your truck, and there was a cigarette butt in the turd you left on the shelf this morning. I happen to know the Winstons have a cigarette habit."

She thinks about this and nods. "Where are they, by the way?"

Her question catches me by surprise. I'd assumed that she had them, but her confusion looks genuine.

"You tell me. They were gone when I got home last night."

Her expression changes from tough to stricken. "They were here when . . ." She pauses, reluctant to confess.

"The gate was standing open when I got home last night."

"I thought I shut it," she says, blinking back tears.

"I know."

"I meant to shut it—"

"The latch is messed up. It could've happened to anybody." I don't like the girl, but her guilt makes me squirm.

She nods and sniffs.

"But my other stuff didn't run away."

"Other stuff?"

"The guitar strap, the camera bag, about a thousand negatives."

She shrugs. "Not ringing any bells."

"Come on, the strap doesn't belong to me, and the camera bag was my mom's."

"So?" Tawny keeps her expression cool. She's trying to tough this one out.

"Please," I say, surprising both of us, I think.

Tawny sighs and sets down her beer. "Okay."

On our way out to the truck Tawny explains that Fritter

instigated the theft—of the negatives, anyway. According to the girl, when she mentioned our plans to print some of the old negatives at the house, Fritter went ballistic and insisted that Tawny make sure that didn't happen. The girl's plan had been to swipe the negatives at some point when we were working in the darkroom, but when I bailed on her and went home with Father Barnes, she instituted an alternate, more punitive plan.

"But," I say, "the dog door?"

Tawny grins. "Pretty cool, right? I'd already done it a couple times since the old lady died. It's quiet here. A good place to smoke and drink beer."

This explains the beer in the fridge and Tawny's familiarity with the house.

"And Fritter wanted the negatives because . . ." I'm hoping she'll fill in the blank.

"I have no idea."

"Why did you agree to help her?" I ask. "Considering all the dog shit you've brought into the library, I thought your goal was to annoy her."

"She said she'd take me off bathroom duty for the rest of the summer."

"And it was worth it?"

The girl shrugs. "That old lady eats a lot of prunes."

Tawny climbs in the truck and then out again, holding Nick's strap and the camera bag. I take them from her, tell her good night, and walk back up to the porch. At the front door, I turn around and look at the girl, still standing next to the truck. From this distance she looks like a little kid waiting for her mother to drive her somewhere.

"What time is it?" I call out.

There's a flash of light as she checks her phone. "Almost midnight."

I don't know why I do it, but I'm pretty sure it has everything to do with the thought of her sneaking into an empty house and sitting there, all alone, trying to learn to drink beer. "Do you have those chemicals you picked up at Gandy Graphix?" I ask.

"Yeah," she replies. "But Fritter made me give her all the negatives."

"I wasn't lying when I said I found some hidden. Let's go see what's on them."

She wastes no time grabbing the sack from the truck and running to join me on the porch. It's dark, but there's enough light for me to make out the stretch of white teeth in her smile.

I'm not mad at Tawny about last night, but I'm not stupid. I make a show of counting the number of strips in the packet before I hand them to Tawny and show her the light box.

"Pick out one strip. We'll print a couple pictures tonight."

She replies, "Three?"

Three is not my definition of a couple, unless we're talking about a Jenna Jameson movie, but I tell her fine.

A few minutes later, she brings over a strip and with a little laugh says, "Let's do the last three on here."

"What's so funny?"

"You'll see."

In the amber glow of the safelight, I explain each step as my mother once explained them to me. I give her the tongs to agitate the print, and when the image starts to appear, she tells me to close my eyes, so I do. I don't have the heart to tell her I already got a peek when I looked through the enlarger.

With my eyes closed all I have left is the sound and the smell of the darkroom. I smile. It's the closest I've felt to my mother in a very long time.

"You know, when I was little, I was afraid of the dark." I'm whispering, but I don't know why.

Tawny makes an amused sound. "Not me. I love the dark. Always have."

"What are you afraid of?" I ask.

For a few seconds the only sound is the soft sloshing of the print moving back and forth in the tray, then she says, "Needles."

I laugh. "I didn't see that one coming."

I can hear the smile in her voice when she replies. "Yeah, well . . . I overcame my fear, I guess. Piercings are cool."

"Plus, I bet they do a great job of pissing off your mother."

She laughs softly. "You still afraid of the dark?"

"Nope."

"So what are you afraid of now?"

I know the answer to this one. I'm afraid of going home to Nick, and then to the next guy and the next. I'm afraid of getting an abortion and I'm afraid of having a child. I'm afraid of booze. I'm afraid of the inevitable, the day I can no longer fight the current. I'm afraid of becoming my mother.

"Drowning," I say, and it's the truth.

There's another quiet space filled with darkness and a chemical smell and memories. If my mother were here, what would she tell us?

"Time to rinse," I say. I sound just like her.

Once we put the papers in the water tray, I lead Tawny into the bathroom, attach the tubing to the faucet and clamp it tight. I leave her to rotate and rinse the prints since this is all still supposed to be a surprise for me. She sighs when I tell her ten minutes, but she doesn't argue. When she returns to the darkroom, I turn on the overhead lights and then stand back and watch as she clips each print on the wire. The photo that Tawny thought was so funny is of a boy, lithe and taut as only a teenage man-boy can be, standing outside, surrounded by trees, his laughing face upturned and his arms outstretched as if he were trying to embrace the whole world. He is wearing nothing but tennis shoes.

"Wow," I say. "He's hot."

Tawny looks at me and frowns. "Don't be a perv. He's like my age."

"That was taken thirty-five years ago," I remind her. "He's probably a grandpa now."

"Ooooh that's right," she replies. "Gross."

I'm not surprised when Tawny asks if we can print some more tomorrow night. I tell her that I have a date tomorrow—a real one this time—and extract from her what seems to be a sincere promise not to break in again, by assuring her that we can print more photos Saturday. That being said, I still plan to hide Nick's strap, the camera bag, and the negatives before I leave this house again. *Once bitten, twice shy,* as Queeg would say.

Before she goes home, I ask Tawny if she might be able to procure me a somewhat illegal item. The girl laughs and tells me it won't be a problem. Since I'm broke, we end up with a you'll-owe-me-one sort of agreement, which pleases her a bit more than I'm comfortable with. Nobody wants to owe a favor to someone who doesn't think twice about carting around dog poo.

Once she's gone, I wander through the house turning off lights and making sure the doors are locked. I put some dog food and water on the front porch and in the back, just in case, and then I walk upstairs. Back in the darkroom, I grab all the negatives and take them over to the light box. With the images so tiny and all the tones reversed it's hard to see details, but as far as I can tell the only obviously interesting one is the naked boy, which is funny, but surely not theft-worthy. I can't imagine what that old woman is after, but if my mother had some juicy photo of Fritter, it's not here. I gather up the negatives and turn off the light box. I can't decide if I'm disappointed or relieved.

Before I leave the room, I look again at the damp prints hanging from the wire. The boy is lovely, of course, but it's the next photo I study with interest. It's of a car, and if I'm not mistaken it's a Malibu from the late 1970s. I'm betting it's a '78 model. I'm betting it was red. The last photo is a picture of the girl who will someday be my mother. She is looking at the camera. At me.

Her smile hints at a secret.

FRIDAY

Every picture tells a story.

CHAPTER 42

It's one of those dreams where I know that I'm dreaming, but I will myself to remain asleep. I'm back at Two Pines, sitting next to Queeg on the steps of a trailer. We're watching my mother feed the seagulls.

She's standing in the gravel courtyard, the pockets of her blue housecoat bulging with bread crusts and cut-up hot dogs. In one hand she holds a drink, with the other she reaches in her pocket, grabs a scrap, and, rising to her toes, tosses the food straight up. Around and around the gulls circle, banking hard, rising and diving, plucking the food out of the hot August air.

Finally, her pockets are empty, but rather than quit, she begins to throw cigarette butts, and gravel, and limes from her gin and tonic. As the birds grab and then drop the trash, their screaming intensifies but still they circle and swoop, circle and swoop, again and again, their mouths open and trusting, never understanding that my mother has nothing left to give.

The phone rings early in the morning. I don't need to look at the screen to know who it is.

"Good morning, Queeg."

"Did I wake you?"

"Of course you woke me."

"Sorry."

He doesn't sound sorry.

"So how did it go yesterday?" I ask.

There's a pause. I can picture him taking a sip of his coffee. I can hear some soft chirping in the background, so I imagine him sitting on the folding lawn chair outside his trailer.

"Bad, but not as bad as I was expecting."

"I called last night, but you were already asleep. I should have called earlier."

"It's okay, sweetheart," he says, letting me off the hook, just like he always does. I hear a faint scratch on his end that tells me he's lit a cigarette.

"Hey, Queeg . . ."

"Hmmmm?"

"When you were married to Mom, did she tell you about any of this? Growing up here, her family, her mother . . ."

"Not much."

"Did she ever mention somebody named Trip?"

"No."

"Did she ever tell you why she left home?"

He sighs. "She talked around her past, Matt, not about it."

I nod even though he can't see me. I understand talking around things. "But after Mom died, you called Tilda . . ."

"I didn't know much, but I knew the name of the town where your mom grew up, so I called around until somebody gave me your grandmother's phone number. It wasn't a big deal. It just required a little effort."

I understand what he's saying. He called. He made the effort.

"Last night I dreamt we were back at the beach," I tell him. "We were watching Mom feed the gulls."

"Sounds like a good dream."

"It was good because you were in it, Queeg." My throat squeezes painfully, and I stop and swallow. "You saved us," I tell him, and it's almost true. He tried hard but failed to save my mother, and I guess he's still trying with me. That's not looking so good either.

There's a pause in which I can hear his measured breathing. "Honey," he finally says, "are you okay?"

"You bet." We both know I'm lying.

"Why don't you just come home?"

I consider telling him how the Malibu is being held hostage; it would be an explanation for my absence that he would understand. But then he'd offer to send money, and it would all get weird because he doesn't have any money to spare. Not to mention the fact that me being here isn't about the money anymore, if it ever really was.

"I've been wondering . . . why did you buy Mom the Malibu?"

"It's a classic."

"I know, but why that car? If she loved classic cars, why not an old Camaro or a T-Bird?"

"We saw one once. On the highway, we passed an old red Malibu. She put a hand against her window and stared at that car like it was a double cheeseburger. She twisted all around to watch from the rear window until we were well past."

"So you—"

"I asked her, and she said that she liked it, that a 1978 Malibu was her favorite car. So I got her one." He pauses, to take a drag from a cigarette I'm guessing, before he adds, "It was probably a mistake."

"Why would you say that?"

"We put more into that car than it was worth."

"But she loved it."

"Yeah well . . . maybe."

"No maybe about it. The very last words she said to me were about the Malibu."

I can hear the smile in his voice when he says, "You're kidding me!"

"I was carrying her equipment out to the car and the last thing she said to me was to be careful not to poke a hole in the seat with the tripod."

"That damn upholstery . . . all those seams. For some reason it had to be tuck-and-roll." His laugh turns into a cough. He pulls the phone away from his face, but I can still hear him struggle. Finally it's over. "Sorry about that," he tells me.

"You need to quit smoking."

"We sure got that car looking good," he says, ignoring me. "All it took was hard work. That's all it ever takes, Matt."

Queeg loves to claim that effort is the cure for every ill, but I don't think he really believes all fixer-uppers can be fixed. He was married to my mother, after all.

"I'm serious about the cigarettes," I tell him. "They're killing you, Cap."

"No point shutting the barn door after the horse is gone."

"You don't know where the horse is," I say, which sounds stupid but we both know what I'm talking about.

"If I get good news from the doctor next week, I'll quit."

"And if it's bad news?"

Another pause and this time I'm sure I can hear him taking a drag off his cigarette and exhaling. "Did you ever find those dogs?"

"They'll come back home," I say, hoping it's true.

"I wish you'd do the same, sweetheart."

"I know," I reply even though I understand that the words he's wanting are, *I will*.

"Is it money? Let me wire you some money—"

"Stop worrying about me and take care of yourself, Queeg. I'm fine." I sit up and pause, waiting for the now familiar nausea to arrive. "I gotta go," I say, hanging up as my mouth fills with saliva. I climb out of bed and head for the bathroom. The simple fact is, I can lie to my stepfather, but it's harder to lie to myself. I'm not fine at all.

With the negatives in my purse, and Nick's strap and my mother's camera bag hidden in the old washing machine in the garage, I feel reasonably safe leaving the house. I don't really think Tawny is going to try again tonight while I'm at Luke's, but better safe than sorry. I grab the borrowed-without-permission yearbooks and a thick American history textbook from the bookshelf in my mother's room, and take them with me out on the porch to wait for Tawny.

I'm heartened to see that most of the dog food I left out last night is gone. Of course it's probably some stray eating it, but I tell myself it's the Winstons. The day continues to improve when Tawny's truck rattles up right on time. Halle-fuckin-lujah. I'm not exactly the skipping type, but there is a definite bounce in my walk as I approach the truck, carrying my purse, the books, and a manila envelope holding the 8" x 10" prints from last night.

Since I forgot to switch my laundry before I went to bed, and therefore my jeans are only now in the dryer, I am wearing another of Tilda's tweed skirts. This one is a trace too woolen for June, and between it and the vinyl truck seat, my thighs are damp and itchy by the time we get downtown. I have Tawny drop me off at the church, explaining that I'll walk over to the library in a few minutes. Amazingly she complies without comment. Apparently we've gone from breaking and entering all the way to reasonably friendly in just one night. I should have had her over for a dark-room lesson earlier.

When we pull up in front of the church, I say, "Did you bring it?"

She nods and pulls a plastic baggie out of her backpack. Inside is a very neatly rolled joint.

I take the baggie and then hand Tawny my mother's history textbook. "Use this as your booster seat and put K through L back in the library."

"Why?"

"If you just stick it on a shelf in Fiction or Biography, Fritter will come across it and think it was misshelved."

She rolls her eyes to let me know she'd like to tell me where to stick it. "You didn't answer my question."

The truth is, even with everything Fritter has done, I hate watching her search for that damn book. But I'm not telling Tawny that. It would be a mistake to show this girl my soft underbelly.

"Because eventually Fritter is going to look in this truck and see that book, and then she's going to be pissed at you, and she'll fire me for not ratting you out earlier."

Tawny bares her teeth in a smile. I'm pretty sure I have just described the exact scenario she's been hoping for.

"I'm serious, Tawny. When I get to the library I'm going to look in this truck, and if that encyclopedia is still in here, I'm going to tell Fritter." I hand her the borrowed yearbooks. "While you're at it, put these back, too."

Tawny narrows her eyes and studies my expression, trying to decide if this is a bluff. Then she scowls and leans forward on the seat to swap the encyclopedia under her skinny ass for my mother's old textbook. I barely get the door shut before she peals out with a smoky roar.

That girl can put on her I-don't-give-a-shit act all she wants, but I know better. Always on the lookout for a new way to antagonize people, to test their affection and find it wanting—the terms used by my high school counselor were Oppositional Defiant Disorder and Low Impulse Control. My face may be less likely to set off a metal detector, but I'm afraid that if I were in her little size six combat boots I'd be pulling the exact same kind of shit she's pulling.

With a sigh I walk to the back door of the church. It's not even nine in the morning and I'm already tired. It's more than a little disheartening at thirty years old to look at a seventeen-year-old and see yourself.

CHAPTER 43

Since Karleen's car is here, I know she's in the church somewhere, so I wander around until I locate her. She's carrying a broom and pushing a housekeeping cart down a long hallway lined with closed doors. I'm not trying to be sneaky, but since I'm rocking my grandmother's skirt with my Chuck Taylors, she doesn't hear me coming up behind her.

"Karleen," I say as softly as possible. Still, she jumps and spins around swinging the broom hard enough that I'm glad I left more than a handle's length between us.

"Steeerike!" I call out as she struggles to control her follow through.

"Shit! You scared me."

"Sorry."

"I think I peed my pants a little."

"Sorry."

She looks me up and down before she speaks. "What are you doing here?"

"I came to say I'm sorry."

"Well congratulations. You've said it three times now."

"I mean about being a no-show yesterday. I lost track of time. I apologize."

She nods slowly. "You're pretty good at this apologizing stuff. I bet you get a lot of practice."

I have to bite my lip not to say "I'm sorry" again. Instead, I hold out my arm. Karleen's brows rise as she looks at the contents of the bag I'm tick-tocking in front of her face.

She plucks the baggie from my fingertips. "Luckily I'm good at forgiving."

She unlocks the nearest classroom, then leads me past the tiny tables and chairs to the bank of windows, one of which she cranks open. She sparks up the joint, takes a hit, and then holds it out to me. I hesitate long enough that she puts it back to her mouth.

"I smoked pot when I was pregnant, and my son turned out just fine."

"Why do you keep talking about pregnancy?" I hold out my hand and she passes the joint to me. I take a small pull, just a little to test my gag reflex. I shudder but stop short of retching. I hand it back and shake my head.

She smiles and points at the manila envelope in my hand. "What's that?"

I open it and pass her the first photo. "This is a picture my mom took, and I was wondering about it."

"It's Trip's Malibu."

"Was it red?"

She nods and hands the picture back. "Is that it?"

I draw out the next photograph and pass it over.

She takes a glance and then quickly lowers it, laughing. "Oh my dear sweet Jesus!" She takes a longer look, trombones it a little, and then lowers it to her side again, still laughing. "Where on earth did you find that?"

"You found it. It was on one of the negatives hidden in the box springs. Is that Trip?"

"In the flesh," she replies.

Our laughter echoes in the empty room. She relights the joint and takes another drag. "That must have been on one of their camping trips," she explains.

"My mother liked to camp?" I'm trying to align that reality to the woman I remember freaking out if she saw a spider.

"No, but your grandmother wouldn't let her date Trip, re-member? They had to get creative. They'd go spend the night out at Cypress Point."

She takes one more look at the photo, still chuckling, then hands it back. "Got any more?"

I hand her the picture of my mother.

Karleen's grin softens to a tender smile. "That's how I still think of her. She was almost always smiling. Did she stay that way?"

I take Karleen's memory of my mother and compare it with mine.

I shake my head. "Sorry."

Karleen frowns and hands back the photo. "Well, at least she got out of here."

"What makes you think where she ended up was any better?"

"Do you know how often my kids had to see me with one of these?" Karleen is pointing at her swollen, purple eye.

"I don't know. Maybe about as often as I had to clean up my mother after she'd gotten pass-out drunk and peed all over her-self."

The second the words are out of my mouth, I wish I could have them back. The expression of tenderness and pity on Kar-leen's face is unbearable.

"I'm sorry," she says. "I didn't—"

"Don't. Please," I tell her. I'm dangerously close to tears. "I just want you to know that you can stop feeling jealous of my mother's life. There were no glass slippers for her, or for me. No magic fairy dust. No happily ever after."

She nods and gives me a minute, turning her attention to the joint in her hands, taking her time to pinch it out and test the end until it's cool enough to slip in her pocket. When she finally looks up at me again, all she says is, "I need to get back to work."

"What was it you started to tell me Wednesday night?" I ask.

She turns away. In profile Karleen looks older, tired. It's easy to see where her cheeks and neck are losing their fight with gravity. I try to remember if my mother's face was softening in a similar way, but I can't.

"You said you knew my mother wasn't pregnant," I remind her. "How did you know?"

She brushes at a few flakes of ash clinging to her shirt. She's still not looking at me. "Did you sleep with Father Barnes?"

"No."

Now she turns to face me, her expression asking if I'm telling the truth.

"I didn't," I say. "I could have. I was going to. But I didn't."

"Why?"

I think about my hand on his leg, the warmth of his lips on mine, how easy it would have been to bulldoze into that man's life. She's asking a good question, one I've asked myself. I wish I knew the answer.

I shrug. "I just lost a taste for it."

Karleen nods slowly, as if I'd actually told her something meaningful. Then she says, "I know your mother wasn't pregnant because she got an abortion the day she left."

Her revelation catches me off guard. Before I can think of how to respond, she continues.

"Your mother and I were on the outs that summer because of Trip, but the two of us had been best friends since third grade. When she called and asked for my help, I was still mad at her, but we had a history. I couldn't refuse." Karleen cranks open another window. The breeze catches a stack of papers at a nearby table. I grab them before they hit the floor and tuck them under a nearby box of crayons.

"When she called she didn't give me any idea what she needed. It wasn't until I picked her up that she told me where we were going. I was surprised—no, *surprised* is too mild a word—I was shocked. We knew girls who'd gotten their problems solved at the same clinic, and your mother had always been very vocal in her disapproval. Hell, who could blame her? Tilda wasn't married when she had Genie, so the idea of choosing an abortion over being a single parent hit a little too close to home for your mom. And yet there we were, on our way to the clinic."

I feel a little sick to my stomach. I wonder if it's the same clinic Dr. McDonald would send me to.

"Did she tell you why?"

Karleen shakes her head. "She wouldn't say a word, not one single word all the way to Tulsa. She wouldn't even look at me."

Karleen goes on, describing the drive, the clinic, sitting in the waiting room while my mother had the procedure. "When it was over, I helped her to the car, and then we drove to a pharmacy about a block away. She waited in the car while I went in to get her pain pills. When I came back out, she was gone."

"Gone? Where would she go? Why would she do that?"

Karleen doesn't want to answer the question. She looks around the classroom, out the window, at her hands. "I said some things . . . things I wish I hadn't."

She glances at me and I nod. I know what that feels like.

"I was angry that she wouldn't talk, angry about Trip, angry about what she'd just done. So I gave her a piece of my mind. Several pieces. And then I said I was going to tell her mother about the abortion." At this, Karleen focuses her attention back on me. "And do you know what your mother did then?"

I shake my head.

"She laughed."

Karleen watches my face for a reaction and she gets one, but I'm not sure what. Confusion? Surprise? Whatever it is, it keeps her talking.

"She acted like I'd just told her the funniest joke in the world. I didn't know what to say, so I just left her there and went inside to get her prescription filled. When I came back out, she was gone. She'd left a note on her seat saying she'd gotten a ride with a friend. I was a little surprised, but mostly relieved, if you want to know the truth. It would have been an awkward ride back to town. Honestly, I didn't think too much of it at the time; people around here are always going to Tulsa for one reason or another. It seemed entirely possible that one of our friends had noticed her waiting and given her a lift home. I mean, where else would she go?"

Karleen sighs and shakes her head. "When I got back to town that day, I should have stopped by her house to drop off her medicine, but I didn't. I went home. I wanted her to start hurting and have to call me and beg me to bring her the pills. She never called and I didn't call her. It wasn't until a week later, when Trip came to see me, that I found out Genie was gone."

Karleen straightens and closes the windows, not realizing—or not caring—that it still reeks in here. I suspect there are going to be some awkward questions come Sunday morning. Once we're back out in the hallway, she relocks the classroom door, and then turns to me.

"Your dogs show up yet?"

"No. Your husband?"

She shakes her head. "He'll turn up pretty soon."

"Might be a good time to change the locks."

She takes the oversize metal dustpan from the cart and clanks it to the floor. "You know, every once in a while your mother would send me a postcard." Karleen bends over, holding the dustpan with one hand, her broom with the other. "Not in a long time, though. Probably twenty years since I got one." She stands and dumps the pan. "I wish I'd written back."

"Do you still have them?"

She shakes her head. "Sorry." Gesturing at the picture in my hand—the one of my mom—Karleen says, "Do you suppose I could have that?"

"Sure." I pass her the photo, remembering something I'd been meaning to ask. "Did my mom bleach her hair?"

The question surprises Karleen. "Yeah. Did she stop?"

I nod.

"She always wore her hair blond."

"Why?"

"I don't know. It was the seventies, straight blond hair was the rage. I don't even know what her real color was, but I do remember that Tilda was fine with her bleaching it—practically insisted that she keep it blond. Hell, my mom wouldn't even let me pierce my ears."

Karleen carefully tucks the photograph into a side pocket of the cart.

"Did you ever tell my grandmother about the abortion?" I ask.

"No."

"Did you tell Trip?"

She doesn't answer that question, but she doesn't have to. Her regret is palpable. She fiddles with her broom instead, picking some cobwebby dust from the bristles.

"You know," she says, "I read a quote once that really stuck with me. It said, 'We are all more than the worst thing we've done.'"

"That's a good one."

She gives me a wry look. "Do you think it's true?"

I weigh my choices—answering honestly versus telling her a comforting lie. Or maybe that's not what I'm weighing. Maybe it's my worst fear against my only hope.

"I don't know," I say and it's true enough.

She surprises me with a quick hug, her sturdy arms strong on my back. "You'd better get to work," she says, but she doesn't let go right away.

When I turn and walk back down the hall, I can feel her watching my retreat. I'm not surprised when her voice echoes behind me.

"It was red," she says.

I turn. "What?"

"Genie's hair. Her natural color was red. I just remembered."

I nod.

"When you find out what made her do what she did, will you let me know?"

Her voice is even, but her eyes are just a little too shiny. I can't decide if she's about to cry or if it's just from the weed.

"What if there wasn't a good reason?" I say.

"What if there was?" she replies.

CHAPTER 44

As far as I can tell it's always windy here, but today it's blowing like crazy. One tug at the big brass handle, and the wind grabs the door out of my hand and slams it open, the loud *boom* reverberating through the library. The occupants of the computer area, our usual little island of misfit toys, turn their heads in unison to stare in my direction. Sheets of paper on the circulation desk come to life, with Fritter, stationed behind the desk, struggling to hold everything down until I get the door closed.

I walk to the desk. "Sorry I'm late."

"Again," Fritter replies, glaring at me, as usual. We're like an old married couple now. I notice that she's got a couple of spooky hairs growing out of a mole on her chin that I briefly—very briefly—consider pointing out.

"Remember, I will be gone this afternoon," she tells me, "so you and Tawny need to prepare the chairs—"

"You're going to a nursing home, right?"

She frowns, irritated by the interruption. "That is correct."

"Visiting your brother?"

Tawny had mentioned Fritter's brother in the nursing home, but it's only now that it occurs to me that he might know as much about my mother as Fritter does.

"I read to a group of the residents, but yes my brother Jonah lives there, so I also visit him."

I stand there as Fritter keeps talking about setting up chairs for the children's story time, but I'm not listening. I'm torn. I'm pretty sure that there's no point in trying to finagle my way into meeting that old man, but at the same time now that I know he's around, I feel like I *need* to talk to him. He is an itchy scab, and Tawny is right. I'm a picker.

"Are you listening?" Fritter asks.

With effort I pull my focus back to the crabby old woman standing in front of me. "Not really."

She makes an exasperated face and sighs. "I was trying to explain that you must move the small tables to—"

"Can I come with you?" I blurt out, surprising both of us.

"What?"

"To the nursing home. Can I come? I'll help. I could read, or I could—"

"Don't be ridiculous. You will stay here and help Tawny—"

"Oh come on, Tawny doesn't need my help." I can't honestly even say why I want to go, but now that I've started I can't resist continuing to push. "And it will give us a chance to get to know each other."

"Well, I'm not—"

"You did say I should associate with a higher class of people."

While Fritter and I have been speaking, an elderly woman has approached the desk.

"Good morning," the lady chirps, setting a book on the counter.

Fritter smiles and returns the greeting.

I pick up the book. "This looks great," I say. "Maybe we should read this one at the nursing home this afternoon."

I see Fritter stiffen. Sensing that I have the advantage, I continue. "Miss Jackson is taking me with her this afternoon to read at the nursing home. She wants to show me how important it is to give back to the community."

The woman beams at us. "Why isn't that nice. Fritter, I'm so glad you're passing along your passion for service."

"When you come back next week," I tell the woman, "I'll let you know how it went."

"That would be lovely," she replies.

Fritter pointedly does not look in my direction while entering information into the computer. She and the lady exchange a few words of small talk. When the woman walks off, Fritter turns to me, frowning. "I don't know what you're up to, but there's no way that I'm taking you with me."

"Well then, maybe I'll just cut out a little early this afternoon. Yesterday I found some old negatives hidden away that I'm dying to print."

She narrows her eyes, perhaps trying to decide whether I'm telling the truth or dropping a hint that I know of her involvement in Tawny's break-in. We stare at each other for an uncomfortable few seconds, each measuring the other's resolve. Fritter is the first to look away.

The rest of the morning passes quickly. When lunchtime rolls around, I cage another apple from the refrigerator in the back room and search the cabinets until I find a package of only slightly expired peanut-butter crackers. I'm staying in for lunch so I can keep an eye on Fritter. I'm half expecting her to find some excuse to go without me.

When the time to leave arrives, I start looking for Fritter. From behind the circulation desk, Tawny gives me the stink eye. "I can't believe you're ditching me."

"Believe it."

"You want to hear something interesting? I get to take a long lunch. Fritter called in a volunteer to cover for me," Tawny says with a sly smile. "I've been assigned a special errand to run as soon as the two of you leave for the nursing home, a certain job Fritter wants me to finish."

I try to hide my surprise. So, Fritter hadn't found what she was looking for in the first batch of stolen negatives. Maybe the ones I still have aren't quite as innocuous as they seem.

I hear Fritter's footsteps on the stairs.

"Good luck with that." I pat my purse where the negatives are safely stashed.

"I wasn't going to do it anyway," she says quietly. "We're still on for tomorrow, right? No rain checks."

Fritter reaches the base of the stairs and walks toward us. I answer Tawny with a nod.

"What are you two talking about?" Fritter asks.

"The weather," I reply.

Tawny grins. Fritter does not.

The old woman gives Tawny a look, fraught with meaning. "You know your duties for this afternoon?"

"Yes, ma'am."

Satisfied, the old woman shifts her sturdy brown handbag from one forearm to the other and then without one glance in my direction walks to the back of the library, through the door and into the parking lot. I follow close behind.

Once we're in her car, Fritter spends a few minutes fixing her hair, tucking up some of the pieces that the high wind has freed from their confinement. It occurs to me that this is it; if I want to apply some pressure to this old woman, right now is the time I could tell her what I know about the break-in. I wouldn't call the cops on her and Tawny, but she doesn't know that. Maybe the threat would be enough to make her tell me what the hell is going on. Or maybe it wouldn't be enough, and I would've played the only card in my hand. Sensing my gaze, she looks over at me, expectantly, as if she knows exactly what I'm thinking and is itching to call my bluff.

I run my fingers through my tangled curls and pretend the challenge in her eyes is about my hair. "Sorry. It's this crazy wind."

She stares at me for another heartbeat before she turns away to fasten her seat belt. "There's a storm coming," she says. "Can't you feel it?"

I do a quick inventory of my feelings: queasy, bloated, and . . . hmmm. Underneath, maybe I do feel something else. Tension, a straining spring, a fraying rope. In my mouth, the salty, metallic taste is back. I wonder if it's fear.

"I don't feel a thing," I reply.

On the outside, Reunion Plaza looks like a resort. On the inside it smells exactly like I expected a nursing home to smell, like disinfectant and burnt onions and pee. For a tiny woman, Fritter walks impressively fast down the hallway, her crepe-soled shoes squeaking on the waxed linoleum tile. I follow with my own sneaker squeak and try to time my steps with hers. When she stops suddenly, I come within inches of slamming into her back.

"What are you doing?"

"Following you."

"Well, stop tailgating," she says, continuing down the hall. I drop back a bit, leaving a couple Fritter-lengths between us.

We stop in front of a half-open door. The old woman steps

into the doorway, blocking my path, but it's easy enough to peer over her shoulder. Inside, the curtains are closed, and a lamp illuminates a white-haired man in a recliner. He's holding a book, but from the way it's resting on his lap it looks like he's been doing more napping than reading.

He looks up. "Who's there?"

She hesitates for a second, then replies, "It's me, Jonah."

I open my mouth to remind Fritter of my existence, but before I can get a sound out, she turns and shoos me away from the door. "Strangers upset him. Why don't you go introduce yourself to the director and tell her you'll start the reading."

I linger nearby, but can't make out words in the murmur of voices within, so, reluctantly, I go find the director. When we get to the activities lounge, there are already several seniors waiting, so I walk through the rows of chairs and wheelchairs to get to the seat in the front that's facing everyone else.

The book I've been handed, *Anna Karenina*, happens to be one that I've read a time or two. It's bookmarked on page 106, well into the story, but before I begin I can't resist turning to the first page and looking at the novel's famous opening line: *All happy families are alike; each unhappy family is unhappy in its own way.* I can still remember how strange I found that sentence when I first saw it as a teenager. I had limited experience with happy families, but even then I understood that unhappy families are less unique than Tolstoy believed. You peek behind the curtains of any household headed by an underemployed single mother with an escalating alcohol problem, and you're going to see a lot of the same sad, angry shit going on.

I've been reading to the group for twenty minutes when I see Fritter slip into the back of the room and take a seat by the door. Her brother is not with her. I clear my throat a few times, and then put on what I think is a pretty convincing coughing fit.

As I anticipated, Fritter stands and threads her way through the wheelchairs to my side. She has one brow raised in a what-are-you-up-to expression, so I work hard to maintain a who-me-up-to-something? look on my face. She's not buying it, but she takes the book and sits in my spot, while I work my way through the napping crowd and out of the room.

I'm guessing from the look on Fritter's face that I won't have long before she comes to find me, so I hurry. When I reach Jonah's room, an aide is just leaving. Her coffee-colored skin is smooth, only the strands of gray along her hairline hint at her age. She looks tired and has a yellow stain across her midriff that I hope for her sake isn't what it looks like. She acknowledges my presence with a smile. "Are you here to see Mr. Jackson?"

I nod, and she holds the door open for me to enter. "He loves visitors," she whispers.

"Why doesn't he go down and listen to his sister reading?"

"He doesn't care for her current book selection. Every time she comes now, he starts in about the evils of communism."

"Tolstoy was a communist?"

The woman laughs softly. "I have no idea. But I'd avoid the subject if I were you."

"Not a problem," I tell her, and it's true. Russian politics are the last thing I came here to talk about.

His lamp is off, and the room is in twilight, illuminated only by the edges of the curtains and the television. Fritter's brother is in bed now, propped up on pillows, the hospital-bed back raised to almost ninety degrees. On the television, a plump chef chops a zucchini.

The old man blinks at me as I enter from the bright hallway. "Back already from reading your manifesto?"

"Hello." I walk to his bedside, extending my hand. "We haven't met but I'm—"

"You came!" His eyes are wide, as he takes my hand in both of his.

"Um . . . yeah. I did." I'm a little taken aback by his reaction, but that aide did say that he loves visitors. I continue with, "I was in the hall earlier with your sister—"

"I thought you'd never come." He's much too excited to see me. He's shaking, his eyes tearing up. He grasps my hand hard with his knobby fingers. "I thought I'd never have a chance to apologize."

I feel a little out of breath in the overheated room. "I . . . uh . . . I think maybe there's been a mistake," I say. "I'm sorry."

"No, I'm the one who's sorry." His voice is hoarse. "I am so sorry. I promise that I never knew. Never. Not until I saw her—"

"What are you doing in here?"

Mr. Jackson and I both startle at this. I twist around and see Fritter standing in the doorway. She's angry. Very angry. I try to step away from the bed, but the old man tightens his grip on my hand.

"Say you forgive me," he pleads. "I have to hear it."

"But—"

"Please. I'm so, so sorry."

I glance at Fritter for help, but she's not looking at me, she's watching her brother, shaking her head slowly. I look down at the old man's trembling hands, nothing but blue veins and bones. I don't know what's going on in his crazy head, but I do know what it feels like to be *so, so sorry*. I step closer and set my free hand on top of his. "I forgive you, Jonah," I say. "Everything is going to be okay."

At this, Fritter steps up and takes her brother's hand from mine. "Enough of this nonsense. It's time for us to go." She turns to her brother, and her voice softens. "I'll come Sunday. I'll bring fudge." She then takes me by the elbow and begins marching me to the door. I have to press my lips together to suppress a whimper as she pinches my skin between her bony knuckles. This little old lady has a mean streak and pretty impressive hand strength to go with it. I make a decision to never challenge her to a thumb war.

We're almost to the door when I notice that the vice grip she's got me locked into has our path lined up with a leg of a portable potty by the door. If she keeps glaring up at me, she's going to walk right into the rolling toilet. As tempting as it would be to let her fall, I'm a little worried she'll take me down with her. Besides, even a mean old lady doesn't deserve a broken hip.

"Fritter, don't—"

"Don't you tell me what to do," she hisses. "I leave you alone for five minutes—"

"You need to look—"

"I'm looking, all right. At an ungrateful—"

"Watch it! You're going to trip—" The words are no sooner out of my mouth, than she catches an orthopedic shoe on the edge of one wheel. She lets go of my elbow at the same moment I grab on to hers to steady her balance, so for both of us, the situation improves. She straightens, yanking her arm from my grasp, but thankfully doesn't try to reestablish her death grip.

We're in the doorway when from behind us Fritter's brother calls out, "Trip? Trip?"

Fritter and I reply in unison. However, I say, "We're fine," while she responds, "He's not here."

CHAPTER 45

Fired?" Luke pauses with a bite of salad halfway to his mouth. "After four days? How did you manage that?"

"It wasn't easy," I admit.

"I've never heard of Fritter firing *anybody*."

I shrug and bite into a slice of cucumber. Greek salads are my favorite, and, with the exception of Wednesday night's somewhat charred dinner with Father Barnes, it's been almost a week since I've eaten anything that wasn't stale, freezer-burned, fast-food, or rubbery soup-kitchen fare.

"With all those teenagers she takes in . . ." He's shaking his head, looking at me incredulously. "Every single one of them a tremendous pain in the ass. Hell, back in the day, I drove her crazy, and she never fired me. Never once have I heard of her firing someone."

"I have my ways," I reply, mysteriously.

Luke grins.

"I have ninja skills when it comes to screwing things up. It's like a superpower only lamer."

He laughs and finally takes that bite of salad.

Luke has gone all out on this dinner, and I am glad to be sitting here eating it. Fritter fired me in the parking lot of the nursing home and then just got in her car and left me there. I had to hitchhike back to my grandmother's house. To add insult to injury my jeans were still damp—stupid antique dryer—so I was faced with a choice of a tweed skirt or velour sweatpants for my date. I almost called Luke to cancel, but then I remembered that all my groceries were still sitting in Father Barnes's refrigerator. In the end hunger trumped embarrassment.

Now, sitting here eating and laughing with this man, I'm ridiculously grateful for the food and the company. He's flirting shamelessly and it feels so good to be wanted that I'm finding it easy to focus on him rather than my itchy wool skirt and my ever-present vague nausea.

Luke's apartment is sleek and modern with everything from kitchen to bathroom set up to accommodate his wheelchair. There are enough pictures on the wall and books on the bookshelf to make it look homey, but the overall effect is a feeling of efficiency and ease. We're both laughing while I tell him the story of how I got sacked. I certainly don't tell him everything, but I do mention Fritter's reluctance to answer questions about my family, and I talk about my visit with her brother in the nursing home. I consider telling Luke about his aunt Fritter's orchestration of Tawny's break-in, but he seems so genuinely fond of the old lady that I hate to be the one to tell him she's a criminal mastermind. Besides, I have the feeling that would just get Tawny in trouble, not Fritter. Who are the cops going to believe—an elderly do-gooder librarian, or a pierced-up juvenile delinquent?

"Let me get this straight," he says. "Fritter fired you for talking to a lonely old man in a nursing home?"

"Well . . ." I equivocate, "it's possible that she interpreted my visit as more of an . . . um . . . questioning, and less of a social call."

"I thought he had Alzheimer's."

"He seemed pretty sharp to me." I decide that mentioning that Jonah mistook me for someone else will not help my case.

"So, did you learn anything useful?"

"Maybe. I found out that *Trip* is Jonah's son."

"That's someone's name?" Luke asks.

"Yup. Trip is one of Fritter's nephews. He was one of her summer projects—maybe the first. And, according to Karleen, he was my mom's boyfriend that summer she left town."

"So Jonah told you about Trip?"

"Not exactly . . ." I sketch out Fritter's almost broken hip, making sure to play up my heroic measures. "And then after she told him that Trip wasn't there, I asked her what that was supposed to mean, and she explained."

"I'm surprised she told you anything after catching you interrogating—"

"Visiting."

"Questioning."

"Okay, questioning," I concede. "Although I never got a chance to ask any questions. Honestly, I think she only told me about Trip because she was a little shaken from her near fall. Did I mention that I saved her from a broken hip?"

I polish off the last new potato on my plate and eye the few remaining on the platter. Luke notices my empty plate and my glance, and pushes both the salad bowl and the platter in my direction.

"Eat."

I serve myself just a tiny bit more, and then say, "So, you were one of Fritter's projects?"

He nods.

"How did that happen? I can't picture you as a juvenile delinquent."

"Why is that?"

"Well . . ." Too late, I realize that I'm thinking of Luke as he is now, neatly trimmed hair, clean nails, wheelchair, wheelchair, wheelchair. What the hell do I know about him or his past? I finally limp in with "You have too many freckles for a trouble-maker," but I'm pretty sure we both know what I'd been thinking.

"Actually, I was a pretty good kid in high school. I partied, but it never got out of hand." He notices that I've finally stopped eating, so he starts to stack the dishes. "After my accident, though, I was a mess." He sets the plates in his lap and pushes back from the table. "Coffee?"

"No, thanks."

"I have decaf."

I shake my head.

"Or would you like a drink? I don't drink, but I've got some brandy here somewhere I bought for a recipe."

"I'm actually not drinking right now either," I tell him.

He glances at me over his shoulder. "AA?"

I shake my head, tempted to answer "PG" but instead I say, "I'm just taking a break."

He grins. "One day at a time."

"Don't you get all twelve steppy on me."

He laughs and wheels into the kitchen. I follow.

"So, Wednesday night I had dinner with Father Barnes."

He glances over his shoulder with one brow raised. "Uh huh . . ."

"No, no, it was nothing like that."

While Luke rinses the dishes in the sink, I describe my evening with Father Barnes, not mentioning my flirting with the priest, but instead discussing his prodigious alcohol consumption.

When I finish, Luke turns his chair to face me. "It's not like he doesn't know where to turn for help. There's an AA meeting twice a week at his church."

"He needs to quit drinking."

"Does he *want* to quit?"

I shrug.

"I'm happy to talk to him, Mattie, but keep in mind, needing to change your life isn't enough. You have to want to change it." Luke's got a funny look on his face. I wonder if we're still talking about Father Barnes.

"I understand," I tell him, and it's true.

"Alcoholics Anonymous saved my life. Well, AA and Aunt Fritter."

"Sounds like a hell of a story," I say.

"It's an awful story," he replies. "But I don't mind sharing it if you want to hear it."

I'm not sure I do, but I can't think of a way to gracefully decline, so I nod.

"I was riding pretty high at nineteen. I'd gotten a baseball scholarship to a junior college that had a good record of getting players into the minors. A month before I left for school a group of us were out driving around." He sighs. "You've heard this story a million times. We were all drunk. The car missed a turn . . ."

"Shit," I whisper. He's right—everyone has heard this story.

"Once I got out of the hospital, about all I did was drink."

"I can imagine."

He gives me a sad smile. "I hope not. I wouldn't want anyone trying to imagine me the way I was back then. So full of self-pity and rage." He rolls to the Keurig coffeemaker and puts a pod in the basket. "The two in the backseat were just a little banged up, I was thrown from the car. The other kid died." He pauses for several seconds before he adds, "I spent a couple years wishing I had, too."

I take a step closer and put my hand on his shoulder. He covers my hand with his own.

"Well," Luke says. "We've talked about me and about Father Barnes." He looks up at me and smiles. "It's time to talk about you."

I laugh. "No way."

"Oh come on."

"I'm not interesting."

"Okay, then just one thing," he says. "Tell me one thing about Mattie Wallace that not everybody knows."

Luke is smiling, his hand still resting on mine, and I know he's showing an interest in me because he's a nice guy and nice guys are interested in more than themselves. Maybe that's why I don't date nice guys. What he doesn't understand is that my past is a lot like the couch in Nick's apartment. On the surface it's fine, reasonably comfortable, the Naugahyde a little scuffed, but presentable enough. But the last thing you ever want to do, and I mean *the very last thing*, is stick your hand down between the cushions and start feeling around.

Luke, however, has gotten personal—his was certainly a between-the-cushions story—and this puts me a little off balance. Frantically, I rummage through my past, searching for an honest story I'm willing to tell, all the while trying to think of a way to sidestep his request without lying or coming off like a total jerk. And then suddenly, Luke provides me with the answer. He begins to trace a slow circle on my wrist with his thumb, and I shiver, feeling my nipples grow hard.

"Not everybody knows I'm good in bed," I say.

He pulls me onto his lap. I have one hand resting on his chest, and I can feel his heart racing beneath my fingers. I'm a little surprised to find that mine is beating fast as well. He runs a hand up my back to my shoulder blades. I lean forward and kiss his mouth.

When I pull away to look at his face, he frowns slightly and averts his gaze. I'm not sure what he's thinking, but there's some worry brewing under that carrottop.

"What's wrong?" I ask.

"Charlie Franklin called today," he says. "We need to talk about it."

Something is up, and from the look on Luke's face it's not something that's going to make me happy. But right now Luke smells like soap and aftershave, and his hand is warm on my back. And he's looking at me as if he thinks I'm something special.

"Can it wait until later?" I ask.

He answers me with another kiss.

I'm nervous. Although I'm certain that the awkward gropings of my first sexual experience will be nothing like what's about to happen on these high-thread-count sheets, I'm feeling a similar flutter of fear. I've never slept with a handicapped guy, and I'm not sure I've ever slept with such a genuinely nice guy either. There's no doubt in my mind that there are a million stupid things I could do to screw this up.

Luke emerges from the bathroom wearing only a pair of blue boxers, and wheels himself to the bed. I was right in my estimation of his build, he looks like a body builder from the waist up, and even his legs, covered in fine red hair, are not as thin as I'd imagined them to be. In one fluid motion he puts his fists on the mattress and lifts himself out of his chair and onto the bed, taking a few seconds to arrange his legs under the covers.

He opens his hand and reveals a condom package, which he tucks under his pillow.

"I knew you were a Boy Scout," I tell him.

"Be prepared," he replies, lifting the covers for a peek. When he sees that I'm naked, he grins and shimmies out of his underwear, tossing it on the seat of his wheelchair.

"I've been hoping this would happen."

"Since when? It seems like all I do is annoy you."

He grins. "Since you handed me a piece of paper that said *twat waffle*."

I laugh.

"I'm still waiting to hear what that was actually about," he says.

"Sorry. We women must maintain an air of mystery."

Luke chuckles, reaching out to cup the side of my face. "You are the most exasperating and ridiculous woman I've ever met."

"But in a really good way, right?"

"The best way," he replies, pulling me to him.

At this most inopportune moment, his cell phone, lying on the bedside table, rings. Luke reaches out an arm and lifts it to his face for just long enough to turn it off, then he drops it back to the table and turns to me.

"Nobody important?"

"My mother."

"Wow. Her calling right now is a little . . ."

"Oedipal?"

"I was just going to say freaky, but let's go with Oedipal. I should have said Oedipal."

"You did work in a library."

"Yeah, I should try to sound well read."

"That's tough, huh?"

"Hey, I was no English major."

"What was your major?"

"Jack Daniel's," I tell him, and it's almost the truth. I didn't go to college, but that's certainly what I concentrated on between the ages of eighteen and twenty-one.

He runs a finger down my arm. He's grinning, and I return his smile, but my misgivings must show on my face, because he reaches over and pulls me into his arms, my head resting on his shoulder.

"What's wrong?" he asks.

I prop myself back up on an elbow and look down at his earnest expression. The light on the nightstand is behind me, my tangled, messy hair making a complicated shadow on the pillow beneath his head. "I'm a little nervous, I guess."

"Why?"

"You're not exactly my type."

A cloud passes over his expression, and even in the dim light I can see his green eyes darken. Anger? Hurt? I'm not sure. I don't know him well enough yet to read the difference.

"You're nice," I hurry to explain. "Dependable. Gainfully employed."

I'm relieved to see his expression clear and a small smile lift the corner of his lips.

"So you only sleep with cruel, flakey losers?"

"Yeah, I mostly date musicians."

"Ah . . ." Luke reaches up and tucks a few strands of my hair behind my ear. "I played the clarinet when I was a kid."

I trace the shape of his smile with a fingertip. "Close enough," I tell him, and then lean over and press my smiling mouth against his.

Luke has one hand steady on my back as the other moves down my neck to my swollen, pregnancy-tender breasts. I try not to flinch, but I must have, because without missing a beat he lightens the pressure until his touch is pleasure, not pain. When he nuzzles my neck and oh so gently rolls my nipple between his fingertips, I begin to suspect that this Boy Scout is going to have no trouble earning a merit badge this evening.

As he pulls me closer for another kiss, letting his right hand engage in an extremely skillful investigation of my lady parts, I slide my hand down Luke's muscled chest. He catches my wrist when I reach his happy-trail.

"Just so you know," he says, "the accident caused a spinal crush injury that damaged nerves, but left some reflexes in place. The nerves that control leg movement are in the same area as the nerves that control psychogenic erections."

"In other words . . ."

"If nothing is going on down there yet, don't think I'm not interested." He pauses to run his hand up my arm, across my ribs. "I am interested," he adds, his fingers tracing a slow path down my belly. "And capable. But usually only direct stimulation will—"

"Like this?" I ask.

He smiles.

It doesn't take long for me to discover that in addition to the agonizingly accurate knowledge of female anatomy he is demonstrating, Luke is abundantly blessed in other areas.

"Good Lord," I say. "Is this weapon registered?"

He grins, pinking up nicely.

I laugh. "Hung like a pony, but blushes like a little girl."

He laughs, too, but keeps his fingers moving.

"You know . . ." My breathing is embarrassingly ragged. "I'm very ready for you to give me that condom."

With a grin, Luke tears open the package and hands it to me. While I'm doing the honors, he reaches back up under his pillow and pulls out a plastic strap, which he then fastens over the base of the condom.

I laugh. "What is that, an adult toy?"

He shakes his head and pulls me on top of him, saying, "Shhhhh."

Belly to belly we lie, his chest hair tickling my ribs. I'm moving slowly, tentatively. He grabs my hips but I resist his efforts to help. "Easy there, Howdy," I whisper. "Don't hurt me."

I feel his chest rise and fall in a chuckle, but to my relief he moves his hands up to my back. I know he thinks I'm joking, but honestly, this man is a Nick and a half. Besides which, I'm discovering that pregnancy has made more than just my breasts overly sensitive.

I've heard it said that even if you're used to driving a compact car, once you size up to an SUV it doesn't take long to start enjoying yourself, and I can tell you that's true. Only a couple of minutes pass before I feel the need to engage in some very unladylike panting and shouting. Luke is smiling, but is awfully quiet the whole time, although he looks extremely pleased with himself when I collapse on his chest.

I feel stupid having to ask, but I do. "So . . . uh . . . are you . . . done?"

His chest moves again in quiet laughter. "I'm finished if you are."

"I mean did you . . . do you want me to . . ." I prop myself up on my hands so I can see his face. He's still smiling, but now he's shaking his head.

He lifts a curl of my hair and uses it to tickle my nose. "Sex is still great, don't get me wrong, but things don't really work like they did before the accident."

"That sucks."

He shrugs. "Not being able to walk sucks, too. But I'm lucky. I'm alive. I'm having a good time when the woman I'm with is enjoying herself."

"Then you must have just had an extremely good time," I reply.

He grins. "I really didn't expect you to be a screamer."

"Shut up," I say, laughing.

"Oooh, now who's blushing?" he teases, and he's right.

I duck my head against his chest, embarrassed. He laughs, and then he wraps his arms around me and squeezes me tight.

CHAPTER 46

It was still raining when I left my mother at the McLeod funeral, and though I hustled, I barely got home with enough time to take a shower and shave my legs before I headed out to Eddy's place. Just as I'd hoped, the lunch date went into overtime. We rolled around on his filthy sheets for a while, drank some beer, ate a frozen pizza, and then finally showed up at the Rusty Nail to work the dinner shift.

My mother called me three times that night—at around eight o'clock, at eight thirty, and then at ten. I didn't answer any of the calls. I had plans with Eddy for later, and I was worried my mother was calling with some random errand that would interfere with that. I'd just seen her that morning, I remember thinking. She couldn't have anything all that important to say.

I followed Eddy back to his place after work and had every intention of staying the night, but I couldn't fall asleep. The faucet in his bathroom dripped, his downstairs neighbors had their television on, and I discovered that sleeping on oily gray sheets was much more difficult than screwing on them. So I dressed quietly in the dark and slipped out of his apartment without waking him. It was late, or early depending on how you look at it. The streets were empty and the temperature had dropped enough that I regretted not bringing a jacket. The sky was finally clear and the moon near full. Steam rose from the gutters on either side of the street, shifting in the breeze, making me drive through misty ghost after ghost.

As soon as I pulled into my apartment complex, I noticed the police cruiser, but I gave it little mind as I parked in my allotted covered spot and walked to my building. The cop car was running, but its lights were off; I could see two officers sitting inside. One turned toward me, watching while I walked past. I was almost to my apartment door when I heard car doors open and shut. I glanced back and saw both officers heading in my direction.

"Shit," I whispered under my breath. I looked back again. They were still coming right toward me. I turned slowly to face them. All I could think of was how sorry I was to have given that cop false information when he'd pulled me over that morning. Lying to a cop is not smart; why hadn't I just told him the truth and taken the damn ticket? As the officers approached, I tried to get a grip. Maybe it's something else, I thought. Maybe they're finally here to investigate the wienie-waggler in the next building.

The younger one wore his police hat and carried an aluminum clipboard case; the other held his hat in his hands. They stopped in front of me and nodded.

"May I help you, Officers?" My voice sounded a little squeaky.

The shorter one wearing his hat spoke. "Are you Matilda Wallace?"

I debated how to answer that question. If this had anything to do with this morning's ticket, it might be better to say *no* and continue to impersonate my mother. But if they already knew I'd lied, or if this wasn't about that at all, and I lied now for no reason . . .

"I'm Ms. Wallace," I finally reply. Safe enough.

"Are you related to Eugenia Louise Wallace?"

Shit shit shit! I couldn't believe it. This *was* about that stupid traffic stop. Who knew cops investigated stuff like this at three fucking a.m.?

"Well . . ." I paused, struggling to think of how to answer this in such a way as to not dig my hole any deeper, while also not acknowledging that there was a hole. To their credit, the officers just waited for my answer. They seemed as interested to see what I would come up with as I was.

Finally I just gave up and said, "She's my mother."

"May we come in for a moment?" the tall one asked, giving his hat a little half spin in his hand.

"Okay . . ." After a few shaky attempts I managed to unlock the door, trying to remember just how filthy the apartment was. When we stepped inside and turned on the light that question was quickly answered. Pretty filthy.

I pushed the newspapers off the couch and waved my arm at the now empty cushions, and then sat across from them in our tatty club chair. I wasn't sure why they wanted to have a chat before arresting me, but if it put those handcuffs off for a few minutes, I was game.

"Ms. Wallace . . ." the shorter one said. "Matilda . . ."

"Mattie," I corrected him. Looking around the apartment I noticed that my roommate Paula had, once again, gathered all the empty beer cans and stacked them into a pyramid on top of the television. Obviously this took much more time and effort than just throwing them away. I suspected she was trying to tell me something.

The cop nodded and then opened his mouth to begin again.

"I'm sorry," I said, preparing to beg for leniency. But I stopped as soon as the words were out of my mouth, because the police officer had also started speaking, and his words had been identical to mine. "I'm sorry," he had just said. For some reason we were both sorry.

He looked at me, puzzled.

I felt my original worry shift to a new one. What the hell was going on? "You first," I said.

The dark-haired cop glanced at the other one and then took a deep breath. "We regret to inform you that your mother was involved in a motor vehicle accident."

He paused, waiting perhaps for me to ask a question, but I stayed silent and shifted my gaze back to Paula's can tower. I was pretty sure I knew what was coming next.

"She died as a result of her injuries," he continued. "I'm very sorry for your loss."

I counted fourteen cans—eleven Miller Lites and three Keystones, which was hardly fair for Paula to have included since it was her boyfriend, Greg, who drank Keystone.

"What happened?" I asked, my voice only a whisper.

"Her car struck a telephone pole. It was a single car accident," the policeman said. "Luckily, no one else was injured."

"Yeah, lucky," I replied.

He flushed slightly and exchanged a look with the policeman sitting next to him. In retrospect, I think the younger man was seeking reassurance; it's possible that this was his first time to do this sort of thing and he was checking with the other officer to see if it was going okay. But at the time I read that glance as some kind of judgment of my reaction, or lack thereof.

I tried to think of something to say, but all I could come up with was, "It wasn't her car."

The young officer said, "Excuse me?"

"She was driving my jeep. She thought it would be easier to drive."

He nodded. "I'm afraid the vehicle is badly damaged."

"She was weak from chemo. She has cancer." I paused and then corrected myself. "*Had* cancer."

"I'm very sorry," the younger policeman said again. And he looked sorry; this was hard for him, I could see that. I wondered if his mother was still alive, if he were imagining having to be on my side of our conversation.

"I shouldn't have let her drive," I said. "It was too soon. She probably got tired, and she couldn't—"

"Ms. Wallace," the older cop interrupted me, clearing his throat. "The coroner will let us know for sure, but I believe that alcohol was involved in the accident."

"Alcohol?" I was confused.

"We believe your mother was driving while intoxicated."

"But she hadn't had a drink in months," I said.

"Until today," he replied.

I looked at the newspapers piled next to the policeman, the napkin with a half-eaten sandwich sitting on the end table. I glanced back over at the television. I remember thinking that I really wished Paula had just this once thrown the damn cans away.

The policemen stood in unison and walked to the door. I followed.

The officer who had done most of the talking turned back and handed me a business card and told me the Community Services office opened at seven. He went on to say that if I wanted to see my mother's body it would be available for viewing with an appointment.

"Do I need to see her?" I asked.

The tall one replied, somewhat cryptically I thought, "That's up to you."

"No, I mean, to identify her."

"An ID was made from her driver's license," said the dark-haired one. He opened his aluminum report case and pulled out a pink slip of paper. "You'll need this receipt to present to property management."

It all felt very businesslike. I glanced down at the paper covered with faded print about office hours and victim's rights. At the bottom a five-digit number had been handwritten in blue pen. "So, how do I—"

"Call the office at seven. They'll answer any questions you have."

And with that they slipped out the door and walked through the dark parking lot to their car. I checked my phone for the time—three fifteen.

My mother's death, which had been visible on the horizon for so long, had now suddenly arrived. I'd be lying if I didn't say that along with the shock, there was perhaps the smallest sense of relief, like an exhale of a breath held just a little too long. With the business card in one hand and the pink paper in the other, I first sat on the couch and then lay down. The cushions still held the warmth of the cops' bodies.

The worst has happened, I told myself. *This is it. This is as bad as it's going to get.*

CHAPTER 47

While Luke and I were tangling his bedsheets, the storm that'd been brewing all day finally broke. We're dressed now and in his darkened living room, standing—well, I'm standing next to Luke's chair—in front of the window. The street glistens with water and the trees whip back and forth in the wind. He reaches up and takes my hand, and for a second I think he's going to ask me to stay over.

"When Charlie called this afternoon," Luke says, "I started to explain your situation, but he already knew all about it. The first thing he told me was to advance you some money."

I'm glad Luke is looking out the window rather than at me. I'm not sure what he'd see on my face right now. "Great," I reply.

Luke nods, but there's something in his silence that tells me he's not finished.

"What was the second thing Charlie told you?" I ask.

"That I'd overstepped my authority when I gave you access to Ms. Thayer's house and the belongings therein."

I'm not sure what to say to that. "Oh" is all I come up with.

"I'm afraid I'll need that key back."

"But all my stuff is still there—"

"Patty will help you pack."

"You mean monitor me to make sure I don't steal anything."

Luke glances up at me but only for a second. "Honestly, I have no idea why Charlie is doing this."

Considering the timing, I'd be willing to bet that Fritter had something to do with it, but I could be wrong. Maybe, unlike Luke, Charlie Franklin *does* do criminal background checks.

"So is this all happening right now?" I ask. "Tonight?"

Luke gives me a small smile. "Well, it was supposed to, and as far as Charlie is ever going to know it did happen tonight. But I talked to Patty and she agreed with me; you can stay until tomorrow morning. We trust you."

"Well, thank you for that."

He shrugs off my thanks. "The paperwork is on the coffee table."

I turn on a lamp and then read and sign the agreement, which says I will use their firm to sell the property, and I must vacate the premises immediately. Lying next to the document is an envelope with a stack of hundred-dollar bills.

"It's five thousand," Luke tells me.

I start to reach for it, but he stops me, saying, "Patty will bring it when she comes tomorrow morning."

"What time?"

"Nine o'clock."

I nod. *This is what you came for*, I tell myself, but it doesn't feel that way to me now. Instead of feeling relief that I can finally leave, a weight settles on my chest. It's a familiar weight, the kind that comes with an opportunity missed, a last chance blown.

"I thought I'd have more time," I say.

"We could make it nine thirty—"

"No, I mean, I was so close."

He wheels his chair over to the couch, joining me in the lamp's pool of light. "Close to what?"

I shrug. "It's pretty clear that for my mother there was a *before* and an *after*, and in between something happened to her. I really wanted to know what that was."

"It's too late to make things better for your mother, Mattie."

"I know." I almost add, *but it's not too late for me.* But then I look again at the money sitting on the table and realize that now it probably is.

"You'll still be in town until your car is fixed, right?" he asks.

"The car is ready. All I have to do is pay."

"I see," he says, nodding. "Well, you still wouldn't have to leave right away if you didn't want to."

"What reason do I have to hang around?"

This would be the perfect time for him to tell me he wants me to stay.

He doesn't.

In the car, I turn on the radio to take the edge off an awkward silence that feels darker than the usual postcoital loss for words. The DJ of the classic rock channel we're listening to must be a mind reader, because he's got some Beatles-music-for-suicidal-types marathon going on. We go from "Yesterday" to "While My Guitar Gently Weeps" right into "Eleanor Rigby." The rain further deepens the mood. Luke's wipers thump steadily, always close but never quite on the beat.

He breaks the silence. "So, about the dogs . . ."

I have a flash of dismay, remembering that they're gone and then worrying that he knows I've lost them, before I realize that he must be asking if I'm going to take them with me when I leave.

"My neighbor wants them," I say.

"Really?"

"Oh yeah. He's a dog person." Who knows? It could be true.

The silence swells again to fill the space, and I'm relieved when we finally pull into my grandmother's driveway. He idles the car up as close as he can get it to the house, then pulls a neatly collapsed umbrella from behind his seat and offers it to me.

I shake my head. "I won't melt," I tell him. "I'm not made of sugar."

He smiles. "You could have fooled me."

His cheesy remark just lies there, wedged between us while we both try to figure out how to end this evening. It feels as if there's something unsaid with us in the car, taking up all the air. My grandmother's house is dark, but JJ's porch lights are on, their yellow glow on my bare legs almost makes it look like I have a September tan. On the radio "Eleanor Rigby" fades into the bouncing guitar of "Blackbird." I can't stop myself from hoping Luke is trying to think of a way to ask me to stay in town for a while.

"I love this song," he says. His face is mostly in shadow, but I can tell he's not smiling anymore.

"Me too," I reply and it's true. Of course we love it. My mother loved it, too. It's the theme song of broken things.

He looks down at his steering wheel and sighs. "The night of my accident . . . I was the one driving the car. It was my fault."

He pauses, but I stay quiet and let him talk. We're in familiar territory now; guilt is an old friend of mine.

"I got probation. I guess they figured being in a chair for the rest of my life was punishment enough."

"I'm sorry," I say.

He looks over at me with a tight smile. "I'm fine. I mean, I'm working at being fine. I've talked to a therapist, to Wayne's parents. I lost my best friend, but they lost a son. They say they forgive me, if you can believe it. It's been ten years." He shrugs, adding, "Things are as settled as something like that can ever be. Someone is dead, and it's my fault. I just have to live with that. There's nothing I can do to change the past."

He sighs and takes my hand in his. I look away, my heart pounding in my chest. When he sees me blinking back tears, he gives my hand a squeeze. He thinks the tears are for him.

"What I'm trying to say is . . . no matter what happened to your mom, it's too late to go back and make it right. You can't save her, you can't save Father Barnes, or me, or anybody else. The only person you can ever save is yourself, and it's never too late for that."

He's waiting for me to tell him that I understand, but all I can manage is a nod. I do understand. I just don't believe it.

I open the car door and turn back, opening my mouth to say *Good night, Howdy*, but then I think of that puppet propped up, his useless legs dangling off Cowboy Bob's lap, and I wonder if that's what Luke pictured every time I called him Howdy. I hope not.

"Good night, Luke Lambert."

"Good-bye, Mattie Wallace," he replies.

I lean over and give him a peck on the cheek and a little smile. And then I reach up and ruffle his hair one last time.

I hurry through the rain to the garage to retrieve the camera bag and strap from their hiding place in the washer, and my finally dry laundry from the dryer. The gate still stands open, the backyard still empty. The bowl of dog food on the front porch also looks undisturbed, and inside the house is even quieter than it was this morning, the air more stale, the stairs steeper.

Up in my mother's room I leave the lights off while I change out of my grandmother's tweed and into my clean jeans and a T-shirt. I walk to the window and look outside. In JJ's house I can see a blue flicker through his blinds that tell me his television is on, but the other houses that I can see are dark. The streetlights look like starbursts through the watery blur. While I stand there, the rain picks up, the wind pushing the drops against the glass until it almost sounds like hail. The fresh smell of the storm seeps in through the cracks in the casement.

A miss is as good as a mile, Queeg likes to say, and he's right. Almost changing my life feels exactly like not changing it at all.

I pull out my phone.

Nick answers on the first ring. It's noisy again on his end, and I remember that it's Friday and he's almost certainly at a gig. He shouts "hang on," so I do. A few seconds later the noise stops abruptly.

"I'm in the alley," he says.

I smile. Nick and I met in an alley behind a bar.

"Remember the night we first met?" I say. "We shared a cigarette, and we swapped stories about our shitty parents. You told me about your dad and how he never came to hear you play. And I told you my story about the time I almost drowned while my mom was busy flirting with her boyfriend. Remember?"

It was cold that night in the alley and I wasn't wearing a coat because I didn't want to cover up my new dress. My friends had stayed inside the bar, but when the band took a break I'd followed the handsome guitar player, Nick, out into the alley. My teeth chattered the whole time I talked about trying to swim to the second sandbar and how I could remember everything except for how I got from the water back to the beach. While I told the story, Nick carefully lifted the cigarette from my shaking fingers and put it to his lips, squinting at me through the smoke. He wasn't shivering. He was wearing a jacket.

"Yeah," Nick replies. "You had on that short red dress."

"Do you remember what you said when I finished my story?" I pause to give him a chance to answer. When he doesn't, I continue. "You said it could have been my mom. That maybe I couldn't see her on the beach because she was already in the water, swimming out to save me."

The phone is quiet. I can't even hear him breathing.

"Nick?"

"I'm here."

"And then you asked me, 'Was her hair wet?' You meant after, when it was all over. You said that if my mom's hair was wet, then I would know she'd been in the water."

"Mattie . . ." His voice is quiet. "What the hell is going on with you?"

"Rico didn't take your guitar strap," I say.

He doesn't respond.

"I'll bring it back. I'm coming home tomorrow."

More silence.

"I shouldn't have taken it. I'm sorry."

I hear him sigh. He's eight hundred miles away, but I don't have to be able to see him to know that he just tilted his head to the left and shrugged his shoulders the way he always does when he acknowledges an apology without really accepting it.

"I've got to go," he tells me.

"Wait," I say. "What would you say if I told you I wanted to have a baby?"

He doesn't reply, but from his end I hear a faint voice and a muffled response from Nick. I wonder who's with him in the alley. I wonder if it's a woman. Maybe they're sharing a cigarette.

"Nick?"

"Listen, Mattie, I need to get back inside."

"You didn't answer my question."

"You want me to answer your question? Okay. I'd say you're fucking crazy, that's what I'd say." He's angry now. I can picture him, his face flushed, his lips pressed together. "I gotta go. We have another set."

"Wait, one more thing."

"What?" He's practically shouting.

"That first night . . . what did I say when you asked me about her hair?"

"Whose hair? What the hell are you talking about?"

"My mother's." My throat is pinched; I'm struggling to get the words out. "Did I say her hair was wet, or dry? I can't remember what I told you."

"Jesus Christ, Mattie, what is *wrong* with you?"

I consider his question. He hangs up long before I come up with the answer.

I read an article once about our instinct for survival, about how even a person determined to kill himself is often betrayed by his body in the end. Feet struggle to find the knocked-over chair, a gag reflex fights the swallowed pills, exhausted arms pull to one side, turning the disconsolate swimmer back, and back again, toward shore.

Giving up is easier for the mind than the body.

Maybe that explains why I open my purse and take out the negatives.

I know it's over. There's not a doubt in my mind. It's been over from the moment I told Nick I was coming home. No, from the moment I saw the envelope full of cash on Luke's coffee table. Or maybe from the moment I got into my car and pointed it west. No. Earlier still. It was over the night my mother died.

For five years I've been fighting the tide, barely keeping my head above water, memories of the past always there, grabbing at my ankles, trying to pull me under. Surely it's time to just accept the fact that sinking is not only inevitable but a welcome relief.

And yet . . .

Here I am, standing once more in the darkroom's amber glow.

CHAPTER 48

I don't have enough paper to print all the negatives, so I print contact sheets to see what I have. Once they're dry, I lay them flat and study the tiny black-and-white images, all the while certain that this is a giant waste of time. I should be packing. I should be sleeping. I should be doing anything other than inhaling nauseating chemical fumes.

There are only a few of my mother since she was usually taking the pictures. But there are several of Trip, a few shots of a lake, some squirrels. Obviously most of the pictures were taken on one of their clandestine camping trips, although part of one roll must have been used before or after, because there's also a good shot of a woman smiling above what looks to be a birthday cake. I decide to just print five, so I go through the sheets and mark the ones I want to enlarge.

Doing this goes more quickly than showing Tawny how to do it. One by one the images appear in the developer: first the woman leaning down over a birthday cake, her smiling face uplit. Then there are three of my mother, and one of Trip—this one a portrait, head and chest. I stack them in the wash tray and carry them to the sink to rinse. In the bright lights of the bathroom, I swish them around looking at one then the other.

The woman sitting at the table with the birthday cake can only be Tilda, my mother's mother. I recognize the setting as the kitchen in this house. She looks to be in her late thirties, I'm guessing eight or nine years older than I am now. She's wearing a floral apron that reminds me of something from a *Father Knows Best* episode, and her short curly hair frames her face as she leans down over the cake. The tickle of recognition I felt earlier changes to a flush of understanding now that I'm looking at the full-size picture in the light. I might resemble my mother around the edges, but I look a lot like this woman, similar enough that someone taking a quick glance at this photo could mistake it for a picture of me with short hair. Comprehension washes over me so suddenly that it's almost a physical response.

Fritter's brother, Jonah, thought he was apologizing to Tilda.

The photo of Trip is a nice one, enough of a close-up that I can see what a handsome boy he was. His expression is serious, his wet hair pushed back from his face. There is beaded water on his neck and chest.

The three pictures of my mother were all taken on a camping trip, I think. I imagine it went like this: my mother taking photos of the woods and of Trip, and then him picking up the camera and taking a few shots of her. My mother is laughing in the first picture, her wild hair blowing around her shoulders. In the second she's mugging for the camera, eyes crossed, tongue out. In the third photo she's not smiling, but instead looking straight at the camera, her brows knitted slightly as if she'd just asked a question. Bra straps or straps from a light-colored swimsuit cross her bare shoulders and her hair is wet and slicked back from her face. More than in the first two, in this photo I can see the woman this girl will become—sad, a little tired, looking for answers. Even the hair is more familiar in this shot, darkened by the water and pulled back rather than loose.

When they're rinsed I carry them to the darkroom and hang them on the wire: Tilda on one end, Trip on the other and the three faces of Genie in between. Standing there, looking at face after face, I realize I'm holding my breath. I step closer and look at the picture of Trip: square chin, long, straight nose, wide mouth with a full lower lip—check. I step closer and then farther away, studying the whole group of damp prints.

Holy shit.

And here it is—mystery solved. I can imagine my mother at nineteen years old, a little bit pregnant, just like me, and standing right where I am now. She's looking at prints of these same photos drying on this same sagging wire, and knowing then what I think I know now.

It's late, way too late to call anyone unless it's with news of death or injury, but I hurry to the bedroom to get my phone anyway. I have to float this theory past somebody. I can't call Queeg this late, can I? Not Nick. Luke? Maybe . . .

When I pick up my phone, I see I have a missed call that came in just a few minutes ago from a local number. I try to call Luke, but it goes straight to voice mail, and I remember him switching his phone off earlier; he must not have turned it back on.

Crap.

I hesitate, looking at the display of that missed call. It's crazy late to return a call from a number I don't recognize, but I'm just too curious not to check it out.

The phone rings twice and then a woman answers. "St. Benedict Episcopal Church."

The voice is muffled, but familiar. "Karleen?"

"Yes. May I help you?"

"It's Mattie."

"Hi," she says, sounding surprised. "What's up?"

"You just called me," I reply.

"Oh. That's right."

"Why are you at the church at one thirty in the morning?"

"Because I thought Father Barnes might have your number in his Rolodex."

Her answer brings me up short. "Rolodex?"

"One of those round things with cards in it—"

"I know what a Rolodex is, Karleen. I also know what a Brontosaurus is, but they're extinct, too."

"Apatosaurus."

"What?" She's making no sense, and her voice sounds funny, her consonants blurry. "Karleen, are you drunk?"

"They changed the name of Brontosaurus. It's Apatosaurus now."

"Karleen?"

There's a pause, then she says, "I couldn't find a Rolodex."

"I'm not surprised."

"So I went through his trash and didn't find anything with your number on it, but when I listened to the messages on his answering machine, there you were."

I find myself impressed by her resourcefulness and her ruthless nosiness. She's Nancy fuckin' Drew.

"And for your information," she continues, "I have been drinking, but I'm not drunk."

I suspect she's wrong about that, but I decide to take advantage of the situation. If she's lucid enough to sleuth out my phone number, she's lucid enough to answer questions.

Thinking back on my visit to the nursing home and my newly

discovered resemblance to my grandmother, I ask Karleen, "Do you know Fritter's brother?"

"I'm sorry I called so late."

"No, I'm glad you did. So do you know Jonah Jackson?"

"Yup. Mr. Jackson used to work on the church van for free until he got too old and sick. I think he's in a nursing home."

"He is. I met him."

"How's he doing?"

"Okay, I guess," I reply. "Listen, did my mom ever meet him?"

"Who?"

I take a breath and back up a little, speaking slowly. "Jonah Jackson. He's Trip's dad, right?"

"Yup."

"So did Jonah Jackson and my mom ever meet each other?"

"I don't see how. He grew up here, but he moved off after college. He didn't move back until he retired. Genie was long gone by then."

Hmmm. Now I'm doubting my theory. "So he never met my mom."

"Not that I remember."

"Not even when Trip was here that summer? Could his dad have come for a visit?"

"Trip's family lived in one of the *M* states . . . a cold one. Minnesota. Michigan." Karleen pauses for a minute and I hear thumping in the background, like she's opening and closing drawers.

"What's going on there, Karleen?"

"Hey, it was Maine. I remember now. And Trip's dad *did* visit that summer. I remember because he brought a Maine snow globe."

I feel the hairs on the back of my neck lift. "Snow globe?"

"You know one of those things where if you shake it—"

"I know what a *snow globe* is, Karleen."

"He brought it for Trip, but Trip didn't want it. I guess it is a pretty lame gift. Mr. Jackson probably shoulda gotten him a watch maybe, or new sneakers, or maybe a baseball glove—"

"So what happened to it?"

"To what?"

I try to keep the annoyance out of my voice. "The snow globe."

"Since Trip didn't want it and your mom was there, his dad gave it to her. It had a lighthouse, and when you shook it instead of snow it had—"

"Birds."

Karleen laughs. "She kept that ugly thing?"

My eyes fill with tears.

"Hang on," Karleen says, and then there are more thuds and banging sounds on the line, louder this time.

"Karleen?" Now I hear only silence on the other end and I worry that I've lost her. "Karleen?" I ask again.

This time she answers with, "Damn it."

"What's going on?"

"I'm looking for a cigarette."

"Can I ask another question while you look?"

"I found matches."

"Great. Listen, what did Trip look like?"

She laughs again. "Why are you asking me? You've seen him."

"That photo is black-and-white. What did he look like in color?"

"Auburn hair. Hazel eyes maybe? Green? Shit. I can't remember. I'm so stupid."

"You're not stupid—"

"Orten says I am."

"Karleen—"

"His hair is gray now, but his eyes should be the same. What color are they?"

"Orten's?"

"No, silly," Karleen replies. "Trip's."

She's obviously had more to drink than she's admitting. "Karleen, how should I know?"

Her reply is lost to a rattling smokers' cough. "Hang on." She sets the phone down, presumably on Father Barnes's desk. I wait, straining to hear. After what feels like twenty minutes, but was probably only twenty seconds, I hear the phone scrape against the wood.

"I'm back," she says. "But I really need to get going." She sounds tired, the slurring worse.

"Wait, Karleen—"

"Hey, I almost forgot what I called to tell you. I found a postcard."

"A postcard?"

"From your mom. I still have one. It has a picture of a beach on the front. And on the back it says . . . shit. I left my glasses at home."

"You can show me later."

"It's okay, I memorized it. It says, *Having a great time with my beautiful daughter. Wish you were here.*"

I wipe at my eyes again.

"Maybe I could come by tomorrow and see it," I say.

She gives me a dangerous-sounding chuckle. "That might not work out so good."

I'm getting a bad feeling about this. "Karleen, what's going on?"

She heaves a sigh deep enough to start another coughing fit. "I need to get home," she finally chokes out. "I need a cigarette. And I should check on Orten."

Something in her voice sets off a warning. "What do you mean *check on Orten?* Where is he?"

"I can't believe I forgot my cigarettes."

"Karleen, answer the question."

"What question?"

"*Orten*, Karleen. Where is he?"

She sighs. "He's at the house."

"Your house?"

"Well, technically it's his house. The lease is in his name. That's what he tells me all the time."

"Are you sure?"

"Well, I haven't seen the lease . . ."

"Are you sure he's at your house—his house?"

"He wasn't moving when I left."

"What?"

"I took your suggestion."

"*My* suggestion? What did you do?"

"I found my old softball bat."

I feel a sickening twist in my stomach. "What happened, Karleen?"

"I hid behind the bedroom door, see, and—"

"Wait. Take it step by step. Start at the very beginning."

"Okay, okay." She sighs and then says, "Step one. Elvis died."

I'm momentarily at a loss for words. Of course, to be fair, I hadn't specified what I meant by *the very beginning*.

"I don't think we have time to start in the 1970s. Why don't you start with what happened after I saw you this morning."

"I am," she insists. "I finished cleaning and then took out the trash. That's when I saw him behind the Dumpster."

"Oh my God . . ." She's talking about soup kitchen Elvis, the man with a cat named Colonel Parker.

"His eyes and his mouth were half open, and flies were all in his—"

"Stop. Please. Stop. I get the idea." I sit down on the bed, hard.

It was her mentioning the flies. That's what weakened my knees and turned my skin clammy and cold. "Okay. Go on."

"The cops came, and they talked to everybody, but they talked to me for a long time. I mean, it's not like they thought I killed him or anything. Elvis still had a tourniquet on his arm, and his kit was laying there, so it was pretty obvious what happened, but they still gave me a hard time. They kept hassling me about my black eye . . ."

"Oh, Karleen . . ."

"It was bad. Anyway, after all that I went home early and . . . Wait. What step am I on? Two?"

"It doesn't matter."

"Step two. Orten came home. He was drunk. And because I was upset about Elvis and the cops, I'd been drinking a little, too. Is that a step?"

"It doesn't matter. Just keep going."

"Okay, step three. No, wait, four?" Her voice sounds even worse, and I'm starting to worry that the slurring is from more than booze—maybe a split lip or missing teeth. "Can we please do this later?" she says. "I really need to get home."

"Wait! Don't go. What if Orten is awake? Call the police— have them go."

"Are you kidding? I've had enough cops for one day."

"But—"

"Besides, I've been thinking . . ."

"Karleen—"

"Don't interrupt me. I've been thinking about your mother. If she'd stayed, Genie never would've let me marry a man like Orten. And if you'd grown up here, you'd have a family."

I'm not sure where she's going with this, but if she's talking at least she's not on her way home. "I had a family, Karleen."

"Just you and your mom? That's not a family. No brothers, no sisters, no grandparents, no real dad, just some asshole bartender you don't even know."

"I have a real dad, Karleen," I tell her, and it's the truth. "His name is Herman, but I call him Queeg."

"If Genie had stayed here and married Trip, you'd have a big brother or sister, and everything would be just fine. I would've gotten over being mad, and Genie and me would have been friends forever." She gives a giant wet sniff. Her voice has gone from drunk-blurry to crying-drunk-blurry. "Instead, now I've got to go home and take care of Orten—"

"You do not need to go take care of that man, Karleen. Just stay where you are for tonight. He's probably fine."

"That's just it," she says. "He was still breathing when I left. I've decided that's unacceptable."

"Hold on now . . ." Holy crap, she's going to kill him. My mind is racing. I need to figure out some way to keep her away from her house. "Did you drive to the church?"

"What do you think? Have you seen the weather?"

"You're in no condition to drive home, Karleen. Let me come get you."

"It's only a couple blocks."

"But if you get pulled over, your whole plan is ruined. Let me drive you. I'll help you with Orten."

"You'd do that for me?"

"Of course I will. I promise. Stay where you are. I'll be there in fifteen minutes."

"But I thought you didn't have a car—"

"I'll use JJ's truck."

"What?"

"He lives right next door," I explain. "He'll loan me his truck." I put a lot more certainty in that statement than I actually feel.

"Mr. Jackson is living there? I thought you said he was in a nursing home."

"Wait a minute, hold on . . ." My mind shuffles facts around, trying to make sense of what she just said. "Are you telling me that Fritter's brother, Jonah Jackson, is JJ, the owner of JJ's Auto Works?"

"Sure. JJ—Jonah Jackson. When he got sick a few years back, his son moved to town and took over the business."

With an almost audible click the pieces fall into place. I close my eyes and picture the boy in the photo and add thirty-five unhappy years to his face.

"Karleen, the man who lives next door to me is Trip, isn't it?"

"Of course," she replies. "How could you not know that?"

"How would I? He never introduced himself. He drives around with the name JJ on his truck, why wouldn't I assume he's JJ? What the hell kind of a name is Trip anyway?"

She chuckles softly. "Jonah Joseph Jackson III. What other nickname would he have?"

CHAPTER 49

Outside, the rain and wind are back in full force. By the time I get to JJ's porch—Trip's porch—my jeans are so wet that I don't know why I bothered to dry them at all. There are lights on, so I'm hopeful that he won't be too angered by my late-night visit. In fact now that I'm up close to his house I hear music. There's a light coming from the window to the right of the door, so I walk over and peer inside. I expect a television, or a stereo, but it's JJ, aka Trip, seated at an upright piano on the far wall of his dining room. The song he's playing is familiar, probably recognizable as something other than the soundtrack of a car commercial by somebody classier than me. It just makes me want to buy a Hyundai.

I rap on the glass with my knuckles. He jumps and spins around, looking in my direction, but I suspect that he's not able to see anything other than his own reflection in the dark glass. I knock again for good measure.

I hear barking coming from inside the house.

He stands and leaves his dining room, so I hurry over to meet him at the door. He opens it a crack and scowls at me over a security chain. At his feet is a Winston, its little pig-nose pressed into the three-inch gap between the door and the frame.

"*You* have the dogs?" I say, feeling a mixture of anger and relief.

He has a strange look on his face as he nods. "Yes I do. One in here and one in the garage."

"The garage?" I lean over and tickle the neck of the dog. It's the smaller Winston. He's snorting and licking my hand. After a final scratch under his chin I straighten and glare at Trip.

"So, you're hiding one in the garage?"

"I'm not hiding—"

"Were you afraid I'd hear them barking?"

"I wasn't—"

"I bet you had a good time watching me worry."

"No, I—"

"Chewing me out for being irresponsible, while all the time you—"

"Damn it, would you just shut up a minute?" he says, with enough force to make me shut up a minute.

"The other dog is in the garage in a trash bag. He's dead. I found him out on the loop."

I look down at the dog still snuffling at the doorjamb. "How'd you find—"

"He was there, lying next to him," he says. "At first I thought they were both gone."

We stare at each other for a second. He's angry and at the same time he's trying not to cry. At least that's what I think is going on, judging from the one eye peering at me above the chain.

"Is this one okay?"

He nods.

"I'm sorry," I say.

"Yes you are," he replies.

The look he's giving me makes it clear just what a sorry sack of shit he thinks I am. But even though I'm not the one who left the gate open, I'm not ratting out Tawny. I'm good at guilt; I've got room left on my shoulders for a little more.

"Thank you, for . . . um bringing them home," I say.

He doesn't reply.

"And I need a favor, a ride, actually. It's important."

Trip laughs, shakes his head, and then before I can say anything else, he closes the door.

At first I assume that he shut it to take off the chain, but after several seconds pass I see the light switch off in his dining room. I'm wrong. He's not letting me in, or coming out on the porch; he's going to bed.

I ring the doorbell, several times, which starts the remaining Winston barking again. And again the door opens a crack, but Trip isn't laughing anymore.

"I really do need your help," I tell him.

"I'm not interested."

"It's Karleen Meeker. She and her husband got in a fight. I think it's bad."

"Orten and Karleen have been trading punches for years without your help."

"But she's waiting for me at the church."

"Is Orten there with her?"

"No."

"Then she's fine." He takes a step back, and I can tell he's about to shut the door again. I quickly wedge my foot in the gap, giving a little gasp when he presses the door into my wet shoe. This trick doesn't work so well with Converse sneakers.

"Please, just this one thing—"

"I don't think so."

"Look, I know you don't like me, and you're pissed at my mom, but—"

"I don't know what you're talking about."

"I want to show you something."

"Not interested."

"But I figured it out," I say, my voice raised against the sound of the storm. "I know why she left you, Trip."

His face changes as soon as I call him Trip. His eyes narrow and when he lifts his hand up to the door, I wisely slide my foot out of the gap. The slam of the door shakes the porch.

I consider my options. I pull out my phone and try Luke, but again it goes straight to voice mail. I think of Father Barnes, but the only number I have for him is at the church—that's no help. And even if I find his home number, I suspect he'll be in no shape to drive. I look at the darkened houses along the street. Would any of them offer a ride to a wet stranger at two a.m.? I don't have Tawny's cell phone number, but I try, with no success, to use my phone to look up Fritter's number—I even call 411 but she's not listed. Shit, don't I have *anybody* else's number?

Ah! An image of a pen gripped in thick fingers . . . I frisk my jean pockets and sure enough there is something there. One pocket still holds the phone book page, which is now just a stiff gray wad, but Gordon Penny's card in the other pocket fared better. It's crumpled and faded from the laundry, but the phone number he wrote on the back is still legible.

A woman answers on the third ring. I convince her to put her husband on the line, but I have a feeling he's going to have some explaining to do later. My conversation with Mr. Penny mainly consists of me pleading with increasing desperation, and him refusing with increasing firmness. He's not interested in helping Karleen, and he's not interested in helping me. As we go round and around I'm wishing that I'd paid more attention to Karleen when she explained Gordon Penny's grudge. It was something about a costume party and a nickname . . . A superhero, I think . . . Maybe . . . I'm almost sure . . .

"I don't understand what your problem is," I say once I've pieced together what I remember. "Flash Gordon isn't that bad a nickname."

There's a silence, one long enough to get my hopes up. And then I hear Gordon Penny sigh. "I was large, even back then, you know." His voice is so quiet I have to strain to hear him. "It was *Flesh*, Ms. Wallace. The nickname your mother gave me was *Flesh* Gordon."

And right there the impossible happens—I feel a stab of tenderness for lip-licking Gordon Penny, or at least the little boy he used to be. I tell him that I'm sorry, and then I try one last time. "Is there anything I can say that will convince you to just let all that go and come help me?"

He hesitates, and for a second I think he's considering it. Then he says, "Sorry, Ms. Wallace. You can't unring a bell."

As if I didn't already know that.

I hear a sound behind me, and I turn to see Trip's door opening.

"You're still here?"

"I still need a ride."

He steps out on the porch. "Who was that on the phone?"

"Gordon Penny."

"Flesh?"

I wince.

"Why were you talking to him?"

"I have his number. He has a car. I need a ride."

Trip looks away, shifting his weight back and forth. He seems to be making a decision. I hold my breath.

"You said you had something to show me?" he asks.

"Wait right here."

I run through the rain back to my grandmother's house, in the front door and up the stairs, muddy water staining the carpet. Up in the darkroom, I yank the prints off the wire, shove them into a plastic trash bag and then hurry back through the storm.

His porch lights are on now, and he's standing by the door, waiting, his white T-shirt glowing an unnatural yellow under the bug lights. Breathing hard, I thump up the four stairs and thrust the bag into his hand.

"What's this?" he says.

"Here." I reach out and dry my hands on the edge of his shirt, which gets me another scowl, and then I open the bag and hand him the first photo.

"Here's my mom. You guys were out camping I think." It's the picture of her laughing, surrounded by trees.

"She kept all those?" He looks a little worried. I think he's remembering his moment of beefcake glory.

"I only found a few," I tell him, keeping my face neutral. I don't need to piss him off any more than I already have.

He nods, apparently satisfied that his modesty has been preserved.

I hand him the picture of Tilda. "See how much I look like my grandmother when she was young?"

He looks at it and then at me. "So?"

"When I talked to your dad today, he thought—"

"You went out to see my father?" Uh oh. He's looking angry again.

"Fritter took me to visit him," I say, which is truthy enough to pass in the middle of the night in a rainstorm when I need a ride.

"Anyway, when I went to see him, he kept apologizing to me over and over. I've never met him before in my life."

Trip looks again at the photo in his hand and then back at me. "He thought you were Tilda."

"He said, *I never knew until I saw her.*"

"I still don't understand what you're getting at."

I hand him the photo of himself, young and serious, staring at the camera, his wet hair slicked back.

"Take a look," I tell him.

He glances at it. "So what? It's me."

"Now this one." I hand him the one of my mother in a similar pose, looking at the camera, her hair darkened from the water and pulled away from her face.

"Hold them side by side," I say.

He studies the photos for a long time before lifting his gaze to meet mine. His face seems to have paled, although it's hard to judge with the jaundiced lighting.

"Eugene Wallace wasn't my grandfather," I say.

He shakes his head. "But . . ."

"Eugene was gay—"

"Gay?"

"Very gay. As in Tilda-walked-in-on-him-and-another-dude-going-at-it gay. So then Tilda got all upset, and your dad gave her a ride, pardon the pun."

"How could you possibly know all this?"

"I got it straight from Eugene's lover. He told me that Tilda caught them together at a party, and that your dad gave Tilda a ride home. I don't know if she and your dad did anything on that particular night—maybe they hooked up some other time. But look at the pictures—"

"That still doesn't mean that Eugene and Tilda never—"

"I know, but think about it—"

"This is impossible—"

"Is it? Tilda was freaked out about you dating my mother, right?"

He nods.

"I thought you looked familiar from the very first time I saw you. I still can't believe I didn't see it until now."

"Damn it, there's no way—"

"Did you look at the pictures? You're tall, and my mom was petite. You had short auburn hair and hers was big and blond. But she bleached her hair; in fact, Tilda practically forced my mother to keep it bleached blond. My mom had red hair, Trip. She had green eyes and you have . . ." I lean forward but the light is too dim for me to make out his eye color. "I don't know. But just look at those black-and-white pictures. With her hair dark from the water and slicked back, and the differences in your sizes taken away, the resemblance is unmistakable."

He looks at the photos again and then back up at me. There are tears in his eyes.

"Why wouldn't she just tell me?"

"What would she have said? 'Hey, guess what? You knocked up your half-sister?'"

"Dear God." With shaking hands, he thrusts the photos at me and then walks to the far edge of the porch. With his back turned, he leans over the railing, his shoulders shaking. Crying? Retching? I can't tell. I glance at my phone to check the time. Shit. This is taking too long.

Finally he straightens, and walks back over, his gray hair wet with rain, sparkling in the harsh light.

"I want you to leave," he says.

"I think when my mom saw these pictures, she confronted her mother, and Tilda told her the truth."

"Go. Now."

"This means I'm your niece."

His eyes narrow and he gives me a look of such rage that I have to fight an urge to flinch.

"You heard me," he says. "Get out of here."

"But I really need that ride—"

"I don't think so."

"Just let me borrow your truck—"

"No way."

"But I told Karleen—"

"That's no business of mine."

"She's at the church right now, but if somebody doesn't stop her, she's going to go back home to Orten, and one of them is going to end up dead tonight."

For a few seconds he considers what I just said, but as I watch, I see his face close back down. "Call the cops," he says, and then he turns and walks to his front door.

"You used to date her. Surely you don't want her dead, or in jail for killing Orten."

"Good night."

"But I promised her I'd come."

"Well, I guess letting people down runs in your family." His hand is on the doorknob.

"Wait, please!"

He pauses.

"I really think my mom thought that leaving was the right thing to do."

"I never got married," he says. "I never had any kids." Shaking his head, he opens the door and then turns back to me. "I spent my whole life believing that love couldn't be trusted."

"If it makes you feel any better, I think my mother did, too."

He steps inside and turns off the porch light. As he's closing the door he looks at me and sighs. "That doesn't make me feel any better at all," he says. And then he's gone.

I wait a few seconds, hoping he'll reappear, but the porch stays dark and there's no noise except the sound of the rain and the gusting wind. The wood beneath my feet trembles with the thunder's roar. Standing here on Trip's porch, shivering in my wet clothes, I am as tired and discouraged as I can ever remember feeling. My muscles ache with exhaustion, my eyes burn with unshed tears.

I carefully tuck the photos back into the plastic bag, and then slide the bundle under his doormat. My uncle's doormat. That secret is his burden now. I don't want it. I've got enough of my own.

CHAPTER 50

It wasn't as if I hadn't been preparing myself for my mother's death. She'd been sick for the better part of a year, and more often than not when her doctors talked about what time she had left, they described their goals in terms of *quality*, not *quantity*. But this was different, not the slow fade I'd been rehearsing, but a sudden darkness. One morning she was standing in front of me, the next she was gone. Her absence felt as sharp as her presence had been—the pain of a phantom limb.

Queeg and I were quiet on the way to the police station that Saturday morning. We were in and out of the property management building in fifteen minutes carrying my mother's purse. We were then directed to go around to the impound lot to see about the car. I didn't want to go; they could have the damn jeep for all I cared, but Queeg insisted. We needed to get the insurance paperwork, he said. I argued that we could do it another day, but he maintained that we had to do it that morning. At the time I was irritated at his refusal to understand how difficult this was for me. In hindsight I think I understand. He had respected my preference not to view her body, but he needed to see something to convince himself that she was really gone.

There wasn't much blood immediately visible, just a broad smear on the cracked windshield and a darker spot on the black upholstery. And there were flies, fat, black flies swarming the seat and the carpet. The front of the car was crushed, the back a jumble of the Christmas gifts I'd bought and left there. The driver's-side door was mangled and hanging ajar, obviously having been pried open to get my mother's body out.

On the floor of the driver's side there was a crumpled receipt, yellow where the folds were above the floor, a deep reddish brown where it rested on the carpet. Next to it was a gray plastic film canister and a small white . . . something . . . a tiny shell, I thought. Or a rock, maybe. I leaned down, waving the flies away, and carefully lifted the receipt, the film canister, and the little rock from the sticky carpet. I remember that it seemed important that I understand the meaning of those objects that had been at my mother's feet, but I don't remember why. The receipt was from the bookstore: *The Caine Mutiny*, $17.95. The film canister felt empty, and I mindlessly tucked it in my pocket. Then I turned my attention to what was lying in my palm, the small white pebble that was not a pebble. And it was not a shell. It was a tooth.

I hadn't told Queeg what the police had told me, that my mother had been drinking. I'd hoped to spare him that. But the whole car smelled of blood and whiskey. When Queeg leaned down to look in the window and saw the two empty bottles on the floor of the passenger's side, he gave a quiet grunt, as if he'd just taken a punch to the belly. With some effort he opened the passenger-side door. Holding up one of the empties, he looked at me wordlessly, shaking his head.

I glanced at the label on the bottle—Maker's Mark—and then back down at my mother's tooth, at the tiny smear of blood it left in the palm of my hand. I didn't speak and neither did Queeg. I'm pretty sure that he attributed the shock and dismay he saw on my face to the fact that my mother had been drinking, but he was wrong. I already knew that she'd fallen off the wagon. But I hadn't known until that very moment that I'd pushed her off.

Queeg pulled paperwork from the glove box and then opened the hatch, telling me to take whatever I wanted. I looked at the mess, the cigar box, the knit hat, *The Caine Mutiny*, the empty bag that had once held those damn bottles of Maker's Mark. In the middle of the disorganized pile was my mother's camera bag, with her camera, a lens, some film canisters spilling out of the top. I took a minute to tuck her gear back inside the bag, and then I lifted it into my arms.

"This is all," I told him.

He nodded and frowned. It was only when he pointed at my hand that I realized that all this time I'd been packing things using one hand. The other was still clenched in a fist.

"What have you got there?" he asked.

With a shudder, I relaxed my hand, letting my mother's bloody tooth fall into the oyster-shell gravel between us. I kept my voice casual when I replied, "Nothing."

Once we settled back in his car, Queeg cracked his window and lit a cigarette to steady his shaking hands. "She promised me," he said. "She promised me no more gin." He took a long drag and then switched his cigarette to his other hand so he could hold it near the window. "And what does she do? She goes out and buys bourbon."

I should have explained. I should've told him that she hadn't gone out and bought anything. I'd bought them. I'd put those bottles in the jeep with my own two hands. I remember wondering, as I sat watching the smoke curl up and out his window, how my mother had known the bottles were back there. Did she get curious and look to see what was in all the sacks? Could she have, like a little child, been hoping to find her own gift? Or maybe she'd braked suddenly and heard the bottles knocking against each other. She would have recognized the sound.

"So," Queeg said, crushing out his cigarette in the already full ashtray. "I'm guessing that she got bad news at the doctor's yesterday."

I glanced over at him, but he wasn't looking at me. He was staring at the jeep. "I talked to her early yesterday morning and she told me she'd moved her appointment to that afternoon," he said. "She promised she'd call and let me know what the doctor told her, but she never called. And I didn't call her. I should have."

Was it possible that she'd gone to the doctor's office alone? When I'd asked her at the funeral to move her appointment back to Monday, she hadn't actually agreed to do so.

Queeg wiped at his eyes and then started the car. "So, what did the doctor say?"

I stayed silent, staring out the window, while my stepfather completed a slow, overly complicated twenty-point turn. By the time we were facing the right direction, I'd made up my mind. My heart was broken, but I had a chance to save Queeg's.

"He told her that the chemo didn't work," I said, and it could have been true. "She didn't have much time left, and it was going to be bad." I took a shaky breath and continued. "In the end, maybe this was for the best."

He glanced at me, nodded briefly, and then put the car in drive. I saw Queeg look at the jeep in the rearview mirror as we pulled away. I didn't look back.

The seat belt was pushing against the empty film canister in my pocket, so I took out the little plastic tube and opened my mother's camera bag to toss it inside. But I heard something, a faint rattle from inside the canister. I pried off the lid and carefully poured the contents out into my hand.

Queeg pulled out of the impound lot and merged onto the street. Reaching over to pat me on the knee, he said, "Everything is going to be okay."

He didn't seem to expect a reply from me; he just switched on the radio and turned his attention to negotiating the traffic. A Phil Collins song was playing, of that I'm sure, but I'm not certain which one. When I think back on it, my memory starts playing "Against All Odds," but maybe that's because it's my favorite Phil Collins song, or maybe it's because the song is so fucking sad.

What I do remember, though, is how the rain started back up right then, the fat drops popping against the windshield, the old wipers squawking and smearing the rain rather than clearing it. And I remember the way Queeg hunched over the wheel, concentrating as he drove, and how the music filled the car, and how I twisted in my seat, angling myself away from Queeg so he couldn't see me cry. And so that he wouldn't notice the two tiny white birds resting on my palm.

CHAPTER 51

And so here I am, sitting on the floor in my mother's room, in her mother's house, mystery solved and nothing has changed. She's still dead. I'm still here.

Karleen's problems aren't my problems. It's time to dry off and go to bed. Tomorrow I can pay Trip, collect my car, and go back to Tallahassee, to Nick, to a clinic for an abortion. By next weekend I'll be at the bar, buying everybody a round of drinks, making this past week into a funny story. It'll be great. It's what I'm good at. It's what I do. It's what my mom would do.

I pull the camera bag into my lap, unzip the inside pocket and pull out the film canister. Again, I pop off the gray lid and dump the contents into my hand. The two delicate white pieces of plastic weigh nothing. When I close my eyes I can't even tell they're there.

Queeg has always told me that the adage *Opportunity only knocks once* is bullshit. "It knocks all the time," he likes to say. "All you have to do is listen for it and open the damn door." What Queeg didn't tell me was that sometimes you can't bring yourself to put your hand on the knob; you're too proud, or too angry. Or too ashamed. Instead you press your ear to the door and hold your breath, listening for the sound of it passing you by. *Next time,* you tell yourself, *next time I'll open it.* But even as you say it you know you're lying, that there's never going to be a next time.

Well, fuck that shit.

I stand, tugging at the knees of my wet jeans. Luke didn't need to tell me that it's too late to save my mother; I knew that the day I held her bloody tooth in my hand. And as far as it never being too late to save myself . . . well, the jury's still out on that one. But I do know one thing for sure: he was dead wrong when he told me the *only* person I could ever save was myself.

Because tonight, I have a chance to save somebody else.

I consider the tiny plastic birds in my hand, and then I tuck them deep into my pocket and run down the stairs. When I open the back door, a wet gust of wind hits me in the face.

Shit.

"This had better get me some good fucking karma," I shout into the night sky. And then I jog out to the garage to get the bike.

It doesn't take me long to realize that this was a terrible idea. It's dark and slick and even with the streetlights, the potholes and gravel aren't visible, so I'm bouncing and sliding all over the place. If I pick up any speed at all, the rain in my eyes makes it nearly impossible to see. Once I get to the park, the trail is smooth, thank God, although the going is still tricky since the park trail isn't lit. Luckily, there's enough vague ambient light to make the black asphalt shine in the darkness. It's slow going, but I keep pedaling. I hope Karleen didn't check her watch after fifteen minutes and leave, because with all the time I wasted trying to get a ride it's already been more than thirty, and I've probably got at least another ten minutes before I'll be there.

When I finally reach the playground at the far end of the park, I start putting on speed, take the right-hand path and pump the bike up to street level. I pop out on the sidewalk next to the street and turn left, angling across to the other side of the overpass, where Shandy and I had our conversation a few nights ago. Head down, I am pedaling hard to keep up my momentum for the next hill.

Perhaps it's because it's so much brighter up on the well-lit intersection than it had been in the park. Or maybe it's because there are still rumbles of thunder and flashes of lightning every few seconds. Or it's just because I'm tired—bone tired. There must be some reason it takes me so long to notice the oncoming truck.

When I do sense movement behind me, I glance back and see it approaching. The pickup has only one headlight, but because of the rain, the light reflects on the street making it look as if there are two lights, one on top of the other. Maybe this is what disorients me enough to make my feet slip on the pedals. Or it could be the sound that the truck is making as the driver tries to stop, the grinding of gears, the hiss of rubber sliding on a layer of oily water. But more likely than not, it's the driver's face, illuminated by the streetlight overhead. It's Trip, his eyes wide with fear, his mouth open in a shout, or a curse, as his truck slews toward me.

I almost make it to the far sidewalk before it happens. My front wheel is nearly to the curb when there's a lurch and a sharp pain in my right knee and then my hip. Suddenly I'm no longer on my bike, but I'm still moving. I pass over the curb and sidewalk and then, after a brief impact of my ankle against the metal railing, I'm off the edge of the roadway and plunging into the deep culvert below.

I am five years old again, and I am flying. No. I am falling. I'm too old to believe in magic, and no wings will save me.

Everything has gone silent, and time has slowed and slowed, and I am falling into shadows cast by the streetlights. I feel the rain wetting my face. Below me I see that what had been a shallow stream under the bridge is now a tide of rushing water. It looks deep and soft, and as my trajectory takes me past the water, I understand that I have once again missed the mark.

I think of Karleen sitting alone in a dark church, waiting for help that's not going to come, and I think of Luke, broken, yes, but still openhearted. In my mind's eye he's grinning at me, blushing pink.

And Queeg—I think of Queeg, and how often he showed his love for me, and how rarely I returned the favor.

I think of my mother.

A girl in a photograph, laughing, her eyes narrowed against the sun. Then with me at the beach, holding my small gritty hand in her own. In her Malibu, red hair whipping in the wind, as she turns her head and looks at me. She smiles.

And then she is seated at the kitchen table, smoking a cigarette, drinking a mug of something I know isn't coffee, and in her outstretched hand are two tiny white birds. "One for you," she says, "and one for me."

And this time I reach out my hand to take one, but now we're at the beach, and I'm struggling in the water, my throat burning, my legs and arms heavy with exhaustion, and suddenly she is there beside me. She puts her arm around my waist and I grab for her, burying my hands deep in her hair. I hold tight to those thick, wet curls, just as I have held tight all these years to my thick, sticky guilt.

And just like that, I understand. She isn't dragging me under. She would never do that. I took on this burden. I'm the one who insists on trying to swim with pockets full of memories as heavy as stones. I'm the one who chose to relive my mother's life as an act of penance. It's not her; it's never been her. I'm the one who can't let go.

And I understand that it makes no difference if her hair was wet or dry, because if she'd been able to save me, she would have. My mother loved me, and I loved her, and she loved her mother, who loved her in return, and in the end we all fucked everything up. And it wasn't because we're bad people. We did it because we're only people, and sometimes that's what people do.

And as the scrubby sloping ground grows closer, I think about Mr. Hambly holding out his trembling hand, palm up, open and ready, and I understand.

And I soften my clenched fist of a heart, and I open it wide. And I give forgiveness—of her and of myself—one last try.

And I let go.

I let *her* go.

I'm close enough to see the yellow of the dandelions peeking out from between the rocks, but I'm lighter now, and the air feels like water on my skin, and I am unafraid. In the rush of the stream below, I hear a voice that at first I think is my own. *Tuck and roll*, it says.

But it's not my voice.

Remember, I hear her call out. *Tuck and roll,* she is shouting after me, as I'm being pushed through the door of the funeral home. And I'm annoyed, and I stop and set down the tripod, and this time I turn to look over my shoulder, and in the crowd I see her face one last time.

Tuck and roll, she is saying, hoping that I will hear.

And I do hear.

And I listen.

And I believe.

SATURDAY
OCTOBER

All's well that ends well.

CHAPTER 52

Sometimes it's tempting to overestimate the importance of the past when predicting the future, to think of yesterday and tomorrow as two points connected by a straight line with a beginning and an end. *Well begun is half done*, Queeg would tell me. *A bad beginning makes a bad ending*. But I've been thinking about that a lot lately, and I'm not so sure. Sometimes *well begun* never has a chance to finish, and every once in a while, a *bad beginning* turns out okay.

Before I went to bed last night I turned on the heat, and its burned, dusty smell is the first thing I notice this morning. On my way down the stairs I'm careful, leaning, maybe just a little, on the banister. My knee still aches most of the time, but if you didn't know about the accident you probably wouldn't even notice my limp. It won't be much longer before I'm back to normal—the doctor's words, not mine. What the hell is *normal*, anyway? Queeg always said that normal people are just people you don't know very well, and as far as I can tell, he was right on the money with that one.

I slip outside and scuttle through the cold wet grass to Trip's yard; the only thing smarter than subscribing to the newspaper is living next door to a subscriber who sleeps later than I do. After I dump kibble into Winston's bowl and Cheerios into mine, I flatten the paper out and flip to the obits page to check the times listed for today's funerals.

About halfway through breakfast my phone rings. I pick it up and say, "Good morning."

"The service is at ten o'clock."

"I know," I reply. "I'm looking at the paper right now."

"You take the paper?"

"Nope."

There's a pause and I smile, waiting to see if that was enough to change the conversation to newspaper subscriptions, or if she'll manage to stay on her original subject of today's funeral. If there's one thing I've come to know about Karleen, it's that her train of thought is easily derailed.

"What are you wearing today?" she says, successfully staying on track.

I consider the question. I'd planned to wear jeans since the only maternity clothes I own are T-shirts, jeans, and a swimsuit in a pastel swirl pattern that makes me look like a giant Easter egg.

"You can't wear jeans," she tells me, putting a wrinkle in my as yet unvoiced plan. I feel pretty sure a swimsuit is out as well.

"Is that some kind of city ordinance? Or just a fashion tip?"

"I saved a couple of my old maternity dresses," she says. "You want stripes or shoulder pads?"

I consider the options, which sound a little like: Brussels sprouts or cauliflower? Leprosy or gangrene?

"Stripes, I guess."

"I'll be there in fifteen minutes."

"Make it thirty," I reply, but she's already gone.

I carry my dishes to the sink and put away the milk. On the refrigerator, tucked under a magnet, is a postcard. On one side, in
my mother's handwriting, it says, *Having a wonderful time with my
beautiful daughter. Wish you were here.* On the other side is a photograph of an empty beach. It could be anywhere, but I like to think
it's Fort Pickens. Sometimes I put it where my mother's writing is
facing out, but today it's turned to show blue sky, water, and sand.
I think there are some white spots in the sky that could be gulls,
but the picture is too faded for me to be sure.

CHAPTER 53

Three of the longest days of my life were spent in Gandy Community Hospital, and I don't make that statement lightly. I once spent three rainy days sick with the flu while camped on a sidewalk waiting to buy Pearl Jam tickets.

The official litany of my latest suffering included a concussion, a grade-one splenic laceration, cracked ribs, a bruised ankle, torn ligaments in my knee, and as ridiculous as it sounds, hip bursitis from the impact. My time in the emergency room has blended into a blurred memory of too much light, too much noise, and not enough pain medication. I can't even tell you if it was one hour or eight spent in that bright misery, but I do remember the blissful dimness and quiet of the private room they gave me, and how I almost cried with gratitude when a nurse finally brought me something for pain.

The morning after my accident a doctor wearing blue scrubs came in and sat on the edge of my bed. He took my hand. "Matilda—"

"Mattie," I said, correcting him.

"Mattie," he replied. "We need to talk about your baby,"

In that beat, in his pause before his next words, I realized two things. The first was that in those pain-filled hours and the drugged sleep later, I had completely forgotten about being pregnant. The second thing was that the accident had surely been too much for it to survive. What stands out in my memory was how gently the doctor held my hand and how surprised I was to feel a push of sorrow in my chest rather than relief. It's not the same, I suppose, to have something taken away as it is to throw it away.

"The baby will probably be fine," he continued. "But we had no choice but to run radiological studies."

At that point he must have read my silence as anger about the X-rays, rather than the surprise it actually was, because he added, "The man at the accident site didn't tell the EMTs that you were pregnant."

It takes me a second to figure out that he must be talking about JJ—oops, Trip. I remember wondering if I would ever get used to thinking of him by the correct nickname.

"He didn't know. Nobody knows."

"He knows now," the doctor replied. "Mr. Jackson informed us that he was your closest relative, so we've involved him in your medical decisions and updates."

"Did he also inform you that he was the one who hit me with a truck?"

The doctor smiled. "From what I hear, he's the one who saved your life. He climbed down the embankment and fished you out of the water, and then he called 911."

"I hit the water?"

"No, you landed on some rocks, but you kept rolling."

"I was aiming for the water," I said.

He laughed softly and gave my hand a squeeze. "We don't always end up where we're aiming, Matilda."

I should have found a way to charge admission; everyone came to gawk at the invalid. Tawny, Luke, Father Barnes, Trip, Karleen—she brought flowers, daisies dyed such a lurid purple that I laughed when I saw them and then moaned, holding my ribs. As it turned out she'd fallen asleep on the couch in Father Barnes's office the night of the accident, and when she woke up and went home the next morning, she found Orten at the kitchen table, drinking a cup of coffee. That day in the hospital, she acted like things were just fine at her house, and she's kept that act up ever since. I wish she'd leave Orten before they end up killing each other, but my wishing won't make it so. Like Luke said, needing to change your life isn't enough. You have to want it, too.

It wasn't until the morning I was scheduled to be discharged that Fritter came to see me. She stepped inside, silent in her rubber-soled shoes, and then carefully shut the door. We've all seen it in the movies—where the villain creeps into the hospital room, holding a pillow or a syringe full of air. Every one of those scenarios flashed through my mind as she approached the bed. Thankfully, I was conscious, and even with my injuries, pretty confident I could take the old woman if it came down to hand-to-hand combat.

But Fritter had confession, not homicide, on her mind. With only a nod for a greeting, she perched on the edge of my hospital bed and started talking.

"Eugene had been in the ground for just over two months when Tilda showed up at my door," Fritter began. "She told me she was pregnant and that the child wasn't Gene's; it was my brother Jonah's. He was away at school at the time, and Tilda asked me for his phone number. Instead of giving it to her, I offered to call him to smooth things over, pave the way for her to break the news. She seemed relieved. She thanked me."

Fritter kept her eyes focused on her hands, and I was glad.

The look on her face was painful enough without having to meet her gaze.

"I thought about doing what I'd promised . . . I almost called him. But I didn't. The next day, however, I told Tilda I had spoken to Jonah, and that he had denied everything."

"Wow," I said, and she nodded in a sad acknowledgment of her appalling douche-baggery, although I suspect those might not be the exact words she would have chosen to describe her actions.

"So what did she do?"

"What could she do?" Fritter replied. "She was distraught, of course, but I had it all figured out. I told her that her only option was to claim the child was Eugene's. She and Eugene had been affianced, after all. Allowances would be made. Besides, with such a tragic story, the shame associated with a child conceived out of wedlock would be overlooked by most. I didn't have to work very hard to convince her. What other choice did she have?"

Fritter shifted her position on the bed and then reached out to carefully smooth the sheet where it had wrinkled. "By the time my brother heard of Tilda's pregnancy it was common knowledge that the child was Gene's, and I'm sure my brother just assumed that was true. After all, if there had been any possibility the child were his, Tilda would have contacted him, rather than accept the burden of single motherhood." Fritter shrugged. "Jonah moved east after college, married, and had a family of his own and then later divorced, and still I never told him the truth about your mother. He never suspected a thing until he came to visit Trip that summer. Genie's blond hair didn't fool him for a minute; one look at her face, and Jonah knew. He came to me and confessed his brief affair with Tilda and shared with me his certainty that Genie was his child, not Eugene's. And God help me, I lied again. I pretended that it was all news to me. I acted shocked."

Fritter's discomfort was obvious. "What else could I do?" she said. "It had gone on for too long. Your mother was an adult, and there was nothing to be gained by telling the truth then. That's what I told Jonah anyway: that your mother was better off not knowing. And that your grandmother might well believe that the child was Gene's, and that telling her otherwise would be cruel. I convinced my brother that everyone would be better off with the secret unexposed."

With a deep sigh, Fritter looked me in the eyes for the first time that morning. "I was scared. If Jonah found out that I'd known all along Genie was his child, he'd never have forgiven me. And Tilda, if she discovered that I'd never even told Jonah . . . well . . . she'd never forgive me either. I'd created this monster of lies, and I had no choice but to keep it alive."

"But then my mom figured it out."

Fritter nodded. "She did. Tilda came to see me, in fact, right after your mother disappeared. She told me how the photographs had exposed the truth, and I urged her to get rid of the evidence. I assured her that Genie would come back home, and that no good could come of having those photos lying around, reminding everyone of the unpleasantness. I think Tilda did throw out the pictures, but she wouldn't touch anything else in the darkroom or your mother's room. She wanted everything to be there for Genie when she returned."

Fritter and I sat quietly for a minute. I suspect both of us were thinking about those rooms so carefully preserved for a girl who would never find her way home.

"And then like a bad penny, I turned up," I said.

Fritter gave me a rueful smile. "And then Tawny comes home one evening and tells me that the two of you were going to develop some old negatives . . ."

"So you sent her to steal them."

"*Steal* is a strong word. I sent her to recover items that didn't belong to you."

"They didn't belong to you either."

Fritter nodded, gently placing her cool hand on my forearm. "The long and the short of it is, I am deeply sorry for the role I played in all of this, and I wanted you to know the whole story. But I'm hoping you won't use this information in a negative way."

"Such as . . ."

"To sully any reputations."

"Sully?" I smiled. Who uses the word *sully*?

"Besmirch. Tarnish."

"I know what *sully* means," I said.

She looked down at her hand, still resting on my arm. "I'll always wonder how things might have turned out differently. You know, Jonah's marriage wasn't a happy one. If he'd known that Tilda was carrying his child he would have married her. Perhaps they would have been happy together."

Fritter shook her head and sighed, her little rounded shoulders even more slumped than before. "To this day I don't understand why I didn't make that phone call."

"I do."

She looked at me, puzzled.

"You were angry and hurting, and looking for someone to punish. I probably would have done the same thing," I told her, and it was the truth.

She nodded and smiled, but it was a small, pained smile. Perhaps using me as a comparison was setting the bar a little too low. And then she said, "If there's ever anything I can do to make it up to you . . ."

To which I replied, "As a matter of fact . . ."

Fritter and I reached an agreement in which I promised to refrain from sullying, besmirching, or tarnishing and she promised to issue a library card to Richard Hambly. Fritter scowled her disapproval at his name, but reluctantly agreed. Getting her to bump up his maximum checkout number was harder. She relented, however, once I reminded her that the more books he took out at a time the less often he'd come in. I'm guessing that Mr. Hambly should never expect a Christmas card from Fritter.

Before she left, I asked for one more favor. I had her open the little closet by the door and get me the plastic bag that held the clothes I'd been wearing when I was admitted. She stood next to the bed while I slid out the jeans, crusted with mud. I checked the pockets. Empty. I pulled out the T-shirt, and when there was nothing left in the bag, I stuck my arm back inside and felt around at the bottom. There, in the lowest corner, in the accumulated sand, I felt a small hard object. I lifted it out and reached back in, but the other one was gone. Looking down at the single tiny white piece of plastic cupped in my hand, I smiled.

"What is that?" Fritter asked.

"It's a little bird."

She leaned in to study it closer. "Doesn't look like much of anything."

"I know," I replied.

CHAPTER 54

Earlier this week a storm came through that swept away the last remnants of summer and today the air is crisp, the sky a watery blue with sunlight so bright it makes the maple trees glow like they're on fire. It's been a long time since I've been in school, but I think I'll always associate this time of year with the optimism of freshly sharpened pencils and limitless possibilities. *Anything could happen*, I tell myself, and it's the truth.

Although someone has obviously tried to clear away the storm debris, the tangle of dead branches pushed against the wrought-iron fence gives this section of the cemetery an unkempt look. A dog barks in the distance, playing backup to the Bible reading.

"Father Barnes looks good," I say.

All I get from Luke is a quick sideways glance. He knows what I'm hinting at, but he's not spilling any beans. I'm curious about whether Father Barnes has sobered up and started going to AA, but whenever I bring up the subject directly Luke's response is to remind me what the second A stands for. My theory has been and remains that since I'm the one who first suggested he talk to

Father Barnes about getting off the sauce, that I deserve to know the outcome of that conversation. Luke's theory is that I should mind my own business. I prefer my theory.

"Don't you think he looks good?"

Luke puts a stern expression on his face, raising a finger to his lips to shush me as if I'm disturbing the ceremony, which is a pretty lame dodge seeing as how we can barely hear the priest's voice from way up here on the cemetery drive.

I'm sitting sideways in the limo passenger seat with the door propped open, and Luke is in his chair parked next to me. Even with my bum knee I could've made it down the slope to the graveside without a problem. But the ground is too wet to easily accommodate a wheelchair, and I didn't want Luke to sit up here alone. We're on the south side of the grave, but the poor graveside mourners face southeast, straight into the sun, and although there's a canopy, the shade it casts is nowhere near the chairs. So most of the guests are wearing sunglasses and that, combined with their dark clothing, gives the impression of a gathering of dangerous badasses. It's only the remarkable predominance of red hair that ruins the effect. It's hard for people with that many freckles to look fierce.

I'm tempted to mention this observation to Luke, but I keep my mouth shut. I think he finds my running gag about Father Barnes and AA only mildly irritating, but talking smack about his family might actually hurt his feelings and that's the last thing I want to do. Besides, I have some skin in this game as well. It's his oh-so-gingery extended family gathered around the open grave. But it's my grandfather they're putting in that hole.

On the way to the after-funeral reception, Luke and I are the only ones riding in the limo, the rest of the family members having redistributed themselves to other cars to give directions to the out-of-towners. The black leather seat is wide enough for four, but Luke sits close to me rather than taking the other window. This is the second funeral I've been to this summer, and I'm pretty sure he knows I'm thinking about that. He reaches over and takes my hand.

When I left the hospital, it was Luke who picked me up, and I stayed with him for two weeks until I could walk without crutches. He took care of me, cooked for me, did my laundry, held me when I woke up sweating from yet another falling dream.

At this point, we're in a kind of holding pattern, Luke and I. Our relationship is clearly more than *friends with benefits*—or I should say remote-cousins-who-the-hell-knows-times-removed with benefits—yet I find myself reluctant to think of him as my boyfriend. Maybe that's because in my experience boyfriends don't stick around for long. Or maybe it's because I still think I'm too much of a pain in the ass to be with a nice guy like Luke. Or maybe it's because for the first time in years, the future feels wide open, and I'm hesitant to make any choice that might narrow that horizon. So I suppose if asked I'd have to say that although I'm happy right now, I'm not aiming to settle down in Gandy with Luke. And yet at the same time I also understand that what the doctor in the blue scrubs told me is true. We don't always end up where we're aiming.

The limo cruises along at a maddeningly solemn pace, and since I don't see any familiar cars on the road around us anymore, I have the feeling we'll be the last to arrive. The reception is at Trip's house, which I'm sure was Fritter's decision, not his. From what I've seen, Trip's idea of entertaining is to put an extra six-pack in the fridge and order pizza. The thought of him hosting a nice reception is so ludicrous I wouldn't have missed it for the world. Good thing I'm invited; crashing it would surely be in poor taste.

We've become something pretty close to friends, Trip and I, although I think he still finds me just the tiniest bit aggravating. And sometimes, at unguarded moments, I catch him looking at me with a deep worry in his eyes. I've told him the fact that he was going to help Karleen counts for something, but he doesn't really hear me when I say it. I think all he can hear is the sound of his truck slamming into me. Of course, I'm not above taking advantage. I've got him mowing my lawn, and we share custody of Winston. During the day when Trip is at work, the dog is usually with me, but when I'm working nights or weekends at the True Value, Winston is next door, stinking things up. For Trip's birthday last week I gave him a bag of potpourri.

And I sold him the Malibu. I think my mom would approve. I never loved that car the way she did, and Trip gave me a great price. Guilt is a superior bargaining tool. The old white Toyota I drive now isn't much to look at, but it runs just fine and already has torn upholstery, so I can relax about that. And every once in a while, if it's been parked with the windows rolled up, it still smells like Queeg.

CHAPTER 55

Queeg didn't have lung cancer as it turned out; the biopsy was clear. What he had was walking pneumonia, the name of which I immediately disputed; *driving pneumonia*, I insisted. Queeg never walked anywhere.

The diagnosis seemed to perk him up, and once he got started on antibiotics, he got better for a while. But although his coughing cleared up, he was still chronically short of breath, so in early July doctors did more tests and found a blockage in his heart. When he told me of the scheduled angioplasty, the very first thing I did after hanging up with Queeg was call Fritter and ask for a loan.

The flight from Oklahoma City to Pensacola was unremarkable, except that it was the first time I'd been on an airplane so it was remarkable to me. Who knew that they could make seats even smaller than the ones on a Greyhound bus? When I arrived in Pensacola, I was astonished again. Nick was there early and waiting for me. Even though I'd called him the night before to tell him when my flight would be in, I was sure he'd be late. But there he was, leaning against his car, his T-shirt a little tighter than it needed to be. When he saw me come out the terminal door, he opened his arms. His body felt familiar, and I hugged him long and hard.

Once Nick and I were in the car, the first thing I did was give him his guitar strap. I'd called him right after my accident and offered to ship it back, but Nick had balked at that idea, worried it might get lost in the mail. I remember thinking that was nuts, but as I sat in that car, watching him run his hands down the strap and then twist around to place it carefully, reverentially, on the backseat, it made perfect sense. He may have never loved me, but he was capable of love, at least for a collector's-item-near-mint-condition-brown-leather-guitar-strap-signed-by-Jimmy-Page-and-Jeff-Beck.

Mile after mile, Nick talked about his band, his job, his new girlfriend, sneaking glances at me as he spoke of her, to judge my reaction. I relaxed in the seat and let his self-absorption wash over me, comforted by the knowledge that I no longer loved this man. In fact, I couldn't imagine how I'd ever thought I did.

When we were getting close to Two Pines, and he'd quieted down a little, I broke the news. I wish I'd had a camera out and ready for when I told him that I was pregnant with his child; I'm not sure I've ever seen a better example of the expression *deer in the headlights*. I assured him that all I wanted was a few signatures to relinquish his rights. He looked relieved and then spent the time from that moment until we pulled up outside the gate at Two Pines explaining why it was very important that his new girlfriend not know anything about it.

Before I climbed out of the car, I leaned over to kiss him on the cheek, but he turned his face and surprised me with a full-on kiss. We both smiled and nodded. It felt like a good-bye kiss, and that was fine. At the chain-link gate, I glanced back at Nick's car, still parked on the shoulder. I lifted my hand to wave, but he wasn't looking at me. He was looking in the mirror, fixing his hair.

Queeg had assured me that the procedure was no big deal, and he didn't need my help, and it was probably true. Although I was off crutches at the time, I had still had a knee brace and couldn't drive a stick, so it was Min He who drove us to and from the hospital. She was the one who went to the pharmacy and the grocery store. Her solicitous behavior toward Queeg didn't exactly bleed over into her interactions with me, but I could tell she was glad I came.

I told Queeg what I'd discovered about my mom's past, but for the most part I kept the focus of our conversations off of me. I assured him that my injury was caused by minor carelessness on my part, that I was fine—no mention of the accident, the hospital stay, or my pregnancy. I told myself it would be better if he were completely recovered before I gave him any surprising news. I told myself that I'd be back for his birthday in September anyway, and by then my belly would be too big to camouflage. The truth, however, is I was too chicken for total honesty. I just couldn't bear to see a look of worry and disappointment on his still exhausted face.

For a week, we just hung out. We watched TV together; we ate together. Only three days after the procedure, Queeg was cleared to drive, so one morning we went crabbing in the bay, baiting the traps with chicken legs and when those ran out, hunks from a little shark somebody had caught and then left to rot in the sun.

We talked about nothing and everything. I told him about some of my new friends in Gandy, about my job at the hardware store, and he told me about a couple of trips he and Min He were planning in the fall. And we talked about my mother. If he wondered why I was suddenly willing to talk about her, he never asked. We spent hours discussing her; I told him as many stories as I could remember from before he met her, and he told me a few about the two of them I'd never heard before. We brought her back to life that week. She lived in our conversations as powerfully as if she'd been sitting in the room with us.

The morning before I left, I asked Queeg if we could leave early and go to breakfast before going to the airport. As soon as we sat down in the sticky booth, I told the waitress that we were in a hurry and she did a good job making it quick. Since Queeg was the sort of person who liked to arrive at the airport extra early, he didn't make much of my request for speed, but when I asked for a to-go box and loaded up my uneaten sausage and a couple of biscuits left in the basket on the table, Queeg raised a brow. I suspect he was wondering if I really planned to take leftover biscuits and sausage through security at the airport, but he didn't say a thing. He's known me for a long time. He was used to me and my steady drip of bad ideas.

Queeg pulled out of the diner parking lot, heading east, and before long there were signs for Highway 30. When we got to the turnoff, I said, "Go south."

"The airport's north," he said.

"I thought we could stop by the beach."

He glanced at his watch, frowning.

"We'll have plenty of time if you'll at least drive the speed limit."

"I'm going plenty fast."

"Are you kidding me?" I laughed. "You drive like a turtle."

"What animal would you prefer?

"I don't know," I replied. "A cheetah. A greyhound . . ."

"A rabbit?"

"Sure."

He smiled and shook his head.

"What?" I asked.

"Nothing," he replied, grinning. And then he put on his blinker, and we crawled onto the exit for 30 South.

It was only nine in the morning but there were already families arriving, staking their claims. At the far end of the beach, a man helped a little boy fly a kite, and a lady was jogging, a wet, sandy golden retriever trotting behind. Queeg and I left our shoes in the car and walked out to the water's edge.

We stood there for a minute, looking out at the horizon. I don't know how often he had come to Fort Pickens but that was the first time I'd been since that Christmas morning with Queeg, when he told me that this was where he'd laid my mother to rest.

"Hey, Captain?"

"Yeah, sweetheart?" he answered, still looking out to sea.

"The tortoise and the hare," I said.

He turned to look at me and laughed. "That took you awhile."

I was laughing, too. "Slow and steady wins the race."

"Haste makes waste," he added.

I don't know if they recognized the Styrofoam box I carried, or if they smelled the sausage somehow, but while we stood there the gulls had been gathering, wheeling above us, calling out, hopeful. I opened the box, divided the contents and held out half to Queeg.

He sighed, grumbling, as always, about the flying rats, but he reached out and took the food from my open hand.

And then we swung our arms in tandem, rising to our toes, tossing one scrap after another straight up into the hot July air.

And the gulls cried out to one another as they circled and dove, circled and dove, again and again, accepting each humble offering.

Queeg and I kept in close touch the rest of that summer. Sometimes he'd call, but usually I'd be the one to call him, and that was a change for us. Although we played our customary roles—I'd tease, he'd laugh, he'd offer advice, I'd ignore it—I think both of us understood why I called so often. I was worried about him.

And then, early in the morning on the last day of August, I got a call from Queeg's number, but when I picked up, it was Min He on his phone. She was talking fast and crying, and I struggled to make sense of her words. But I heard her say Queeg's name, and then she said *sorry*, and I knew he was gone.

It was Labor Day weekend and hard to get a flight, but I shouldn't have worried. In the three days between her phone call and my arrival, Min He had taken care of everything—the obituary had been published, the death certificates ordered, and she had even, in accordance with his wishes to not be embalmed, already had Queeg cremated. He was waiting for me in a plastic box sitting on his kitchen counter. It was early evening when I arrived, and Min He invited me to her trailer for dinner. She wasn't exactly what I would call friendly, but I appreciated what she was doing. She was helping me because Queeg would have wanted her to. In the end, it was our love for him that mattered to us both.

I turned down her offer of her sofa bed, and asked instead for a key to Queeg's trailer. On the way from her trailer to his, I stopped by the metal table and chairs and sat down. It was much warmer than it had been when I'd last sat at this table with Queeg, but the damp air and the smell of the salt water felt the same, and when I closed my eyes I could still hear the gulls.

After the small memorial service, attended mainly by other

elderly residents of Two Pines, I drove Queeg's car to his attorney's office. The will was simple: there wasn't much, but it was mine. Perhaps the biopsy scare in June had gotten him thinking about his mortality because he'd sold the house—the one he'd lived in with us, then rented out, first to my mother and then after her death to other tenants. And he'd sold his trailer to Min He. Once I took what I wanted of Queeg's belongings, she planned to move it to the other side of the park to replace one of the old rentals. The thought of his trailer ending up back there, where we all began, still makes me smile.

Once everything was settled, I ended up with his white Toyota and almost ten thousand dollars. I signed a bunch of papers, one of which gave his attorney the right to act in my behalf regarding the estate. Once the death certificates were issued, the attorney would transfer funds, charge a small fee—it was all good. As I was leaving I asked the lawyer if when it was settled, he could please cut a check to Min He for $200. He agreed without even asking me why.

So I drove the Toyota back with Queeg's ashes buckled in the passenger seat. The trip from Pensacola to Gandy is only thirteen hours with a functioning transmission. But they were a long thirteen hours.

Right now Queeg sits on a shelf in the closet. The remaining tiny snow globe bird is sitting there, too, on top of Queeg's box. Sometime after the baby is born and I'm flying solo again, I'll drive Queeg back to Florida and take him out to Fort Pickens. I'm going to put him and that little white bird to rest in the sea with my mother. I'm going to invite Min He. I think she'll come.

CHAPTER 56

As I suspected Luke and I appear to be the last to arrive at the reception. Trip's driveway is full of cars and there are several up and down the street. I hop out of the limo and start up the walk, but Luke is stuck, waiting for the driver to reassemble the wheelchair. The poor driver's face is flushed, his meaty hands shaking as he tries to match up the parts. I feel like I ought to stay and help, but Luke gestures for me to go on. He's nice that way.

I smell Tawny before I see her. The undeniable odor of marijuana gets stronger as I approach the door. Tawny is seated cross-legged, leaning up against the house.

"Seriously? On the front porch?"

"Fritter's in the kitchen," Tawny croaks.

This makes sense to me only because I know that the layout of Trip's house is almost identical to my grandmother's, with the kitchen windows opening directly onto the back patio.

I squat down next to the girl and hold out my hand, and she instinctively passes the joint to me. Rather than take a hit, which is obviously what she expected me to do, I snub it out and hand it back, saying, "You have a job to do, remember?"

When Fritter asked me to take some photos at the reception, my first question was whether Tawny would be coming back for the funeral. When it was determined that she and her mother would be in attendance, I immediately recruited the girl to assist me. It would have been easier to just do it all myself with my digital camera, but film photography is a dying art, and Tawny is going to forget everything I taught her this summer if she doesn't get more practice.

The girl tucks the joint into her pocket. "You know what you are?"

"I have a feeling you're going to tell me," I say.

"You're a *fun-sucker*. You go through life just sucking all the fun out of everything."

"I've been called worse—by you, mostly. Now get in there and get some candid shots."

Tawny heads straight to the food platters on the dining room table, but I keep walking. I see Gordon Penny talking to a group of men, and I quickly avert my gaze and do my best not to capture his attention. I know if he sees me he'll come talk to me about next week's closing, and I don't want to deal with his gloaty smugness today.

To say that I'm less than thrilled about him buying my grandmother's house would be an understatement. But his offer was more than fair—the best I was going to get, according to Charlie Franklin—so after a sleepless night or two, I finally just said *fuck it* and signed the contract. The fact is, my mother is long gone from that house and so is Tilda. They've moved on and now it's my turn, albeit to a somewhat less final destination. I found a garage apartment a couple blocks from here that suits me fine. And I must confess, there's a small part of me that finds some real pleasure imagining Gordon Penny's surprise the first time he tries to shower in that house, struggling to squanch his massive body under my grandmother's miniature showerhead.

I weave through the crowd until I reach the kitchen. Fritter is in here alone, her back turned to me. She's rinsing out a glass pitcher, and the light from the window over the sink casts her sturdy shape in a dark silhouette, yet turns her hair into a glowing silver corona.

Hearing the snap of my camera, she glances over her shoulder and sees me standing in the doorway.

"What on earth are you wearing?" she says.

"The circus is in town. I'm the tent."

That elicits a tiny snort of laughter from the old woman before she reverts back to her naturally crabby state.

"Don't lurk in the doorway. Come here and make yourself useful."

"Okay, Aunt Fritter."

She winces at the word *aunt*. I smile. I never bother to call Trip *uncle*, but I can't resist tweaking *Great Aunt* Fritter when nobody else is listening. I might never get tired of reminding her that she's related to a low-class, tent-wearing, no-goodnik like me. I join her at the sink, but I don't make myself useful. I just lean against the counter next to where she's working.

She glances at the camera hanging around my neck and says, "Thank you."

"My pleasure," I reply, and it's the truth. I'll never have my mother's love of photography or her talent for it, but the camera feels good in my hands. Familiar.

"I'm sorry about your brother," I say.

She nods. "It was his time, but it's never easy."

"I know," I say, because I *do* know.

"And for what it's worth . . ." She pauses to clear her throat. "I am grateful that the two of you spoke. I think believing he'd apologized to Tilda gave poor Jonah some measure of peace."

"You didn't seem all that grateful at the time."

"Well, that might not have been my finest moment." She opens cabinets until she locates a canister marked *Sugar*. "But in my defense you were being very sneaky."

"True," I admit.

"And nosey."

"You're right."

"And annoying. And pushy."

"You can stop anytime now."

"Well," she tells me, "all I can say is, the acorn doesn't fall far from the tree. You may resemble Tilda, but you are Genie all over again."

My first instinct is, as always, to argue with that statement, but this time I just smile.

"I can only imagine how much trouble a child of yours is going to be," Fritter adds, but her stern tone is tempered by the hand she tentatively reaches out to place on my belly. I set my hand over hers, positioning her palm on the spot where I've felt recent movement. When the little person-to-be inside of me bumps and shifts under our touch, Fritter and I share a smile.

"I'm putting her up for adoption," I say.

"Her?"

I shrug. "According to the doctor."

Fritter gives my belly a gentle little pat and then resumes her kitchen duties, crossing to the refrigerator to pull out a large paper bag. "Adoption sounds like a good idea. Although, I suspect you're too hardheaded to do anything that sensible."

"I can't be a mother," I say. "I'd screw it up."

The old woman laughs softly. "Doesn't everybody?"

Before I can reply, Trip pops his head into the kitchen. "Luke is here. I think that's everyone. It's time for the toast, and then we'll take pictures."

"Give us ten minutes," Fritter says.

"What are you two doing?" he asks.

"It's bad luck to toast with water," she explains. "And not everyone drinks alcohol." She looks at me meaningfully, and I nod. I'm not puking anymore, but I'm not smoking or drinking either. Considering her ancestors, this poor kid is probably already destined to be a fuckup. I don't need to make her life any harder than it has to be.

Fritter pushes the paper sack in my direction and hands me a knife. I turn and look at what she has assembled on the counter—a bowl, a pitcher, a sugar canister, a paper sack of . . . I pull the bag closer and look inside, knowing what I'll find. Leaning in close I take a deep breath, expecting a scent as sharp as the yellow fruit's flesh, but I'm pleasantly surprised. The lemons smell good. Sweet, even.

ACKNOWLEDGMENTS

Picture an awards show, and a young woman (who's never eaten a doughnut in her life), standing breathless at the podium, an award clutched to her sequined chest, desperately listing names as the shut-up-already music swells. Now take away the stage, cameras, music, award, podium, sequins, youth, and doughnutless body. What you have left is what she and I have in common: amazed happiness, a long list of people to whom we owe a debt of gratitude, and the panicked realization that we'll never be able to name them all.

I'm betting there are people who should be on this list but aren't, and if you're one of them please accept my sincere apology. Also, please understand that I'm exceptional at guilt. I've almost certainly discovered the omission and feel even worse about it than you'd want me to. (Admit it: that does make you feel a little better, doesn't it?)

So here it goes:

Thank you, Jillian Verrillo, editor extraordinaire, for loving my book enough to take it on, for your astute editorial suggestions, and your perpetual good humor. I could not have asked for someone more fun to work with. I'd also like to thank everyone else at HarperCollins and Harper Paperbacks. Cal Morgan, editorial director, and Amy Baker, associate publisher: thank you for believing in this book and working so hard to make it happen. Thanks to design manager Jamie Lynn Kerner for the beautiful interior design, copyeditor Jane Herman for your adroit fact-checking and ninja comma skills, proofreader Audrey Sussman for your keen eye, and production editor Sherry Wasserman for your management expertise and attention to detail. To cover designer Joanne O'Neill, thank you for your creative energy and collaborative spirit; to managing editor Dori Carlson, thanks for keeping it all moving smoothly; and to publicist Leigh Raynor and the marketing team, Kathryn Radcliff-Lee and Mary Sasso, I'm grateful for your resourcefulness and your tireless efforts on this book's behalf.

Jeff Kleinman, agent *ne plus ultra,* thanks so much for your wisdom, patience and steadfast advocacy. You were and still are the agent of my dreams. And to the rest of the Folio Literary Management team and Jita Fumich—thank you for your help.

I'm grateful for the time taken and suggestions given by the readers of the early drafts: Sandy Ebner, Hallye Terrell, and Lisa Love, plus Carrie Bedford, Maryvonne Fent, Michael Jacobs, Ed Markel, Camille Cira, and the other members of the Ongoing Workshop. Thank you, Sue Garzon, for the book's title, and instructors: Shelley Singer, Dennis Foley, Dana Adams, and Michael Murphy, for your advice and encouragement. Thanks to photographers Judy Bankhead and Tom Hargrove for the darkroom advice; any mistakes remaining are my own.

To the friends who've enriched my life, and the friends who've helped save it, a thank you hardly seems like enough. I'm not naming names here for fear of leaving someone out, but I don't have to, right? You know who you are.

Thanks to my children, who are now delightful adults. You have given my life great meaning, and my head gray hairs. Mike, Stephen, Katherine, and Corey, I love you all. (That's what she said.) Oh, and a special tip of the hat to Katherine for all the inventive profanity. (How often does a mother get to say that to her daughter?)

And finally I'm grateful to Leonard, my husband and best friend. We've been together our entire adult lives, yet amazingly you're still putting up with me (even after the cat fence) and for that I am blessed. Truly, miracles abound.

About the author

About the book

Insights,
Interviews
& More . . .

Read on

Meet Melissa DeCarlo

MELISSA DECARLO was born and raised in Oklahoma City. Growing up she wanted to be a writer, an artist, an actress, and one of those people wearing bright yellow helmets who get to climb telephone poles. Then one day she looked around and discovered that she was all grown-up with a degree in computer science and working in an office where she had to wear panty hose every day.

But sometimes in life, as in the best stories, do-overs are possible. Melissa now lives in East Texas with her husband and a motley crew of rescue animals. She learned how to paint and sculpt and has worked as a freelance writer, grant writer, and graphic designer. She's even done a little acting in community theater. But after she managed to break her foot climbing a flight of stairs, she decided that climbing telephone poles was probably a bad idea. She no longer even owns a pair of panty hose.

Some of Melissa's favorite things are reading, writing, making art, hanging out with her husband and their awesome grown-up kids, and watching that YouTube video of the goat that sings like Usher. *The Art of Crash Landing* is her first novel, but some of her short fiction and essays have appeared in online and print literary magazines. You'll find links to a few of these and who knows what else at www.melissadecarlo.com. ❧

Inspirations, Explanations & Extrapolations
A Short Quiz

Judge a man by his questions rather than his answers.
—Voltaire

Circle the correct answer:

1. Mattie's stepfather, Queeg, was inspired by:
   (a) The author's grandfather who probably wore sock garters at some point but, by the time the author knew him, was a gentle, confused man who called her *sugar lumpkin* and once set fire to the curtains with his pipe.
   (b) The author's father who didn't wear sock garters but who was a fan of pithy sayings, garage sales, and naps in his La-Z-Boy during golf tournaments.
   (c) The old guy who works at the tire store (sock-garter status unknown) who, upon seeing the author reading in the waiting room, remarked that he had "just finished readin' a darn good little book" and then went on to explain that the darn good little book he'd just finished readin' was *Anna Karenina*. Needless to say, the author did her best to hide both her surprise and the cover of the extremely pulpy sci-fi novel in her lap. ▶

(d) All of the above (plus all the other gentle, funny, and surprising old men she has known).

2. Buttercup, the class guinea pig, was inspired by:

(a) The guinea pig that the author promised her parents would be no trouble at all, but that was, as it turned out, pregnant, which taught the author (and her parents) that three guinea pigs really are a fair amount of trouble.

(b) Some other rodent, although probably not a pregnant one.

(c) Why am I even giving you a third choice? I'm pretty sure you've got this one figured out.

3. In addition to dyeing poodles and taunting Gordon Penny, in which of the following shenanigans might Genie and Karleen have been involved?

(a) The petroleum jelly–coated toilet seats in the bathrooms closest to the teachers' lounge.

(b) The weekly dose of dish soap in the fountain in front of the Gandy Municipal Building.

(c) The two dozen crickets purchased for the science lab's iguana that were somehow released up in the ceiling tiles rather than the lizard's terrarium.

(d) The boring sign in front of Earle's Self-Storage that had read EXTRA SPACE 4 LEASE HERE! that was livened up late one Saturday night to read SEE ALPACA SEX HERE!

(e) And then the next weekend to HERES A SEX TRAP!

(f) Then PLEASE CHEER 4 SEX!

(g) All of the above (and more).

4. Mattie seems a little clumsy at times. The author just might be prone to falling:

(a) From balconies

(b) Off bicycles

(c) Up stairs

(d) Off horses

(e) Down mountains

(f) All of the above except for the one about balconies, although now that the author is looking at the frankly quite impressive list of non-balcony things she has managed to hurt herself on, she's decided that staying off balconies is probably a very good idea.

5. Why were both of Tilda's dogs named Winston?

(a) She really, really liked the name Winston.

(b) They weren't, but her eyesight was bad and she had trouble telling them apart, so she called them both Winston.

(c) It's complicated. ▶

Inspirations, Explanations & Extrapolations *(continued)*

6. Photography is:
    (a) One of the author's skills.
    (b) Not one of the author's skills, but she's pretty sure it could be if she wanted it to be.
    (c) I mean honestly, how hard can it be?
    (d) The author's family and friends would like to mention that the author has an alarming tendency to say "How hard can it be?" before discovering exactly how hard something can be, but after having dragged aforementioned family and/or friends into some ridiculous project. It's best to never mention the words "cat fence" to the author's husband. Seriously.
    (e) b and c and oh, okay, d. But in her defense, the cat fence sounded like a great idea, and besides, how was she to know that although it would do a terrific job trapping squirrels in the yard (which certainly made the dogs happy), the cat would learn how to climb up the side of the house and over the roof within a week of the fence's installation?

7. When it comes to beach vacations the author:
    (a) Is intimately familiar with weedy trailer parks.

(b) Has driven past a few on the way to the nice hotel/condo/house rental.

(c) a and then b because although the author's parents did place a very high value on frugality (especially when it came to family vacations), the author and her husband were not that frugal (especially when it came to family vacations). The author's children have yet to thank her for that. A card would be nice. Or candy. Or chocolates.

8. Will Mattie end up settling down in Gandy with Luke? Might she keep the baby?
(a) Yes.
(b) No.
(c) You tell me.

9. Poor Mattie's life was a nomadic, chaotic mess. The author's life is/was:
(a) Similarly chaotic.
(b) Mostly normal.
(c) Completely normal.
(d) Is there even such a thing as normal?

Answers:

1. Mattie's stepfather, Queeg, was inspired by:
(d) All of the above.
Although my dad was probably the primary inspiration, he ▶

wasn't Queeg. My dad was his
own man, a builder and an
attorney; a watcher of *Hee-Haw*
and an expert maker of French
toast; a stubborn man who
tenderly cared for my mother as
she sickened and ultimately died
from emphysema. He died in
1999 of urothelial carcinoma
of the kidney, which, like
emphysema is directly related
to smoking. I wish they hadn't
smoked. I miss them both
every day.

2. Buttercup, the class guinea pig, was
inspired by:
(a) The guinea pig that the author
promised her parents would be
no trouble at all . . .
My guinea pig was named
Tabitha and lived with us for
many years, making her little
oooeek noises and happily eating
her atlfalfa pellets and the
carrots I'd feed her while she sat
in my lap and watched television
with me. (Yes, we found homes
for her two babies.)

3. In addition to dyeing poodles and
taunting Gordon Penny, in which of
the following shenanigans might
Genie and Karleen have been
involved?
(g) All of the above (duh!).
In all fairness, the city fountain
had never been cleaner, the

crickets singing overhead added a pleasing, albeit temporary, outdoorsy ambience to every lab assignment (the Bunsen burners seemed like tiny campfires), and the new covered sign Earle finally bought was much nicer than the old one. If Genie and Karleen had been asked about any of these events, surely they would have replied, "You're welcome!"

4. Mattie seems a little clumsy at times. The author just might be prone to falling:

(f) All of the above except for the one about balconies, although . . .

Okay, ready? Bicycles: Long story, but I somehow didn't learn to ride a bicycle until I was in my early twenties, and so, although technically, I *can* ride a bike I'm much better off not doing so. Stairs: I once broke my foot running up a flight of stairs (*prancing* up the stairs, according to my husband, but we disagree on this point). Horses: Seven stitches in my scalp. Mountains: I have skied and snowboarded and have, after a few trips to the orthopedist, come to the conclusion that some people are simply not meant to go fast down icy slopes. ▶

5. Why were both of Tilda's dogs
   named Winston?
   (c) It's complicated.
       Tilda did, indeed, name a dog
       Winston (the larger, less farty
       dog) after the music store she
       missed so badly. Every week at
       the senior center's afternoon
       dance, Tilda discussed Winston
       with her regular dance partner,
       George. One Saturday George
       told Tilda he had bought a
       French bulldog of his own,
       although Tilda couldn't help but
       note, from a less reputable
       breeder.

       When a massive stroke felled
       George, no one in his family
       wanted the dog. It was only after
       Tilda's offer to take the animal
       was accepted that she learned
       George had also named his dog
       Winston. She wondered at the
       time whether this hinted at
       some poignant, unexpressed
       affection for her on George's
       part, or merely an appalling
       deficit of originality. Publicly,
       Tilda bemoaned her late dance
       partner's lack of imagination,
       but her secret heart couldn't
       stop remembering the warmth
       in George's eyes, and how they
       were exactly the same color
       blue as her favorite cardigan.
       She never changed the dog's
       name.

6. Photography is:
    Yeah, well. Okay, probably the less said about all that, the better.

7. When it comes to beach vacations the author:
    (c) a and then b because . . .
    When I was a child and we went on family vacations to the beach we always stayed in a mobile home park. At the time I thought it was fun, although I suspect my mom was less than thrilled to have KP duty even on vacation. Once after we'd all gone crabbing, my dad made the mistake of leaving all the crabs we'd caught alive in a bucket out behind the trailer long enough for me to name them all. Then I cried about their fate until my dad finally drove me, and the crabs, to the pier so I could dump them all back in the ocean. Yes, even as a small child I was a pain in the ass.

8. Will Mattie end up settling down in Gandy with Luke? Might she keep the baby?
    (c) You tell me.
    I'm serious. I don't know what happens next, because these characters aren't mine anymore. They're yours. They're ours.
        Some days I like the idea of ▶

Inspirations, Explanations &
Extrapolations *(continued)*

Mattie raising that little girl with help from Luke and all of their family and friends in Gandy. But then sometimes I prefer the thought of Mattie getting in her car and taking that trip to California that her mother and Karleen never made. Maybe it would be a mistake to settle down before she's figured out what she really wants from life. I do know that Mattie no longer feels an urge to self-destruct, but beyond that? I don't have a clue. Do you? I'd love to hear it! Contact me on Facebook or via my website, and give me your best guess.

9. Poor Mattie's life was a nomadic, chaotic mess. The author's life is/was:

    (d) Is there even such a thing as normal?
    I grew up with married parents in an average house in a middle-class neighborhood in Oklahoma City. I lived in the same house from four years old until I went to college. My parents drank, yes, but they weren't alcoholics. In our house there was not too much shouting, I'd say an average amount of laughter, and a lot of love. But, this was real life and not a television series. Things

weren't perfect. I was the youngest of three children, the middle sister was disabled and my brother, the eldest, went to Vietnam when I was nine and came home a heroin addict who spent the rest of his life battling addiction.

My parents, my brother, and my sister are all gone now. I'm the last one standing, the only one left to tell stories about my dad's naps in front of the television, my mom's paintings, my sister's sweet smile, my brother's struggles, and ultimately my own.

Although the events and people in my book are certainly fictional, the themes—difficult family relationships, addiction, guilt, shame, redemption—have been as real in my life as my pet guinea pig and the sound of the oyster gravel in the trailer park popping under the tires of my dad's 1973 Buick LeSabre. So, has my life been nomadic? No. Chaotic? Sometimes. Messy? Yes, yes, and thank God, yes. Yours too, I'm betting. ∽

"A dazzling debut that truly soars . . . featuring [a]
heroine readers won't be able to stop falling in [love with]."
—CAROLINE LEAVITT, *New York Times [bestselling]*
author of *Is This Tomorrow* and *Pictures [of You]*

Broke and knocked up, Mattie Wallace has got all her [worldly possessions]
crammed into six giant trash bags and nowhere to go. [She]
really is turning into her late mother, a broken alcoholic [. . . one]
choice she didn't make.

When Mattie gets news of a possible inheritance left by a grandmother she's
never met, she jumps at this one last chance to turn things around. Leaving the
Florida Panhandle, she drives eight hundred miles to her mother's birthplace—
the tiny town of Gandy, Oklahoma. There, she soon learns that her mother
remains a local mystery—a happy, talented teenager who inexplicably skipped
town thirty-five years ago with nothing but the clothes on her back. But the girl
they describe bears little resemblance to the damaged woman Mattie knew, and
before long it becomes clear that something terrible happened to her mother. The
deeper Mattie digs for answers, the more precarious her situation becomes. Giving
up, however, isn't an option. Uncovering what started her mother's downward
spiral might be the only way to stop her own.

"A whole lot of heart, soul, and humor. . . . You won't stop
reading until all the great mysteries of Mattie's messed-up life have
been unraveled by the ever-wise Mattie herself."
—JESSICA ANYA BLAU, author of *The Wonder Bread Summer*

MELISSA DeCARLO was born and raised in Oklahoma
City, and has worked as an artist, graphic designer, grant
writer, and even (back when computers were the size of re-
frigerators) a computer programmer. *The Art of Crash Landing*
is her first novel. Melissa now lives in East Texas with her
husband and a motley crew of rescue animals.

HARPER
An Imprint of HarperCollinsPublishers

Cover design by Joanne O'Neill
Cover image © by mishkom / Getty Images
Author photograph © Batten Photography,
Tyler, Texas

Discover great authors,
exclusive offers, and more at hc.com.

Fiction

$6.00

9 780999 757352

ART OF CRASH LANDING

EAN

0915